A FAIR EMIGRANT.

A FAIR EMIGRANT

A NOVEL

BY

ROSA MULHOLLAND
AUTHOR OF "MARCELLA GRACE: A NOVEL"

PHILADELPHIA
H. L. KILNER & CO.
PUBLISHERS

CONTENTS.

A FAIR EMIGRANT.

CHAPTER I.

ALONE IN THE BUSH.

ARTHUR DESMOND, an Irish gentleman, left his native country under unhappy circumstances, in the year 18—, and found his way to Minnesota, where, following as far as white settlers had then ventured, he took land, built himself a wooden house, and began life in solitude. Though quite a young man, a grey look of blight on his countenance and a dejected droop in his walk told plainly that whatever might be the mainspring of the energy that kept him labouring from morning till night, and from night almost till morning again, with little sleep and no recreation, hewing down the woods and turning up the virgin soil for future harvests of gold, there was at least no hope in his toil. Young though he was, he was a broken man, who, with a canker in his heart that could not be cured, had isolated himself voluntarily from the society of his fellow-men.

Hope put out of the question, the motive for his persistent labour was not far to seek. A man of keenly sensitive organisation, of fine rather than strong brain, he was well aware that for one like him a load of unsurpassed mental agony is not to be borne except

face to face with nature, alone in some of her magnificent solitudes, and under the yoke of such bodily toil
as leaves little leisure for consecutive thought. Obeying
the instinct for self preservation, he had taken hold of
the only means that could save him from the doom of
insanity.

He had brought nothing with him to the backwoods
but his workman's clothes and tools, the miniature
likeness of a woman, and a packet of letters which he
wore sewn round his neck till they began to crack in
the folds and fray at the edges, and, later, deposited in
a small box of pine-wood carved rather skilfully by
himself. He never looked at the miniature and he
never read the letters, but when he came in from work
his first glance was towards the casket, and at night it
was placed with his revolver by the side of his lonely
bed.

His beard grew long and untrimmed, and white hairs
began to creep in among his dark locks. He held little
intercourse with men, yet whenever a human being
passed his way, whether white traveller going to or from
St Paul, or Indian straggler from far out on the prairie
that stretched from his door to the horizon, the wayfarer
was sure to receive kindly hospitality from the lonely
squatter in his log-built home. The cries of animals,
the songs and calls of birds, and the ring of his own
axe were often the only sounds he heard for weeks.
Sometimes the concert of the woods and the murmured,
exquisite music which Nature makes for herself in her
great solitudes charmed the grey look of blight from
his face, or the sumptuous colouring of the primeval
scenes around would fascinate his eye and smooth away
the furrow that agony had already dug deep between
his brows. And it was these momentary relaxings of
too taut a string, these almost unnoticed yieldings to

the great mother's power to soothe, that saved his reason and enabled him to give continuity of purpose to his work.

Whatever may be the motive of long and determined devotion to labour, it is generally rewarded by a harvest of success. Arthur Desmond saw his work begin to prosper and its profit to teem upon him before he had realised that any other result was to be expected from his toil than the dulled state of memory which had enabled him to keep sane. All that he had touched seemed to turn to gold, and, as he saw it pour into his hands, he asked himself bitterly: "Of what use is this to me? What am I going to do with it?" He flung it into the earth again and forgot it, but when another year had passed it returned to him doubled and trebled. Again he buried it in his wider and wider-spreading meadows and fields, and again it found its way back to him with an increase that made it more burdensome than ever.

Master of a vast and fertile territory, he still lived in his log-house, content with that rude harbour for his own person, while his granaries and farm-buildings multiplied and extended. No comfort came to him with his success, no joy in his riches, nor hope for happiness in his future years. To his farm-servants he was a liberal and kindly employer, to those with whom he dealt in business upright and fair, but no man grew intimate with him or called him friend.

At last an event occurred which made a change in Desmond's forlorn life. Returning one evening after a solitary day with his gun in the woods, he found two travellers at his door waiting to ask his hospitality for the night. They were father and daughter, had come from St Paul, and were on their way far out into the Indian country. The man was a travelling merchant, who had dealings with the Indians, and the girl was his only child. Both had evidently seen better days, were refugees from more civilised lands, belonging to the large class whom folly, wrong, or misfortune reduce to beggary every day. The girl was beautiful, with that peculiar, delicate beauty which speaks eloquently of gentle blood. Arthur Desmond, seeing her standing at his door, with the setting sun burnishing her golden hair and lighting up her pale face, was struck by her loveliness, but only as he was struck daily by the grace of the flowers that sprang up through the grass on the prairies. Had the heart within him not been dead he might have fallen in love with her. As it was, he looked at her with interest, and his melancholy brow unbent as he led her into his home.

She was ill with weariness, quite unfit for the journey she had undertaken rather than remain behind her father in the city of St Paul. Next morning she declared herself able to proceed; but the two men, looking at her, saw that if she did so it would probably be at the cost of her life. The father was deeply distressed and uncertain what course to pursue, but his host came to the rescue.

"Leave her here," he said, "and she will have time to rest and recruit her strength while you are away. Your journey accomplished, you can call for her as you return. The wife of one of my most trusty servants shall wait upon her, and she shall have every care so rude an establishment as mine can afford."

This seemed the only reasonable solution of the difficulty, and though the girl wept and clung to him, her father insisted on her accepting Desmond's hospitality. Promising to return soon, he mounted and travelled away across the prairie, looking back and waving his hand to her till he was out of sight. And then the girl crept trembling to her seat at Desmond's fireside.

The delicate courtesy with which her host treated his young guest proved that he had been born for other scenes than that of the wild prairie and the backwoodsman's hut; and as the girl gathered strength and was able to walk a mile, hoping to meet her father returning from his journey out West, and as week followed week and the father did not appear, Desmond forgot his own sorrows in devising means to occupy her mind and keep her from observing the unexpected and unaccountable length of his absence. It was long before the terrible likelihood dawned upon her that he had met his death among the Indians, and that she should see him no more. At last passing travellers from the Indian country brought certain news that he had been killed by some of the savages, whom he had been imprudent enough to offend.

After the first agony had exhausted itself, the desolate creature raised her head and proposed to set out with her broken heart for St Paul, there to seek a livelihood for herself, but as little as a dove is fit to fight among hawks, so little able was she to carry out her gallant intention. So thought Arthur Desmond, looking on her stricken face and transparent hands; and yet he knew not what to advise. She could not stay with him, and there was no woman to whose care he could think of confiding her.

On the night before her proposed departure for St Paul, as she sat opposite to him at his fireside for the last time, with her slight hands folded in her lap and a look of patient determination on her child-like face, a strange trouble for her came down upon Desmond and a sense of remorse, as if he alone were driving her out into the dangers and miseries of a hard world from the safe shelter of his home. Violently agitated, he rose up and went into the woods, where he wandered all night, a prey to the most unhappy thoughts, beset by intolerable memories, torn with the struggle to cast off the claims of a cruel past, to free himself from the power of its dead hand, which, after so many years, still clutched murderously at any pale hope that might venture to spring up in his heart. Flinging himself on the earth, he sobbed in the solitude and darkness, not even a star to witness or a bird to overhear, nothing to intrude on the sacredness of a strong man's secret agony. At dawn he rose up with the marks of the conflict on his face, and went slowly back to his dwelling, where at the door stood already the conveyance which was to take his visitor back to St Paul.

"My dear," he said, taking her by the hand, "I cannot bear to see you go. There is one way by which you can stay with me, if you will. I am a careworn, broken man, and you are a young, fresh, and lovely girl, but we are both lonely and unfortunate. Can you make up your mind to marry me?"

The young wife bloomed across her husband's desolate life like a wind-flower in the fissure of a rock; and though she could not bring him actual happiness, yet the sweetness of her nature and her tender adoration of him comforted his starved and frozen heart, and his gratitude for her love and faith in him amounted to passion. She knew little of his early life, and understanding that the subject was painful, did not press for further information. With a woman's instinct she had divined that some other woman had broken the heart of which the noble wreck was her own; but that any darker cloud than that cast by a cruelly disappointed love had ever rested on him, she did not live long enough to find out. After one happy year she bade good-bye to the forest shades, the sunny prairies, and her idolised husband—leaving an infant daughter in her place.

When Bawn, the child, was ten years old, Fate made another raid on Desmond's small store of hard-earned happiness. For his girl's sake he fell into one of those sad blunders which men in his position so often stumble upon. At a distance of some miles from his own possessions a family of French settlers had established themselves, and of the group was a middle-aged spinster of bustling and active turn, who soon showed a lively interest in Desmond and his motherless daughter. Looking on his far-spreading fields and teeming granaries, the thrifty Jeanne quickly resolved to share that extraordinary prosperity which seemed so little appreciated by the melancholy Arthur. How she managed it is needless to relate, but in a very short time after she had made up her mind, she became stepmother to Desmond's little girl.

Desmond soon discovered that in his solicitude for his child he had been led into an irretrievable mistake. Jeanne was a masterful woman, and rather than fight with her, the man of hapless fortune was fain to let her have things her own way. The wooden home which had satisfied him and his girl was deserted, and a fine new dwelling-house was built. All the ways of life were changed for father and daughter. Servants were scolded and well looked after, abuses corrected, waste was put an end to, and peace for ever banished from the Desmond fireside. A governess was engaged for Bawn—not a day too soon, certainly—all the prairie maiden's pretty wild ways were condemned, and a good education was energetically administered to her.

In submitting to the new state of things Bawn was influenced by her all-absorbing love for the father, whose sole consolation she knew herself to be. She was now a woman, emancipated from her stepmother's control, yet living on the most friendly terms with her father's wife. Within the big house Jeanne reigned paramount, and every one bowed to her will; but deep in the wild woods, lost in the lonely wildernesses of the forest, father and daughter held their meetings and their councils, and were as happy as Desmond's recurrent fits of melancholy occasionally permitted them to be.

CHAPTER II.

THE SECRET OF A LIFE.

" Bawn ! Bawn ! "

Mrs Desmond was calling loudly in her deep contralto tones to her stepdaughter from the front door, shading her eyes with her hand from the strong sunlight that flooded the land—light that intensified the beauty of everything, suggesting corn, wine, and oil, overspreading flowers, teeming fruits.

" Where can that girl have got to, and her father out of the way as well ? I don't know what would have become of Arthur Desmond's goods if I had not taken them in hand ! Shouldn't wonder if she was over in the log-house encouraging him, as usual, in his whims."

Jeanne crossed the flower-laden sward towards the old wooden house, smothered in bloom, which still stood at an opening of the woods some distance from the new house with its gardens. Jeanne, though quick and energetic, was plump and portly, with a swarthy skin, keen black eyes, and intensely black hair. She was dressed in a calico wrapper of red and white stripes and a large Holland morning-apron with pockets, in which she jingled her keys, and looked neat, thrifty, active, and aggressive.

" Coming, Mother Jeanne ! " cried Bawn from within the log-house, where she was busy arranging her father's books, weapons, and various belongings, and beautifying the place in a way of her own. Desmond had forbidden the old wooden home to be swept away, disputing on this one point the will of his wife ; and he used it as a sort of den, his only substitute for a club.

"A pretty state of things !" panted Jeanne. "Here is a man from St Paul about wheat, and nobody to speak to him but myself. I'm sure if I did not work myself to death I don't know what would become of us all."

"Is not the steward to be had ? "

"Oh ! of course, if you leave it to servants. Give me the man who looks after his own business."

"Father laboured long years, and now his hair is white," said Bawn, with a pathetic vibration in her voice. "I think we may sometimes manage without troubling him."

"Well, I'm sure it's not for my own benification I trouble ! " snapped Jeanne, who, having all her life been accustomed to French on one side and English on the other, often unintentionally coined words of her own to suit her momentary convenience. "And pray, is it by your father's ordeal that you spend so much time in this old hutch ? "

Bawn laughed. "Come, now, Mother Jeanne, look at these exquisite roses. Smell !"

"It's no kind of use talking to you, Bawn. Here is a question of so much for wheat, and—and there you are offering me roses to smell, as if nothing was needed in this world but a nose ! but you are too old now for my tutition."

"The business is done by this time, I warrant," said Bawn, placing the despised roses in a glass on her father's reading-table, where, amid a litter of his favourite books, stood the old wooden casket which he had fashioned and carved so many years ago. "And you know, Jeanne, even if sixpence a bushel less than

possible is had for the wheat, we can well afford the
loss—better, perhaps, than the dealer who buys it."

Mrs Desmond drew back a step from her stepdaughter and eyed her with contempt.

"I do believe," she said, "that you are at heart a
Communist, or a Vincent de Paul, or something of that
kind. You don't know how to grasp your own and hold
it tight when you have got it. You would let everyone
be as rich as yourself. You seem to think whatever
you have got more than you actually need must have
been taken from somebody else, and that you are bound
to restitute it."

"Jeanne, Jeanne! I can't help laughing. Fancy
what you would do to me if you caught me at it!
But seriously, dear, you know we are actually rolling in
money."

"And if we are, how much of it is owing to my care?
Not, I'm sure, that I want it for myself. I've no
children to think of, and it is only for your father and
you I need toil. From morning till night I wear the
flesh off my bones——"

Bawn bit her lip to hide a smile. A good deal of
the said flesh still adhered to the framework of Mrs
Desmond's abundant person, but Jeanne could not
have been happy without her chronic grievance of
perpetual overwork.

After her stepmother had bounced away Bawn went
on smilingly with her occupation, and, when it was
finished, set out to meet her father on his return from
the forest, where he had been wandering alone since
morning. This had been one of Desmond's bad days,
when the ghost of his past—a ghost that would not be
laid—dogged his steps, voices none but himself could
hear tormented his ears, and faces long unseen pursued
him, gazing on him with eyes of hate or turning away

2

from him in loathing.   On such days all the old agony
grew young again within him, a cruel mist rose all round
him and cut him off from his actual world, blotting out
even Bawn's comfortable countenance.   His gun and
dog were the only companions he tolerated at these
moments, and, ranging the woods from morning till
evening, he did battle in solitude with his foes.

Now, toiling homeward through the forest, he carried
the marks of the conflict on his face and in his gait, in
the dull pallor of his skin, the sunken, dark eye, the fine-
drawn lines of pain hardening a mouth naturally sweet,
the pinched look of his features.   Yet even with this
blight upon him he had a peculiar air of nobility all his
own.   The snow-white hair waving over a forehead
which was that of an idealist, and the dense darkness of
his eyes and brows, would alone have given him distinc-
tion in a crowd.

Coming slowly through a long aisle of shade, he
looked up and saw Bawn waiting for him in the full
sunset light at the nearest opening.

"Thank heaven!" he sighed to himself, feeling like
a man who, having toiled all night through stormy
breakers, finds that he is suddenly in sight of shore.

"My darling, I almost took you for a goddess of the
woods, what with that white gown, your May-blossom
face, and all this shining hair!"

"That comes of reading poetry and romanticising in
the forest, Daddy dear," said the girl, giving him a loving hug.   "I wonder is there a goddess of Matter-of-
fact among their deityships?   Look here!"   And, linking her arm through his, she drew him forward.

A fire had been kindled on the ground, and a steam-
ing gipsy-kettle was slung above it.   On a little stand
near were cups and saucers and a dish of newly-baked
cakes.

"Your favourite cakes, sir, and the tea is just made. Now sit down and give an account of yourself, you unsociable, rambling, unaccountable darling of an old Daddy!"

"Give me your tea first. Thank heaven for tea! No, I cannot tell you where I have been. So many miles away, my girl, that you never could follow me."

"Ah!" said Bawn quickly, "if you would only try me."

Desmond looked at her in surprise, and the hues of life that had stolen back to his face paled away again. It was the first time Bawn had ever hinted at a desire to intrude on his secret.

"No, no, do not mind me," she cried, seeing the effect of her words. "I would rather break my heart than give you one extra pang."

"My little girl! my poor little girl!" said Desmond, startled at her passionate tones. "You break your heart! That would be the worst thing that Arthur Desmond, with all his ill-luck, was ever guilty of."

"My heart is pretty strong," said Bawn stoutly. "It could bear a good deal, if a good deal were laid on it. Emptiness is the one thing that could hurt it—like Mamsey's boiler, that cracked with heat because it was not kept properly filled."

Desmond rose and paced up and down for a few moments, a flush on his thin cheek and a strange excitement burning in his eyes. Bawn went up to him presently and put her arms round his neck.

"You shall not tell me anything if it distresses you," she whispered.

Desmond clasped her in his arms and looked fondly in her eyes.

"My only joy and comfort! there is much I would willingly confide to you, if I thought my confessions would not damp and blight the young glory of your life. You are still so young—"

"I am twenty," she said quickly ; "and I feel so old that I cannot believe I shall ever grow any older. Trust my ripe age, father—at least if it will help you, as I often think it might, to share your painful memories with another. As for damping me—why, I am not easily crushed. Jeanne says I am like an indiarubber ball : the harder you try to put me down the higher I spring up again,"

"I have always intended you should know my whole story, Bawn—after my death. You know the wooden box that stands on my table ? "

"Yes."

"It contains papers that will be yours when I am gone ; letters belonging to my youth, a portrait which you will cherish, and a statement written out in my own hand—my history, jotted down from time to time on sleepless nights. If you strongly desire it you shall have that statement to-morrow, and after you have read it we will talk the matter over, if so be you do not shrink from or suspect your old dad."

"Father ! " flinging herself into his arms. "Shrink from you ! Suspect you of anything but what is noblest and best ! "

"Ah ! Bawn, there were others who loved me, and yet cast me out."

"Fiends ! " muttered Bawn, tightening her soft arms round his stooping neck.

"No, not fiends, dear. Stanch, true men, and a sweet, soft woman like yourself."

"Are they still alive ? "

"I think so. I hope so ; yet for my own sake I ought not to wish it, seeing that released spirits may, perhaps, know all truth."

"Is there no way of making it known to them before their release?"

"None. And if there were I would not seek it now."

"But I would."

"You?"

"Do you think," said Bawn, unclasping her arms from his neck and linking her hands behind her back, while she leaned forward and looked into his face—"do you think I could live in the world for the fifty years or so I may possibly stay in it, without finding out those people and making them ashamed of their conduct? If there be a lie against you living in the world, I will take it in my own hands and strangle it."

She laid her white, firm palms together as she spoke, and knotted her fingers as if she were in reality wringing the life out of a viper.

Desmond smiled his sweet, melancholy smile.

"Now, who could think there was so much passion in my smiling Bawn? My dear, you speak of an impossibility. The error went too deep; has strengthened its roots in the soil of time. There are lies, Bawn, that will walk up to the judgment-seat clothed like truth, and only at the crack of doom shall their faces be unveiled."

Bawn looked away into the depths of the twilight forest with an obstinate light of determination in her deep grey eyes.

"Daddy," she said presently, putting her hands on his tall shoulders and bringing her face close to his—"Daddy," kissing him, "what do they call the thing that you were accused of? Don't"—kissing him again—"be afraid to tell me. I can't wait till to-morrow."

"It was murder," said Desmond, with a blanching face.

"Oh the fools!" cried Bawn, holding her warm cheek firmly against his. "The fantastic idiots! To think of a man like this in connection with such a crime!"

"No, Bawn, none of them were fools."

"Then there was a villain among them," insisted Bawn.

"May be so, my dearest—may be so. But all that lies among the mysteries that will never now be solved."

"Why?"

"Because death is always sealing up the lips of truth."

"Are *all* the actors in your story dead?"

"I told you just now, my daughter, that I do not know. For long years I have not had the heart to make an effort to inquire. Very long ago I used to receive, from time to time, letters from one who promised to send me word if anything in my favour came to light. As his letters ceased, I believe him to be dead. In the course of thirty years death will have reaped a big harvest from every inhabited land of the earth. He will not have spared the spot where the tragedy of your father's life was enacted."

They walked up and down together, Bawn with her cheek against his shoulder and her hands clasped over his arm. The round, yellow moon rose above the darkening tips of the trees and cast a misty radiance over the distant prairie. Odours of cultured flowers mingled with the sweets of hay, the breath of cattle stole towards them at times, and the low, burnt-out fires of the sun smouldered and died in the forest thickets.

"I know all this happened in Ireland, of course," said Bawn. "It was not in your own south, where you were born? Was it in those beautiful northern glens you have sometimes told me of?"

"It was there. On an evening as lovely as this, in the midst of scenery far more beautiful, more picturesque, in the flush of my youth—a youth full to the brim of happiness and hope—my bitter doom came down upon me. But ask me no more to-night, my darling. To-morrow everything shall be told."

CHAPTER III.

" AND now, dear," said Desmond, "as I have given you my serious promise, let me go my own way for the rest of the evening. I want to look over the papers in the old wooden box in the shanty, to put them in order for your reading. Don't expect to see me again till to-morrow morning, and tell Jeanne I shall not come in to supper. I shall spend most of the night at my task."

"I fear it will be a painful one," said Bawn, beginning to tremble for the consequences of her own boldness.

"Not so painful as it might have been. Your faith and confidence have given me courage, and, after a life-time of silence and isolation with my trouble, your sympathy is very sweet. Already I feel happier than I believed it possible I could ever feel again. Little daughter, you have comforted me."

"Daddy, I hold you to be one of God's martyrs."

"That is wild talk, my darling. Only to-night do I realise fully how wicked I have been. I have suffered morosely, without admitting the blessedness of suffering."

"I cannot wonder."

"My daughter's trust has broken my pride. I freely pardon all who injured me. Go, now, my precious one, and pray for me if you would help me."

"I am always praying for you. Sometimes I think

I hear the angels grumbling, 'Here is this Bawn again, clamouring about her father!'"

"Continue your violence, my dearest. A most unusual hope and happiness have descended upon me to-night."

"Thank Heaven for it! And after this we shall be so happy!"

Then they parted, Desmond going to his shanty and Bawn returning to the house, where she baffled Jeanne's inquiries about her father, merely saying that she had seen him, and that he would not return in time for supper. Retiring early to her room, the girl remained long on her knees trying once more to weary out the patience of the angels. In the vigorous hopefulness of her healthy youth she was not satisfied with asking resignation and peace for her martyr, but demanded comfort the most complete, a crown of happiness the most absolute, to make amends for long years of desolation and pain. How strangely such vehement prayers are sometimes answered only those can know who have dared to utter them.

Having made her demands of Heaven, Bawn lingered still, looking out of her window, her eyes resting on the sleeping, sombre woods, the dreaming prairie spanned by the star-sown sky, the white, moon-silvered gables and roofs of the homestead. A dog bayed in the distance, a faint lowing came from the cattle-sheds, and the geese gabbled in the farm-yard. Echoes of whistling and faint laughter floated up from the fields, where some of the labourers were amusing themselves. Red fire-side lights shone under the eaves and made the moonlight more white, more ethereal by contrast.

While her eyes took in the beauty of the night her heart swelled with indignation as she thought over her father's communication of the evening, and asked herself in amazement what kind of men and women these might be whom he had described as good and true, yet who could believe him a criminal, and, driving him away from them deliberately, could lose him out of their lives for evermore. Stupid, base, inconceivable beings! There was no word in her vocabulary strong enough to express her contempt and disgust for them. So patient, so kindly as he was, and so quietly brave in spite of that amiable weakness of character which his daughter felt in him, and which made him more loveable in her eyes! Why could he not have forgotten them? Why could he not despise them as she did? To think that, after all these thirty years, the memory of their love should live so cruelly within him and would not die!

"Oh! that he and I could go back among them," she thought, "and force them to believe in the truth. I am not blighted and heart-broken, but young and strong, and full of faith. I would walk into their homes and reproach them with their falsehood. I would tell them of his noble, gentle, and laborious life; of how the poor come to him for help, and the rich entrust him with their interests. I would ask them to look at his sad eyes, his white hair, and I would say, 'Is this the man you branded and drove out from you?'"

Flinging herself on her bed, she cried herself to sleep, and soon slept the undisturbed slumber of pure and perfect health. After some hours she wakened suddenly, with a strange, startled feeling, a belief that her father had been standing at her bedside the moment before her eyes had opened, that he had bent over her and spoken to her. Even when wide awake, and aware that this must have been a delusion, a dream, she felt uneasy, as though intelligence had been given her that something unusual had happened. Dawn was already making objects dimly visible in the room, giving them that ghostly aspect which all things take at the first sign of the approach of another day, and, wondering if her father had returned to the house, she lay listening, thinking it possible his entrance might have wakened her. All was still, and, with an anxiety that would not be controlled, she rose and went to the window commanding a view of one end of the log hut. The faint star of light which she could always see when he was there at night, was burning still. How long he was lingering over that painful retrospection! How tired he would be to-morrow! Full of a tender concern for him, she dressed quickly, went noiselessly down the staircase, and let herself out of the house, with the intention of persuading him to give up his vigil, and of preparing some refreshment which he might take before going to his much needed rest.

She was soon at the door of the shanty, and, finding it unfastened, went in, calling softly to her father that it was she.

There was no answer. The light on the table was burning low with a flicker that seemed to struggle with the encroachments of the dawn-light, and she could see her father's figure sitting in his chair by the table, his head leaned slightly to one side and resting on his hand. His other hand lay upon some papers which were before him on the table — the letters he had taken from the casket, which stood empty by their side. Her first impression was that he had fallen asleep—no unnatural consequence of his long day's wandering in the open air, followed by hours of vigil. She hesitated, unwilling to disturb him, and waited, expecting to see him wake or stir.

The lamp flickered out, and the daylight grew

stronger in the room. Desmond's face was in shadow and his attitude was one of such perfect repose that his daughter felt no alarm, only remained patiently standing at the window, debating whether she should return to the house and prepare some coffee, or wake him first and persuade him to accompany her.

It struck her at last, with a vague sensation of chill that the room was unnaturally still, that she had heard neither breath nor slightest movement from the figure in the chair since her entrance into the hut. The moment after this vague alarm had seized her she was by her father's side, kneeling at his chair, and looking fearfully and scrutinisingly into his face.

Something she saw there made her start with a cry of fear and anguish, and seize him by the hands, which were stiff and cold to her touch, like hands of the dead. The noble face was grey and rigid, with an awful look, which even the sweetness on the lips and the peace on the brow could not soften. Had death indeed found him in this moment of forgiveness and contentment, and had the brave heart broken while thus reviewing in a tender spirit the evidences of the wreck of its happiness? How Bawn regained the house and summoned aid she never knew, but in a short time every remedy that could be brought to bear upon the apparently lifeless man had been tried, and not without effect. He recovered at last from what was proved to have been a long and very deathlike swoon.

The next day the swooning returned, and the doctor from St Paul whispered to Bawn that, though her father was stricken with heart disease, yet if properly cared for and saved from all anxiety, he might recover so far as to linger, an invalid, for years. It was a shadowy hope, and all but Bawn admitted it to be so. No better sign of the seriousness of his case could have been given than Jeanne's unwonted control over her tongue, or at least her tones; for had her husband been likely to recover, she would not have so spared him. As it was, she did all her grumbling in her store-rooms and dairy, where she lamented much that she was so soon to be a widow after all the pains she had taken to be a wife.

Meanwhile Bawn sat by her father's bedside, looking neither despairing nor melancholy. A run round the garden, morning and evening, kept a speck of colour the size of a carnation bud in her cheek, so that Desmond should not say she was wearing herself pale with her constant and devoted attendance on him. With smiles that never failed—smiles, sweet and penetrating, that had a restoring power, like good wine— she tended, cheered, and amused him. If good nursing could bring back any half-dead man to life, then Arthur Desmond must soon have arisen and walked. For some time he hoped with Bawn that he should do so, but little by little he learned from his friend, Dr Ackroyd, how small was the amount of such expectation he could dare to indulge in. Making up his mind to die, he felt no regret, except for the sake of the beloved daughter he was leaving behind him. Watching her sitting at his window, at work on nice things for his comfort, to be worn, as she fondly hoped, in the coming winter, which he knew he should never see, he remarked the beauty of her face and form, and the signs of an ardent though controlled nature which were so clearly visible under her serene and smiling aspect. In her pale-blue linen dress and bunch of field-daisies he thought her so charming that nothing could be added to her beauty. What would become of her when he should be laid in the earth? Rich, handsome, good, with a mind cultivated far beyond those with whom she was ever likely to come in contact, how was her life likely to be spent? Ah! if he might be spared yet a few years longer, the time he had hitherto spent in selfish, retrospective sorrow should be used in the endeavour to pilot his darling into some secure harbour for life. He would make a trip to Europe—take her, not to England, but to those Continental places where varieties of people are to be met. Who would recognise him now or remember his story? It was not possible but that some good man, her mate in heart and mind, seeing her, should love this dear Bawn; and, a shelter having been found for her, what mattered about the rest?

Then, having travelled in imagination as far as Europe, Desmond's thoughts went further still, and the face of another woman became present to his mind. After half-an-hour of dreaming he sighed heavily.

"Daddy, what is ailing you?" said Bawn, with all her heart in her eyes.

"I have been thinking, dear, it is a pity I told you—all I told you that evening. What is the use of it now? The bitterness is gone, for ever gone. Under the shadow of death's wings all things take an even surface. I have often thought to ask you about the letters and papers, dearest. I was reading them when I got this blow—"

Bawn's heart always stood still when he would speak like this, calmly, of death. But she answered in her cheerful way: "They are all safe in the casket. I have not looked at them."

"Better not look at them at all, then, my dear—at least not till I am gone."

Bawn left her seat and knelt by his bed, laying her head on the pillow beside his.

"Do not talk so," she said, "if you would not kill me. You are going to be well, and then we will forget and be happy. And I must read those letters, though not until you bid me. I have a presentiment that in the course of my years I shall meet those people who spoiled my father's life; and I should like to know all about it."

"Dreams, my darling—dreams. How should you ever meet with them; and what could come of it but pain?"

"I don't know how I shall meet them, but I have a long time to live in this world, and they are in it, too —some of them, surely—and there is no knowing how things may happen. And as for pain, there might be pain, indeed, but the truth might come out of it."

"Well, dear, I feel that I have no right to deny your request in the matter, having told you so much as I did. You know the worst, and if your mind will run on the subject, it may be well, as you say, that all the circum- stances should be known to you. Open the casket when you like, and make your own of the contents."

"May I speak to you of this again when I have done so?"

"Dear, I would rather not. My life has been lived, my burden borne. Peace has come to me at last, and I will not give it away again. Make what use you please of your knowledge in after-years, but smile and prattle to me now while I am with you. I have done with the past, and let us think of it no more."

Bawn was afraid to move her head lest he should see the tears dripping down her cheeks. His perfect peace, forgiveness, satisfaction, wrung her heart more than the most bitter complaints could have done. The peace of approaching death was upon him, though Bawn would not have it so. How sweet it would be when he should get quite well and would talk like this, about what in former days had been a horror not to be shared or softened! After a long time of silence, she ventured to withdraw her head from the pillow and steal a look at his face. She thought he had fallen asleep, and so he had; only she need not have feared to awake him, for though his eyes were fast closed, his spirit was already awake in eternity.

CHAPTER IV.

FROM THE PAST.

THE second winter after Arthur Desmond's death had come round, and his grave was covered with snow. Bawn, having lived through one tragic year, was trying to begin another with patience, which was the more difficult to her as Jeanne had begun to wear a gold locket and bracelets, and to entertain friends and relations who in her husband's lifetime were not welcome in his home.

One clear, frosty evening she came slowly downstairs from her own rooms, where she had of late lived almost entirely, and looked wearily through the windows as she passed them, up at the keen stars and across at the forest darkness, lingering, loath to enter the drawing-room, and yet resolved to conciliate her stepmother, whose wrath she often excited by her avoidance of the obnoxious cousins and friends.

As she sat down by the fire in the lamp-light she looked very unlike the blooming, vigorous Bawn who had lived so full a life at her father's side. Near her were the books he and she had read together, but she did not read, nor did she sew much, though a work-basket stood at her hand with varieties of material for such feminine occupation.

"Bawn, I wish you would talk a little," said Jeanne, pettishly. "It makes one fidget to look at your quiet-ness. And I want particularly to have some communication with you. Very seldom indeed you allow me to set an eye on you."

"Well, Jeanne, you cannot say you are lonely. You have company that pleases you better than mine."

"That may be, miss. As you say, I am not fitted for a lonely life. Now you, for instance, judging by your ways, are fond of mooning all by yourself, and so you will find it easy to grow into an old maid, as, from your demeanour to gentlemen, I see is your intent. But I can tell you I am of a different character and am not going to follow your example."

"Jeanne," said Bawn, with a gleam of her old smile, "you always will make me laugh. And I daresay it is good of you. I have not smiled for a long time, I think. How, dear Jeanne, could you manage to turn into an old maid?"

"Oh! you can make pleasantries, can you, though you were so angry at my Cousin Henri's clever jest the other day, sweeping out of the room like the goddess Dinah!"

"Don't, Jeanne—don't remind me of it, please," said Bawn, a slight frown crossing her fair brows. "I fear I am not as good-tempered as I used to be. I am growing irritable; don't provoke me till I can get back to my natural ways. Some day when your Cousin Henri is tired of coming here you will find me less unamiable than I am now."

"No, he will not cease to come here, miss; as long as I please he shall come here. And that reminds me. I was going to tell you—I suppose you are aware—that I am a widow a year to-day."

"Yes," said Bawn sadly, and she shivered and drew nearer to the fire.

Bold as Jeanne was, she grew a little nervous as she tried to proceed with her communication. Bawn's utter

3

obtuseness took her by surprise and made what she had to say more difficult. Could not the girl guess what was coming? On the contrary, her eyes had fixed themselves on the fire with an abstracted look. She was evidently not thinking of Mrs Desmond at all.

"I want to tell you, if you will listen to me," said Jeanne, desperately, "that I am not a woman to have her life blighted by one man—"

Bawn was now sitting bolt upright, startled more by the simper that had come upon her stepmother's face than by the woman's words.

"Hush!" she said sternly, and threw out her hands as if to stop further conversation.

Jeanne shrank back, shocked by the look on the girl's face.

"I am acting for the best in all our interests," she said, whimperingly, and flourishing a handkerchief of black some inches deep.

Bawn bent her head with one deep sob, and there was silence in the room for some minutes. The younger woman struggled with her grief and disgust; the elder fumed and told herself that she would tell her news that evening, no matter how disagreeable her stepdaughter might be.

"If you would not always intercept me I would tell you what I want to say," she burst forth at last. "Well, then, I am going to be married."

"Married!" repeated Bawn, mechanically.

"You will be jealous, I suppose, that I have had the first offer; but, indeed, I assure you Cousin Henri is serious in his intentions, too."

"Married!" repeated Bawn to herself. It seemed she could not be persuaded that the woman whom her father had dignified with his name could be in earnest in making such a statement.

"Yes, I tell you. The young man is a patriot of my own."

"Young man!" murmured Bawn, more and more amazed.

"And why not a young man? I suppose you mean to predict that I am not a young woman. Have I a grey hair in my head any more than you, miss?"

Bawn was silent while all the truth pressed upon her. Jeanne was but a year her father's widow, and she was going to become the wife of some vulgar acquaintance.

"I know what you are thinking of, of course," pursued Jeanne. "The house and farm are yours, and you can turn us out of them if you please. But if you would only be reasonable, Bawn, and think of Cousin Henri, we might all live here together and make our fortunes again and again."

Bawn was thinking and did not hear her. After all, the woman was only following her natural instinct in returning to the coarse associations from which Desmond had withdrawn her. Let her go. A few minutes' reflection assured the girl that this ought to be a relief to her rather than anything else. Only it would leave her, Bawn, so solitary.

Jeanne's last words rang upon her ear, and the meaning of them came back to her after a few minutes.

"Put me out of the question," she said quietly; "and please do not mention your cousin's name to me again. I will think the matter over, and tell you what I shall do about the house and farm."

"You could never work it," cried Jeanne, "and a manager would be sure to rob you."

And this was all that was said on the subject then.

When Bawn laid her head on the pillow that night, she felt a bitter sense of renewed desolation which she knew to be in reality meaningless, but which had to be suffered, nevertheless. Jeanne, disagreeable as she might be, was the only creature to whom she was bound by any tie. She had shared the past with her, and to part from her utterly was to break the last link that bound her to it. Yet this was what had to be done, and there was only one generous and sensible way of doing it. The most rational thing that she, Bawn, could do would be to leave this great place, in which she could not think of living alone, to her who had been mistress of it so long, who knew how to manage it and thrive in it. Yes, she must go forth out of her home, and find herself a shelter elsewhere.

Upon this decision she slept; but in the middle of the night she awoke suddenly, as if some one had called her. It seemed as if a voice had spoken in her ear, saying: "Why not go to Europe—to Ireland? Why not carry out your old idea of seeking for your father's friends and enemies?" As a strong light springs up in a darkened room and reveals all the details that had been only hidden and not annihilated in it, so the thought that had roused her from sleep showed her the deep desire and unshaped purpose which sorrow and weakness had held dormant in her brain.

Excellent idea! To what better account could she turn her time and the wealth which her father had left to her? Here was a new interest for her life, and closely linked with the beloved who had suffered, and was at rest.

She rose, lit her fire and lamp, and unlocked the drawer where a year ago she had, with heavy tears, deposited her father's old wooden casket. In proportion as the contents had been precious to him they were precious to her, but until now she had not trusted herself to look at them. Now she eagerly unfolded document after document, as if she would find between their pages light and instruction to carry out the plan she had conceived.

Under the papers was a miniature portrait, the face of a beautiful girl—soft blue eyes, a cloud of dark hair, face like a blush-rose, mouth and chin tender, but weak. The dress was of conventional elegance in the fashion of a bygone day.

"You are the woman who loved and yet condemned him," she said to the pictured face. " Poor weak creature, I pity you! Perhaps you married a man who was really bad, and so suffered for your sin ; or may be at this moment your heart is broken by the evil ways of a son. If so, you are justly punished for not knowing a good man when you saw him."

The fair face smiled undisturbed by her reproaches, and Bawn wept.

Desmond's own notes and statement ran as follows :

" I solemnly swear that I am not guilty of the crime laid to me ; that I had no act or part in the death of Roderick Fingall, who lost his life on the mountain of Aura, in the Glens of Antrim, on a May evening in 18—. Even if I were capable of the crime, I had no motive to urge me to it.

" It is true we both loved Mave Adare ; but she had given her promise to me, and I never dreamed of doubting her. The circumstances were these : Roderick and I had been good friends enough till he learned of my engagement to Mave, and then he took a dislike to me, fancying I had supplanted him. He had never spoken to her of his love, nor had she suspected it ; but he thought she understood him, and mistook for a deeper feeling what was only sisterly friendship for himself. This she declared to me, and I believed her ; but he chose to hug his grievance and fancy himself wronged.

" Neither Roderick nor I was rich, but accident had for the moment given me a probable advantage over him.   An old man from Barbadoes had turned up in the Glens, and, though the Adares, Fingalls, and I were unconnected by ties of blood, he was related in a distant way to each of us.   He boasted of having made a large fortune, and, having returned to bestow his bones in his native land, intended to bequeath his money to some one of his kindred.   He constantly declared that he would not divide it, but would leave it to whichever of his relatives pleased him the best.   This was, perhaps, intended to put all on their mettle to be good to him, though it might have had the effect of keeping some at a distance.   I may truly say I did not think of him at all, so absorbed was I in my happiness as Mave's accepted lover and in the daily enjoyment of her companionship.   Still, in some way — why I never could tell—a report got abroad that 'Old Barbadoes,' as he was called, had taken a fancy to me and intended to make me his heir.   People said that when Mave and I were married he could benefit both Adare and Desmond by giving us the bulk of his wealth.   I declare that neither she nor I believed there was any foundation for this gossip, nor did we allow ourselves to wish it might be true.

" The rumour had the effect of making Roderick more restless and irritable.   In the bitterness of his disappointment all the generosity of his nature seemed obscured for the time, and he was heard to say that Mave had preferred me because I was the favourite of ' Old Barbadoes.'

" He was a good fellow at bottom, though of a passionate temper and a little melodramatic in his ways, and Mave and I did not despair of winning back his friendship in time.   But death barred that.

"I was a stranger in the Glens, and my small patrimony lay in the south of Ireland. Father, mother, and sister being dead, I was the only remaining member of my own family. After my mother's death I had been induced to visit Antrim, which was her birth-place, and there I spent the happiest as well as the most terrible months of my life. Mave, in the midst of her family, seemed to me like a wild rose blooming in a poisoned atmosphere ; for the Adares were strange people, proud, thriftless, and of a morbid turn of mind, who, with failing fortunes and extravagant habits, considered themselves above the degradation of any kind of work. The men led idle and unwholesome lives, and were hated and feared by their poorer neighbours and dependants. I delighted in the thought of taking my Mave out of the strange company of her people, away from the gloomy hollow of the mountain which was her home, and bringing her to my bright little Kerry domain. We should not have been rich, but I was full of plans for earnest work, for building up my fortunes by determined industry. I said to myself, 'Idleness is the rock on which so many of my class in my country split and go to wreck. I will steer clear of it.'

"Roderick Fingall's statement that Mave had been influenced by the fact of my being 'Old Barbadoes'' favourite stung me more than any other of his taunts, and on one or two occasions I spoke angrily of his impertinence and carelessness of the truth. Mave did her best to soothe me, and seemed, I thought, unnecessarily fearful of a quarrel arising between us.

"I will make a plain statement of what occurred, as far as I know, on the evening of Fingall's violent death.

"There had occurred that day between Mave and me something like a misunderstanding on the subject of Roderick, and I was a good deal vexed in spirit when

I set out to take a long ramble across the mountains, hoping to walk off my ill-humour.

" I had done so. Heaven is my witness that I had forgotten all bitterness by the time I found myself climbing the side of Aura. My mind had gone gladly back to the contemplation of my own happiness, and, full of hope and joy, I felt my veins thrilling with the glory of the sunset, often so magnificent among those Antrim hills. I had no thought of unkindness towards any one when I saw Roderick Fingall approaching me with bent head and gloomy eyes; I felt nothing but pity for his disappointment, self-reproach for having allowed myself to be irritated by the expressions of his morbid jealousy. He was walking to meet me, without having perceived my approach, and, thinking himself alone in this mountain solitude, had allowed his face to express unreservedly the bitterness of his soul. Filled with compassion and compunction, I disliked the idea of surprising him, and began to whistle that he might be warned of my nearness to him.

" He misunderstood me and took my whistling for a sign of triumph and derision, as I found when, a few moments afterwards, we passed face to face on a narrow path above a steep and ugly precipice.

" ' So,' he said, ' you have come to dog my steps even here, to flourish your confounded good fortune in my face !' or words to that effect.

" ' No, indeed, Fingall,' I said. ' I had no such thought. We have met by accident. Let it not be an unfortunate chance. I feel no ill-will towards you. I wish to God you felt none towards me.'

" I thought I saw a gleam of relenting in his eyes as I went on.

" ' We were once good friends; let us be so again. I never knowingly did you wrong, and if I have caused you pain it is a grief to me. On some points I believe you to be mistaken. You will live to find it out.'

"He looked at me scrutinisingly. I think he was beginning to believe in me. The bracing, brilliant mountain air, the glorious sunlight, the ennobling beauty of the scenery around us were all in my favour, and I felt it. He looked up, and threw the hair from his brow. I saw that a struggle was going on between his natural generosity and the evil spirit that had got possession of him. Finally his eye sought mine.

"'God is around and above us,' I said; 'let not this glorious sun go down upon our wrath. Fingall, why cannot we be friends?'

"I stretched out my hands towards him, and he made a movement. As God is my judge, I do not know whether he intended to advance towards me in friendship or to retreat in denial of my appeal. His step backward may have been an involuntary one; the next moment he might have flung himself forward into my arms. My memory of the look in his eyes assures me that to do so was his intention. But he stood upon treacherous ground. In the excitement of our feelings neither of us had noticed that he had backed while speaking to the very edge of an abyss. He took one fatal step and vanished. I heard his cry as he went whirling down the precipice—then all was silent. . . .

"I hurried down the mountain in a terrible state of agitation; met some people and told my story, and we went in search of him. He was found quite dead. At the inquest I gave my evidence, and a verdict of accidental death was returned. His family were in a frantic state of grief. He was his mother's youngest and favourite son, and the calamity threatened to deprive her of her reason. So deep was my own affliction that it was some time before I began to perceive that people were looking askance at me. Some one was whispering away my fair fame. A nameless horror rose up beside me, dogged my steps, haunted me like an evil spirit; when I tried to grasp it, it slipped through my fingers and vanished. I resolved not to see it, tried to forget it, ascribed its existence to my own over-excited imagination; but still the reality of it was there, asserting itself at every opportunity. At last one day with a sudden shock I came in front of it and saw its face, ghastly with falsehood and corruption. It was believed that I had murdered Fingall! . . . .

"The whisper grew and swelled into a murmur so loud that I could not shut my ears to it. Even in Mave's tender eyes there arose a cloud of doubt. Her smile grew colder and colder, and a look of fear came over her face when I appeared. I became aware that I had a powerful though secret accuser, who, while assuming to screen me, was all the time gradually and persistently blasting my good name.

"There came a day when I could bear it no longer, and I went to Mave and asked an explanation of the change in her manner towards me. I said I knew there were evil rumours in circulation concerning me, but I should not care for them, I could live them down, if only she would bravely believe in me. At once I saw my doom in her averted eyes. It seemed that, whoever my accuser might be, he had her ear and that her mind was becoming poisoned against me. Seeing the despair in my face, she burst into passionate weeping; but when I drew near to comfort her she shrank from me. In the agonising scene that followed I learned that some secret evidence had been laid before her which she considered overwhelming. Timorous and gentle I had known her to be, but that she could be so miserably weak and wanting in trust of me, whom she had chosen

and dignified with her love—of disloyalty like this I had not dreamed. I went to her brother Luke, who was the dominant spirit in that unwholesome household, stated my case, declared my innocence, and asked him, as man to man, to help me to free myself from this curse that was threatening to blast me. I found him cool, reticent, suspicious, professing to be my friend, unwilling to say anything hurtful to me, but evidently firmly convinced of my guilt. He said that, for the sake of old friendship and of his sister's former love for me, they were all anxious to screen me from the consequences of what had happened. I answered that I wanted no screen, only to come face to face with my accuser. He smiled slightly, saying that that I could never do.

" I left him feeling as if I had been beating my heart against a rock, and for some time longer I held my ground, lying in wait for my enemy, striving to kill the lie that was slowly withering up the sap of my veins ; but as air escapes the clutch of the hand, so did this cruel calumny fatally and perpetually elude my grasp. As the wretch doomed to be walled up alive watches stone placed upon stone, building up the barrier that separates him from life, so, slowly and surely, I saw the last glimpse of light disappear from my horizon. One day I rose up and shook myself together, and owned that I could bear it no longer. I went to Mave for the last time, and, finding her still possessed by the belief in my guilt, I bade her an abrupt farewell and went forth like a lost soul out of her presence. I shook the dust of the Glens from my feet, and departed from the country without taking leave of any one. Strange looks and wags of the head had so long followed me, that I believed scarce a man in the place would have cared to shake hands with me. I was looked on as a murderer, who, for certain reasons of old friendship, had been allowed to escape justice, but whose presence was not to be desired in an honest community.

"To understand fully the general abhorrence in which I was held, one would need to know the character of the Glens people. A murder had not occurred among them within the memory of man, hardly a theft, or anything that could be called a crime. The people had their faults and their squabbles, no doubt, but they were, on the whole, a singularly upright and simple-minded race, who kept the commandments and knew little of the world beyond their mountains.

"I went forth from among them with the brand of Cain on my forehead, to go on with my life as best I might in some spot where rumour could not follow me. No man bade me God-speed. Every one shrank from my path as I walked the road, and doors were shut as I passed them by. In all this there was only one exception. As I walked up Glenan with my heart swooning in my breast and my brain on fire, a woman opened her door and came a little way to meet me. Her name was Betty Macalister. She had been a servant in the Fingall family, and had recently married and gone to live in Glenan. Doubtless she knew the whole tragedy as well as any one knew it, but she opened her door and came out and offered me a drink of milk, which, I suppose, was the best way that occurred to her of expressing her good-will. My first impulse was to dash it from her hand and pass on. How could she dare to be kind, when Mave—? But a look in her homely eyes, which had an angel's light in them at the moment, altered my mood. I took the milk and tasted it, and returned it to her with thanks.

"'Good-bye, Mr Arthur,' she said, 'and God defend the innocent!'

"I could not answer her. I looked at her silently, and heaven knows what she saw in my gaze. She threw her apron over her face and rushed sobbing into the house.

"I went to London, where I stayed till I had effected the sale of my little property in Kerry, and the home that was to have been hers and mine was made over to strangers. All that time I walked the streets of London like a man in a nightmare. So long as I kept walking I felt that I had a hold on my life, had my will in control; but when I sat down, the desire for self-destruction rushed upon me. I believe I walked the entire of London many times over, yet I did not know where I walked and remember nothing that I saw. During this time I wrote to Luke Adare, telling him I was going to Minnesota, and would send him my address when I arrived there. I was not going to behave like a criminal who had been glad to be allowed to escape. If at any future time I were to be wanted by friends or enemies, they should know where to find me.

"After that Luke wrote to me, once to London and two or three times to Minnesota. There was nothing in his letter which seemed to require an answer, and I did not answer him. Indeed, it was, and is still, a wonder to me that he wrote as he did to a man whom he believed to be a murderer, and one who would not even confess or regret his crime. There was a sympathising and pitying tone in his communication which surprised me, for Luke was no tender sentimentalist. He gave me no information about home; he never mentioned Mave. What was the reason of his writing at all I could never make out.

"I received one other letter from the Glens, and that **was** from Betty Macalister, to whom I had also given

my address, having an instinctive feeling that if anything were to turn up to clear my good name, she
would be more likely than Luke to let me know."

Bawn here turned to Betty's letter, which was as
follows :—

"YOUR HON. DEAR MISSTER ARTHUR :

"This comes hoppin' you are well as leaves me in
this present time the same and husband. The hollow
fokes is not doin' well. The ould Misster Barbadus he
left all he had to Misster Look. The ould house luks
bad an' Miss Mave she dozzint walk out at all. The
gentlemen has quare ways an' the people dozzint like
them a bit better nor they did. There was great doin's
for a while, but the munny dozzint last with them, A
think, for the ould place is lukkin' bad now. My man
an' me sticks to you thru thick an' thin, but yure better
where ye are.—Yures to kommand,

"BETTY MACALISTER."

This epistle, which bore a date ten years after
Arthur's departure, Bawn read over and over again,
and one piece of information it contained struck her as
remarkable : "Old Barbadoes" had left all his money
to Luke Adare—the money which it was supposed
would, under other circumstances, have come to Arthur,
as his favourite.

The next letter she opened was from Luke himself.
He wrote :

"I hope you are doing well, for in spite of all that
has happened I feel a deep interest in your welfare.
The New World is before you, and your story cannot
follow you there. Indeed, it is hushed up here, for all
sakes, though it never can be quite forgotten. You

may yet be a prosperous man, outlive the past, and make new friends. I shall always be glad to hear of you, and to know what you are doing, &c., &c., &c.—
"Your sincere well-wisher,

"LUKE ADARE."

The remaining letters were very much in the same strain, expressing a desire to know something of the exile, and showing a leniency towards him as a murderer, which was hard to understand. Some of them contained reproaches of Arthur for not having written to give an account of himself. "Only that Betty Macalister has had a line from you, I should think you were dead," he wrote under the latest date of twenty-five years ago. It was evident that Desmond had never gratified the curiosity of this anxious friend.

Bawn was very apt to jump, rightly or wrongly, to a conclusion, and by the time she had folded up all the papers and replaced them in a box she had made up her mind that Luke Adare was the person who, for his own selfish ends, had whispered away her father's good name, and blighted the lives of both sister and friend. Arthur a murderer and banished, and Roderick Fingall dead, the inheritance had devolved upon Luke as the eldest of the Adares.

"And this frail creature," she said, studying Mave's portrait again, "this was a tool easy enough to work with. Had you been a brave, true woman, ready to stand up in his defence and fight the lie with him, he might have been able to hunt down the liar and clear himself before the world. But you quailed and deserted him, you coward! Luke was the villain and you were the fool!"

The greater part of that day Bawn spent riding alone over the prairie, revolving and maturing her project as

she went, considering the details of it and the dangers
and difficulties it might include. That evening she
walked up to Mrs Desmond in the drawing-room and
said, in a tone of simple friendliness:

"Jeanne, I have made up my mind to let you have
the house."

Jeanne was amazed. She had made her demand,
well aware she had no right to make it, and without
expecting to find her audacity so quickly rewarded.

Bawn continued: "I am going to St Paul in the
morning to speak about it to Dr Ackroyd."

Mrs Desmond was instantly alarmed. She did not
like the interference of Dr Ackroyd, who would make
it a matter of business. "Why need he interfere
between us?" she said. "Cannot we make our own
arrangements? You are of age."

"I wish to consult him," said Bawn, quietly. "It is
not long since he was my guardian. And you forget,
Jeanne: it will be necessary for me to find some shelter
for myself when I leave the place to you."

"This is very provoking of you," cried Jeanne, "to
talk as if I wanted to turn you out. Why can we not
all go on together?"

"Let that be; it is my affair," said Bawn. "I have
other plans for my future."

"Now, what plans can she have?" thought Jeanne,
looking round the handsome room, and running over in
her mind all the goodly possessions and advantages she
was gaining by Bawn's generosity. "It must be that
she means to go to Europe and figure as an heiress at
the fashionable places." And Jeanne thought, with an
impatient sigh, of how admirably that part would have
suited her, if she had just been twenty or thirty years
younger, and had not acquired the passion for making
money.

CHAPTER V.

A WILFUL WOMAN.

THE next day Bawn made a journey into St Paul to consult her guardian.

Dr Ackroyd had been her father's oldest friend in Minnesota, and the only man who had ever approached to anything like intimacy with him. At a time when the doctor had been hardly pressed by pecuniary troubles, Desmond's generosity had laid the foundation of his ultimate prosperity—a fact which he had never forgotten.

"Doctor," said Bawn, walking into the snug room where he and his wife were sitting, "I have come to talk to you on business. You know I am a woman of business capabilities now—twenty-one years of age last month."

The doctor nodded. "Yes, yes; she has found it all out. I was her guardian a month ago, Molly, but now she will be for taking the bit in her own teeth, no doubt."

"I have a pretty good fortune, haven't I, Dr Ackroyd?"

"As pretty a fortune as any young woman in America, I should say at a guess; and that is saying much. Come, now, what do you want to do? Trip away to Paris, and all the rest of it?

"And quite natural too, Andrew, at her age, and with such a fortune and such a face!" said Mrs Ackroyd, a motherly old lady, with whom Bawn was a favourite.

4

The same thought was present in the minds of husband and wife as they looked at Bawn's fine, fair face, with its grave sweetness and a certain majesty of womanly dignity which in her most thoughtful moments sat on her brow. At such moments her coil of golden hair looked like a royal crown. Now, as she gazed into the fire, seeing something which they did not see, they easily fancied her in brilliant rooms, shining in white satin or some such raiment, with crowds of adorers hovering round her. They knew the sort of thing that happens well enough. Many a lovely young heiress sails from America and gets turned into a countess or a marquise before many summers have poured their choicest flowers into her lap.

"Yes, I have been thinking of going to Europe," said Bawn, "though not to Paris."

"It is the gayest place and the prettiest," said the doctor. "Of course there are the summer resorts——"

"I was not thinking of gaiety, nor even of prettiness," said Bawn, "though the place I mean to go to is, I believe, beautiful enough. But if it were the ugliest place on earth, and the dullest, as it probably is, I should want to go all the same."

She spoke musingly and looked into the fire, seeing in the burning wood fairy glens, and mountains with giddy paths from which a false step might hurl a man in an instant—mountains with lonely hollows of their own, and secret paths dark enough to overshadow a human being's life.

The doctor gazed at her in astonishment. "Come," he said, "I give it up."

"Doctor," said the girl suddenly, looking at him straight, "did it ever strike you that my father had had a great trouble in his life, one that must have been more than the ordinary kind of trouble?"

The doctor's face changed. " I always thought it," he said gently.

Bawn turned red and then quite white. " It is true," she said ; " and the journey I want to make has reference to that trouble."

She paused and hesitated.

" My dear," said Dr Ackroyd, "if you have anything to say to me in confidence, my wife will go away."

" No," said Bawn firmly, stretching out her hand to the old lady, who was regarding her with deep concern. " I can trust you both, if you will bear with me."

Mrs Ackroyd stirred in her chair with good-natured emotion and a little curiosity, and, wiping her spectacles with the hand that was not in Bawn's grip, put them on, as if they would help her to see well into whatever was going to be laid before her.

Bawn went on speaking, white to the lips, but with firm voice and calm eyes :

" My father left his country, you know, as a young, quite a young man. Well, he left it under a cloud. Some enemy had whispered away his good name and blighted his life. He had friends, and there was a woman who had loved him and was to have married him ; and they one and all—good God ! can you believe it ?—they one and all cast him out of their lives, withdrew their faith and their friendship from him, and sent him across the world with a broken heart and spirit— poor heart that nothing could ever heal ; noble spirit that is free from pain at last !"

Grief brimmed over Bawn's sad eyes as she finished. She suddenly covered her face and sat drowned in tears.

Her friends did not worry her with questions and consolations, only suffered the floods that had opened to wash themselves away ; and the girl said presently :

"There, that is over. You are very, very good to listen to me."

"Now," she continued, with a light leaping into her eyes and determination straightening the quiver of her lips, "I know that he had an enemy who slandered him, or all this could never have happened. He himself believed that he was the victim of circumstances, but I do not believe it. Certain notes and papers have been put in my hands to read, and I have formed my own conclusions from them. I shall never rest till I have sifted the matter to the bottom—in as far as it can be sifted," she added, wistfully, "at the end of thirty years."

"Ah! that is it," said the doctor with a smothered sigh. "And, my dear child, I don't want to contradict you—I feel with you intensely—but how, if at the time he found it so impossible to clear himself, how do you dream of being able to do it now?"

"Not by walking into the country, into the houses of those people, and saying, 'You are my deadly enemies. I am Arthur Desmond's daughter, and you calumniated my father. Confess your sins, or I shall—I shall go back crestfallen where I came from!'" said Bawn, with lips relaxing into a little smile. "No; that is not my plan. I think I have been studying to acquire the guile of the serpent during the last few days, and I have laid a little plot which I cannot put into execution without the assistance of a friend."

"Well?" said the doctor looking at her inquiringly. "Continue."

"I intend," pursued Bawn, "to go to the place—a secluded spot it was; and I believe, I have been told, it is not the sort of place that changes much—a glenny and mountainy place such as we read about but do not see here."

"I know," said the doctor, nodding, and instantly seeing pictures in his memory ; for he, too, was an exile and loved Scotland.

"I shall go there," said Bawn, "not in my own name and character, but as the orphan daughter of a farmer, an emigrant, who, from what she has heard from her father about his native land, has taken a fancy to see it and live in it. She has brought her small fortune—say five hundred pounds, her father's savings—to invest in a little farm such as a woman can manage. In this way I will settle down among those people, as near them as possible, and, without exciting their suspicion or putting them on their guard, will try to get at the long-hidden secret, strive to unearth the too long buried truth. When I succeed I shall disclose my identity, pour out the vials of my wrath upon the false or good-for-nothing friends, shake the dust off my feet—and come back here to you."

"A pretty romance, my dear, but about as wild and impossible as pretty."

"Do not say so."

"What do you propose to do if you find it beyond your power to get at that long lost truth?"

"Come back here all the same, only worsted," said Bawn ; "but it will be long before I confess myself beaten. A number of people must be dead first."

"And if you find them all already dead?"

"That is not likely," said Bawn quickly. "Not in such a healthy country place, where the people live long. I have thought it all out, and the chances are with me."

Dr Ackroyd was silent. Wild as the girl's scheme was, he saw she was completely in earnest, and he knew her long enough and well enough to have had experience of a character indicated by the shape of her broad, fair brows and certain expressions of her clear grey eyes and good-tempered mouth. There had always been a simple and intelligent directness about her intentions and a robust fearlessness in carrying them out that made such a proposal from her somewhat different to what it might have been coming from any ordinary impulsive, romantic girl, who would be pretty sure to give up her plan in disgust and dismay after a first tussle with a few uncomfortable obstacles. He admitted to himself that, if any girl could carry out such an enterprise, no better one than this could be found to undertake it. But of what was he thinking? All the strength of his influence over her must be exerted to prevent her entering on such a wild and uncertain path.

He was sufficiently a man of the world to know what had never entered into the saddest dreams that ever flitted through Bawn's golden head—to be well aware that there existed a possibility, if not a likelihood, that Arthur Desmond had been really guilty of whatever crime or transgression had been laid to his charge. During all the long life that he had spent in this new country Dr Ackroyd had met with a great number of men who in their youth had blundered into evil, and had either come out here of their own free will or been sent by their indignant friends to begin life afresh where their past was unknown. And why might not Desmond have been one of these? He would prefer to believe, with Bawn, that the man who had lived here so stainless a life and suffered so deeply had been guiltless from the beginning, and the victim of malice or a mistake. But the entire faith of Bawn's heart could not make its way into his. Not only did he see the probability of failure for her enterprise, but feared that she might be met by some overwhelming testimony to his guilt—guilt long expiated, and perhaps for ever forgotten had not her rash and loving hand rooted it out from the past which had buried it. Might not even a bright and strong creature like this be felled by such a blow?

These thoughts trooped quickly through his mind, and Bawn watched the changing expressions of his face.

"Well," she said quietly, "you are not going to oppose me?"

"My dear," he said, "I will oppose you with every argument, with all the persuasion, I am capable of compelling to my aid. Had this occurred some time ago I should have been in a position to forbid you absolutely to carry out so wild an intention. As it is, you are your own mistress. I cannot control your actions. I can only beseech you to take an old man's advice, and *let the dead past bury its dead.* Your father is at rest; the waves of time have rolled over his sorrow. You need never come in contact with any one who knows anything of his story. In any other plan for your life, in any indulgence you can imagine, I will help you to the best of my ability; but I cannot see you act in a way which I believe would be the ruin of every prospect you have in the world."

"I have no prospect," answered Bawn, sadly. "What could I do with my life while this shadow rests on it?"

"Your idea is overstrained. By and by you will form new ties—"

"Never!" said Bawn, solemnly. "Even if I wished it, and it were likely, never could I till this cloud is cleared away."

The doctor was startled and silent. He had not been told what was the nature of the wrong thing of which Desmond had been accused, and the look in Bawn's eyes at this moment suggested that it was something even worse than he had imagined. But he spoke cheerfully.

"Pooh!" he said; "you are in a morbid humour.

Put off the consideration of this matter, for a time
at least. You will change your mind; you will give
it up."

"I will never give it up," said Bawn, her soft lips
closing and tightening with resolution. "The wish has
gone too deep. There is nothing else to live for in my
life."

This was the beginning of a struggle which lasted for
two months between Bawn and her ex-guardian, and at
the end of that time Dr Ackroyd felt himself obliged to
lower his colours and let the girl have her way. Rather
than allow her to follow it without help or protection of
any kind, he was forced to yield and take the affair into
his own hands. Step by step she gained upon him; bit
by bit she got all her will. His first concession included
the proviso that he was to be allowed to take her across
the ocean himself, and that, before he suffered her to go
seeking her fortune in that unknown spot towards which
her desires were carrying her, he was to pay a visit to
the place as a tourist, take note of how things stood
there, gather information about the people, and make
up his mind as to how far her plan for coming among
them was safe and practicable. To all this Bawn un-
easily consented at first, fearing much that such protection and precaution might excite attention and
frustrate her aims. Fate in the end decreed that she
was to go her wilful way and perform her pilgrimage
according to the programme she had at first marked out
for herself. A dearly-loved child of Dr Ackroyd's was
discovered to have fallen into a dangerous state of
health, and he found it impossible to leave her. Bawn
must either go alone or not at all. She chose to go.

"You can put me on board and give me in charge to
the captain," she said; "and when I land, if I find any
difficulty, I can telegraph to you, and you can telegraph

to your English friends, whom I will not go near if I can help it. This will surely be protection enough for a steady young woman like me, of the class to which I shall belong. Nobody will mind a simple farmer's daughter. How many poor girls come out to America every day to earn their bread under circumstances so much worse than mine! If I were travelling with you I should be always betraying myself; and if, as you say, 'the world is so small,' somebody would be sure to see me who might meet me afterwards and find me out."

Her friends felt themselves unable to restrain her. After all, their own child was their first consideration, and Desmond's daughter was impatient to be away. Jeanne was married, and Bawn felt herself pushed bodily out of her home. There was nothing more for her to do here except to procure an outfit of very plain clothing to suit the station of life she had chosen, to make some money arrangements transferring a few hundred pounds to an Irish bank, and, leaving her fortune in Dr Ackroyd's hands, to say good-bye to the dear old home and to the beloved grave where peacefully her father slept.

CHAPTER VI.

AFLOAT.

"I WAS a madman to let her go," muttered the doctor, taking off his hat and wiping his troubled brow. '"I ought to have had her committed to a lunatic asylum first."

"I don't see how you could, dear," said his mild, literal wife, "as she is not mad. People would have thought you were plotting for her money."

The doctor groaned. "There is no help for spilt milk," he said. "So wilful though so sweet a specimen of womankind I never knew. She has turned me round her finger like a skein of worsted. God send it may not yet be the breaking of our hearts; for if anything happens amiss to Bawn we can never hold up our heads again."

That triumphant young woman, having looked her last through tears at her receding native shores, had now seated herself in a convenient nook on deck with her face oceanwards, and was regarding the boundless, glistening vista before her with a strange and solemn delight. It was her first introduction to the sea. Most of us behold that great wonder first from afar off, then we make acquaintance with it piecemeal; some blue sandskirted bay becomes dear to us, or we learn to worship it from purple-clad cliffs, with the gulls riding on the green waves beneath at our feet. But Bawn had suddenly been lifted from her forest and prairies, and flung, dazzled and amazed, upon this illimitable world of waters. As the view became wider, and the ocean became more and more a living, all-absorbing presence to her mind, regret, courage, hope, loneliness, confidence, all of which had been shaking her and inspiring her by turns, alike vanished and were forgotten, and she sat breathing in long, deep draughts of salt air and delight, enjoying her young existence with the joy that is the inheritance of sea-birds.

She had planted herself in a corner, so that her back was to the other passengers on board, whose tramp, tramp as they took their walk up and down the deck, and the occasional sound of whose voices, fell on her ear but did not disturb her privacy. She was right in the front of the vessel, all her being going willingly forward with it, her face set outward towards the horizon of sea and sky behind which lay the secrets she had tasked herself to penetrate and the lands she had never seen. The books with which the doctor had supplied her were untouched. Who could read in a world of such ever-shifting, ever-shimmering enchantment? Leaning well forward, her firm, white chin set in the pink hollow of her hand, she let the hours go by without once turning her head to see how it fared with the humanity behind her. The only person who for a minute engaged her notice during those first morning hours was a man who had got further even than herself into the very end of the vessel, and, mounted on a heap of ropes, gazed for some time out seaward through a glass. She observed that it was a straight, well-built figure, and that the profile had a clean-cut outline. Long before he had done gazing through his glass Bawn had forgotten him and was again looking out, out far, with fascinated eyes at the glittering, ever-shifting boundary lines of the realms of light towards which the great heart of the steamer was straining and panting. As he turned to spring from his vantage-ground of coiled ropes the man glanced towards the figure that had sat so persistently motionless during all the first hours of the voyage— hours when people are generally so full of fidgets and so eagerly speculating on the chances of desirable acquaintance among fellow-passengers. Evidently this person, young or old (her back had looked young, though muffled in a shepherd's plaid scarf and broad-brimmed black straw hat), desired to become acquainted with no one, for she deliberately set her face from all. It was not for the purpose of seeing what that face was like that he had scaled the height of the rope-heap, but, having glanced at it once, he stopped a moment, gazing, and then, though she had not been conscious of him at all, involuntarily lifted his hat before he sprang lightly back on the deck.

At evening he noticed her again, thinking : " I wonder how much longer that girl will be able to sit still ? Will she keep in one position for eight or nine days to come ? "

On the instant the wind carried off her hat and a quick hand caught it, and Bawn stood facing her fellow-traveller sooner than he had expected, her smooth gold head laid bare, its locks ruffled with the breeze, and her fair cheeks dyed a rich damask, partly with surprise, partly from the flame-coloured reflections in the air.

"Thank you greatly," she said with unaffected gratitude, receiving her hat from his hands.

"You must take better care of it."

"Yes; if it had gone what should I have done ? I have not another," said Bawn gravely, and then smiled as the image of herself sitting on deck hatless for the rest of the journey rose before her.

"I will tie a string to it for you. On board ship and on the top of a mountain there is nothing else of use.

Allow me. I know the right place to fasten it," taking
the hat from her hand.

"I have never been at sea before," said Bawn, "and
so I could not know."

Bawn was standing in the red glow of the sun,
heavenly fire in her grey eyes, her face gleaming in cool
tones against the rose dusk of the sky, like that of some
fair saint set in an old jewelled window. Her new
acquaintance was not observing her, busied with his
good-natured exertions.

"There!" he said, lifting his glance, "that will—."
He stopped short, gazing at her in surprise.

"Good heavens, how beautiful! And who sent her
off to cross the ocean alone?"

"That will hold," he went on quickly, as Bawn took
the hat and put it on her head, suddenly remembering
that she had resolved to make acquaintance with nobody,
and had been specially counselled to keep young men
at a distance.

"They will always be wanting to do things for you,
my dear," good Mrs Ackroyd had said; "but if you
allow them it will end by their getting in your way, so
that you won't know how to get rid of them." And
Bawn, thinking with a shudder of Jeanne's cousin Henri,
the only young man she had ever come much in contact
with, had believed she should find it very easy indeed
to prevent them from coming within yards of her. But
this person was not like cousin Henri.

She made her hat fast, and with a great effort checked
the pleasant, sociable feeling that had been growing on
her, threatening to loosen her tongue and make her
feel at home with this stranger.

"I am greatly obliged to you," she said in a voice
that sounded suddenly cold, and then, making him a
bow, the manner of which was never learned on the

prairie and must have come to her by inheritance, like the sheen on her hair, she withdrew into the shelter of her corner again, and resumed her old attitude of solitary reserve.

He felt his dismissal to be a little abrupt, and yet, continuing his walk about the deck as if nothing had happened, the man was no way displeased at it.

"What a brute I was to stare at her like that!" he reflected. "If I had seen another fellow do it I should have knocked him down. Had she not curled herself up in her corner after it I should no longer feel an interest in her. I wonder how long it will be before she allows me to speak to her again?"

The next morning before going on deck, Bawn provided herself with books and some knitting. Her chief desire at present was to pass unnoticed and unquestioned on the voyage, as there was danger to be dreaded from even the most harmless intercourse. Some one might come to identify her as her father's daughter, and make her known to some other who might probably cross her future path in that yet unknown region towards which she was so eagerly travelling. She thought of her friend of the evening before, and decided that to no one's curiosity would she make the slightest concession, beyond a statement of the fact that she was a farmer's daughter from Minnesota and alone in the world. The man was a gentleman and would hardly ask questions; but things leak out in conversation, and she knew herself well enough to be aware that the most difficult part of the task she had assumed would be the concealment it was bound to entail. For though she owed no confidence to any one, it is so much more pleasant to be frank.

She had scarcely got the needles arranged in her knitting before she perceived that one of the many pairs of passing feet had stopped beside her, and there was her friend of the evening before, cap in hand, regarding her with as much deference as if she had been a queen.

"It is cold to-day, and it is going to be colder. Will you allow me to open your rugs and make you a little more comfortable?"

Bawn looked at him kindly, and for a moment was so inconsistent as to be glad to hear any voice breaking on her solitude; but the next she remembered that here was a possible enemy, who, after some time, if he got encouragement, might, voluntarily or involuntarily, become aware of her identity. Before she had had time to make up her mind whether to repulse him or not, he was stooping over her rugs and shaking them out. "You had better take this chair," he said, bringing one forward. "You will soon get tired of your camp-stool."

Spreading a rug over a chair, he bade her sit on it, and wrapped the warm woollen stuff about her feet. All this was done so quickly and easily, that she felt dismayed to observe how soon her power of keeping people at a distance had deserted her, another person's power of service having put it to rout. Prying and officiousness she had prepared herself to deal with, but genuine good nature is not easy to repulse. Feeling at once the improvement in her condition, she felt bound to admit it with thanks.

"I am glad you have books," he continued, picking them up to place them beside her. The "Count of Monte-Christo" and "Hiawatha" were two of the volumes bought almost at random by Dr Ackroyd at the bookstall. "'Hiawatha'—ah! I meant to have gone out to that country, had not business called me home sooner than I expected. Have you read the poem, or do you know the Dakota country?"

Bawn bit her lip. She had a strong misgiving that

farmers' daughters of the class to which she wished to belong did not read poetry, yet how could she deny her acquaintance with the poem, every word of which had been read to her by her father lying under the forest trees ?

"My home was in Minnesota," she said, "and I have seen the Falls of Minnehaha ; and—yes, I know 'Hiawatha' pretty well."

The words came forth reluctantly. How lamentably she was breaking down at the very beginning in the acting of her part! Should she ever learn to conceal or evade the truth ? But the stranger was not thinking of her, but of the book.

"I read it long ago," he said, "and everything concerning the Indians always possessed an interest for me. I must read it up again. Have you any objection to hear a little of it now while you work ? "

Bawn breathed a silent sigh and pricked her finger. Was this man going to make her acquaintance in spite of herself ? Oh! if he were only like cousin Henri, how easily she could snub him ; but, as it was, she could not think of any form of denial which would not seem like downright rudeness on her part in return for his politeness.

"Do not let me fatigue you," she said, making one great effort to discourage him, but he only answered, smiling :—

"It will be a new kind of fatigue, that will savour of rest. My limbs have been well exercised of late, my tongue not at all. If I do not bore you—"

"No," said Bawn with unwilling truth, and keeping her eyes on her work.

"If I do not look at him at all," she thought, "perhaps there will be less danger of his remembering afterwards what 1 am like."

The reading began. An earnest, deep-toned voice took up the rhythm of the poem and gave forth the words as if they were set to music, and a mist came over the listener's eyes as the sound of the familiar lines awakened painful memories in her heart. She had wanted to forget everything but the future; and was this a good or an evil spirit that had crossed her path and baffled her intentions? Sometimes she missed the sense of what was read while enjoying the melody of the voice and the pure intonation of the words, uttered with an accent a little foreign to her ears. Of course he was a foreigner. Had he not spoken of being called home on business? The certainty of this brought a feeling of relief to the girl as she listened. If he were only an Englishman returning from a trip to New York, not having been as far as Minnesota, never having met with or heard of her or hers while on American soil, what reason had she to imagine that discovery of her identity by those from whom she wished to conceal it could ever overtake her through his agency? None, if she could only be wise and control her too candid tongue. Whatsoever she represented herself to be, as that and nothing else must he accept her. Considering this and the extreme unlikelihood that, having parted on reaching Great Britain, they should ever meet again, Bawn felt the anxious strain upon her mind relax and her heart rise high within her. She raised her eyes fearlessly, and for the first time took accurate note of her companion's appearance. The blue cloth cap which had replaced the hat he had worn last evening was pushed back a little, showing the whole of a broad forehead, the upper half of which looked white above the sun-tanned brownness of the rest of the face. His crisp, dark hair would have been curly if not so closely cut, and he wore a thick brown beard that did not hide a

somewhat large and sensible mouth. His eyes were
deep-set under strong brows, and almost sombre in
colour, though readily emitting flashes of fun. It was
altogether a practical and keenly sympathetic face,
with humour lurking in all its little curves. Just now a
slight languor, expressive of his enjoyment of the rest
he had spoken of as desired by him, lent him a character not always his own. Seeing that her observation
was unnoticed, Bawn studied him with care for some
moments, and made up her mind that he was worthy of
her interest. A pleasant and most unwonted feeling of
the suitability of their companionship grew on her, and
as she plied her needles she glanced at him again.
This time his eyes met her stolen investigating
glance.

> " Minnehaha, Laughing Water,
>   Loveliest of Dakota maidens,"

he was saying as he raised his dark eyes to take an
equally stolen and investigating glance at his silent and
industrious auditress. She said she had come from the
Dakota country, she had stood beside the Falls of
Minnehaha ; and some analogy between the fair face
that looked up at times and out to sea beyond him
with an expression in the wide grey eyes that he could
not fathom, some fancied resemblance between this
present maiden and the Laughing Water of the woods
and prairies, had doubtless occurred to his mind and
caused him to glance at her, unexpectedly meeting her
gaze.

Bawn, aware of all the cool observation that had
been in her own gaze, reddened, and said quickly: " I
have been thinking."

" Yes ! " said her companion, glancing away, plant-
ing himself more firmly on his elbow, and speaking in

the most matter-of-fact voice. "So was I. You were
going to tell me——"

"Nothing."

"I beg your pardon. Look! Did you ever see anything so marvellous as the sun on the wings of yonder
flight of birds?"

"Wonderful!" said Bawn, shading her eyes with her
hand, which was not yet browned and reddened by
farming labours as she could have wished it to appear.
"How fast they go! They will be there long before us."

"There? Where?"

"Oh! anywhere. Great Britain, I suppose." She
was unwilling to name Ireland, lest in the very tone of
her voice as she pronounced the word he should hear
her whole history.

"Are you so very anxious to have the journey over?"

"Yes," said Bawn, fervently wishing she could fly
after those birds and reach her destination at once,
escaping perilous *tête-à-têtes* with strange and possibly
inquisitive people.

"I do not feel at all impatient," said her friend with
the blue cap ; "though, if I were properly alive to consequences, I ought to be, for I am bound to be in
London on the morning of the eighth day from this."

"Why, then, not have sailed on an earlier date and
given yourself more time?"

"Why not, indeed, except that Fate plays us curious
tricks? I thought to have done so, but, owing to an
accident, I arrived at New York in great haste only at
the last moment before this steamer sailed. However,
I am of a philosophic turn of mind, and I said to myself, 'I will take this disappointment as a stroke of good
luck. Who knows what may turn up on the way to
make me glad that I was disappointed?"

A satisfied smile brightened on his face as he spoke,

and, though he was looking out to sea and not at her, Bawn felt that he meant to convey that he was already grown pleased with the existing state of things, and, partly at least, because he had found a companion in her. She could not reflect his contentment. Why need his voyage have been inconveniently delayed only, it would seem, for the purpose of embarrassing her?

One grain of comfort she did extract from his statement however. "He is not Irish, at all events," she thought, "and, once I land in Queenstown, will, in all human probability, never cross my path again." Reflecting on this, she unbent her brows a little and consented to become a trifle more friendly.

CHAPTER VII.

ACQUAINTANCES.

WHEN lying awake in her berth that night, Bawn, reflecting on the swiftness and pleasantness with which her day had flown by in the society of the person in the blue cap, acknowledged to herself that she had very foolishly departed from her original plan of making acquaintance with no one on board, allowing no one to intrude upon her privacy. She was running a great risk in permitting herself a friendly intercourse with this individual. True, she had been very careful, had given him no clue to her identity. He did not know her name—not even the name she had chosen to bear during her stay in Ireland—and she now made a firm resolve that she would not betray it to him. He had certainly not shown any curiosity, though on one occasion she fancied he had given her an opening to mention her name, possibly wishing to know it as a matter of convenience. She was well aware that she had passed over the opportunity, and that he had noticed it, and it hurt her that she had been forced to be so secretive. But then had she not entered on a course which would necessitate the utmost secretiveness ? Bawn sighed as she thought of how ill she was in this respect fitted by nature to play the part she had undertaken, but reflected that she must make up by determination for what she lacked in other ways. In arranging her plans she had never calculated on the likelihood of her caring

much for what others might think of her, being fully
persuaded that the loneliness and singleness of her own
purpose would be sufficient to carry her through every
difficulty. And now already she winced because she
had not been able to be perfectly frank with an acquaintance of forty-eight hours.

"Well," she thought, "the only way to avert this
danger is to keep him at a distance. It will be but a
matter of a few days. To-morrow I must begin by
staying away from deck all day."

And, having settled the affair in this way, she slept
profoundly.

When the morrow arrived it was hard to keep to
so unpleasant a line of conduct as that on which she
had decided. The sun shone, the breeze was pleasant.
Down-stairs she felt in prison, but still she stayed
below in the places inaccessible to gentlemen. She
appeared at table in her place beside the captain, and
at lunch her friend of the blue cap hoped she had not
been ill, and told her how delightful it was on deck
to-day. Bawn was obliged to admit that she was not
ill, but stated her intention of resting in the ladies'
cabin all day. Her friend looked surprised.

"You are not ill now," he said. "I never saw any
one look more healthy, more undisturbed by the sea.
But if you begin to stay down-stairs you will make
yourself ill."

"I hope not," said Bawn, serenely, and passed into
the prison to which she had condemned herself.

The day passed wearily. All the unpleasantnesses
of the sea now forced themselves upon her. Her companions were sick, or unmanageable children who could
not be trusted long on deck, and a few of those women
who, no matter how good the passage, are always
grievously ill on a voyage. She tried to pass the time

by making herself useful and agreeable, but when
evening came she felt jaded and depressed for want of
the abundance of fresh air to which she had been always
accustomed. As soon as it was quite dusk, she concluded that she must breathe freely for a little while
before settling to rest for the night, and went boldly
up on deck.

It is too late for "Hiawatha," at any rate, she thought,
as she leaned over the ship's side and rejoiced in her
freedom. The stars crept out one by one, the phosphor-
tracks gleamed on the water, the breeze was wild and
fresh, and the watery world boundless around her. Her
heart widened within her, and her nervous little fears
took to themselves wings and flitted away into the
night. How foolish she had been to feel afraid of any
creature! A certain power within her—that power of
heart and brain which gave her temper its buoyancy
and strength—had been suffering cramp all day, and
now recovered its vigour, so that she was able to turn
with a quiet smile on hearing the now well-known and
importunate voice at her side.

"I ask your pardon," said the Blue Cap, "for trying
to interfere with your good resolves this morning. I
had no idea you were sacrificing yourself for the benefit
of others. I heard one lady singing your praises to
another just now, telling how you had been acting as a
sister of mercy all day."

"I did not stay for the sake of others, I am sorry
to say," she answered quickly; "I was thinking only of
myself."

"I fear I bored you yesterday with 'Hiawatha.'"
His tone was penitent, but Bawn's quick ear detected
a something which suggested that there was a sly
gleam of humour in his eyes as he spoke. It seemed
that she was making matters worse. Not having been

clever enough to pretend to be ill, nor yet to allow it
to be supposed that charity towards the sick had altogether influenced her, she had led him to suspect the
truth, and to imagine himself formidable enough to
frighten her out of his presence.

" No," she answered, " you did not bore me," thinking
how very much pleasanter yesterday had been than
to-day, and how ungrateful she certainly was.

" Thank you After that I may venture to ask you
to take a turn up and down the deck. A little exercise
before sleeping will be quite as good as a little air."

" I dare say it will," said Bawn readily, and, feeling
as if she was making some amends for her bad treatment
of a friend, she accepted his arm, and threaded with
him the groups of other peripatetics, feeling unaccount-
ably at home with this stranger in the crowd.

" How clear the stars are to-night ! " he said. " That
is one of the best things about being at sea, one gets
such a fine view of them all round ; and if one only had
a powerful telescope—"

" Yes," said Bawn, gladly, " how I wish we had ! "
And by the sound of her voice her companion knew
that his choice of a subject of conversation was a lucky
one. It had not been made without deliberation, and
had been selected among others that occurred to his
mind as being furthest off from this world of cares and
dangers, secrets and sorrows, and less likely to scare
away his reticent fellow-traveller from his side. That
this lonely girl, with the frank, true eyes, had some good
reason for wishing to keep her own counsel and to pass
unknown through the crowd was evident to him ; and
though he wished to cultivate her acquaintance, and,
if possible, make her voyage more pleasant for her, he
was anxious also that she should not feel embarrassed
by his companionship. Therefore he did not ask her

where she had been and whither she was going, how
much she had seen of this beautiful and interesting
world, and what particular part of it she was now
expecting to see, but suddenly placed a ladder of escape
from such questioning at her feet, and mounted boldly
with her to the stars.

"I suppose you understand something of astronomy,"
he said. "I used to know a little, but I confess I am
beginning to forget it."

"I don't know much more than the names of the
planets. I am a farmer's daughter, and astronomy can
hardly be expected of me. Some of the constellations
seem like old friends when I look up at them."

The Blue Cap here overcame a temptation to draw
out the farmer's daughter a little, even to the extent of
ascertaining what portion of this wide earth her father
farmed, and he felt that he had gained a victory over
her distrust of him when he heard her make even so
vague a statement as to her circumstances.

"When I was a youth," he said, "I used to think I
would like to have a star of my own, a country-house
among the cool fields above, and a sort of celestial
estate, which I could manage in my own way, without
so much trouble as one is obliged to take thanklessly
enough here."

"Rather a solitary state of grandeur to live in."

"Oh! I did not mean to be there alone. I was to
rejoice in the love of some angelic being, an inhabitant
of the star, who was to be as far above mere ordinary
women as my star was above the earth."

"You are not so romantic now," said Bawn, smiling.

"No; I was thinking a little while ago, just before I
saw your head appear above the stair yonder, that those
dreams of mine were a long way off, and that it made
me very old to remember them; and also," he added, as

if half to himself, "that I am now fain to be content to mate myself among the daughters of men."

Bawn said nothing, but the query naturally arose in her mind, had some charming daughter of men already taken possession of his heart, and, while speaking like this, was he thinking of her? And for the first time it occurred to Bawn to think of him as a person with a story of his own, with a home, with pursuits, occupations, loves, and friendships. He was no longer only a troublesome shadow haunting her to her sore annoyance and perplexity, but an individual who interested her and had the power to make her forget herself and her own affairs. On the instant she felt that she would have liked to ask him some questions, but, being so resolutely uncommunicative herself, upon what pretext could she look for anything approaching to confidence from him? She remained silent with the surprise of these new thoughts.

They continued their walk mutely, each wrapped in reflection. The stars waxed brighter overhead, the night-breeze blew freshly against them. Most of the passengers had gone down to rest; a few sat clustered in dark groups, or tramped up and down deck like themselves. The watery world lay dark, restless, and mysterious around, and Bawn experienced the pleasant feeling of comradeship — a feeling which gradually grew on her.

"I have been thinking," said the Blue Cap, "how very wide apart our thoughts have probably flown while we have been walking the last three lengths of the deck. Your hand was on my arm, but who shall say where you were carried in the spirit?"

"Or you? I shall never know where you have been, nor you where I have been."

"I will tell you, if you give me the slightest en

couragement, all that I have seen and said during the last five minutes."

"That would hardly be fair, for I am not willing to be equally communicative."

"You have guessed rightly; I should look for some return. But then a very small fragment of your thought would purchase a large proportion of mine."

"Well, then," said Bawn, "part of my thought—not the whole nor even a large share of it—was this : I wondered to perceive how two utter strangers like you and me could become so friendly, enjoy each other's company, exchange thoughts, and all the while remain perfectly ignorant of each other's lives, past and future, and content to be so ; and that, having made acquaintance, we should immediately afterwards pass out of sight of each other and be thought of no more. You see I have not met many strangers, or I suppose such a thought could not have dwelt on my mind."

"Life has often been compared to a journey," said the Blue Cap, "for the reason that people meet and part thus at all points, exactly like fellow travellers. Now, my thought was simpler than yours; for I was trying to—merely trying to—think of you as a farmer's daughter, and, for the life of me, I could not do it."

"I told you the truth," said Bawn, quickly.

"The truth, the whole truth, and nothing but the truth ?"

"Not the whole truth. My statement was correct, and that is all."

"What an extraordinarily beautiful radiance has that phosphorescence upon the water!"

"Yes; but I am tired. It is time for me to go below."

He turned at once, and led her silently to the top of the stair. As Bawn stood on the steps and looked up to bid him good-night, her face appeared fairer than ever in the fresh twilight of the starry night.

"By what you said just now," he said, looking at her attentively, "did you mean to hint that perfect oblivion of each other must necessarily descend upon us once we touch our mother earth again? Why should the sea be so kind and the land so harsh? Is there any reason why we should not continue to be friends?"

"Every reason," said Bawn, decidedly, as she disappeared out of the starlight into the well of shadow gaping for her.

CHAPTER VIII.

THE next morning Bawn made up her mind that she would not be a coward any longer. She fancied she had given the gentleman to understand that she wished to remain unknown, and therefore might feel herself secure. After what had passed he could never press her for information about herself. Upon these terms she was willing to be friendly, and might accept the pleasure of his companionship occasionally.

Going on deck, she found that he had already prepared a comfortable seat for her, and he soon installed himself at her feet.

"Shall we return to the Indians?" he said, looking about for "Hiawatha."

"No," said Bawn, fearing that this might lead to more personal talk concerning her home and native State.

"You dislike the Indians?"

"I have known much about them that is noble," she answered evasively, and then closed her lips and fastened her eyes upon her work.

"I suppose you have been to Paris?" said Bawn, suddenly, raising her head and looking at him calmly. She had made up her mind to dash into any subject that would lead far from her own future and past. Paris would do. A man would be sure to have plenty to say about Paris.

" She is going there, perhaps," thought the Blue Cap,
"and I wonder in what capacity ?   American women
sometimes make the Grand Tour alone, and I have
heard that even charming young creatures will do so
in case they have no male relations to travel with.
Perhaps she is going to be a governess there ; but no,
in that case she would have professed more knowledge
of astronomy.   She may be a princess in disguise
travelling to meet her friends, who will bring her out
in Paris to the delight of their world.   She has been
warned to avoid all young men as dangerous, and
therein lies her mystery.   Yes," he said, pushing back his
blue cap and showing that broad forehead, the uncover-
ing of which increased the look of strength and reliability
which belonged to his face—" yes, I do know Paris as
well as most foreigners of my age.   And for one who
has friends there, what a charming place it is !   You
will find it a delightful entrance to the European world."

Bawn bit her lips to prevent words of explanation
crossing them.   Why should she tell him that she was
not likely to see Paris or to mix with any gay world ?
If he persisted in disbelieving that she was a farmer's
daughter, and chose to think of her as a young lady
débutante on her way to Paris, why, let him do so, and
it would be all for the best.   That he should be himself
a frequenter of gay cities seemed to lessen the chances
of their meeting again.

" I wonder have I hit the mark ? " thought the Blue
Cap, watching furtively the humorous smile that gleamed
in Bawn's eyes as she resolved to mislead him.   " What
affair is it of mine that I should trouble myself about
it ?   If I were only sure that her circumstances were
safe and happy, and that a pleasant future lay before
her, I certainly should not let curiosity disturb the
serenity of my mind."

The breeze was fluttering round Bawn, ruffling the hair about her temples and ears, bringing a rosy colour to her face, and sometimes carrying her skeins of silk a little way out of reach, to be captured and returned to her hand by her watchful companion. It happened that a small white handkerchief also fluttered forth from her lap and was whirled into the Blue Cap's face. Catching it as it made a sudden wheel round and tried to escape over the ship's side, he was about to return it to its owner when a very distinct word of four letters caught his eye, embroidered in the corner. "Bawn" was daintily and flowerily stitched on the delicate bit of cambric in the place where ladies mark their names.

"Is it your Christian name?" he asked eagerly. "Come, there is no confidence in that. I will forget it again, if you like. But let me know it for a few moments. What a curious, uncommon name is Bawn! Perhaps the famous Molly Bawn was your ancestress?"

"Yes," said Bawn placidly. Yesterday she would have been distressed at this slight accident, but, having accepted the rôle of a *débutante* on her way to Paris, she was rather pleased than otherwise at having been detected as the owner of a lady's pocket-handkerchief. It was testimony to the fact that she was a wealthy demoiselle travelling (unavoidably) alone to France, where her friends waited to receive her, and behaving with proper reserve towards chance acquaintances by the way. This was precisely the impression which the sight of the bit of embroidered cambric produced on the Blue Cap's mind, and as Bawn, after a stolen glance at his reflecting face, assured herself of the fact, a sense of the humour of the situation grew on her, and a sly, repressed smile curled her lips.

Her companion saw it and fancied it told him she was not sorry to be found out, after all; that she had been willing to tease him. And now he felt willing to tease her.

"Now that I know your Christian name," he said, "I am bound to tell you mine. It is Somerled—almost as strange a one as yours. After this we shall be more comfortable. It is a great advantage to have a name to call one's friend by."

"Strangers do not call one another by their Christian names, especially when one is a man and the other a woman."

"But we are hardly strangers, are we? On board ship friendships spring up so rapidly. And then you and I, being each solitary, are thrown upon one another more than in an ordinary case. However, this is, of course, subject to your approval. I will not pronounce that pretty name of yours without your leave, not even with a 'Miss' before it—for you see I have come to the conclusion that you are not married."

"No, I am not married," said Bawn, with a look of extreme surprise that the question could have occurred to any one.

"I thought so by your fingers," said Somerled, smiling with great satisfaction, "It is always pleasant to know that one has guessed aright. I do not like to think of how I should have felt had I been told that I must address you as Mistress Bawn."

"What difference could it have made, after all?" said Bawn demurely.

"Ah! who knows? What difference could it have made? It is impossible to answer such a question. Somehow I should like to think that when I meet you again in Paris there will be no devoted husband hovering round you. I would like that our open-air, breezy friendship might continue undisturbed by any new element."

"Why do you think we shall meet in Paris?"

"Because I have friends there, and I sometimes visit them. I know I shall find you out, radiant in satins and laces, perhaps with your head already turned by flattery. Indeed, I shall then perhaps have only the past to live upon. For I shall find so many newer friends gathered round you that I shall scarce get a word."

Bawn was silent, suddenly carried back to the evening when Dr Ackroyd had concluded that she was bent on coming out in Paris as an American heiress. "What do you want to do with your fortune?" he had said. "Trip away to Paris, and all the rest of it?"—declaring the French capital to be the gayest and prettiest place for her. Suppose she had been able to put all memory of her father's wrongs out of her mind, and to do as the good doctor and his wife had thought but natural she should do? She might have been now really on her way to the pleasantest city in the world, under suitable protection, and likely to meet this young man, as he expected, in those brilliant *salons* of which she had so often heard tell. And suppose that after months and years he were to prove that he really valued her friendship as much as he now appeared, perhaps pretended to do, and suppose, and suppose—! For a few moments she saw herself surrounded with these fair circumstances, and thought that, had they been realised, she could have been glad at the prospect of meeting this blue-capped Somerled again. Such a position, which had been so possible to her and was now so impossible, appeared to her for a minute sunned by such happiness as she had never yet imagined. But it was only for an instant. The dark forests of her old home rose sombre and forbidding out of the background of her thoughts, and in the well-known leaf-strewn hollow which they

6

shaded she saw the lonely grave that held all that had
been dear to her in life, and which appealed from its
solitude and silence to the fidelity of her nature. Those
dazzling scenes which were so familiar to her new
friend, and which she could imagine so well, were not for
her ; that gay and brilliant Bawn whom she had seen
just now moving light-hearted through the crowd was
only a phantom of herself, an impersonation of the most
volatile side of her nature. No, the world of Paris
must live on without her, as it had always done, and,
alas! was but too well able to do. She had bound herself to live on the shady side of life, under the gloom of
mountains, in the shadow of concealment, with the
sorrow and wrong-doing of the past always present to
her mind.

"Do not look so grave," said Somerled. "Have I
been too familiar in my manner of talking to you ? If
you are displeased, tell me, and I will vanish for this
day."

"No," said Bawn, brightening. "You need not go
I fear I should now feel lonely if altogether left to
myself."

This speech was the result of her reflections, which
had just proved to her how completely apart their
future paths must lie, and how utterly unlikely it was
that they should ever meet again in this world.

He glanced at her gratefully, with that bright smile
which always looked so good as well as gay.

"And what about the cross children and the sick
ladies?" he asked. "With them you could not have
been lonely."

"It is far pleasanter here."

"Even with me as a drawback ?"

"Even with you as a drawback."

"For the life of me I cannot bring myself to be sorry

I missed the boat I ought to have sailed by, though for your sake I ought to regret it. I have seen several charming persons gazing at you with benevolence, and looking daggers at me. That old gentleman with the flowing beard, for instance, is dying to oust me from my position as your knight and to step into my shoes. Had I not been here he would have spread your rugs and carried your camp-stool."

"That prosy old gentleman who worries the captain with questions all dinner-time?"

"The very man. I see you might have found him almost as much a nuisance as myself." •

And so the day wore away, and the Blue Cap, as he walked up and down deck that evening at dusk, told himself that the gold-haired young woman with the broad brow and firm mouth, whose peculiar look of strength, humour, and sweetness had fascinated him, was really surrounded by no unpleasant mystery, but was only as reticent and dignified as maidens ought to be.

He wished he could ask her plainly to tell him her name, antecedents, and real position in the world. At first he had fancied that she had a downright fear of his acquiring any such information concerning her, but now it seemed to him that she only took a sly delight in withholding it. He concluded that it did not matter to him at present how silent she might be, but resolved that before they left the steamer he would persuade her to be more communicative. He remembered with a little vexation that she had shown an utter want of interest in his affairs and no curiosity even to learn his name. That they should part in this state of ignorance and indifference was not to be thought of. Three days of almost hourly companionship with this girl had made him feel that he did not want to lose sight of her. And yet he acknowledged that there was in her a certain power which would enable her to baffle him, if she pleased.

While his mind was still occupied with these reflections he saw Bawn come forward as if to meet him, walking with a quick step, and seeming to have some word of importance on her lips. But no, she had not seen him, though she paused at the ship's side close to the spot where he stood. At this hour he was generally down below and she was resting in the ladies' quarters, and she evidently had not expected to see him. He noticed that she held in her hands the little, delicate cambric pocket-handkerchief which he had picked up and restored to her in the morning, and saw her deliberately tie it up in a knot and drop it into the sea. He watched her with surprise. Was it for having accidentally revealed to him her Christian name that she thus punished the otherwise unoffending bit of cambric?

The truth was that Bawn, having unwittingly allowed it to get among her new and plain belongings, and having used it unawares, had now resolved to get rid of it, considering that, though it had served her this morning by setting her fellow-traveller's speculations on a wrong track, yet it was an undesirable possession for a person of the class to which she wished in future to belong. And meanwhile the young man, observing her, felt his former wonder at her great desire to remain quite unknown revive, and did not venture to speak to her as she turned away without seeing him, and went straight down stairs again for the night.

CHAPTER IX.

ENEMIES.

"WHAT a nice sort of hotel this steamer makes!" said the brown-faced, dark-eyed man who called himself Somerled. Again it was early, bright morning, and he was sitting idly watching Bawn's white hands plying their knitting-needles. "I should have no objection to go on as we are going for ever, or at least for ever so long—that is, if we could only stop at some port now and again and have a good walk. A man wants to stretch his legs occasionally, but otherwise——"

He broke off abruptly, and, as Bawn did not answer, began to whistle softly an air which she knew well, one of the Irish melodies with which her father had early made her familiar. As the strain stole across her ear, memory supplied the words belonging to it :

> "Come o'er the sea,
> Maiden, with me,
> Mine through sunshine, storms, and snows:
> Seasons may roll,
> But the true soul
> Burns the same where'er it goes."

"Are all American steamers as nice as this one?" asked Bawn, interrupting the whistling at the end of the first part of the melody.

"Well, the only other one of which I have had any experience was not at all nice. It was an emigrant ship, and perhaps you do not know all that is included in those two words."

"You came out to America in an emigrant ship?"

"I have succeeded in getting you to ask me a question at last," said the Blue Cap, smiling genially.

"You need not answer it unless you please. My organ of curiosity is not a large one."

"I have noticed that you are a remarkable woman. But I am willing to be questioned. I have been hoping you would ask me many questions about myself."

"I cannot do that, because I am not anxious to make confidences on my own part."

"As I have said, perhaps more than once, I am well aware of it. At present I am not disposed to molest you. I own I should be glad (as, I think, I have also said before) if a large amount of confidence on my side were to purchase even a small scrap of yours. But that shall be just as you please. It is a breach of good-breeding to ask personal questions, nevertheless I tell you plainly I shall not be willing to shake hands and say good-bye to you when this voyage is over without knowing where and by what name I am to find you again. I do not make friends and drop them so easily as that. I should not say so did I not perceive that you have made up your mind that I am a gentleman."

"Were I not satisfied on that point, I should not sit here day after day talking to you."

"Then, having accepted me as a friend, why be so exceedingly reticent with me?"

"You always speak of our being friends, while in reality we are only chance acquaintances."

"But life-long friendships are begun in this way."

"Must I tell you downrightly that there are reasons why we can never be friends after we leave this vessel?"

"I will not believe it without explanation," he answered after a slight pause, and in a low voice whose earnestness contrasted with his hitherto gay, careless manner. A slight flush had risen on his brown cheek. Bawn grew a little paler, but silently continued her work, her heart throbbing with the consciousness that the thing she most dreaded had happened.

She had drawn on herself the notice of a person who might want to know too much about her, and thus increase the difficulties in her way. Reflecting on her curious position, she asked herself why she could not tell him the little tale about herself which she had prepared for the enlightenment of those with whom she must come in contact after reaching her destination—inform him that she was the orphan daughter of an Irish emigrant, who was bringing her father's savings to Ireland to invest them there in a farm, which she intended to work by her own exertions? Why could she not narrate this little story to one who was at once so interesting to, and so greatly concerned about, her? Partly because she found it easier to annoy than to deceive him explicitly in words, and partly because she would not be driven into laying her future open to an interference which might possibly thwart her plans. As she quietly reviewed her position and strengthened her resolve to remain unknown, the Blue Cap's look of disturbance gradually disappeared, and, quitting her side, he walked away to a distance and leaned over the vessel's edge. Presently she heard him whistling the second part of the air which she had interrupted, and to which her memory again supplied the words:

> " Let Fate frown on,
>   So we love and part not ;
>   'Tis life where thou art,
>   'Tis death where thou art not."

Then he went and talked to one of the sailors, and half an hour passed before he returned to her.

"You have not told me yet about the ship," said

Bawn, with a conciliatory smile. "I do wish to know how you came to be there, and I am willing to pay for the information with any little experience of my own that you will think worth listening to."

"Good!" said Somerled. "That makes me feel better. I have been savagely cross for the last half-hour. How I wish I had a longer story to relate to you! It will be told too soon. I simply went out to America with some hundreds of emigrants, that I might know by experience how they are treated on the way; we hear so many complaints of the sufferings of the poor on their voyage out to the New World. And I had reasons for wanting to know."

"I see; reasons like mine, that are not to be told."

"Exactly. Not until I see my way more clearly towards selling them at a profit."

"I can guess yours easily enough. And so you made common cause with the poor. Mr Somerled, I will shake hands with you without waiting for the moment of leaving the ship."

"Even though we are only chance acquaintances," he said, with a brilliant change of countenance, taking the firm, white hand that had suddenly dropped the needle and outstretched itself to him. Bawn's eyes were turned full on him, glistening with moisture and overflowing with a light he had never seen in them, and thought he had never seen anywhere, before.

"I shall always remember you as a friend," she said, carried away by enthusiasm, and with a kind of radiant solemnity of face and manner.

"Will you? Perhaps among your dead?"

"If you knew how precious are my dead," she answered, with a sudden darkening of all her lights, "you would be proud to be admitted into their company."

"That may be, but I would rather be in the company of your living," he said, dropping her hand which he had held. And Bawn, wishing she had been less impulsive, picked up her needles again and became busier than usual with her work.

"I want to hear more of your emigrants," she said presently, as serenely as ever. "How were they and you treated, and what have you been doing for them?"

"To the first question I answer, 'Badly.' To the second I must admit, 'Not much.' I hope, however, to be able to say something about the matter in Parliament one day."

"Are you in the English Parliament?"

"You are surprised at the suggestion that so dull a fellow could hope to get admittance there. But sometimes it is easier to please a nation than a woman."

"Do you expect to please a nation?" asked Bawn, elevating her eyebrows slightly.

"Not exactly, perhaps, though. I hope to get on pretty well with that small section of one which will be made up by my constituents."

"And the nation will go down before you afterwards?"

"Perhaps less than that may content me, though I have my ambitions. However, I am not in Parliament yet. And now, having confessed so much, it is time for me to receive some small dole from your hands."

Bawn's face fell. "What can I tell you? I have seen a prairie on fire; I have spoken to an Indian chief—"

"All my experiences pale before adventures like those," said the Blue Cap, trying to read the changes in her face.

A great change had come over her, for, in thinking of her past, events of one sad year had suddenly arisen before her mind.

"I have aroused painful memories," said Somerled, gazing remorsefully at her colourless cheeks and troubled eyes.

"You would drive me back upon them."

"Do you mean that you have experienced nothing in your past but what is painful?"

"I do not say that," she said, brightening up again. "But what is there to tell about happy days? They slip through our fingers like soap-bubbles, glistening with all the colours of the rainbow. How can we tell what has made the days so happy or the soap-bubbles so beautiful? Common things—mere 'suds,' as the washerwoman calls them—catch a glory from the sunlight and vanish. And when they have vanished, what has any one to say about them?"

Somerled sat gazing at her with a slight frown, observing how cleverly she always contrived to give him a ready answer without enlightening him at all, to talk so much and convey to him so little. Without saying more he got up and walked away, and after a while she saw him down at the other end of the deck playing with some children, hoisting the little ones on his shoulders and setting the bigger ones to run races along the deck. She heard his merry laugh among theirs, and noted the fact that her disobligingness had not the power to annoy him. Why, she asked of her common sense, should she allow herself to be bullied or wheedled into running risks for the sake of momentarily gratifying the curiosity of an idle and inquisitive fellow-traveller? She would not do it. Let him stay among those children and their lady relatives (there were one or two pretty girls among them) for the rest of the voyage. His doing so would certainly be an unexpected relief and advantage to her.

Having finished playing with the children and con-

versing with their mother and young aunts, the Blue
Cap pulled a book out of his pocket and threw himself
on a bench to read. What he read was a very unsatis-
factory chapter, and all out of his own head. He did
not like that girl, after all (his reading informed him).
There was too much mystery about her, too deeply
rooted and watchful a reticence for so young and
apparently simple a woman. She must have some
strong, almost desperate, reason for closing her lips
so firmly when he tried to beguile her into speaking,
for changing colour so rapidly at times when he pressed
her, as if she feared he would perceive the very thought
in her mind.

He turned the pages of his book impatiently, and
owned that he would give much to see the thought
lying behind that wide, white brow, which seemed expressive at once of the innocence of the child and the
wisdom and courage of a woman experienced in life
What was the story, what were the scenes in the back
ground of her youth which were accountable for that
sad look starting so often unawares into her eyes?
With what sort of people had she lived, and whither
and to whom was she travelling now in the great, giddy
world of Paris? Well, what did it matter to him?
He had no intention of falling in love with her. He
had never fallen thoroughly in love in his life, and he
was now thirty years of age. Two or three fresh, pretty
faces of girls he had known floated up from his past and
smiled at him as he made this declaration to himself,
and yet he persevered in the avowal. He had liked
them, flirted a little with them, been very near falling
in love with them; but either he had been too busy
setting his little world to rights, or they had lacked
something that his soul desired, for he had certainly
never as yet given the whole heart of his manhood into
the keeping of any feminine hands.

As yet he had not seen the woman to whom he could give up his masculine liberty ; and still, while he em-phatically stated this to his own mind, he distinctly saw a vision of Bawn sitting knitting at his fireside, the light of his hearth shining on her fair face, into which colour and dimple would come at the sound of his voice, and his care and protection surrounding her with a paradisi-acal atmosphere. When, at the end of his chapter, he found this picture before his eyes, he flung away his book in something like a passion, and got up and tramped about the deck.

No, he was not going to fall in love with a nameless, secretive, obstinate-tempered, wilful woman. His wife must be open as the day, transparent in thought, and with all her antecedents well known to the world. She must be of a particularly yielding and gentle disposition, and have exceedingly little will of her own.

CHAPTER X.

MISLEADINGS.

" Do please tell me more about Paris," said Bawn, with
a sweet beseechingness in her eyes and voice, and her
lips curling with the fun of leading him further and
further astray in his speculations concerning her. " If
you knew how impatient I feel to see it ! "

" Which is true enough," she thought, " only I am not
at all likely to gratify my desire."

" It is not the place for a person of your disposition."

" How is that ? "

" The French are a nation not remarkable for
frankness."

" And you think my natural reticence may increase
in Parisian society ! Now, that is not kind. I have
heard the French character charged with untruth rather
than reserve. I have told you no falsehoods, and I
might, if I would, have satisfied your curiosity with a
dozen."

" True. That is something. How many days have
we yet got to live ? "

" On board ? Four, perhaps, or five, I think."

" Four will finish the voyage for those who land
at Queenstown."

" In what part of England is Queenstown ? " asked
Bawn, demurely.

" It is in Ireland—the first British port at which
we touch. But for you and me, who are going on to

Liverpool, there remain five whole days to enjoy each other's society."

"Do not let us quarrel away our time, then," said Bawn, persuasively. "Five days would be very long if we were to keep making ourselves disagreeable to each other all the time."

"Five days are but a short space for happiness out of a lifetime," said Somerled, brusquely, with an ardent, angry glance at her downcast eyelids.

"Yes, they would be," she said quietly, "but let us hope that few lives are so unhappy as not to possess a larger share of happy days than that."

She heard him shift in his seat impatiently, but, being busy with a dropped stitch, she naturally could not see his face.

"Do you intend to travel on to Paris alone? I hope there is no offence in a gentleman's asking such a question as that of a lady. The journey from Liverpool to Paris will be a troublesome one. Perhaps you will allow me to give you some hints for its safe accomplishment."

"Certainly," said Bawn, raising her eyes and looking at him straight, while she controlled the corners of her lips with difficulty. "There will be no one to meet me at Liverpool."

"I will write out a little memorandum of what you are to do after you have got out of my reach," he said. "I suppose, as we shall both be going on to London, you will allow me to escort you so far."

"If I step into one car there is no reason why you should step into another, unless, indeed, you want to smoke—"

"We call them carriages in England."

"That is nicer. Carriage sounds so much more like a private conveyance."

The Blue Cap was silent. His imagination played him a sudden trick, and showed him a certain well-know private conveyance drawn by certain favourite horses, within which were seated a man and a woman, and the man was taking the woman by a certain well-known road to his home, as his wife. The man who held the reins was himself, and the woman was this golden-tressed, aggravating, unimpressionable Bawn.

"In London I shall certainly have to bid you good-bye," he grumbled.

"Until we meet again in Paris?"

"So likely that I should find you!—asking about the streets for a person of the name of 'Bawn.'"

"Is Paris as nice a place as they say for buying pretty things—clothes and jewellery I mean?" said Bawn, in the most matter-of-fact manner.

"Oh! yes; first-rate for all that kind of thing. And so this is what your mind has been running on for the last ten minutes?"

"Why should it not?"

"Why, indeed? For no reason. Only I fancied you were not the kind of woman to let your mind get totally absorbed by clothes and jewellery."

"Men are never good judges of the characters of women."

"Probably not."

"In my case you have had ample material from which to form your conclusions. Why should a young woman come all the way from New York to Paris, if not to attend to her wardrobe and general personal decoration? Have you not heard that American women pine for this opportunity from their cradle upwards? Now, I feel sure that the very first morning I awake in Paris" (she paused, thinking that such a morning would probably never dawn, or that, if it did, the hour was so far away as to be practically nowhere in her future), " I shall make a rush to the shops before breakfast, just to see what they have got for me.   And I shall probably spend the half of my fortune before I return to my hotel."

" I am really disenchanting him now," she thought. " How disgusted he looks."

" Your hotel !   Do you mean to say that you intend to stay alone at a hotel ? "

" I certainly did not intend to tell you so.   You betray me into forgetting myself."

The Blue Cap looked pale and displeased, and Bawn bent over her knitting and bit her lip, thinking, with a sting of regret, that she would rather he had not obliged her to shock him so much.

" Do you not know," she said, "that American women go where they please and do what they have a mind to ? "

" I have heard a great deal that I do not like about certain females of your nation.   But I did not expect to see them looking like you."

" Why ? "

" Why ? why ?   Your face, your manner, your gestures, your slightest movement, all express a character directly opposite to that which you are now making known to me."

" It is always so with us," said Bawn, gravely.   " Our appearance is the best of us.   We are not half worth what we look."

" So it seems, indeed.   With your peculiar brow and eyes and glance, I did not expect to find you harbouring the sentiments of a French grisette."

" My stepmother was half French," exclaimed Bawn.

" Your stepmother !   That does not give you French blood, I suppose," he said impatiently.

"Neither does it, when I think of it. But might it not have taught me French ways?"

"And opened up the path to Paris for you."

"You are so quick at guessing that I need to tell you nothing."

"And so you have been dreaming all this time about clothes and jewellery," he reiterated contemptuously. "When you were sitting looking out to sea, as I first saw you, with a peculiar expression in your eyes which I had never observed in any eyes before, and yet seemed to recognise when I saw it, I must conclude now that you were merely pondering the fashion of a new necklace or the colour of a gown."

"You recognised the expression of all that?" said Bawn, in a tone of keen amusement. "This leads me to think you have sisters, or cousins, or a wife—"

"I have no wife" (crossly).

"How fortunate for her! A man who would fly in a passion because a woman gave a thought to her dress would not be a pleasant husband."

The Blue Cap scowled. "I hope you may get a better one, madam."

"I devoutly hope so—if ever I am to have one at all, which is doubtful."

"I dare say you would rather continue to go shopping about the world alone."

"I admit that I find liberty very sweet."

"So I have concluded. Do not imagine that I could desire to deprive you of a fragment of it."

Bawn laughed gaily. "Oh! no," she said. "Your ideal woman (who lives in the clouds, by the way, and will certainly not come down to you) will never know the colour of the gown she has on. But seriously, Mr Somerled, why have you changed so much for the worse since you first began to talk to me? You spoke of the

7

pleasure of meeting me in the gay *salons* of Paris, and you did not suppose I should walk into them in my travelling dress ? "

"And seriously, madam, why have you changed so much for the worse since you first allowed me the privilege of talking to you ? Then you had the face of an angel, with the thoughts of an angel behind it. You have still the face—"

"But the thoughts, translated into words, have proved to be the thoughts of a—"

"Milliner."

"I thought you were going to say 'fiend,' but it is the same thing, since bonnets and gowns are anathema."

"How shall I make you feel that you have bitterly disappointed me ? " he said, looking at her with a mixture of anger and tenderness.

"It is," said Bawn, gravely, "silly in a man to expect to meet an ideal woman—that is, an angel—in every female fellow-traveller he may chance to encounter."

While she said this her grey eyes took an expression he failed to read, and a pathetic look which he could not reconcile with her late conversation crept over her mouth. Perhaps the thought arose almost unconsciously in her mind that, under other circumstances, she would have been pleased to have encouraged that delusion of his with regard to the angel that might possibly live in her.

Yet when she lay down to sleep that night she congratulated herself on her success in lowering the inconvenient degree of interest which this stranger had so perversely taken in her. Why could he not have devoted himself to the children and their pretty aunts, who always seemed so pleased to speak to him, and so saved her the trouble of baffling his curiosity ? For that curiosity alone was the cause of his devotion to her she was resolved to believe, electing to deny that any genuine liking for herself strong enough to influence him could have sprung up within the limits of so short an acquaintance. And then certain looks and words of his which gainsaid this belief occurred to her memory, insisting that here was a good man who was wanting to love her if she would let him. If such was indeed the case, then had she so bound herself to a difficult futrue that she could not turn her steps and allow herself to be carried on to a happier destiny than she had dreamed of?

Ah! of what was she thinking? Forget her father and her determination to clear the stain of guilt from his beloved name? Confess the whole story to this stranger, merely because he had assumed the position of her guardian for the moment; because he had eyes that could charm, now by their grave tenderness, and now by their electric flashes of fun, and was also the owner of a sympathetic voice and a thinking forehead? Was she to own that by merely putting forth his great powers to attract, he had been able to overturn all her plans, and that she was ready to await his disposal of her heart and fortune? Oh! no—not even if he, being the gentleman she took him to be, could continue to interest himself about her, once he knew of the cloud that rested on her father's memory.

CHAPTER XI.

FURTHER MISLEADINGS.

NEVER had there been more perfect weather for a journey, so far, but on the sixth day a gale met the good ship in the teeth. Bawn made this a pretext for staying in her cabin all day, and the Blue Cap weathered the storm on deck, feeling that he could not ask her to face it with him, and anathematising the mischance that had lost him some of those hours which he had now begun to count as precious beyond price. Towards evening, when the wind was still howling and the steamer pitching, he could no longer control his desire to see her, and went down to look for her.

"Ask the young lady with the golden hair if she will speak to me," he said to the stewardess. So strictly had he respected her intention of keeping her name unknown to him that he had taken no measures to discover it from any other than herself. He would learn it only from her own lips.

She came to him at the foot of the stair, looking unusually pale, but quiet and unalarmed.

"The worst of the storm is over," he said, looking at her with a glow of gladness in his dark eyes that made her heart beat faster. "You must be tired to death of that cabin by this time. Every one has been sick, I suppose, and everybody cross but yourself. Come up on deck, and I will take care of you while you get a little air."

"Yes," she said readily. Why should she not go?

Her thoughts had been troubled with him all day, and she found such thinking a very unwise occupation. Better go with him and brace herself, if not him, by disenchanting him a little more than she had yet done. There were now only two days of the voyage yet to come, and after they were past she should see him no longer.

He drew her arm within his and piloted her to a spot where she could sit in safety by slipping her arms under some ropes, which kept her lashed to her place.

"You have not been frightened?" he said, in a tone which made her suddenly repent of having exchanged the stifling cabin for the airs, however grateful, of heaven.

"No; I am not easily frightened, I think, and I am not much afraid of death, perhaps because I can never realise it for myself. I am so young and strong that I suppose I hardly believe I have got to die. And just now life seems more alarming to me than death."

"Why?"

"I cannot tell you."

"Is it because you fear the shops of Paris may disappoint you?"

"The shops?"

"Have you forgotten the shops which contain your heaven?"

"True. Oh! yes, of course. There may be things, you see, in those shops which I may not be rich enough to buy."

"Bawn—"

"Do not so call me, please."

"Why?"

"You said you would not unless I gave you leave."

"And will you not give me leave?"

"No."

"I beseech you to allow me."

"I cannot. It hurts my dignity too much."

"Do you think I am a man who could bear to hurt your dignity?"

"I do not think you are; but, at all events, I will not allow you to be. Do you think any nice woman would allow a mere fellow-traveller, the chance acquaintance of a week, to fall into a habit of calling her by her Christian name? Because I believe you a gentleman I have, being alone and in peculiar circumstances, accepted your kindness——"

"I have shown you no kindness; I have simply loved you from the first moment I looked upon you."

"You must not say so."

"Why must not I say so? I am free, independent, able to give a home, if not a very splendid one, to my wife. Till now I have not cared to marry because I never loved a woman before as I love you. I have told you no particulars about myself, neither my name, nor where is my place in the world, nor any other detail which a man lays before a woman whom he asks to share his lot. I have avoided doing this out of pique at your want of interest in the matter and your persistent silence about yourself."

"That is a silence which must continue."

"Oh! no. Give me at least a chance of winning your love in time. You do not positively dislike me?"

"No."

"Nor distrust me?"

"No."

"Then why should you thrust me so terribly away out of your life?"

"Because I have to go my way alone, and I cannot allow any one to hinder me."

"Those are hard words coming from so young a

woman. Do you mean that you have pledged yourself never to marry?"

"I have not so pledged myself."

"You are not engaged to any other man?"

"No."

"You have no mother nor father to exercise control over your actions?"

"I am quite alone in the world, and as free as air."

"Then let me tell you that you are in need of a protector and of such a love as I offer you. I believe you are going to seek your fortune in Paris; for I have made up my mind that you are not rich."

"Why?"

"Do wealthy young ladies travel across the sea alone? Good, noble, and true ones may do so, but the wealthy bring keepers and care-takers in their train. Then, though your dress is neat—as fit, and more charming and becoming than any other lady's garb that I see or have seen—it is not the apparel of a woman of property."

"I do not like sealskin; it makes me too hot. I am too healthy and vigorous to wear fur."

"You will not admit that you are poor, but it is one of the things about you that I know without your telling."

"I am not a woman to marry a man merely to get out of a difficulty."

"God forbid! I think I should not care for you if you were. You are, rather, a woman to reject what might be for your happiness, from an exaggerated fear of being suspected by yourself or others of any but the purest motives for your actions."

"I am capable of making up my mind and sticking to it. And I do not wish to marry."

"Never?"

" I will not say never. I think I hardly seem to believe in my own future. The present—I mean the present of a couple of years or so — is everything to me."

" And your reasons for all this you absolutely will not tell me, not even if I were to swear to devote myself to assisting you in any enterprise you have got on hand ? "

" I spoke of no enterprise."

" No, but all you say implies that you have one. There is some difficulty before you, and it is your romantic fancy to meet it single-handed."

" If that is your theory, what becomes of the salons and the shops ? "

" It may be a difficulty that lies among salons and shops. How can I imagine what it may not be ? Can it·be that you think yourself under obligation to enter some convent ? "

" No ; I fear I am not good enough for that."

" Then what can it be, in which the services of a man might not be acceptable, if not useful ? What reason ought there to be why you and I should part, as utter strangers part, and never see or hear of each other again ? "

" Some of the reasons I cannot tell you, but one may be enough. You want to persuade me to marry you ; and I do not want to marry you or anybody else."

" You could continue. to refuse me ; or time might change your mind."

" It would be exceedingly inconvenient to me if I were to change my mind."

" You mean that you are afraid of that ? "

" I am a little afraid of it."

" Upon what grounds, if I may dare to ask ? Do you distrust your own powers of endurance, and dread

to be betrayed into marrying for a motive you consider unworthy, the weak desire to escape from a
dilemma ? "

" Not that."

" Are you afraid you could learn to love me ? "

" Yes."

" My God ! And after such a confession you expect
me to give you up ? "

" You will have to give me up," said Bawn sadly.

" O my love ! do not speak so hardly. You have
admitted too much."

" I fear I have, and you ought not to have wrung it
from me. You ought to have been satisfied with my
earnest statement that I am doing the only thing that I
can do."

" Bawn, you do not know what you are saying. As
well say that two people in the flush of youth and
health would be justified in casting themselves, hand-in-
hand, into the sea to drown together. You would condemn us, with the love and happiness that are in us, to
sudden death at the end of this journey which has been
so fateful for us both. Do you really desire that we
should never meet again in this world ? "

" I do not desire it. But I know that it must be."

" Never ? Have you considered all that that word
'never' means ? It is not absence for a year or for
twenty years ; it is entire blotting out for evermore. '

" It may be," said Bawn, " that in years to come we
may happen to meet again."

" And your difficulty may then be cleared away ? "

" It may be so, or, on the contrary, it may have deepened so terribly that I shall be glad to see that you
have married and made yourself happy in the meantime."

" You are a heartless woman."

"Am I? It may be well for me if I can prove to myself that I am."

Silence fell between them. The gale had abated and the sky had cleared. He could see the expression of her face as she looked straight before her with a downcast, wistful gaze. There was such sorrow in her eyes—those tender and brave grey eyes which had seemed to him from the first moment he had met their glance to be the sweetest in the world—as made his heart ache to deliver her from the mysterious difficulty with which she was so sorely beset. That she had some great struggle before her he no longer doubted; that she was in the hands of people whom she hated and was ashamed of, he feared. He did not for a moment question her own individual goodness and nobility of purpose, but his very faith in her made him the more alarmed for her sake. What might not such a girl undertake if she could only get hold of a motive sufficiently lofty and unselfish!

That he should lose her out of his life through her fidelity to some worthless wretch or wretches, in some way bound up with her fate, made him feel wild; and yet, even as he gazed at her face, it seemed to grow paler and paler with determination, as, knitting her soft brows, she pushed away her regrets and strengthened her resolution to adhere to her own plans.

How, Bawn was asking herself, could she tell this man that she was the daughter of one who had been branded and banished as a murderer? How could she persuade him to share her certainty that her father had been wrongfully accused? And even were he to prove most improbably generous, and were to accept her faith and say to her, "Be you henceforth my wife and nothing more," could she then forget her father and his life-long anguish, and utterly relinquish her endeavours to clear his name in the eyes of the little world that had accused him ?

No, she could not bring herself to say, "I am the daughter of Arthur Desmond, who lived under a ban for having taken the life of his friend." And even if she could thus run the risk of being rejected as the child of a murderer, she would not give up her scheme for throwing the light of truth upon his memory.

After all, what was this man to her, this acquaintance of less than a week, in comparison with the father who had for twenty long years been the only object of her worship? Let him take his ardent dark eyes, his winning voice, and the passionate appeals and reproaches elsewhere. She could not afford to yield up her heart to his persuasions.

CHAPTER XII.

LOVERS.

BAWN got up the next morning fully determined that she would not allow herself to love this lover. Her heart might be shaken, but her will was firm. She was not going to give up the prospect for which she had sacrificed so much and struggled through so many obstacles, at the bidding of a person who last week was unknown to her. His eyes might grow tender when gazing at her, his hands be ready and kind in waiting on her, his companionship pleasant, and his voice like music in her ears, but she could not change the whole tenor of her life because those facts had been accidentally made known to her. She should certainly miss his face at her side, and his strong presence surrounding her like a Providence, but none the more was she willing to bestow on him suddenly the gift of her future. And there seemed to her no medium course between surrendering her entire fate at once into the hands he was outstretching to her and putting him back into the shadows of the unknown from which he had so unexpectedly and awkwardly emerged to cross her path.

And now she thought, as she finished dressing, there was only this one last day throughout which to keep true to her better judgment. To-morrow the captain expected to touch at Queenstown, and she must give her friend what she feared would be a painful surprise. She would bid him a short good-bye, and leave him to finish his voyage as though such a person as herself did not exist in the world.

"People who fall in love so easily," she thought, " can surely fall out of it again as quickly. By next week, perhaps, he will be able to complain of me to some sympathising friend, and in a month I shall be forgotten as completely as if I never had appeared on his horizon."

Such was Bawn's theory of loving. Love ought not to spring up like mushrooms in a night, but should have a gradual, reasonable, exquisitely imperceptible growth, striking deep roots before making itself obtrusively evident. Her father was the only person she had ever seriously loved, and her love for him had had neither beginning nor end. How could a mere stranger imagine that in the course of a week he had learned absolutely to need her for the rest of his life ?

In the meantime the man who called himself Somerled had passed a wakeful night. While Bawn in her berth summoned up all her resolution to resist for yet another day, and thus finally, the fascination which she unwillingly acknowledged he exercised over her, he lay and remembered but one saying of the woman who had suddenly risen up in his life and at once widened his heart and filled it with herself. She had admitted that she feared to learn to love him, and to his fancy the admission meant all that his soul desired. A girl who was afraid to cultivate his acquaintance, lest she should end by loving him, must already, he thought, almost love him ; and a girl with so soft and young though so determined a face, having made such an admission, must surely be capable of being won by perseverance. He feared that he had shocked her delicacy by speaking to her so suddenly, but he told himself that the urgency of the circumstances excused him. He chafed to see how his chances of success were lessened by the mysterious difficulties of her position, and he set himself seriously to guess what that position and those difficulties might be. Looking at the case all round and recalling other words of hers besides those few which it made him so inexpressibly happy to dwell upon, he summed up all the evidence he could gather as to her circumstances, and before daylight broke over a foaming sea he thought he had made a tolerably good guess as to her purpose and the trials she felt herself bound to meet alone. For some reason which she believed to be compelling she was making her way to Paris to endeavour to earn money, not, as he conceived, for herself, but for the sake of some other person or persons. And he thought he had hit the truth when the idea flashed into his mind that it might be her intention to become a singer or an actress.

The idea made him sick. An actress going through training on a Parisian stage! He could not rest after the suggestion came to him, and got up and walked the deck, and was so walking and chafing when Bawn appeared.

He did not know it was the last morning on which he should see the trim, womanly figure, the fair, oval face under the round black hat, the little, strongly-shod feet coming to meet him steadily and gallantly along the windy deck. No presentiment forewarned him that by the same hour next day he should be labouring under the sorrow of having lost her out of his life for evermore.

At sight of her his mind became suddenly filled with the one exultant thought that here she was still safely within his reach, and not to be lost sight of, even at her own most earnest bidding, unless death should lay hold of her or him and frustrate all his hopes. He would throw over the urgent business that had brought him hurrying back across the ocean, and which was waiting for him in London to be dealt with at a certain hour. He would throw anything, everything else to the winds, follow her to Paris, even (if it must be so) unknown to herself, be informed of her whereabouts and her circumstances, and after that leave the sequel of his wooing to the happier chances of the future.

His face was flushed, his dark eyes shining with the force of his determination to compel happiness, as he came forward with his morning greetings. She accepted silently and meekly the support he offered her in her walk, feeling warmed and comforted by his presence and protection, while thinking remorsefully of the necessary treachery of the morrow.

"Since daylight," he said, "I have been watching for you. I almost began to fear I had frightened you away, and that you were going to spend another day among the babies and the sick ladies."

"I should have been wiser had I done so," said Bàwn. "I am not easily enough frightened."

"You would not have been wiser. You are able to take care of yourself—to hold your own against me. When you yield to my persuasion, to my counsel, you will do it with your eyes open, with the sanction of your own judgment."

"Shall I?"

"I have been wanting to talk to you."

"You talked so much yesterday that I do not imagine you can have anything left to say."

"You have no idea of my talking capacity when you say so. I could talk for a week, if you would only listen to me. But if deaf and cruel miles were to come between me and your ears, then I feel that I could almost become dumb for the rest of my life."

"Almost? That is, till some other young woman, like or unlike me, should be found willing to listen to you for yet another week—perhaps for months and years."

"Bawn, look at me!"

"Why should I look at you?" she answered gravely. "I know very well what you are like; and I am greatly in earnest in saying I would rather you would talk of something else. After all I said last night you ought not to go on speaking to me like this."

"And after all I said to you last night you suppose I can talk to you of nothing but the weather until the moment for parting with you arrives?"

"It would be better for yourself and kinder to me if you were to do so."

"You think, then, that I am going to lose you so easily?"

"I know you will have to lose me. You had better make up your mind to it, and talk to me for the rest of the time only about Paris and the shops."

"And the theatres?"

"And the theatres, too, if you like. It would greatly amuse me to hear something about the theatres."

"You would rather be amused than loved."

"Anything is better than to encourage the continued offering of what one cannot accept."

"Perhaps you cannot accept what is offered because you have a preference for theatres."

"I do not understand you."

"An idea has occurred to me which seems to throw some light upon your mystery. You are going to Paris, perhaps, to prepare yourself for the stage."

Bawn blushed crimson, and her change of colour did not escape her companion's eye. It was caused by vexation that he should imagine her influenced in rejecting him by what seemed to her such an ignoble and insufficient reason, but he took it as a sign that he had hit upon the truth, to her sudden embarrassment and chagrin.

"You are dreaming of going on the stage. This time I have guessed aright."

"I will not tell you," said Bawn, now as pale as the foam-fleck that touched her cheek. Let him, she thought, follow this false scent if he would. It would lessen the likelihood of their meeting again.

"Great heaven! You upon the stage!"

"What do you find so shocking in the idea? Suppose I am what you have taken me to be, a poor young woman with her bread to earn in the world, why should I not go upon the stage? Have not good and noble women been actresses before now?"

"I am not going to allow it for you."

Her hand trembled on his arm, and she turned her head away that he might not see the expression of her eyes. She was unspeakably grateful to him for the words he had just spoken. Good women, greater women than herself, might spend their lives upon the stage, but such an existence would, she admitted, be intolerable to her.

"Pray how do you intend to interfere to prevent me?" she said after a pause.

"I do not know," he said, with something like a groan. "I cannot tell how I am going to find you and save you from such a fate; but I warn you I will leave no stone unturned in trying to do it."

Bawn withdrew her hand from his arm.

"You mean that you will follow me—persecute me?"

"Persecute you? No! Guard you from yourself—perhaps yes."

8

"Guard me!"

"Save you, may be, from the consequences of your own innocent rashness and romantic daring."

Here he had hit home. The romantic daring was truly hers, and only Heaven could know what the consequences of it yet might be. As Dr Ackroyd had warned her of trouble as the issue of her wilfulness, so now was this other man threatening her with the dangers of that future to which she was obstinately consigning herself. Yet as she had resisted the lawful authority of the old friend, so much the more would she refuse to yield to the unasked counsel of the new one. Her father and his good name and his fair memory were and should be more to her than the approval of either—more than her own happiness, or her own liberty, or her own ease.

But an overwhelming sense of the responsibility she had taken upon herself pressed on her suddenly, and made her feel more ill in body and mind than she had felt since first setting out upon this path of her own seeking, which already she began to travel with so much pain. Why she should be so shaken at this moment she could not tell. Dr Ackroyd was now more to her than any other person in the world, and yet his representations had not moved her as the entreaties and reproaches of this audacious stranger were moving her. She drew her hand quickly away as he sought to replace it on his arm, and stood aloof by the side of the vessel, looking silently down to the flowing of the water.

He saw that she suffered, and thought she was giving way before the urgency and honesty of his desires. She was acknowledging him in the right, and searching for a path by which she might allow him to approach her. He saw her firmly-closed hand relax and drop by her side, and that stern knitting of the soft, white brows, which at times gave her the look of an angel of justice rather than of tenderness, gradually smooth itself away. Tears gathered under her eyelids.

He drew a step nearer to her.

"What are you thinking of now, Bawn—my Bawn?"

"Not yours, nor any other's," she said, shaking her head sadly. "I belong, I can belong, to no one."

"Not even in that far-off future which you hinted at once?"

"I ought not to have spoken of any future of my own. My future is in bondage to another."

He drew a long, hard breath. He felt impatient and sick at heart.

"Then you have not always told me the truth."

"Always."

"You were engaged to no other man, you preferred no other man, you had no parents or relations who could control you—have not these statements all been made by you? Did you not tell me you were your own mistress, free as air, unfettered by any other will than your own?"

"I told you all that, and it was true."

"And yet your future is in bondage to another?"

"I cannot explain these things without telling you of matters of which I have bound myself not to speak."

"You are a riddle and a mystery, and you have broken my heart!" he cried with sudden passion. "I wish to Heaven I had never seen you!"

"That is what I have been wishing every day since you first spoke to me," said Bawn, in a low, trembling voice, while she threw back her head with dismay in her eyes and defiance in her gesture. "It is what from the first I have wished to make you feel."

"Good Lord! do you, then, hate me?"

"No; I wish I did."

"O, my dear! do you know what you imply by those words?"

"I do not know, and I do not want to know."

"I am going to tell you."

"You must not; you shall not, for I will not hear you!" cried Bawn, and with a little wail of pain she dropped her face upon her hands, leaning over the vessel's side. Then he turned away and left her, and walked about by himself at the other side of the ship, gloating over the admission which her words had again made to him.

He remembered with satisfaction that he had yet some time before him in which to overcome her resolution to work upon that growing inclination towards himself which he thought he saw in her, and which she feared and strove against. Who could this person or those persons be to whom she was so bound, to whom the disloyalty that bought her own happiness would be a crime? It could not be a right or just bondage with so much mystery attached to it; for he was now convinced of the existence of some serious reasons for her silence as to all her circumstances, future and past. He was sure that she trusted him enough to be willing to confide in him, if betrayal of others were not involved in her confidence. That she was going upon the stage he hardly doubted now. She had not denied it. Poor, and anxious to earn money, what so likely as that she, being young and beautiful, should hope to make a fortune by that adventure? He was sure that she was clever, ready to believe she would be able to carry the world before her, and he chafed with impatience as he thought that the next time he saw her she might stand behind footlights, and under the eyes of a too critical or of a delighted crowd.

The bell rang for breakfast, and Bawn moved away

and disappeared. When he next saw her she was seated by the captain's side, as was usual at meal-times, and chatting to him pleasantly. But her face was unusually pale.

"We are going to have a return of fine weather," said the captain. "We shall probably be in Queenstown in the morning."

"Do many of your passengers land at Queenstown?" asked Somerled, reflecting with satisfaction that Bawn was not one of the number.

"A good many," said the captain, and Bawn held her breath, expecting he would say something polite to the effect that he was sorry that she was one of those to whom he should have to say adieu on the morrow. But someone addressed him on the moment, and the opportunity passed.

After breakfast she asked herself if it would not be better were she to stay in the ladies' quarters for the whole of this long day, only going on deck for a few minutes in the evening to bid a final farewell to her friend. But no, she could not see that she was called upon to act so harshly, now that the very hours of their friendship were numbered. She would enjoy this one day of companionship. The future would be long enough for separation and silence.

He met her as usual as soon as she appeared, and led her to a retired seat.

"That young pair only met first when they came on board, and I am sure they are engaged," said a girl to her mother.

"They seem to differ a good deal while they talk," said her sister, "and the man often looks disturbed, if not angry."

"She plagues him a good deal, I fancy, though she looks so sweet and smooth," said the first girl.

"She has some trouble, I think," said their mother. "I have seen tears in her eyes when she thought nobody was looking."

"That must be very seldom, for the man is always looking."

"He is a distinguished-looking fellow, and I hope he is not getting himself into any foolish entanglement," said another lady sitting by.

"He is old enough to take care of himself. The girl may be in more danger," said the mother.

"You need not be uneasy abôut her. She is a young lady who can carry her point, equal to the management of more than a flirtation, and able to carry it to a satisfactory conclusion."

"Perhaps all the more to be pitied on that account. If a girl of that stamp takes her own affairs in her hands too early she sometimes makes a wreck of her life."

"She seems to be quite her own mistress, at all events, travelling from America all alone. For my part, I am fond of girls who try to get under somebody's wing," said the other lady, who meant no unkindness, but who suffered from overmuch conscientiousness, and was accordingly inclined to be censorious.

That Bawn at present felt her own wings strong enough to carry her there was no doubt, and it was for this reason that she had consented to spend her last day on board in company with the man who had declared her to be so necessary to his life, and yet whom she was quite resolved never to see again. And in the meantime the man, resting on the admissions she had already made him, had begun to hope in earnest, and relied on the many hours that were yet before them to break down at last the barriers she had built up between their future lives.

"Bawn," he said, "I want to say several things to

you." He paused, and she did not check him for calling her by her Christian name, though he gave her time to do so. He thought this a sign of relenting, but in reality she was only thinking that he might call her what he pleased to-day. The wind was carrying the sound away from her ears even as it was spoken, and would never return again bearing his voice. Once she was buried in the mountains, this man, who led a busy life out in the world, a dweller in London, a frequenter of Paris, would certainly never stumble upon the paths of her retirement.

"I have been thinking deeply all night about the mystery that surrounds you."

"How greatly you exaggerate! Surely a little reticence need not be magnified into mystery."

"I do not think I exaggerate. I believe your trust in me, which you have avowed, would have overcome your reticence before now if something more than mere personal reserve were not included in your silence."

"What, then, do you think of me?"

"That you are cruelly bound to some other person or persons, and that generosity to them, to him, or to her, whom you believe to have the prior claim upon you, is the cause of your reticence. I am sure that loyalty to some one has sealed your lips and fettered your movements."

"Should I not be unworthy your regard did I forget such prior claims—granted that they exist?"

"Bawn, give up this lonely enterprise."

She started visibly, and looked at him with wide-open eyes. The words struck her like a blow, and it was some moments before she could reassure herself with the remembrance that he knew nothing of her intentions and alluded to a fancied scheme which had originated in his own brain. Her eyes fell, and she was silent. Neither did he speak, being occupied in adding this look which he had surprised from her to the other scraps of evidence he had gathered as to her lot.

"I cannot give it up," she said at last, feeling a certain relief in talking of her own affairs, under cover of a misunderstanding, with this friend of to-day, who yesterday was not, and to-morrow would not be. "I am bound by loyalty, by love, by pity, by the energy and fidelity of my own character. My motive is strong enough and sound enough to bear me through what I have undertaken. It is an older acquaintance than you. God grant it may prove as good a friend !"

"Believe me, it will not," he urged, looking at her expectantly, as if he thought the longed-for confidence was coming at last. "Happiness is not to be looked for from it, comfort it will have none, difficulty and disappointment will follow persistently in its train."

"Ah, you evil prophet !" she cried, with something between a laugh and a sob. "It may be that you are right," she added. " My enterprise is, however, my life ; and with it my life shall be overthrown."

A red spot burnt on her cheek, and the look on her face smote him with remorse.

"I would not forecast evil for you," he said, "even if you persist in putting me out of your future. No matter to what shadows you may have devoted yourself, there will still be an escape for you somewhere into the light."

"I shall not be easily crushed, I can tell you. So long as the sun shines and the breeze blows there will always be a certain vigour and gladness in my veins," she answered, smiling one of her sunniest smiles upon him.

"It is getting cold, I think," he said, as a chill from the heart ran through his stalwart frame. It was hardly easier to him to picture her in a future of sunshine which he could never share than to imagine her falling away from all the promises of her young life for need of the protection that he could give her.

"I think it is turning cold," he said abruptly. "Have you any objection to walk a little?"

CHAPTER XIII.

TREACHERY.

During all the rest of that day Somerled exerted himself to amuse and entertain his companion. That sob in her voice, that flush under her eyes, when he had predicted evil for her, had frightened him, and he sought to banish unhappy recollections. He was a man who hitherto had not needed to make much effort in order to be beloved. Now that he was deliberately and earnestly trying to be lovable, he felt some hope that he might not ultimately fail.

Assuming boldly that they were to meet again some day in Paris, he chatted pleasantly of the delightful hours they might spend together there. They would go to the old churches in the mornings and to the theatres in the evenings; in the day-time explore the quaint old quarters so full of interest. How the bells on the horses' necks would ring, and how the animals' hoofs would click on the asphalt pavement! What visits they would pay to the shops, the picture-galleries, the old museums and palaces! Bawn laughed and asked a hundred questions, and as the day went past it seemed as if they had been riding and driving, seeing sights, and making purchases together, instead of walking up and down the deck of a steamer all the time, or sitting upon two camp-stools facing each other. By evening it seemed to her as if she must have spent a week in Paris, and she could hardly persuade herself she had never been there. This day seemed to have added a year to their acquaintance, so much pleasure, so many experiences had they shared between them.

It was not until the dusk began to fall that Somerled ceased talking and allowed her to find herself again in the steamer, with the waves running beside them, and another day of their companionship fled, bringing them so much the nearer to their final separation. Of how near it had actually brought them he did not dream.

It was an unusually clear, starry night, every one on deck and in the highest spirits. Our two friends sat in a quiet corner facing the breeze. Bawn's hat had fallen back on her shoulders, and her face looked pale and grave under a cloud of ruffled golden hair—not the same eyes and mouth that had been laughing so gaily all day. She was asking herself whether the moment had come for telling him that they must part to-morrow morning.

"You are looking now," he said, "like that statue of Diana in the Louvre. All this day you have had quite a different face. But now you laugh and dimple up, the likeness to the Diana is gone."

"I have always been so very much alive I cannot imagine myself like a statue."

"Bawn, at what door am I to knock when I go—say a fortnight hence—to look for you in Paris?"

"At no door," said Bawn, all the laughter and dimples gone.

"Then I am to give up my business and accompany you to Paris now?"

"Is that the alternative?"

"I think it is. Look at the matter as I will, I can come to no other conclusion."

She shook her head.

"It simply comes to this: I cannot make up my mind to lose you out of my life."

"A week ago you had never heard of me. A fortnight hence your business will fill your mind and I shall be forgotten."

"You do not think so. Your heart must tell you the reverse. A week has done for me what the rest of the years of my life cannot undo."

"What can I say to you that I have not already said ?"

"Half-a-dozen words—the number of a door, the name of a street, the name of a person, all of which you have kept carefully locked up behind your lips."

Bawn turned pale. "If you knew all I could tell you, you would turn your back upon me at once and go your way. But I will not allow you so to reject me. It costs me a great deal to say this, and I had not meant to say it. I had, and have, good reasons and to spare to give you without this one; but perhaps it will satisfy you more than all the rest."

"It does not satisfy me, simply because I cannot accept what you have said as the truth. I must judge of your obstacle with my masculine brain before allowing it to stand. I can imagine no barrier between you and me except such as cannot possibly exist."

"I assure you again, that if you knew my story you would part with me willingly. I would spare you a great deal of pain. More I cannot say."

"Then I repeat that I will not be frightened away by something of which I know not the form nor the meaning—a nursery bogie mooing in a dark corner. I refuse to believe that an obstacle is insurmountable unless I have touched and examined it, and measured my strength with it. Bawn, listen to me once for all. I am a man who does not make up his mind on a subject without having thought it out. I have made up my mind about you. My judgment approved of you even

before my heart desired you. You cannot shake my
faith in yourself, and nothing that is not yourself, nothing that does not destroy my belief in you, can
influence me to withdraw the claim that I have laid
upon you. In addition to this I may say that I am a
man who desires only a few things in this world, but
what I want I want quickly—that is, I know very soon
when an object has become necessary to my existence.
Yours are the first eyes of woman that ever assured me
their light was necessary to my life. Because I am
threatened with some mysterious shadow behind your
back, shall I weakly consent to extinguish such a light—"

He broke off abruptly, and Bawn was silent.

" Unless," he went on, " you tell me that you hate
me, that under no circumstances could you think of
being my wife, I will exert every faculty I possess to
make your future one with mine."

She wrung her hands together, and still said nothing.

" Bawn, you do not tell me that you hate me."

" I cannot tell you that, for it would not be true."

"Then you are going to tell me where we may meet ? "

" No."

" I will not ask you to betray any one. I will not
intrude on your privacy or seek to alter your plans.
Only let me know where and at what time I may see
or even hear from you. The moment may come when
you will be glad to call on me for help."

He took out his pocket-book. " My address is written
here—two addresses, in fact, one of which will find me
at my club in London and the other at my home. I
will give them to you in exchange for a couple of words
from you—a number and a street in Paris."

Bawn suddenly felt all her resolution giving way, and
a desire to have that leaf from his pocket-book take
possession of her. But her will was not yet overcome.

She clung on to her preconceived intention of keeping her own counsel, even while at the moment she could see the force of none of her reasons for so doing.

"How do you know," she said lightly, "that I shall be in Paris at all? It is as likely that I shall go to London or Vienna."

Her words and tone jarred upon her own overwrought feeling as she spoke, and nervousness made them seem even more heartless than they were. They had the effect she intended them to have, that of startling her companion and breaking up the dangerous earnestness and persuasiveness of his mood.

He flushed as if he had been struck. "Ah!" he said, "I have misunderstood you, after all. You are a heartless coquette, and your reticence is a mere trick to torment me."

"Why did you not perceive that before?" said she. "I have not tried to impress you with a high opinion of my character."

"No, you have not tried, but you did it without trying. The fault was in myself. During the past few days I have forgotten that some time ago I found you an empty-headed and disappointing woman. The idea returns to me——"

"Perhaps in time to save you."

"As you say, perhaps in time to save me."

"If so, I shall rejoice to have freed you from delusion. I shall have done you one good turn, at least, before we part," said Bawn, smiling, though with straitened lips.

"Doubtless you know how to rejoice over the follies of men who are deceived by the beautiful mask that Nature has given to your ungenerous soul!" he cried angrily. "I——"

A little gasp from Bawn checked the rush of his words. A bolt had fallen suddenly on her heart, her head. She threw out her hands blindly and fell stiffly back in her seat.

"Good God! she has swooned," he exclaimed in amazement and dismay. He laid her flat upon the bench and flew for an old lady who had shown her some kindness before.

"I thought she would be ill before all was over," said the old lady, bathing her forehead and chafing her hands. "Very few escape. It is nicer to be ill at first and enjoy yourself afterwards. There, she is better. She must get down-stairs at once."

"Will you lean upon my arm?" said Somerled penitently.

"Yes," she said. And together they made their way below.

She turned to him at the cabin-door and put her hand in his.

"After this," she said, "you will promise to think no further ill of me?"

He answered by silently raising her fingers to his lips.

"Never any more?"

"Never."

"Thank you, my good friend. Good-night."

As Bawn slipped into her berth and laid her head on her pillow, she told herself that the struggle was over, that this startling episode in her life was finally closed. But the man, who returned to the deck and paced there under the dark heavens till the small hours of the morning, told the wind and the stars jubilantly that this gold-haired, grave-eyed, sweet-mouthed woman was his own, that she loved him in spite of the shackles that bound her, and through the cloud that hung around her, and that, with youth and love on his side, he would baffle the whole world to make her queen of his heart and of his home.

The stars paled, the breeze grew colder, the dawn broke and showed the green coast of Ireland lying between sky and sea. The passengers were all asleep; no one on deck was much excited by the sight of the grey and green, hazy shore except a home-sick sailor-lad who was hoping soon to feel his mother's arms about his sunburnt neck. The man Somerled had flung himself on his berth an hour before, and was sound asleep in the expectation of a happier morrow than had ever yet dawned for him. The stopping of the steamer did not wake him, neither did Bawn's light feet as she passed up the stairs and crossed the deck, selected her luggage from the pile that had been hoisted from the hold, and inquired at what hour the earliest train would leave Queenstown for Dublin. As she walked about, waiting for the necessary arrangements to be made before she could touch land, her eyes turned anxiously towards the stair, as she hoped or feared, she scarce knew which, to see the well-known dark head appear above the rail. Surely the noise, the trampling over-head, the shouting and hauling, would awake him and he would come on deck to see what was going on. If he were to come to her at this last moment what foolish thing might she not possibly say or do? Never before had she found herself so near the undoing in a moment of all that her deliberate judgment had accomplished with so much forethought and pains.

A few words of thanks to the captain and of good wishes from him, a vain effort to frame a kindly message of farewell to be delivered by him to her friend, and then, with the unspoken words still choking her, Bawn was hurried into the tender. She arrived at the railway station just in time to catch the earliest train, and was soon flying with the birds away across Irish pastures.

CHAPTER XIV.

PASTURES of dewy green, hills of buttercups and daisies, flecks of water with heaven in their depths, and red and black cattle grazing amongst sedges and yellow lilies, streaks of dark bogland fringed with tawny weeds, soft, violet ridges of far away mountains, all wreathed in shifting sunshine and shimmering mist, passed swiftly before Bawn's eyes as she whirled through the butter-fields of Erin. Could anything be more different from the lofty solemnity of the dark pine forests, the far-stretching flatness of the prairie lines?

There was a long day's travelling before she stepped out of the train, and was conscious in the clear darkness of rugged hills, a bay with dusky shipping, twinkling lights, and a smell of fish and tar.

Arrived at the little hotel recommended to her by Dr Ackroyd, she was conducted by the honest woman who owned it to a tiny room with space just sufficient for herself and her trunk.

As she sat at breakfast the next morning in the little hotel parlour, with her hat and shawl beside her, the door opened and a gentleman came in. Then she noticed that breakfast was laid for a second person at the other end of the table, and the man, whose tea and toast were placed opposite to hers, sat down in the place that was prepared for him and stared at her.

She reflected that farmers' daughters cannot expect to have everything as ladies would wish, and serenely

9

went on with her breakfast as if no one had come into the room.

"Would you like to see yesterday's paper?" said the man; and then Bawn had to look at him for a moment. He was a stoutish, pompous-looking person, holding himself very erect, his eyes of a light watery blue with a puffiness under them, head a little bald, with a fringe of light coloured hair, a heavy mouth shaded by a heavier moustache, and hands that were fat and unnaturally white.

"Thank you," said Bawn; and, taking the paper, she held it so as to screen herself from his scrutiny.

"Ye didn't mind the major, did ye?" said the landlady apologetically afterwards. "He's a fine man an' a rich gentleman; but he's a good hand at starin', isn't he? My Mary complains of it when she has to wait on him, and she isn't as handsome as you, mem. If it had 'a' been one of the Fingalls, now, ye'd 'a' been quite at home with them; but Major Batt isn't so nice for a young woman that does be travellin' all her lone."

One of the Fingalls! Bawn's heart gave a sudden throb as the name fell on her ear. That strange, long week at sea dropped suddenly out of her life, and she was her father's daughter again, with his good name in her hands.

She had hardly taken her seat on the long car when Major Batt came out of the inn, looking larger than ever in a huge ulster and soft hat crushed down over his puffy eyes. He approached the little green car with the silver harness, but, instead of mounting it, said a few words to his servant, and then, coming up to the public conveyance, hoisted himself with some difficulty into a place by Bawn's side.

She thought regretfully of how his burly figure would probably shut out her view of the coast scenery. To try to see beyond him would be as bad as looking over the shoulders of a crowd. Travellers round the Antrim coast are few, and no one else appeared to claim a seat on the conveyance. The driver cracked his whip and the car rattled out of the town.

"You see," remarked the major, "I could not think of letting you travel all alone on this beastly car."

"Thank you," said Bawn; "but it was quite an unnecessary attention. We Americans are accustomed to take care of ourselves."

"I may say, in the words of the poet : ' Lady, dost thou not fear to stray, so lone and lovely along this bleak way ? ' "

A sudden turn in the road brought the wide ocean to their feet—a magnificent sheet of shifting silver guarded by shining white limestone cliffs, stretching away in curve after curve into a fairylike distance. Major Batt sat with his broad back squared against the scenery, and his little watery blue eyes fixed upon all of Bawn's face that was visible through the thickest of gauze veils.

"I am a stranger," she said, "and this kind of scenery is new to me. Have you any objection to letting me see it ? "

"I was just going to advise you to lift your veil," was the reply.

"It is one of our American inventions—the newest help to the eyes. I can enjoy my view better with it than without it."

"With such admirable assistance, you ought to be able to see through me."

"Perhaps I can," said Bawn, quietly, "but I am none the less anxious to change seats with you."

"Think what an unpleasant move for me. The view would engage all your attention, and I should have none of it."

Bawn was silent for a few moments, and then, finding the major's eyes still relentlessly fixed on her, she leaned back and said to the driver :

"Will you be good enough to stop a moment ? I wish to change my seat."

The driver was at her service in an instant ; the major laughed a little and muttered something, but offered his assistance, which was not accepted, and Bawn, placed at the upper end of the car, where she could keep her face turned away towards the scenery, felt herself victorious over her obtrusive fellow-traveller.

Nevertheless the major still continued to make himself as objectionable as he could, following her up the slightly sloping side of the car as far as was possible, though invariably getting shaken down to the lowest corner again by reason of his own considerable weight.

"I never could see anything in scenery myself," he said presently. "The only view I care about is the view of a pretty face. And you," he continued, as Bawn made no reply, intent on watching the shifting curves of the silver cliffs folding and unfolding far ahead—"you have just deprived me of one of the finest prospects I ever gazed upon."

As he spoke he had edged himself up the side of the car and come as close to Bawn as he could manage. "Did you speak ?" she said, turning suddenly. "This is not a good place for hearing, though capital for seeing. The wind carries your voice over your shoulder, I suppose."

"And your face over your shoulder, I suppose," he grumbled, as the back of Bawn's head was again presented to him. At the same moment, by an artful touch, she let loose the ends of her veil, which were driven into his face by the breeze.

"Confound it !" she heard him ejaculate, and he was suddenly shaken away from her and settled down in a heavy deposit at the lower end of the car. Looking round again, she saw him manipulating one of his eyelids and patting it with his pocket-handkerchief. A corner of the veil had gone into his eye.

"I am afraid you have got something in your eye," she said, serenely. "It is dusty for the time of year."

"Ah! true; so it is."

"And limestone dust is particularly irritating. What a pity you do not wear a veil like mine."

"Thank you; yours has been enough for me," he growled, trying to look as if nothing had happened, but winking wildly.

After this Bawn had peace for some minutes; but, the eye getting better, the major's spirits revived, and his pleasantries continued.

"Now, I am sure we have met in America," he began. "I spent last summer there, and ever since I saw you first this morning I have felt certain we were excellent friends in New York."

Bawn reflected a few moments and then said: "I wonder to hear you say so, for small-pox usually changes one so much; especially when one has only just recovered from it."

"Small-pox! *You* only recovered from small-pox. But you have no mark of it whatever."

"I can scarcely rely on your flattering opinion, as you have not seen me in a good light without my veil."

"You must have had it very lightly."

"I cannot say I had; but if so, it is all the worse for the person who takes the infection from me. He will be sure to catch the fiercest kind of it."

The major, who had been edging up the car, suddenly stopped his ascent, and was gradually, this time unresistingly, shaken down to the bottom, where he sat aghast.

"But you ought not to be going at large," he said; "it is highly wrong."

"One must go somewhere for change of air, or one cannot get well; and in a thinly-populated country like this one hardly expects to come in contact with people."

"Do you think it is very infectious?" asked the trembling major.

"Well, I shall never sit beside a recovered patient in a train again; that is all I can say," said Bawn, sighing.

"But perhaps you never were vaccinated?"

"O dear! yes. But I am a firm believer in the new theory that vaccination only makes you more susceptible," said Bawn, tucking her veil about her face, and turning away to hide her smile.

Meanwhile Major Batt sat ruefully looking askance at her from the other end of the conveyance, occasionally casting anxious glances behind to see if his own car was coming into sight.

"I think I shall walk a little," he said presently, with a comical attempt at ease of manner. "These outside cars are a confoundedly cold means of locomotion. Driver, stop! Let me off."

Off he went, and the car went on without him; and Bawn, looking back, saw the trim little green car hastening from the distance, and the stout major trudging gallantly to meet it.

After that the two strong horses drawing the "long car" thundered along under the overhanging limestone walls with Bawn as the only passenger. The sea washed green and pellucid over its white shingle, and clouds of silver smoke rose and filled the air with a curious fragrance from piles of burning kelp that smouldered on the shore. Few living creatures were to be seen, but here and there a cottage appeared in a hollow or on the summit of a cliff.

"There's Aughrim Castle, miss," said the driver, who had been silently chuckling over the discomfiture of the major, and now thought it his duty to entertain the lady. "That's where Lord Aughrim lives, miss, barrin' when he's away from home, which is mostly always."

"Then we have got into the Fingall country," said Bawn, looking round her eagerly.

"Oh! faix we have, miss. Furdher on ye'll come to Glenmalurcan, where the gineral and his family does be livin'. Leastways the gineral's dead, God rest his sowl; but the family's there to the fore, a'm proud to tell ye."

CHAPTER XV.

SISTERS.

A FEW days later two members of the Fingall family stepped out of the post-office of the little town of Cushendall and stood in the village street with disappointment strongly depicted in their faces. They were two slight young figures, clad in costumes and caps of Donegal frieze, wearing strong boots on their little feet, and carrying sticks somewhat like alpenstocks; two girls exceedingly unlike in appearance, and yet with a sisterly resemblance to each other.

"It is too bad, Shana dear, isn't it?" said the fairer and softer-looking of the two, fixing a pair of wistful blue eyes on the other's face. "How can we make them answer us? What can we do?"

"Do?" cried Shana. "Nothing but endure their silence. To think of our putting our ancestors in print, vulgarly trying to turn them into money, and having them scorned for our pains. I suppose it serves us right for the sacrilege. O Rosheen! what would Flora say if she knew of it?"

"But she would have had to know if the story had been published and become famous," said Rosheen. "We could not have gone on living with such a secret on our minds."

Shana knit her brows in impatient thought, and then suddenly tossed her head with a little peal of careless laughter.

"We must try again, I suppose," she said. "Waste some more paper and another bottle of ink."

"Perhaps we put too much war in it. Stories that get published are generally chiefly about marriages, I think," suggested Rosheen, timidly.

"And evidently the publishers won't allow us to strike out a new line," said Shana. "They would rather," she added contemptuously, "hear about the courting and marrying of the silliest person in the world than read about the brave doings of a hero like Sorley Boy. I would not humour them even if I could," she went on, with a brilliant damask glowing in her brown cheeks. "I will write about nothing but heroes and battles. Now come along, dear ; I have to call to see Betty Macalister, and to buy some tapes and pins at Nannie Macaulay's.

As the two girls turned their faces to the sunshine and set off walking, the difference between their faces, which were so much alike, became more distinct. Shana was a brilliant brunette, brown as a berry, with a delicate glow under her skin, a curling cloud of dusky brown hair, eyes dark, keen, and sweet, set in a forest of softening eyelashes, and an eloquent and character-istic mouth. Rosheen was fair, a little freckled, with hair decidedly auburn, and eyes of baby blue. Their noses were short, their brows low and smooth, and their little dimpled chins had been cast in the self-same symmetrical mould.

The village of Cushendall lies in a hollow among mountains, four cross streets, with a strong old tower in the middle, and a stream from the hills winding among trees to the sea. A savour of turf-smoke pervades it, and it is not so clean as it ought to be. Tiny shops show all sorts of odds and ends which country folks need to buy, and up one hilly street are a few dwellings

of the genteeler order.   As the two girls walked down
the village street every eye beamed on them.   In the
sight of all, from the shopkeeper standing in his doorway to the children making mud-pies in the gutter, the
fresh-faced, free-stepping maidens were as princesses of
an ancient line, daughters of the ancient chieftains of
the glens.   Nodding to every one they met, they passed
through the village and out upon the varied upland
that led towards the vale of Glenan.

All around them lay swelling knolls, Tivara, the
cone-shaped, fairy mount, rising with fantastic mien
among its fellows, looking fit ground for elves to dance
upon, as they do on moonlit nights.   Little cots and
humble farm-houses nestled in their clusters of trees,
their white walls gleaming here and there in the folds
of the cultivated hills, and circling around and above
these lower highlands the greater mountains rose with
their dark rough crowns and broad sides, and their
curved and curious peaks.   A rich, sombre purple hung
round Tibulia's beak-like crest, and over towards
Cushendun a long sweep of mountain, rugged with
shrubs and heather, had caught a warm crimson
flush.

The girls came down along the dark red road cut
through high sandstone cliffs to where Red Bay sweeps
with one majestic curve round the opening into Glenmalurcan, away to the great Garron rock, and suddenly
they espied a small green car with a fast-stepping horse
and silver harness coming to meet them by the cross-
road that skirts the shores of the bay.

"O Shana! Major Batt," murmured Rosheen in
dismay.

"Now, Rosheen, your fastest walking!" returned
Shana ; and the two little frieze-clad figures went at a
pace that would not have been amiss at a walking-

match. The green car was, however, too much for them, and met them at the angle of the bay.

"Miss Shana! Miss Rosheen!" cried an unctuous voice, and the owner of the car flung the reins to his servant and sprang off with as much agility as could be expected from a person of his build.

"This is an unexpected pleasure!" he went on after greeting them with much effusion, trying meanwhile to keep up with the inconvenient swiftness of their pace. "I have just paid a visit to Lady Flora at The Rath. My disappointment was great at not finding you at home. I thought of asking permission to join you in a ride."

"We do not ride now," said Rosheen regretfully. "We have given up our horses."

"Then I hope you will allow me. I think I can mount you, if you will be so good, sometimes."

"Thank you," said Shana sturdily; "but we much prefer our walking. A horse can't scramble up banks and climb rocks with you as we want to do when we come out."

"No, certainly," said the major, glancing nervously at the rough bank beside him and hoping she would not expect him to escort her immediately to the top of it. But Shana was thinking of something entirely different.

"Major Batt," she said with sudden and unusual earnestness, "I am going to ask you a serious question."

The major, for some reason best known to himself, changed colour and felt a glow of pleasure and curiosity, and at the same time wished himself safely back upon his car.

"The times are awfully bad," continued Shana. "Everybody is suffering; but some people must suffer more than others."

The major. had become very red. "I hope—I trust
—" he stuttered.

Shana silenced him with a magnificent wave of her
little hand.

"I am going to ask you if you know anything at all
of the old people who are still living at Shane's
Hollow?"

"Nothing whatever," said the major promptly. And
his countenance cleared.

"I thought, as you are the person who bought up the
last remnant of their property, that you might have
had some dealings with them which would enable
you to tell me whether they are really starving or
not."

"Starving!" said the fat major. "Starving, Miss
Shana, is a very uncomfortable word to make use of,
especially in connection with people who once held
their heads high in the county."

"It suggests that we may all come to it. You,
however, need not fear it, for a long time at least," said
Shana, with a little laugh, which the major did not
altogether like. "I don't think any of us need fear it,"
she added, "not even Rosheen and I, for we should
turn into honest work-women first. But seriously,
Major Batt, do you know of any means that those
poor old people have got of keeping the wolf from their
door; for their door does open and shut still, I believe,
though half of the roof is gone."

"I should say," said the major jocosely, "that they
are so accustomed to the wolf that they could not live
without him. But seriously, as you say, I only know
that some two years ago they had a little money
invested somewhere, though not more than enough
to give each of them a meal in the week. I have
reason to believe that, with their usual time-honoured

improvidence, they have sold out that moiety of property and eaten it up in a lump."

"Then they have nothing left," cried Rosheen in dismay. "They will die in that hole, and we shall all
feel like murderers."

"My dear Miss Rosheen, I never heard your gentle
lips make use of such strong language before," said the
major, suavely. "If fools will commit suicide, I don't
know how they are to be prevented."

"They used to eke out their existence in various little
ways," said Shana. "I have heard all about it from
'Hollow Peggy.' Mr Edmund cultivated a scrap of
land behind the old garden walls, where nobody could
see him, and so they had potatoes and vegetables. Mr
Paddy broke stones in a cave, gathering them off the
hills and breaking them with a hammer. Afterwards
he sold them to Alister and others for the roads, pretending he had a contract for supplying them. These
were the only industries they attempted ; lately, I fear,
even these have come to an end. Mr Edmund broke
his leg a short time ago by stumbling down a hole in
the ruined house, and the doctor carried him off whether
he would or not, to the poor-house hospital. Mr Paddy
is disabled by rheumatism—"

"They will all die ! " broke in Rosheen piteously.

"Let us hope not," said the major, buttoning up his
coat and speaking with a certain nervous decision.
"Old people reduced so far can live upon so little."

"The worst of it is," continued Shana, "that their
pride is so great that they will absolutely accept of no
assistance."

"It is the best thing I have heard about them yet,"
said the major, with increased decision of manner.

"They will not take help from any private source, nor
remove to the poor-house. The doctor removed Mr

Edmund almost by force, because he could not risk his own life wandering through the ruin in search of his patient. The sisters and brothers look on his removal as the last calamity that could have befallen them. They would be the Adares of Shane's Hollow as long as they live, and be buried by torchlight when they die, as has always been the custom of their family."

"And they will really accept no aid ? "

"They were tried at Christmas with money and clothes, but all was sent back, with the politest of messages and thanks."

"It is decidedly the most creditable thing I ever heard about them," reiterated the major, with satisfaction.

"I think differently," said Shana. "When people are old and destitute they ought to own their mistakes and practise the one virtue left to them—humility. To me there is something ghastly, absolutely inhuman, in their pride."

"You will hardly overcome it now, however," said the major.

"I think we ought to go on trying," said Shana, solemnly ; "and that is why I have spoken to you, Major Batt. Will you join with Alister in asking some other gentlemen to look after the case of the old people in the Hollow ? "

"I would do anything in the world for you, Miss Shana—" began the major gallantly.

"Not for me," she interrupted, quickly, "but for Christian charity, Major Batt. When I waken in the night I think I hear the voices of those poor old creatures crying in the wind, 'To work I am not able, to beg I am ashamed.' Ought we to let them die like rats in a hole ? "

"Miss Shana, you are an angel !" burst forth the

major; "and I will do anything I can. But I warn you, I believe they have some means of existence, or they could not afford to indulge their pride."

"You do not know them," persisted Shana. "You are a comparative stranger in the country, so often away, while I have been living near them ever since I was born. Their pride is great enough to sustain them through the pangs of death by hunger. It separated them from all who were once their friends. It will be inexorable in consigning them to a horrible grave."

"I do hope you are wrong Miss Shana, for your sake as well as for theirs. I never saw you in so doleful a mood before. Let us talk of something pleasanter. Of course you go to Dublin for the Castle amusements."

"No," said Shana, "we have made up our minds to stay at home this season. It seems to us hideous to go about dancing and junketing while the country is in such a miserable state."

"And besides—" began Rosheen.

"We require no besides," said Shana, quickly.

"But there is no disturbance in our part of the world," urged the major.

"This island is not so large but that we must all feel what occurs in any part of it," returned Shana. "There have been sad doings on Lady Flora's property in the west, and we are feeling it to the marrow of our bones."

"Lady Flora spoke as if she expected to take you to Dublin, if not to London."

"Did she?"

"And so I will hope to meet you shortly in gayer scenes. And now, as I am dining with Lord Aughrim this evening, and have a long way to drive, I must tear myself away from your charming society, and wish you, reluctantly, good afternoon."

He swung himself on to his car, which had been following him all the way, and after he had driven off the sisters walked some way in silence. Then Shana said : " Laugh, Rosheen ! Let us have a laugh ! I feel as if I had been putting both my hands into Major Batt's pockets. How I did frighten the poor creature ! I am curious to see what he will do for the Adares. It will be a fight between his gallantry and his prudence."

" He will have something to think about all the way back to Lisnawilly, at all events," said Rosheen joyously ; and then both girls laughed out loud peal upon peal of fresh young laughter, with which they seemed to cast off all the troubles that had been oppressing them since morning.

Their walk lay now along a narrow road at one side of the valley of Glenmalurcan, which runs up between two stretches of mountain, wide at its opening where the bay washes its feet, and narrowing gradually for two long miles to the point where the hills fold together and a fairy waterfall bursts from the upper rocks, whirls over the ash and nut trees in its way, and leaps into a tarn in the heart of an exquisite dell. The stream from the waterfall descending to the sea divides the vale as it flows, and the birds fly across it from mountain to mountain. Just now the opposite crags of Lurgaedon were red with sunlight, while a deep shade dropped down from the black-purple crags above the road travelled by the sisters, darkening all that side of the glen with one majestic frown.

The valley is fairly cultivated, and white gables show here and there among clusters of trees. An old bridge across the river indicates the course of an ancient road winding down the centre of the vale. As the girls proceeded swiftly along the narrowing road the trees grew thicker, and the view was gained only in enchanting glimpses between overhanging boughs.

A cawing of rooks began to be heard from the thickly-wooded distance, and their cries gradually swelled into a clamour as the girls got right under a huge mountain crag that loomed above the tunnel of trees they were threading and threatened to drop down upon their heads.

And here they entered the tall, old-fashioned gates of The Rath, and passed down the shady avenue, emerging suddenly before the front of the house into all the dying splendours of sunset.

CHAPTER XVI.

A SISTER-IN-LAW.

LADY FLORA FINGALL sat in an easy-chair before the fire with a book on her lap, a work-basket at her feet, and tea set forth, with its equipage of ancient silver and delicate china, on a spindle-legged table beside her.

She did nothing but look into the fire, however; for, though the setting sun made red bars along the sashes of the small, high windows, yet the drawing-room was already almost dark but for bright patches of sunlight of fantastic shape that flecked the many-cornered walls.

It was a pleasant reflection to Lady Flora's rather frugal mind that she had been able to furnish her drawing-room according to the approved mode of the day without having recourse to the fashionable upholsterer. To bring such persons and their productions across the Antrim mountains would have been a difficult and expensive undertaking, and she had simply had recourse to the garret at The Rath, out of which she had brought forth as pretty specimens of the spindle-shank tribe as any to be met with in Oxford Street. The old brown carved chimneypiece running up to the be-wreathed ceiling, which had been an eyesore to her when she came as a bride to The Rath, had of late become a treasure; the old dado, which she had papered over long ago, was now restored and repainted; and all the grandmother's cupboards and elbow-chairs and stacks of brass-handled drawers, which had mouldered under the eaves, disgraced and forgotten for so many years, were, with the help of a little beeswax and the village carpenter, at this moment looking handsome and dignified among sunflowers and peacocks' feathers in this ancient, home-like, and very comfortable apartment.

Lady Flora was a plump little woman, with a good quantity of fair hair, a white hand, a pretty foot, and a sharp and ready tongue. Her dress was elegant but not expensive, for she had a wonderful knack of getting good things cheap. Even the richly-wrought shoes which decked her little feet had been made at small cost by a poor old bankrupt shoemaker, who endured his reverses in a back street in Paris, and were fashioned out of a morsel of Indian embroidery which had been sent her by a wandering friend.

" I am glad to see tea," said Shana, taking off her hat and shaking back her curly, brown locks. " We had nothing for lunch but one of Nannie Macaulay's stale buns. And I am so thirsty ! "

"You ought to be tired," said her sister-in-law, poking the fire till the flame lit up the darkening room ; " but you look bright and bonnie ; and I heard you laughing immoderately as you came past the windows."

" Oh ! yes ; we met Major Batt," said Rosheen, " and he always makes us laugh."

" Major Batt is an extremely agreeable and sensible person," said Lady Flora ; " but I confess I never looked on him as a humourist."

" No," said Shana, with a sly smile, as she put down her emptied cup ; "he only inclines to make humourists of other people. How he did button up his coat to-day when I talked about money, poor dear ! " And Shana

walked across the room with her chin pushed out and
set up in the air, and fingered energetically at the
buttons of her jacket.

"How very unlady-like!" said Lady Flora coldly.
"And pray, Shana, why did you talk to Major Batt
about money? I hope—"

"You need not hope, Flora," said Shana abruptly;
"you know I am hopelessly outspoken, and I did ask
Major Batt for money."

Flora sat up in her chair, her plump lips parted, her
keen, pale eyes fixed upon Shana with horror.

"Yes," said the girl, carrying her replenished cup to
the fireside and seating herself on a stool by her sister-
in-law's side, "I asked him to do something for the poor
old bodies in the Hollow."

Lady Flora sank back in her seat. "I am relieved,"
she said. "I thought—"

"I don't want to know what you thought, Flora.
Your thoughts and mine are seldom the same."

"I am happy to say you are right there," said Lady
Flora sharply. "But there—tell me about Major
Batt."

"He buttoned up his coat," said Shana, sipping
her tea.

"By which remark you mean to imply, of course,
that he is careful of his money; and I admit that he
is. It is one of the virtues I admire in him. In this
wretched spendthrift country, where people hardly ever
think of to-morrow, a prudent man is a jewel to be
prized."

"Major Batt needn't think so very much about to-
morrow. His to-morrow will not be so long as some
other people's, and he has no one in particular to
succeed to his money and lands."

"Major Batt will marry," said Lady Flora, complacently turning a pretty ring on her short, white finger, and looking as if she was almost betraying a secret.

"Has he been making a confidence to you, Flora? He told us he had been here," said Rosheen, sidling up to her sister-in-law with a roguish look.

"What funny entertainment Major Batt's little confidences would be!" mused Shana, gazing into the glowing coals, which threw a hundred mischievous reflections into her dancing eyes.

Lady Flora ignored this observation and turned to Rosheen.

"I can't exactly say that," she said with an air of reserve, "but he gave me to understand a great deal."

"He generally does leave a good deal to the imagination of the listener when he talks," said Shana.

"Ah!" said Lady Flora, smiling archly, "there will come a day, perhaps, when he may find words enough to satisfy every one. In the meantime, Shana, I think that, prudent as he is, he will respond to your appeal to his generosity."

"I hope he may, for the sake of the poor old Adares," responded Shana readily; but her colour became heightened and a look of displeasure passed across her expressive brow.

"For somebody else's sake," said her sister-in-law quietly. "I will not say for which of you."

"You have fallen asleep at the fire and dreamed a bad dream," said Shana gravely. "Forget it, Flora."

"I never dream," said Lady Flora. "And I had Major Batt here all to myself for more than an hour."

"Poor Flora!" said Shana, with a heavy groan.

"I must say he thinks much more highly of you both than either of you deserve."

"Did he come to say he would marry, he didn't care

which?" laughed Shana. "Come, Flora, you don't mean to say you would sell us to Major Batt?"

"Unfortunately, he cannot marry both of you," said Lady Flora, a spot of anger reddening her cheek; "but if either of you were to refuse such an offer I should— wash my hands of you."

"Let me ring for a basin and some scented soap on the instant," said Shana seriously.

"Shana, you only say these things for the sake of appearing clever. I know you value money, for I have heard you wishing you were a man, that you might make it. And all I can say, now that we are on the subject, is, that if so excellent an opportunity should occur of providing for either of you, you will not be so mad as to put it away. With my children in the nursery, and little or no rents to be had; with Alister so weak in his dealings with the people, and all expenses to be covered by the income of such money of mine as happens to be invested in English securities— with this state of things staring me in the face, I will say that it would be extremely inconsiderate, not to say ungrateful, if either of you were to refuse to become settled advantageously in life.

Shana's cheeks were now glowing like the coals in the fire. She drew away her hands, with which she had covered her face while her sister-in-law was speaking.

"I own, Flora," she said earnestly, "that it is very hard on you having me and Rosheen to do with, now that our fortune which our father left us is gone; that Alister's property also should be so embarrassed, and that we should all depend on you—"

"You know I would wish to deny you nothing," interrupted Lady Flora; "but with my own young children—"

"I have thought about the children—I am always

thinking about them," said Shana, with burning eyes; "and, believe me, Flora, Rosheen and I intend to provide for ourselves."

"Major Batt is a capital *parti*," said Lady Flora. "And I am sure I should not have spoken to you so plainly except for your own good; and I expect that when he asks he will not be discouraged."

"As you say, he cannot ask to marry us both," muttered Shana meditatively.

"One will be enough; but as I am not at all sure which of you he prefers, I desire that you will both be prepared," said Lady Flora.

Rosheen pouted and hung her head. Shana rose and walked to the window, and stood looking out into the growing darkness for a few moments, then came back to the fire and said distinctly:

"If Major Batt makes choice of either of us, I hope it will be of me."

"Come now, that is better," said her sister-in-law in pleased surprise. "I always knew, Shana, that you had a fund of good sense somewhere if you would only condescend to make use of it."

Rosheen stared at her sister in astonishment, but said nothing. Shana rested her elbow on a ledge of the mantel-piece and went on:

"But I warn you, Flora, that I do not believe he is thinking of doing anything of the kind. In spite of his mature years and, let us say, solid appearance, Major Batt is fond of flirting, or doing something that he fancies is flirting. He is one of those persons who always put before them to achieve the most difficult enterprises, and so he is always trying to make himself agreeable—"

"By the way," interrupted Lady Flora, "I told him he might expect to meet you in Dublin."

"That you must not think of, Flora. Ball-dresses and all that expense at such a time!"

"That is my affair," said Lady Flora graciously.

"No, Flora," said Shana, drawing her sister's little hand through her arm, "it is my affair and Rosheen's. This, at least, must be left to ourselves. We will not go. It is bad enough to eat the children's bread—"

"Nonsense!" said Flora shortly. "How exceedingly literal you are! Who talked about bread? I must say it is very unamiable of you to take me up so sharply. And now I advise you to go away and dress. Alister is in his study, buried, as usual, in a book all day—would not even come out to talk to the visitors. Oh! that reminds me—what does bring that engineering young man, that young Callender, about the place so often? He was here again to-day."

Shana and Rosheen had reached the door, and Shana turned suddenly round and looked steadily at her sister-in-law.

"I suppose he comes because Alister asks him," she said. "I am sorry we did not see him."

"I consider him rather an intrusive person," said Lady Flora coldly, but avoiding Shana's shining eyes. "I do not like him, and I do not object to let him see it. There, do not keep standing in the door-way, girls. Bernard is coming in with the lamps."

The two young sisters went, linking together, up the dark old winding staircase, dimly lighted here and there by an old-fashioned lantern, and descending a few steps on the other side of the first landing, entered their own particular apartments. These were first a long room with a slanting ceiling and low walls, and a small, square window at each side, set up high under the eaves. This was their old school-room, which, as they no longer needed a governess, they had

turned into a sitting-room, making use of their own
ingenuity and needlework, to effect some considerable
improvement in its arrangements. It was a very old
room; the walls were panelled in dark brown; the
windows had deep brown seats; the sunflowers, of the
girls' own making, on the short, brown stuff curtains
made a grateful gleaming of gold in the brownness of
the place. The furniture was ancient and worm-eaten,
and the long, dark, oaken schoolroom table, with its
row of drawers, still held its time-honoured place all
down the middle of the floor.

A large bottle of ink and some pens stood upon it,
and a row of old book shelves held a store of shabby-
looking books. Two pretty work-boxes stood on the
table, and a basket of apples and an old-fashioned china
jug full of brilliant winter leaves. A peat fire burned
low on a flagged hearth, and Shana knelt before it and
began to take turf logs from a large wicker basket by
the fireside and set them on their ends on the tiles.

Rosheen came and knelt beside her, and they laid
their heads together.

"Shana, why did you say you hoped Major Batt
would make choice of you?" said the younger sister in
a whisper of reproach and awe.

"Because, darling, I should be able to fight my
battle better than you," said Shana.

"Flora thinks you meant that you would accept him."

"I am sorry, then; but she ought to know me better.
I merely said what occurred to me to say."

They were silent a few minutes, each feeling the
sympathy of the other, and then Rosheen said:

"O Shana! if Shanganagh Farm were only let!
That would bring us a little income of our own, and
we need not feel so dreadfully when she talks about
the children."

"Even in that case we should still be dependent," said Shana; "though of course it would be better than nothing. But nobody is coming to take Shanganagh while the times are so bad, and I fear, I fear the times are not likely to mend."

Shanganagh was a farm on an upper level of the mountain, about half a mile from The Rath. It was a part of a property left to the girls by their father, and had been lying unlet for the last two years. All the land belonging to them except this lay in disturbed districts, and it was the last blow to the sisters when Shanganagh was left on their hands.

"Nobody is going to take Shanganagh," repeated Shana. "The people are all flitting to America, and this place is so far out of the world."

"What are we to do then, Shana?"

"Something," said Shana with a frown, and kissed her sister hastily and stood up. And Rosheen said no more just then. She did not always know what to make of Shana.

Then they rose and went up a few steps to their bed-room, a very large room, plainly furnished, but adorned with all the little odds and ends of prettiness that girls love, with two white beds in opposite corners, and a tiny crib in between for the use of their eldest niece, who was the darling of the young aunts. Here they assumed their well-worn black silk frocks and the simple pearl ornaments left them by their mother, and returned to chat by their sitting-room fire till it was time to go downstairs for dinner.

Alister Fingall, sitting at the foot of his dinner-table, seemed for the first few minutes to be still living in the book that had enchained him all day. He was a slight fair man with dreamy eyes, and a sweet lazy smile. In the company of others he required time to come to the surface of the conversation. After he had eaten his soup his eyes rested with pleasure on the fresh faces of his young sisters, gleaming and glowing with the pure cool tints which are produced by exercise and mountain air.

"Any news in the village, girls?" he asked. "I hear you have travelled half the county to-day."

"No news," said Shana, "except that Betty Macalister talks of giving up her holding and emigrating. She cannot see her way to paying her rent."

A shade crossed Alister's face.

"Betty must not go; anybody but Betty. Who is her landlord, by the way?"

"Major Batt," said Rosheen, with a stolen glance at Lady Flora.

"She can go to the Land Court now like others," said Alister, "and get her rent reduced, if it be too high."

"I must say," said Shana, "that I don't think Major Batt is to be particularly blamed in this matter, for Betty seems to think that she and Nancy are unable, on any terms, to manage their land."

Lady Flora gave Shana a glance of approval.

"Major Batt is a most worthy gentleman," she said, "and, unlike some others, will be able to stand against the worst attacks of the Land Court. His fortune is too substantial to be undermined by any number of defaulting tenants."

"'Others' meaning your unhappy husband," laughed Alister. "What a pity we were not all born to an inheritance in the Three per Cents. like you, Flora!"

Lady Flora arranged her bracelets and said nothing, and the children came into the room for their share of dessert. There were six of them, the eldest being Duck, a little maiden of eight, who walked straight up

to her Aunt Shana and fixed a pair of inquisitive eyes
on her face.

"Where were you all day, Shana?   The house is not
nice when you are out all day."

"What will you do when I go away altogether,
Duck?"

"I will go with you," said Duck, emphatically, and
dived with her head under Shana's elbow.

"Duck, you nearly upset Aunt Shana's raisins into
her lap!" said her father.

"It was Shana's own hand that was shaking, papa,"
said Duck.   "I saw it before I poked her with my
head."

That night the wind roared as usual round The Rath,
coming down with many a swoop and rush from that
near, overhanging mountain, and hurtling strangely
over the girls' low, slant-roofed rooms.   A sound as of
blowing of organ-pipes was going on in the chimney,
and Shana and Rosheen lay awake listening to the
rude, familiar music, while Duck lay sound asleep in her
crib between them.

"Shana," said Rosheen, in a pause of the wind, "why
does Flora dislike Willie Callender?"

"Say *Mr* Callender, Rosheen.   It is not nice, dear,
to call young men by their Christian names."

"But we know him so well.   What does Flora see in
him to dislike?"

"He has no money in the three per cents," said
Shana, grimly.

"O Shana!"

"Nothing but an honourable name and a profession,"
continued Shana; "so what is there for any one to like
about him?"

"I should think," said Rosheen, "that when a young
fellow has such a pleasant face and such a kind, gentle-

manly manner any one might get on without disliking him."

"Well, dear, he is nothing to us, so we had better not talk about him."

"I am sure he thinks a great deal of you, Shana."

But Shana pretended to be asleep.

Rosheen was soon asleep in reality, and, after lying long awake thinking, Shana got up and, lighting her lamp, dressed herself. Passing by Duck's bed, she held the light above the little face, and then knelt beside the child and kissed her tenderly.

"Eat your bread, my darling?" she murmured in an aggrieved whisper. "Stand in your light? Encroach on your little worldly inheritance? No, my Duck, your Shana has more pride for herself, more love for you than that! Come, then, Shana, and try what the storm will tell you this lively night!"

She passed into the sitting-room and closed the door of the sleeping-chamber softly behind her. Shading her lamp and rousing up the fire, she opened a drawer in the old school-room table and took out some paper and pens. A cup of strong tea stood ready on the hearth to scare away the natural sleep from her young eyes. Having drunk this, she settled herself at the table and listened for inspiration in the hurtling of the wind.

"Rosheen was right," she said. "There ought to be love in it. But how can I write on such a subject?" As she listened a tale of love and sorrow and struggling grew out of the sobbing voices round the window and came to her. A smiling face with fair curls, a manly young face, a cheerful voice came across her thoughts — not the sort of hero for a harrowing tale.

"I must make my hero exactly the reverse of that

vision," she said with a smile, and then, as the wind
bullied on through the trees and piped weird ditties
through the ancient sashes, Shana drooped her head on
her hands and struggled with a serious and unexpected
difficulty—that of keeping a certain living individuality
out of the interesting tale she was hoping to write.

CHAPTER XVII.

GRAN.

TOR CASTLE stands on a breezy height a quarter of a mile inland above the bold promontory of Tor Head, opposite the Mull of Cantire. Here have dwelt for generations the elder branch of our Fingall family, at present represented by a young man, cousin of Shana and Rosheen, and by his grandmother. Gran, a striking and well-known figure in the district, is also grandmother to Alister and his sisters, and a fond greatgrandmamma to Flora's children.

Between The Rath and Tor Castle lie miles of beautiful country : romantic Glenariffe and Glenan, the lovely shores and strange caves of Cushendun, the rugged and splendid headlands of Cushlake, with their rocky climbs and flowery ravines. Far below Tor Castle the waters of Moyle wash the rocky walls of the great Tor Head—fairy Moyle, haunted in days of eld by the enchanted swans, the Princess Fionnuala and her brothers. Scotland looks so near that, on a fine day, one would think a ferry-boat might bring one across in a quarter of an hour, and from the windows of Tor Castle the exquisite outlines of the hills of Jura show their fantastic outlines on the bosom of the glittering sea.

Gran is the real head of the clan Fingall, loved by rich and poor. Her tall, spare, and still active figure is often seen moving from cottage to cottage about Tor, her stately old head with its snow-white curls stooping to enter at their lowly doorways. She is a rigidly upright, God-fearing, and charitable soul, kind rather in her deeds than her words, though a rare tenderness sometimes shines out of her keen and penetrating eyes. A slight degree of sternness in manner and demeanour deceives no one as to the quality of her heart, and it is never forgotten that she has known a terrible sorrow in her life.

On certain days the whole of the Rath family were accustomed to come all the way from Glenmalurcan to spend a day and stay a night with Gran. At other times Tor Castle was empty and silent enough, even when Rory, the master of Tor, was at home—he and Gran making but a small family to occupy it; but when The Rath people appeared it became as busy and merry as a hive. Such stirring visitations were the delight of the old lady's life; and preparations, in the airing of rooms and providing of sweets and good things for the children, were begun many days before the expected guests arrived.

On a bright May day the usual migration from The Rath to Tor was taking place. Lady Flora had gone early in her brougham with the nurse and two youngest children, leaving Shana and Rosheen and the elder babes to follow, walking, and riding on the family car.

The drawing-room at Tor had not been restored and re-restored like Lady Flora's; the ancient furniture had performed no journeys up and down the garret-stairs, had known no period of ignominious seclusion: there it stood just where it had been since the beginning of all things, as might be imagined—the old bureaus, and tables, and china-presses, and sconces, black with age and bright with well-polished brass. The round, convex mirrors which Lady Flora had once thought so hideous, but worshipped now, hung where they had always hung, except when removed for purposes of cleaning; the carpet was so worn that, but for rugs adroitly spread, it would have shown too plainly the marks of its valuable antiquity; the curtains had no particular colour left in them, but had a ghostly dignity in their folds better than the richness of many modern fabrics. The well-wrought brasses about the fireside shone with a comfortable splendour when the fire glowed all across its width between the high-shouldered pilasters and carved panels of the time-darkened chimney-piece.

All the chambers at Tor were furnished in the same style of unquestionable antiquity. They and their contents seemed as old as Tor Head and the waves that beat against it; and they suggested the truth that more dignity than money belonged to the inheritance of the ancient clan Fingall. Gran, who prized every stick and stone in the castle, saw nothing amiss; but Flora perceived keenly with her more worldly eyes that Rory would have to marry an heiress, as Alister had done, if only that he might restore and replenish his ancient home.

Even in bright May weather the breeze that blows up from the great Tor is sharp and cool, and Gran and her granddaughter-in-law sat in two grim arm-chairs facing each other by the fire. Gran looked like some old queen in a historical picture, with her white head posed against the carving of her high-backed chair, and her long black draperies flowing round her on the floor.

"I am glad you arrived first," she was saying, "because I want to talk to you apart from the girls. If Manon comes here I should not like them to have heard a word to the prejudice of her or her mother."

"Certainly not," said Lady Flora; "and I do not

11

know why any one need be prejudiced. You did not like her mother when you knew her as a young woman, but her grandmother was your friend. The girl is of good birth and an heiress. Why should she not come to you, if her mother wishes it ? "

"Why should she not?" said Gran reflectingly. "But then why should she do so ? I mean, what is the reason for her wishing it ? Aimée was a young woman I could not bear—sly, untruthful, cold-hearted."

"But she was charmingly beautiful and married the son of a wealthy marquis," laughed Lady Flora; "and that ought to cover a multitude of sins."

Gran sighed and fingered the letter she had in her wrinkled hand impatiently. Hers was not a worldly mind like Lady Flora's, and she had not been thinking of the position of this mother and daughter who were putting themselves forward to claim her friendship, but of their moral worth. It had once been a trouble to her that she could not like the daughter of the friend of her youth, and now it was vexing her that she might have to dislike the granddaughter as well. True, the grandchild might reproduce the estimable and loveable qualities of the grandmother; but then why did Aimée, the mother—so worldly, so cunning, and always, in former days, so unsympathetic with Gran herself—now ask to send her child under her roof, into the undesirable seclusion of the Antrim highlands ?

"I cannot guess her motive," said she, folding and unfolding the letter. "Manon is handsome and an heiress, and in France, in Paris, she ought to have the world at her feet. The grandmother is long dead—the only link between me and this mother and child; and even while she lived, Aimée took but little interest in her mother's friend. And now she writes to me like this :—

"'DEARLY LOVED FRIEND OF MY DEPARTED MOTHER:—My darling Manon, of whom you have heard tell as the heiress of her grandfather, the late Marquis de ——, husband of your dear friend my lamented mother, is now of age, and the world is full of snares and attractions for her. I have taken a strange fancy, sentimental if you will, to place her under your care for some few months, before launching her on the dangers and pleasures of life—'"

"There!" cried Flora. "What would you have more unworldly than that? If not very wise herself, she has a high opinion of you, and would like her daughter to have the advantage of your friendship."

A little colour stole into Gran's dear old face, partly at the suggested praise of herself, and partly with pleasure to think that Aimée's motive might, after all, be a high one.

"I do not consider myself a very good person, Flora. I tremble to think of how much better I might have been if I had tried."

Flora made a little mouth behind her fan. In her opinion Gran was a great deal too good—"too high-flown," as her granddaughter-in-law would have called it.

"Any virtue I have had has been too much of a negative kind," the old lady went on. "One cannot be very bad, always looking at Tor Head and the sea. But I would be glad to think that Aimée had some delusion on the subject, for better a mistake of that kind than no desire to look up to any one. Aimée has lived in the midst of the gay world, with its snares and temptations, and her daughter will probably do the same—"

"Why?" asked Flora coolly, putting down her screen and looking Gran in the face. "If Manon comes here with her mother's graces, her French noble birth, and her grandfather's money, why need she ever return to France, except for a visit, as Rory's wife?"

"Flora!" exclaimed the old lady, grasping both arms of her chair and looking indignantly at her grand-daughter-in-law.

"Dear Gran, don't fly up the chimney with horror at my depravity. I don't mean that we are to entrap and capture the young woman, force her into a marriage behind her mother's back; but all I can say is that, under the circumstances, such an event as Rory's marriage would be very likely to ensue from Manon's stay in his house. When her mother sends her here she knows that there is an unmarried master of Tor, thirty years old, and if she makes inquiries she can discover that he is not unattractive—"

"Stay, Flora. You run away with me. I fear I was thinking of wrong to Rory more than wrong to Manon."

"The heiress of a marquis, young and lovely!" exclaimed Flora.

"We have yet to judge of the personal charms of Mademoiselle Manon," said Gran. "I was thinking of her qualities of heart and head. I put the heart first, you see, Flora, though I do like a woman to have a few grains of sense."

"So do men, dear Gran," said Flora, with a slight sneer. "Such a thing was never heard of, you know, as a man marrying a pretty face with nothing behind it. They always inquire about a girl's brains and right feelings before they look at her eyes or feet."

Lady Flora set up her own pretty feet before her on a footstool as she spoke, and Gran glanced at them and then at her face with a little sigh. But the mistress of The Rath had not meant at all to imply that she herself had neither brains nor heart.

If," began Gran, slowly and earnestly, after a pause —" if Manon should prove to resemble her grandmother rather than her mother, and if she and Rory were to love one another, I should be happy to see such a marriage; but if she be worldly, vain, and deceitful " (Gran frowned as if confronting a well-remembered image which rose before her mind's eye), "rather then would I see Rory dead than standing by her at the altar."

Lady Flora shrugged her shoulders and glanced round the bare, faded, noble old apartment.

"At all events," she said, "I do not see how you can refuse to receive the granddaughter of the friend of your youth. Rory is in London at present, and as the girl is coming there with friends he can escort her across the Channel. He will thus have an opportunity of discovering even sooner than ourselves whether she is a wretch or a saint."

"Of course, as you say, I cannot refuse to receive her," said Gran gravely; "but, at all events, I will write to her mother at once to tell her exactly how I am circumstanced here, and warn her of how little the girl can expect in the way of entertainment."

CHAPTER XVIII.

THE BACKWOODS-WOMAN.

WHILE Gran came to this conclusion the rest of the family from The Rath—nurses, children, and aunts—were proceeding along the romantic road towards Castle Tor. Shana and Rosheen, being capital walkers, only needed "a lift" now and again, and when within about a mile of their destination they sent on the roomy family car without them, keeping Duck by their side at her own urgent request.

As the girls trudged along, laughing, talking, glowing with exercise, a figure appeared suddenly on the slope above them and began rapidly to descend—a fair-haired young man, who pulled off his cap as he leaped to the road and stood smiling before them.

"O Wil—" began Rosheen, and checked herself, glancing at Shana.

"How are you, Mr Callender?" said Shana, gravely, giving him her hand.

"It is so long since we have seen you!" pouted Rosheen. "What have you been about?"

"Mr Callender called yesterday when we were out, Rosheen, and he has been so busy. It is very hard and absorbing work bringing a narrow-gauge railway down the side of a mountain, is it not, Mr Callender? Rosheen does not consider," said Shana, briskly.

"It is not, perhaps, as hard as it looks," said the young engineer, who did not feel as if he had much to say just for the first two or three moments. A few minutes ago he had been walking through the heather with sad enough thoughts, and lo! here he was looking in the face that was everything to him in the world.

"O Rosheen!" cried Duck, "do get me some of those sky-flowers down in the hole there!"

"Nonsense, Duck! Sky-flowers!"

"Flowers like bits of sky, I mean. O Rosheen!"

"If I get you three will they content you?"

"Six," said Duck. "I do so love them."

"Three!"

"Twelve!"

"You little extortioner! There, I will get you six, but not one more, for the rest are too far down." And off scampered aunt and niece, dropped over the roadside bank, and began to do what Duck called "slithering" down the seaward slope, while Shana and Callender walked on together.

"Miss Fingall—Shana!" began the young man eagerly, "I want to tell you, if I may, why I must for the future refrain from visiting at The Rath. I have thought much about how to tell you. I had hoped yesterday to find an opportunity; I was disappointed then, but chance now favours me. I hope it is not wrong of me to speak—at all events, I must. I cannot allow you to think I am careless of seeing you, even if you do not care—"

"I do care," said Shana, abruptly. Then she added, "I like to see my friends."

"Ah! your friends. Well, Lady Flora has been so cold to me, has, in fact, so snubbed me on several occasions when you were not present, that I feel I cannot again force myself into her house. When your brother invites me I will come gladly, and endure Lady Flora's slights, but I cannot enter The Rath uninvited any more."

"You are right," said Shana, quietly.

"O Shana! if I may say a little more. Ah! I will say it, come good or come ill. Shana, I love you. Unfortunate beggar that I am, with my fortune yet to make—Shana, I love you, I love you!"

A flash of brightness and colour suffused Shana's face, and she trembled, but she said nothing.

"I know I am an idiot to speak, for I dare not ask you to marry me now. I dare say I am very wrong. I may be a dreamer to hope I may one day be able to give you a place in the world worthy of you. At present I can say nothing except that I love you, and perhaps I ought not to say it. But, Shana, I love you, I love you!"

Shana had conquered her trembling and lifted her grave, dark eyes steadily to his.

"And I love you too, Willie Callender," she said with a still earnestness of manner, as if she were uttering a vow. "I am glad you have spoken to me, and you need not fear to have done me a wrong."

"O my love! I do fear it, I do fear it."

"Come good or come ill, I am yours," she went on steadily, "whether you can claim me or not. If you were to die to-morrow, and I were to live to be a hundred, I should never love another man."

"Shana! Shana! do you know what you are saying? Do not say it rashly. I shall live on your words, and work on the strength they will give me."

"I have said it," said Shana, a radiant smile breaking over her face. "I have given my promise to you, Willie Callender," she went on, as they stood with clasped hands, looking in one another's eyes, "and now my life will be full of light, and my future glorious. Come when you like, stay away when you like, I will welcome you, wait for you, trust you, work with you. Now here are Rosheen and Duck, and we must go on to Castle Tor."

" Are you going to leave us so soon ? " cried Rosheen, as she saw Mr Callender turn away from Shana.

" The men are waiting for him yonder on the road," said Shana. " He is out surveying, and has no more time for us."

" Good-bye, Rosheen ; good-bye, Duck," said Callender wistfully, and as he raised his hat his eyes flew back to Shana's, still shining with the light his impulsive words had kindled in them.

" Good-bye," he repeated in an altered voice, and was gone.

" How oddly he looks ! " said Rosheen. " What could you have said to him, Shana, in such a little moment to make him like that ? "

Shana smiled. " Perhaps I told him not to break his neck leaping down hills," she said. " One can say a good deal in a little moment, sometimes."

" It is a good deal, from you, to express even so much interest in him as that," said Rosheen, " so I don't wonder it overwhelmed him."

" I hear hoofs ! " said Shana abruptly. " Duck, do you think papa can be coming ? "

Duck believed it possible, and in a few moments Alister Fingall rode up and sprang from his horse, crying :

" I have good news for you, girls. Guess——"

" Major Batt is married," said Rosheen with sudden solemnity.

" No," laughed Alister ; " as far as I am aware, he is still in a position to flit from flower to flower."

" Betty Macalister has got her rent."

" Hopelessly wrong. I see I must tell you. There is an offer for Shanganagh Farm."

" The farm ! "

" Alister ! What delightful news ! "

Alister stood smiling at his sisters, watching their pleasure grow as they realised the welcome truth. That the letting of the farm was very important to them he knew, but of all it meant to their proud young spirits even he was unable to imagine. Independent bread, a shield from Flora's taunts, power to look Duck and her following unremorsefully in the eyes, composure of mind with regard to the fate of the novel just begun— these were but a few of the boons which the rent of Shanganagh, paid regularly every half-year, would bring into the lives of its young-lady landlords.

"What kind of tenant are we to get?" asked Shana, radiant. "And will he pay?"

"It is not a he," said Alister. "It is a she."

"Really!" But of course she has a man of some kind to act for her."

"It seems not; and there is nothing very odd in a woman taking a farm, if only she knows how to manage it. Miss Ingram writes:—

"Writes? Have you not seen her?"

"I only got her letter just before I left, and thought best to show it you before seeing her. She is in lodgings at Nannie Macaulay's."

"Where has she dropped from? We were in Nannie's a few days ago."

"She is an Irish farmer's daughter from Minnesota, come to Ireland with the little savings that her parents left her. She wants to live in the country of which she heard so much from her father. Immediately on arriving she made inquiries about lands to let, and applied at once for Shanganagh."

"Without seeing it?"

"Oh! I believe she has been to see it. These Americans lose no time; and from the tone of her letter I gather that she is a woman who knows what she is about. She thinks she understands farming; and let us hope that she is right."

"What women these Americans are! I suppose she is a sort of female grenadier."

"No matter what she is, if she be solvent. Her only reference is to a Dr Ackroyd, in St Paul. She is willing to wait till I can get an answer from him."

"Is it necessary to wait?"

"We may be able to judge about that when we have seen and heard her. She offers either to come to interview me at The Rath, or to receive me at Nannie Macaulay's."

"Oh! let her come to The Rath," cried Rosheen. "I do so want to see an American farmeress!"

After this news, Shana and Rosheen were impatient to return to The Rath, and the days at Tor Castle with Gran seemed longer than such days were usually found. Shana had a great deal on her mind, and longed for the seclusion of the old schoolroom in which to think out her thoughts. Here she had not a moment alone to realise the fact that Willie Callender had spoken to her, and that her life had gone out of her own keeping. Smiling quietly at Flora from the opposite side of the great Tor hearth-place, she wondered what her sister-in-law would say or do if she knew what had happened to her that day. But Shana was not much afraid of Flora. And the letting of Shanganagh made it easier to be brave. Alister left Tor the morning after he had brought his news, promising to see the proposed tenant and to invite her to come on a certain day to The Rath.

"Ask her to come in the evening," said Shana. "Major Batt is dining with us, and her visit will be a welcome interruption. And all hours must be the same to a farmer who has travelled from Minnesota."

Back in their own sanctum, the sisters hugged one another and laughed aloud. That heaven should have sent them an American farming-woman to pay them the rent of Shanganagh and make them independent of Flora, seemed too delightful to be true. On the eventful evening of her expected visit they dressed early, even though Major Batt was in the drawing-room, and hurried into his presence, eager to get a word with Alister about the heroine of their dreams.

"Well, what is she like?" asked Rosheen, sidling up to her brother as soon as he appeared.

Alister's face was twitching all over with fun.

"As like a backwoodsman in petticoats as anything you can imagine," he said. "Big, brown, and bony. Swings her arms as if she was accustomed to carry a hatchet, and walks like a dragoon."

"Exactly what I pictured her," said Rosheen, triumphantly.

"I did not think she would be quite so bad as that," protested Shana; "I fancied her a short, thick-set person with a knowing expression and a nasal accent."

"Add the knowing expression and the nasal accent to my first sketch," said Alister, "and you will have her to the life."

"I don't think you need have brought her here," complained Lady Flora. "A person like that ought to be dealt with in an attorney's office."

"I am not an attorney and I have not got an office, and you know I never take more trouble than I can help. It is easiest to do the business in my own way. If she bullies us too much Major Batt and I will be able to manage her. Eh, Major?"

"Oh! certainly; anything you please," said the major, nervously. "Though in the case of a woman—"

"American females from the backwoods hardly count

as women, major, do they?" said Alister. "Oh! by the way, girls, I told her you could put her up for the night."

"For the night!" A look of blank dismay overspread the faces of the three ladies, dismay developing quickly into indignation on Lady Flora's countenance.

"Most inconsiderate," she pronounced. "Where do you think we could put such a person?—unless she will go among the servants."

"There is the brown room," suggested Shana. "If she has been invited we must welcome her."

Lady Flora turned her bracelets on her white wrists, which, with her, was a sign that all the family knew. What the savage man means when he dances his wardance, that Lady Flora meant when she turned her bracelets. She would not have that American farmeress sleeping in her house.

"If you are afraid," said Alister, "we can lock her in and put a couple of the dogs outside her door."

A peal of the bell was heard, and everybody started.

"By Jove! there she is," said the master of The Rath. "I begin to feel nervous. Only that Major Batt is here—"

"Don't be ridiculous, Alister," said his wife. "As you have brought her here, you must make the best of her. Only please send her word that the car must wait. I will not have her here for the night."

"It's Miss Ingram, sir. Wants to see you, sir," said the butler confidentially in his master's ear.

"Will you receive her in the drawing-room, Flora?" asked her husband; and then, seeing the bracelets turning, he said to the servant:—

"Show her into the library. I will be with her immediately.

CHAPTER XIX.

IN THE ENEMY'S CAMP.

BAWN stood on the hearth in Alister's library, looking round her with the most lively interest. She had now been several days in the Glens, and had walked and been driven in various directions, making acquaintance with her father's country. Each evening she had returned to Nannie Macaulay's, and mounted the bit of narrow stair that led to her nest over the needle-and-tape shop, with her heart and imagination vividly impressed by the scenery through which she had been moving all day. All over it she saw the sorrowful details of her father's history, and every creature she met on the way seemed an actor in the tragedy of his youth.

Afraid to ask many questions, lest those around her should guess her identity and purpose, she contented herself with hearing the general remarks of the car-drivers, and encouraging Nannie Macaulay to gossip when she brought her her tea. Like most people who live absorbed in one idea, she fancied every word and look of others bore in some way on the question so present to her own mind. How could persons who had once known or heard of Arthur Desmond outlive their interest in him, or suffer the life of the present moment to thrust him and his story far into the background of their thoughts?

Now she had penetrated into the very camp of the enemy, and stood upon the hearth of a Fingall. Nannie

Macaulay had not been slow in pouring forth, almost unasked, the pedigree of Alister, the master of The Rath, and of Rory, master of Castle Tor. Her own wit and previous knowledge had discovered the exact relationship between these living men and the Roderick whom Desmond was supposed to have killed. Nannie had not mentioned the murder, nor touched at all upon the tragedy. She had only hinted at it by saying that the old lady at Castle Tor had known a terrible sorrow in her life. And Bawn knew that Gran must be the mother of Roderick, and that Alister and Rory must be the sons of his brothers, now dead.

In making her way from American prairies to Irish glens she had not counted upon coming at once into such close contact with the family so intimately connected with her father's misfortunes, the descendants of those "friends" who had condemned and forsaken him. When Alister Fingall, seeing her young and a lady, had asked her to come to The Rath and there conclude the arrangements for the farm with his sisters, her landlords, she had at first shrunk from accepting his invitation, disliking to enter his house. Curiosity, however, had overcome her hesitation, and she was here.

Now she stood under the roof that must have sheltered her father on many a happy day before the horror came. These walls had heard his laugh, these old books must have been touched by his hands. This fireside, towards which she instinctively stretched her fingers after the chill drive on an outside car through the evening mists of the glen, must often have reflected its flame in his eyes and welcomed him freely among its own. And the friends who had sat here by his side had deserted him in his misfortune, had cast him forth out of their home and their hearts.

She withdrew herself from the warmth of this fireside

of a Fingall, and stood aloof, frowning round the quiet, comfortable room with its book-lined walls, felt-covered floor, reading-lamps, reading-desk, and pictures.

Here they had dwelt, the cruel ones, all this time, happy, honoured, beloved, and at ease, while he whom they had persecuted wasted his life in an alien country, pining under the calumny with which they had helped to load him. After a few minutes these thoughts so grew and wrought in her mind that had she been left much longer in the room alone she might have walked out of it and made her escape from the house. Fortunately for her reputation as a sensible woman, very desirable to her at present, she was prevented from so acting by the entrance of Alister Fingall.

" Miss Ingram, pardon me for keeping you waiting. My sisters will be with us shortly. In the meantime sit down, please, and let us discuss our business. Have you thought over all I said to you this morning ? "

" I have thought it all out long before this morning, Mr Fingall. One does not cross the ocean without knowing why one comes. The desire that brought me here was to possess a farm in Ireland. You have a farm to let, and I will give you the rent at which you value it."

" You are very young and—excuse me for being so personal—very fair to enter upon so bold and independent an undertaking."

Bawn inclined her head with a stately movement, and a slight look of impatience crossed her smooth brows.

" If your father " (Bawn started) " had lived he would probably have advised a different course. I am older than you, and I have young sisters. I should not like to see one of them place herself in the position you are so anxious to take up."

" Your sisters are young ladies, Mr Fingall, brought

up in luxury and holding the place of ladies in the world. I am a farmer's daughter, hardily reared, understanding my father's business and wishing to practise it, and with no family traditions to be hurt by my plebeian occupation."

Alister Fingall observed her attentively as she spoke, and followed the imperial wave of her white hand, from which she had forgetfully removed the coarse glove it pleased her to wear. He thought the would-be tenant of Shanganagh Farm did not look exactly like a humble farmer's daughter. However, he could interfere no further on the score of the girl's apparent gentility. His remonstrances took another form.

"Farming is different here from what you have seen in Minnesota, and you will be obliged to trust servants to manage your business. If you lose your money in a year or so, have you considered what you will do?"

"I will not lose it," said Bawn, with decision. "And, at all events, I have made up my mind to try this venture. However, if you think me an unsafe and uncertain tenant, please say so at once, and I shall seek for what I want elsewhere."

"I have no objection to you as a tenant—on the contrary. It is not easy to let land just now, and a solvent tenant is highly welcome to my sisters at this present moment. Anything I have said to dissuade you has been for your own sake alone."

He spoke with an accent of sincerity which Bawn, despite her prejudice, could not mistake. But she said to herself that she did not want his friendship, and that she had already repaid his courtesy by explaining to him her views with regard to her own position—a piece of confidence which she had intended vouchsafing to nobody.

"As you have quite decided, I will now introduce

12

you to my sisters," he continued, and rang, and sent a request that the young ladies would come to the library.

Shana and Rosheen came into the room, each in her own characteristic manner. Rosheen hovered behind her sister, glancing inquisitively into the room, half frightened and half hoping for fun. Shana held her head well back and her eyes well open to take in the whole situation, and resolved that this brawny back-woods-woman who had come to their rescue should be treated as a friend, however disagreeable she might unfortunately be.

Both sisters paused speechless on the threshold at sight of Bawn, whose heart at once throbbed involuntary approval of these fresh, sparkling-eyed, white-armed girls in their graceful though well-worn black silk frocks, and their simple and virginal ornaments of pearl.

" Miss Ingram, these are my sisters, the Miss Fingalls, who will be your landlords. Shana, this is your new tenant—if all goes well. Miss Ingram will not be dissuaded by me from the difficulties and responsibilities of farming."

" I am a farmer's daughter," said Bawn, turning on the two girls a warm, broad smile which lit up her whole face, and showed it in a new aspect to Alister. " I cannot persuade Mr Fingall of all that that means. I have taken my little fortune in my hand, and I wish to turn my American gold into Irish butter and wheat. If you will trust me with Shanganagh, Miss Fingall, I will do my best to prove a desirable tenant."

Shana had by this time recovered from her astonishment.

" Forgive me for staring at you," she said pleasantly, "but I expected to see such a different person." And she cast a reproachful glance at Alister.

"To tell you the truth, Miss Ingram," said her brother, "we were all dying with curiosity to see a backwoods-woman. And we could not picture her without a hatchet."

"Will not a spade do?" said Bawn, with a smile. "I shall be at work with that implement soon."

"Not with your own hands?" protested Rosheen, who had been standing rapt in admiration at Bawn's changing countenance and golden hair.

"Perhaps you will be so good as to come and see," said Bawn, forgetting her enmity to the Fingalls for the moment. She had never seen any one of her own sex look so temptingly companionable as these charming girls. "At all events, if you will give me the key of Shanganagh I will enter into possession at once."

"But who will live with you there?" cried Rosheen.

"I think I have found some one. The person with whom I lodge recommends" (here Bawn grew grave and cold) "a Mrs Macalister and her daughter. They were thinking of emigrating, and will be glad to take a home with me instead."

"Betty Macalister!" cried Rosheen, clasping her hands. "O Shana! what a shower of good luck at once!"

"I am exceedingly glad," said Shana, fixing grateful eyes on her future tenant. "You hardly know what good you will be doing there. And Betty is a faithful soul."

"Yes," said Bawn, the grave look on her face deepening almost to sternness, "*I believe she is a faithful soul.*"

The brother and sisters noticed the sudden alteration in Bawn's countenance and tone, and thought her mind had been crossed by a sense of her own loneliness among strangers.

"And now will you come upstairs and take off your hat and shawl?" said Shana, quickly resolving that she would brave Flora's displeasure rather than send this delightful stranger back through the miles of Glen to Cushendall that night. She must be warmed up and made to forget her loneliness. Rosheen, always an admirer of her sister's superior audacity, heard her now with satisfaction.

But Bawn was not to be suddenly led into the bondage of friendship like this. The mention of Betty Macalister had recalled her to herself, and reminded her of her cause against this house.

"You are very kind; but my car is waiting and I must go. I have business in the morning which must be attended to."

And in spite of renewed and pressing invitations she got upon her car and was driven from the door of The Rath.

"Well, have you dismissed the backwoods-woman?" asked Lady Flora, who, notwithstanding her interest in Major Batt, was rather tired of her *tête-à-tête* with him.

"O Flora! what a pity you did not see her," cried Rosheen. "She is simply glorious!"

"With ugliness?"

"With beauty."

"Alister, has this girl gone crazy?"

"She has lost her head about Miss Ingram evidently. What would have become of the major, if we had introduced her here? Our new tenant is a young woman eminently fitted by nature for the breaking of susceptible hearts."

"Is she really handsome?"

"Really."

"And young?" asked Major Batt.

"And young."

" And what is she going to do at Shanganagh ? "

" Waste her money, I am afraid ; but as she will not be advised, we must allow her to pay us the rent. You might as well have been civil to her, Flora."

" I do not like handsome women who go gadding about the world alone," pronounced Lady Flora. " When did she get here, and how ? "

" Oh ! a few days ago, and by the car round the coast."

" Humph ! " said the major. " My dear Fingall, I think I know the lady. It was extremely improper for her to come here. She has just recovered from the small-pox."

" *Small-pox !* " cried Lady Flora, horrified.

" I travelled on the car with her, and she told me of her misfortune," said the major. " A handsome young woman, as you see her through a veil."

Shana and Rosheen laughed and exchanged glances.

" I think Miss Ingram has her wits about her," said their brother slyly. " Are you sure she did not want to get the car to herself, major ? "

" I am very sure she did not,"' said Major Batt stiffly.

" At all events, this decides me that I will not have her coming here," said Lady Flora. " Small-pox in a household like this ! Audacious creature, to subject us to such a risk ! "

CHAPTER XX.

SHANGANAGH FARM lay on the opposite side of Glen-malurcan, looking from The Rath. To reach it one followed the old road by the river up the middle of the glen, and turned off into a by-road or "lonan," climbing the hill by easy zigzags, between hawthorn-hedges, to the bit of table-land midway up the mountain, on which the farmhouse stood. The beetling crags hung imme-diately over it as over The Rath, but the farm lay full in the sun—green fields, old mossy orchard of gnarled apple-trees, strips of tillage, and a house with white-washed walls and yellow thatch.

Except for a few scrambling, fragrant cabbage-roses, rakish larkspurs, and ragged, spicy gilliflowers rooted long among the apple-trees at the end of the wild slip of orchard, there was not a flower about the place, as Bawn remarked, missing the flushing flower-growths to which she had been accustomed.

Here, if she wanted colour, she must lift her eyes to the opposite mountain-ridges and view the violet and saffron tints, the orange and rose and crimson hues, cooled by greys, infinite in variety of depth, which hung for ever between the plains below and the mid-heavens above her head. Now that it was nearing summer, the whole vale of Glenmalurcan, from its mountain-tops to the sea, was steeped in colour. Of the ponderous gloom of its winter days Bawn as yet knew nothing.

Inside, **the** house consisted of four rooms, opening out of one another on a flat, and a dairy and store-room behind. The house-door led straight into the kitchen, and off the kitchen was Bawn's sitting-room, and off that her bedroom. Overhead was a servant's apartment, under the roof, and a loft for apples, and for the hanging up of sweet and bitter herbs in bunches to dry from the rafters. Of this simple dwelling Bawn and her. serving-women, Betty Macalister and her daughter Nancy, took possession during the week that followed Miss Ingram's visit to The Rath.

Having with much difficulty procured sufficient furniture, the new tenant went to work to try and make what she called her "shanty" a little habitable; and it was well this occupation lay to her hand, as, her fields being already sown, she had little outdoor employment in this season, and disliked the idea of sitting down to think.

Even as it was, while she stained her parlour floor brown, and waxed it bright, and spread it with the goatskins of the country, she found it hard to keep the sailing away for ever of that steamer out of her mind, to suppress a voice in her heart that accused her of treachery to a friend.

Where had those ardent, dark eyes sailed to out of her life, and what bitter things against her was that brave, brown man thinking now as he reflected on the trick she had played him?

Well, he was gone. One cannot both have one's loaf and eat it, and she had swallowed her bread, sour and bitter as the mouthful had been. She had thought the swallowing of the morsel everything, but it had left a taste on the mouth which was neither nice to endure nor easy to get rid of.

Even so, would she give up the position she had now

gained, the footing on which she stood, the hope of accomplishing her purpose which seemed already floating all round her in this mountain atmosphere? As she hammered a nail home in her house-place she declared no, she would not own to any desire that she had been weak enough to relinquish her enterprise, or suffer herself to wish for a moment that she was back on the high seas, with still the option of holding, for life, the lover who had so strangely, suddenly, extravagantly loved her.

When a few unexpected tears dropped on the nails she drove in, almost as heavily as the blows of her hammer, she told herself they had welled from the depths of her heart solely because she was lonely, homesick, all forlorn in a land of strangers; and also because, curiously enough, now that she was here in the scenes so long dreamed of, had kindled her hearth-fire on the mountain-side looking towards Aura, had spoken with the descendants of those whom she considered her father's enemies, she found it more difficult to realise certain dire events in the past than when sitting by a solitary grave on the now far-distant prairie.

The people here all seemed so utterly unconscious of Desmond's tragedy. Even Betty Macalister kneaded her cakes and arranged her pots and pans as if all memory of it had passed away from her mind.

For what, then, had Bawn come here, after all? To what end had she quenched for ever a light that had unexpectedly shone on her out of a stranger's eyes, warming her who had not known herself cold till the warmth was withdrawn?

These were sore questions, such as she had never thought to be beset with, and for the moment she was not able to answer them.

And meanwhile, as she was at work with her women,

putting her house in order, cleaning and polishing, and arranging her scanty furniture, a storm broke over the mountains and rolled down the glens, hiding away the opposite ridges behind sullen cloud and tattered mist, and lashing the walls of the farmhouse with a scathing rain. A noise like thunder roared in the wide chimneys, angry drops hissed into the fire, and in the midst of the tempest Bawn wrestled with her own regrets, which were as fierce and unexpected in their onslaught on her heart as the assault of the elements on her dwelling.

But Betty and her daughter proceeded with their tasks as if nothing was the matter, only called to each other a little more loudly than usual, so as to be heard above the hurly-burly of the wind and rain.

No one came near the farm for a week, and when the week was at an end Bawn had grown visibly thinner, and thought that she must already have lived a year by herself at Shanganagh.

CHAPTER XXI.

BETTY SPEAKS.

At last one day the wind ceased to bully, the rain dripped and stopped with many a wild sob, and late in the evening the clouds opened overhead, and a great, broad, burnished moon looked over at Bawn from The Rath side of Glenmalurcan.

Never before had night appeared to her in such lovely and romantic guise. She went out and walked up and down before her door, trying to fathom the o'ershadowed glen with her eyes which magnified the height of the dark mountain ridges against the moon-illumined sky; to measure the depth of the apparently bottomless valley, the bottom of which seemed to have been swept away into the bowels of the earth. She was in a new world, as new to her as the ocean had been, with the worshipping lover it had brought to her feet and carried away with it again into infinite obscurity.

Do what she might, this reality would not seem real. This promised land which she had striven to reach, and had touched, would not feel solid under her feet. Something had risen to make mischief between her and herself of a month ago. " It cannot be that this will last !" she thought. " If it should last, what is going to become of me ? Does one's own imagination ever baffle one, even after every tangible thing has failed ? "

All her romance had been born with her and was of a well-braced, close-knit fibre, quite opposed to weakly sentimentalism. It was so well disguised from herself in its garb of home-spun that she neither fostered it nor

was afraid of it, and only knew it under the name of
common sense.

Her father being her hero, and his troubles and
wrongs having always being sufficient to feed the flames
of her young enthusiasm, she thought herself the least
likely woman in the world to fall at the feet of any
other idol, to concern her whole being about any mere
beginner of a man whose story should be all in the
future instead of in the past.

That women with purposes will make fools of themselves by hurling their whole souls into the identity of
some masculine creature, losing their individuality of
heart and intention, she was not unaware, but she had
not classed herself with the women who so act. Having
triumphantly escaped from her importunate fellow-
traveller, she had proved herself self-contained and not
easily interfered with ; and now because of a week of
loneliness, shut up with a tempest, her will seemed to
have gone off its wheels, her imagination was playing
her wild tricks. Was she even seeing ghosts, or what
the Irish call "fetches"—

For, turning sharply to take a fresh turn on her rude
terrace above her fields, she thought for an instant that
she saw Somerled of the steamer coming swiftly along
the path to meet her.

There he was, his height, his gait, his brown face
looking pale in the moonlight now grown dim behind
a cloud-veil, his deep-set eyes darting anger. She
thrust out her arms before her to push away the vision,
and as she did so a thought of her father and Roderick
Fingall on Aura flashed across her mind. Was it a
man who had passed so near her, or had she really gone
crazy and fancied that one of the gnarled old apple-trees
had moved ? She stepped quickly inside the open
door and nearly stumbled over Betty and Nancy, who

were sitting on three-legged stools by the threshold,
bent, like herself, on enjoying the sudden beauty of the
night.

"Mistress, what's the matter with ye?   Did you see
a ghost?"

"Have people the right to come past here at night,
Betty?"

"They haven't the right, but they take it—makin'
foot-pads and short-cuts up the glen."

Bawn came forth again and began resolutely to think
of her work as she walked.   To-morrow she would
begin to make butter, comparing ways and methods of
her own with those of her handmaidens.

"Nancy," said Betty's voice, coming distinctly to
her across the silence of the night, "if it was the banshee
I heard a minute ago I wouldn't wonder.   Many's the
time this week I thought of the ould Hollow cratures.
How much of the roof fell in, d'ye think, this wheen o'
days back?   I always know by the banshee when one
o' them's gone.   Sich a screech as she let the night the
poor gentleman died in the poorhouse!   An' small
blame to her to be mad at the disgrace.   But there was
sich squeals in the storm itsel' all this week back I
couldn't tell whether she was cryin' or not."

Bawn listened.   The "ould Hollow cratures."   The
"Hollow fokes" of Betty's letters written so long ago to
Desmond in Minnesota; this very Betty, sitting here so
tranquilly on her three-legged stool and maundering
about the banshee!   How was it to be believed?   In
what way was she to join these broken fragments of life
past and present, and patch them into any whole thing
and make them hang together?   The woman must be
speaking of the Adares of Shane's Hollow.   Some of
them were alive, as Bawn had learned, and still living
in the ruin of their home over yonder behind that black

ruggedness of mountain, not so far away either when you consider "foot-pads" and "short-cuts."

Was it not to make the acquaintance of these crumbling remains of a rotten humanity, to wring their secret, if they had a secret, out of their faithless souls, that she had crossed the sea? If they had a secret? Of course they had a secret. Bawn threw up her hands and pushed the ruffled gold hair away from her feverish forehead. If they had not a secret, or if Luke Adare should be dead—should the banshee have already screeched for his soul's flight from its long purgatorial imprisonment behind yon mountain—then, again, she must ask herself why in the name of Heaven had she been so mad as to come here, wandering over the ocean to search a casket that had already been rifled, disembarking secretly at Queenstown, stealing away from a friend like a thief in the night—

"Betty," she said abruptly, "you are always talking about 'hollow people.' Do you mean people hollow inside like a penny whistle? You make me exceedingly curious."

Hitherto she had been afraid to ask questions of Betty. Many good opportunities she had deliberately lost during the past week, always feeling that her time would come, and fearing to do anything rash. Now she spoke with what she considered extraordinary cunning.

"Lord love you, misthress, they're hollow enough, I'm feared, if you mane emp'y. But Hollow 's the name of a great ould place that wanst was. A great, grand family in their time, miss. Nancy and me were talkin' about them."

"And why are they hollow, if it means empty?"

"I was manin' hunger, misthress, savin' your presence."

"Tell me about them, Betty; I want to hear a story."

"Och! misthress dear, sure you're young an' hearty

an' well-to-do in yourself, an' you little know what it is
you're axin' about. It's an ould story, an' badness is
the best of it. They were great an' grand, but cracked
with pride; and pride always gets a fall, I'm thinkin',
from Lucifer down to Luke Adare. Sure the father of
them wouldn't take money from the tenants, wouldn't
touch it with his fingers, till his steward had washed it
in a basin before his eyes. No good comes of insultin'
the poor o' God. Then the sons had the curses o'
women draggin' round their feet, an' where could their
road go to but down-hill, anyway? It's at the bottom
they are now an' sure enough. They're shut up in the
trees yonder so long by theirselves that the very dogs
has forgotten them. Nobody but Peggy an' the banshee
takes any heed o' them. The world's that set away
from them that I would walk over there to look afther
them a bit myself, only for the rheumatis an' a grudge
I have against them. Many a grudge is against them
as well as mine. But mine's enough for myself."

Bawn gazed on the picture which at Betty's suggestive
words had sprung up in vivid colours before her eyes.
It seemed there were other tragedies in the world besides
Arthur Desmond's. The Adares of Shane's Hollow
would not appear to have fattened on their ill-doing.
But what about Betty's well-treasured grudge against
them? Come, now, let her be bold and probe for
Arthur Desmond in an old woman's memory.

"What is your particular grudge?" she asked care-
lessly. "Did they turn you out of their house, or
anything of that kind?"

"Och! dear, no. They never were my landlords.
Little land they've held these long years back; it all
went from them: too many graves they put in it.
But they were sore an' hard on wan I had a regard for,
long before you were born, misthress. An' I could

never forget it to them, though it was none o' my business."

"Tell me about it, Betty. I love to hear tales about long ago."

"Well, it's such an ould story, misthress, an' most people forgets about it, an' wants to forget it, too, on account o' the Fingalls. You're a stranger here, an' I wouldn't like you to be talkin' about it."

"I have nobody to talk to; and, as I am a stranger, I feel curious."

"Surely, surely. An' why shouldn't I tell you about poor Misther Arthur—God be good to him?"

"Poor Mr Arthur!" Bawn's heart thrilled and her eyes grew moist. She had touched the link that connected the father she knew with the tragedy of his youth, had heard his name familiarly pronounced by one who had spoken to him in the day of his trial. There was that in the old woman's tone pronouncing those three words which hinted of unforgotten sympathy. Bawn hardly restrained herself from throwing her arms round Betty's neck and crying, "Faithful heart! tell me about my father." But she was learning to place a bar between her actions and her impulses.

"Who was he?" she asked, as soon she could attune her voice to the tone of a mere gossip.

"He was a young gentleman from Kerry that come here; soft in the tongue an' sweet in the eyes, so he was, an' made our hearts jump with the pleasant way he had. An' Miss Mave over there in the Hollow— good Lord! to think what she was then an' is now— she took him for her sweetheart, as any young lady he had 'a' fancied couldn't ha' helped doin'. An' they might have been happy an' rich—though the Adares was goin' down-hill even then—for there was a quare foreign gentleman—"

"Old Barbadoes," thought Bawn.

"With a dale o' money, that was thought to be goin' to lave all he had to the pair. But, ochone; to think o' the muddle that everything got into with them. Roderick Fingall, away at Tor" (here Betty dropped her voice), "he was for Miss Mave too, an' went clane mad because she took up with Mr Arthur Desmond; an' he was a bullyin' fellow, though good-natured enough when he was at himself. The long an' the short of it was that the two young men were both walkin' on Aura wan evening, an' *somethin' took place*, an' Roderick's dead body was found at the bottom of a precipy. It got whispered about that Arthur murdered him to get him out of the way, partly on account of Miss Mave, and partly bein' afeared ould Barbadoes would lave him the money; for there was always great talk about which of the three he would lave it to."

"Who were the three? Arthur Desmond, Roderick Fingall—"

"And Luke Adare. The ould man had give out that wan of jist them three should get his money."

"Well?"

"Faix, I don't know what way to tell you about it. It would take bigger words nor I know how to use. Poor Mr Arthur was hunted out of the country for the murder; even Miss Mave—Heaven forgive her! she has put in her purgatory since—she believed the lie against him—"

"Was it a lie?" asked Bawn sternly.

"'Deed an' nobody but a fool would ask the question. I beg your pardon, misthress. I forgot you were a stranger an' not born at the time. Anybody that ever knowed him would know it was a lie."

"But these people knew him—the Fingalls and the Adares."

"Ay; an' it be to be the divil that bewitched them. Some people praised them because they wouldn't lay han's on him; though may be it would ha' been betther they had, for then he could ha' spoke up for himself. Anyhow, they let him go under a bad name, an' he took himself off to America an' never was heard of no more."

Bawn stood silent for a few minutes, struggling with her heart. At last she took up her questioning again with a steady voice.

"It is a very sad story, Betty. What did the young lady do after he was gone?"

"Just fretted herself into an ould woman, she did; wouldn't look at man of mankind, but sat in a corner like a dummy, while her brothers was sportin' an' spendin' about the world, an' up an' down the country, pickin' up all the curses that money could buy. For ould Barbadoes, he left Luke his fortune. Roderick and Arthur were both out of the way, and to be true to his word he was bound to lave everything to Luke. But little good it did the Adares; they only sunk it in more sin an' sorrow. It ran through their fingers like sand; an' before many years was out they were as pinched as ever they were before. There they are now, beggars that's too proud for the poorhouse. It's a'most enough to make a body forgive them, so it is, in spite o' their sins; though wan would need to be nearhand as good as God himself to do that same. Och! dear, sure if the poor's poor, it was the Lord that made them poor, an' that's their comfort; but when the rich makes themselves poor with wickedness, there's no oil at all can be got out o' *that* crule rock o' desolation."

Bawn's mind was not in a condition to pity the Adares. It was fit and proper they should be miserable.

18

Her thoughts ran on to the conclusion of Arthur Desmond's story.

"Has nothing ever occurred since to throw light on the mystery of Roderick Fingall's death?" she asked. "If Arthur Desmond did not kill him, how did he die?"

"Troth an' nobody knows, barrin' he fell down the clifts. As for light, it would take light from the other world to clear people now of believin' that Arthur done it. As I said before, if they had took him an' put him on his trial he might ha' had a chance; but whispered guilt's the hardest to get shut of. He was too proud to defend himself from what he was not openly accused of. He held up his head as long as he could, but when he saw Miss Mave was gone against him like the rest I think it crushed him like. He got a down, melancholy look, an' the people said it was guilt that ailed him. You see there was Roderick Fingall's mother an' brothers, an' whatever was the reason, *they* were firm set on believin' that Arthur had murdered Roderick. They were that mad they could hardly be kept from tearing him in pieces—

Bawn stepped forward suddenly with a wild glance at the talking old woman.

"Is anything the matter with you, misthress?"

"I am only horrified at this story. Don't mind me, but go on. Was there no one in all the place to take his part?"

"Nobody but Luke Adare. I raged an' swore myself; but quality dozzint mind a poor body like me. It was said that, only for Luke, Arthur would ha' been laid han's on an' hanged. It was the only good turn I ever heard o' Luke—"

"The villain!" burst forth Bawn. "He knew that if Arthur Desmond had been put on his trial the character might have been cleared that *he* had whispered away!"

Betty stared at her mistress in astonishment.

"Whisht!" she said. "Sure, as I said, that's what many's the time I thought myself. But Lord, my dear, don't you take the whole of it so terribly to heart. It's an ould story now, an' may be poor Mr Arthur made himself happy afterwards in another country. He was young enough to get over the trouble, and he had no bad conscience, I'll go bail, to keep him down. America's a grand country, from all I hear, for puttin' everything right that goes wrong in other places. There's not so many crooked turns in it as there is here; all's plain sailin' and plenty of room. Whether he's there now or with God above, he's safe an' well, I'll be bound, an' a young crature like you, that never seen him, an' come into the world long after his trouble, needn't be vexin' so sore about him."

"It's a story that would pain any one," said Bawn, trying to control the passion that Betty's recital had roused in her.

"Och! dear, it pained many's the wan; but a stranger like you oughtn't to feel it so bad."

"No," thought Bawn; "she is right. A stranger like me oughtn't to feel it so bad. If I show feeling about it I shall attract attention."

She turned her back on Betty and gazed over at the black mountain behind which lay Shane's Hollow with its sins and secrets, and then suddenly wheeled round on the old woman with a smile.

"At all events you have told me a story," she said— "just what I wanted. You see we Americans have a way of wanting to know about everything. My father was an Irish farmer—an emigrant, as I told you before —and all the old stories of the hills and the people interest me. I'd like to hear more about the Adares, and Fingalls, and Arthur Desmond ; but it is late now. Another time you must tell me more."

"Nancy," said Betty Macalister to her daughter that night in bed, "the misthress has a good heart. There she was in a red-hot passion, all about poor Mr Arthur Desmond thirty long year ago. An' she may say what she likes about being only a farmer's daughter, but she's a rale lady. That comes of bein' born in America, I'll be bound. All the shillin's is pounds there, an' why shouldn't all the women be ladies ?"

"If the Lord hadn't sent us the rheumatis we might have gone there an' been ladies, too, you an' me ; an' I might have wore my parasol, like Kate Maginnis, that only went out last year," grumbled Nancy, half-asleep.

"Spake for yourself," said her mother. "I'd rather have the rheumatis in ould Ireland than wear a parasol in America. An' I'm thinkin' America has done well enough for us when it sent us a misthress like yon—"

Bawn went to rest feeling that Betty had administered to her the tonic she had been much in need of. Somerled had sailed quite out of sight in his steamer, and the real hero of her dreams, Arthur Desmond, with his sorrows and wrongs, had arisen again to fill his rightful place. As she laid her head on her pillow she was free from the bewildering pain that had shaken her for days, and in the arms of her old and settled purpose she fell asleep, satisfied that in outwitting her troublesome fellow-traveller she had escaped a very formidable danger.

CHAPTER XXII.

THE sun shone, and Bawn was herself again.

Never had she risen from sleep more serene, fair, and healthful in mind and body than on the morning after her first sifting for treasure-trove in the dust-heap of Betty's memory. The jewels of faith and mindfulness so easily turned up there lay in her palm and beamed in her eyes. With Betty at her side, unconsciously to guide and warn her as she proceeded with her enterprise, she was in a better position than she could ever have hoped for as a stranger here. She would make Betty's recollections her chart and compass as she steered her way through the difficult waters which, in her cockle-shell boat, she had so daringly undertaken to navigate.

Buoyed up by the belief that a new power had been placed in her hands, she felt the clipped wings of her courage grow and spread again. That vivid interest in her own dramatic adventure which a week's storm seemed to have quenched rose again like a little sun on her imagination, and gave its wonted colouring and light to her thoughts.

With pleasure she assumed the print dress and large Holland apron, covering her from shoulder to ankle, in which she could feel like the dairymaid she intended to be. Her strong, coarse shoes and knitted worsted stockings were put on with triumph; even the little, common pebble brooch which fastened the strip of snow-white collar round her throat was evidence in her favour as a daughter of toil. Having arranged the milk-pans on the well-sanded shelves of her dairy, discoursing all the time to Betty and Nancy about butter and cream, as if to get the best price in the market for those commodities was the only thing worth living for, she walked down through the sunshine to the orchard with its fringe of flowers, to get a bunch of something fragrant to place in a jug in the dairy windows.

"Shana," said Rosheen, "there is Miss Ingram. Isn't she a pleasant sight?"

The sisters were coming up the fields at a rapid pace, their eyes roving joyfully over grass, trees, and chimneys of the little farm, which was to them as the mill that was to grind their bread of independence. While its action had been paralyzed they had choked at Flora's table; but now, lo! the wheel was turning again, and nobody's crust need stick in their throats. This thought of theirs gave an increased radiance to Bawn's face and figure in their eyes as she turned, with her hands full of gilliflowers, and saw them approaching, glanced hastily over the part she intended to play, and advanced with eager steps to meet them.

"Young ladies, it is kind of you to come to see me."

"We wanted to make sure you were not blown or washed away," said Shana. "The storm has been a rough one. My cousin, Mr Fingall of Tor, crossed a few days ago, and was nearly wrecked—as nearly as is possible, that is, in the Holyhead packet. A French young lady whom he escorted to visit my grandmother gives a doleful description of her terror. You must have borne the full brunt of the wind here at Shanganagh."

"I think we did; but you see I have held my
ground. Will you not come in, young ladies, and rest
a little and eat something ? "

"We have just been wondering whether you and
Betty have got a morsel of food between you."

"Potatoes and tea have been our chief nourishment
up till now, but this morning we have been making
some butter. Betty is downcast because I insist on
using a barrel-churn, Miss Fingall. What is your
opinion on the subject ? "

"I am as ignorant in the matter as your gable-wall,"
said Shana solemnly; "but if you are going to introduce improvements it will be lucky for the glen
How exquisitely clean you have made the whole place!
But you want some more furniture. There is going to
be an auction near Cushendall; perhaps you will allow
me to drive you there."

"That would be too great an honour, Miss Fingall.
I think I shall do as I am pretty well. Farmer-women
from our backwoods are accustomed to rough it, and I
shall have time enough to furnish when I have made
my fortune," said Bawn gaily, as she moved about the
room in her dairymaid's apron, spreading a snow-white
cloth with the best eatables she had to offer—home-
baked scones, eggs, tea in a little brown earthen teapot,
cream and fresh-churned butter, and the roses and
sweet-smelling gilliflowers in a bowl in the middle of it
all.

"If you treat us like this we shall be coming here
every day," said Shana, "devouring your produce. But
please, Miss Ingram, allow us to wait upon ourselves."

"That would hardly be proper," said Bawn demurely.
"I shall be happier if you will allow me to keep my
own place."

Shana looked at her with a puzzled expression.

Nothing could be better assumed than Miss Ingram's air of humility and accustomedness to service, and yet to the shrewd girl observing her there was something unreal about it. A thought passed through her mind somewhat like Betty's conclusion on the same matter—a reflection that, in a well-to-do country like America, where education is cheap and prosperity widely spread, the people of lowly station may be more highly civilized than with us. But Shana, who was fascinated by the stranger, and eager to be friends with her, was not inclined to magnify the distinctions of birth between them. A certain marked difference it must make, of course, for Shana, with all her liberality, was a Conservative; but it need not go so far as to keep Miss Ingram standing like a servant while she poured delicious cream into Shana's cup of tea.

"What is your place?" asked Shana smiling.

"The place of a tenant with his landlord," Bawn said, with an answering smile. And then she added gravely: "You must remember that I am a humble working farmer, Miss Fingall," looking at her bared arms and her apron, "while you are a young lady of gentle blood."

"You do not speak at all like a common farmer person," said Shana.

"I try to behave nicely in the presence of my betters," returned Bawn, with an irrepressible gleam of fun in her eyes. "But I do not mean that I am quite uneducated."

"I suppose America is a very levelling place," said Shana.

"Very."

"Well, I do not object to that if all the farmers' daughters are like you. And the next time I come I hope you will sit while you are making my tea. If she will not promise that, what am I to do with Gran's invitation, Rosheen ? My grandmother sends you a message, Miss Ingram, to beg you will come one day and pay her a visit. She appreciates the boon that your coming has been to her granddaughters—"

Bawn cast down her eyes and smiled demurely. The patronizing tone of the invitation pleased her well. If she could fit fairly into the place of an inferior among these people her work would progress the more easily.

"She is very kind."

"She is generally very lonely, and always glad to see a visitor. At present my cousin Rory is at home, and a young lady is staying there, and Tor is more lively than usual. My cousin will take us about a little and show you that side of the country."

"That would be too much trouble, Miss Fingall."

"Oh ! Rory is always ready to do anything good-natured," said Rosheen. "We have been telling him already about you, and he is quite interested in the idea of a woman's doing so clever a thing as you are doing. And he has been to America, too ; only just come home."

"He went in the interests of the emigrants," said Shana, rising and buttoning her gloves. "He wanted to inform himself thoroughly as to how they are treated on board ship. He is going to make a fuss about it in Parliament. That will give you an idea of what he is made of, Miss Ingram. He will not think it much trouble to show you the caves and the headlands."

"It was a gallant thing to do," said Bawn, with a sudden vivid recollection of having heard another man say that he had taken a similar step and for the same purpose. The coincidence struck her as remarkable, but she had not time to think of it, as her guests were about to leave her, and kept talking to her all the way across the fields and through the gate that opened on the boreen that was to lead them to the old road by the river down the glen.

But after they had been some minutes out of sight she asked herself:

"Do all the young men of the British Isles go out in emigrant steamers to learn how the emigrants are treated, and with the intention of talking about it in Parliament?"

She stood looking over her gate, which was all out of joint, one shoulder up and one down, and, still gazing at the road along which Shana and Rosheen had just tripped out of sight, she felt a lively desire to go to Tor, and see this other man who had the same aims in and ideas about life as Somerled of the ocean steamer that had sailed away from her. And while her thoughts thus went out to the unknown Tor, her eyes marked the wild beauty of the peep of mountain road descried under the arches of trees festooned with boughs of the scarlet-berried ash. How richly, vividly green were the hedges, with their fringes of grass and ferns encroaching on the way! What a delicious touch of purple lurked at the bottom of that leafy tunnel, boring into infinite distance! Three little red cows had taken shelter from the afternoon sun beneath a row of bushy, thick-set oaks, and stood knee-deep in a golden pool, making foreground for a gray mountain bluff half swathed in ragged clouds, dazzling with light and blotted with transparent shadow.

Bawn, whose eyes were accustomed to wider and more monotonous pictures, delighted in these sparkling vignettes of scenery, fresh, crisp, and deep-coloured, and full of a wayward variety.

An hour later she was watching her men, the only

two labourers she had as yet picked up to keep her
land in order, who were filling the gaps in the thorn
hedges through which neighbourly sheep and goats had
been accustomed to jump every day, just to see that the
Shanganagh crops were coming up, and to test, by
tasting, the excellence of the corn.

She was in the act of looking over the hedges to
comfort a large ewe, who, with two little lambs at her
heels, was standing with disappointed meekness beyond
the fast-closing gap, when the sound of wheels caught
her ear, and she saw a car coming up the road—
a little green car which she thought she had seen
before.

She tilted forward a large white sun-bonnet that had
been hanging by its strings on the back of her neck,
and placidly went on watching her men with one eye,
and consoling the motherly ewe with the other.

"Miss Ingram—you see I have heard your name—I
intended to send in my card, but—a—meeting the
mistress before I reached the threshold—a—I may say
I am Major Batt, of Lisnawilly, and I have called to
pay my respects to a fair stranger—a—to inquire if I
can be of any assistance in helping you to stock—a—or
furnish—a—or anything of that kind."

"You are too good, Major Batt," said Bawn from the
depths of her sun-bonnet. "May I ask if you have got
anything to sell? I want a number of good milch cows
—as yet I have only got one—a fast-trotting pony and
some kind of light cart or phaeton in which I can drive
myself about, some farmer's carts and a couple of strong
horses, a few honest and industrious farm-servants, a
quantity of rakes, spades, pitch-forks, and other imple-
ments, and a multitude of cocks and hens."

"Really, Miss Ingram—a—I did not call altogether
with a view to business, believe me, yet perhaps I can

accommodate you. I have two fine heifers, an excellent
pony, and my housekeeper has a farmyard full of
turkeys and geese. But, as I said before, this visit is
meant to welcome the fair tenant of Shanganagh Farm."
And he looked towards the house, as if he would
suggest that they should repair thither, that he expected
to be received under her roof.

But Bawn was not going to have Major Batt in her
shanty.

"You must excuse me," she said; "I cannot leave
my work, but if you would like a little refreshment, we
churned this morning and there is some excellent
buttermilk."

"Miss Ingram—a—I consider buttermilk as excellent
nutriment for pigs."

"Oh! is it? Thank you for the hint. Anything of
that kind is so precious to me. By the way, as you
have mentioned them, perhaps you would look at my
pigs, Major Batt. Pigs seem to be creatures most easily
procurable in Glenmalurcan. Andy will show them to
you, if you would like to see them. Andy, show Major
Batt to the pig-stye."

Andy dropped a great armful of dry thorn, with a
covert grin at his comrade, and saying, "This way, sir,"
trudged off with the unwilling major expostulating and
grumbling in his wake.

"Now, Andy," said the latter, as they paused at the
new wooden piggery which had been built during the
last few days within a desirable distance from the house,
"tell me, what do you think of her?"

"Tundheranouns! sich a beautiful crature niver walked
about a stye. Didn't I sell her to the misthress myself?
The makin's of as lovely flitches as iver hung out of a
roof."

"Tut, man! I was speaking of your mistress."

"Oh! bad scran to the bit I understood you," said Andy. "It's not for me to be passin' remarks on the likes o' the misthress. It's aisy enough to see what *she* is."

"Not when she wears that sun-bonnet, eh, Andy? Now, tell me, like a decent man, is she pitted with the small-pox or not?"

Andy burst into a roar of laughter, and then, eyeing the major slily, said:

"Oh! begorra, major, ye have hit the nail on the head. An' it's a tar'ble pity, isn't it, now? Only for them pock-marks—bad luck to them!—she'd be as purty as she's good."

"I have won my bet, then," said the major triumphantly, patting his pocket as he strutted away from the pigs to take leave of their inhospitable owner, "though 'pon my soul I am not sure that I am glad, after all. There is something aggravatingly interesting about her American insolence."

"The impident ould naygur!" said Andy to himself, as he followed him back to the field, "to be passin' his remarks about her at all, at all. He'll be laughed out of his skin for this, thank God! or my name isn't Andy."

"And, O Major Batt!" cried Bawn, still from the recesses of the sun-bonnet, calling after the major, who was marching towards the gate, half-offended and half-elated, "I will have that pony and those turkeys and geese."

"What is the matter with you, Andy?" she said, turning once more to her labourers, where they had begun to fill another gap.

"Nothin', misthress. The laughin' takes me that bad sometimes that I do shake as if I had the policy [palsy]. Oh! murther, murther, misthress! I forgot to give the major his butthermilk."

"Would he not have liked it, Andy?" asked Bawn gravely.

"Troth, an' it's a taste of Inishown he'd have been likin' bebther."

Bawn said no more, but thought she would ask Betty in the evening what was the meaning of the word Inishown.

CHAPTER XXIII.

BAWN was busy feeding Major Batt's turkeys, which, with the pony and some other chattels, had duly arrived from Lisnawilly and been paid for at the highest market price, when a boy put a note in her hand, saying he had run with it all the way from Tor Castle. Gran had written the invitation for which Shana had prepared Miss Ingram.

All the clan Fingall were evidently full of curiosity to see something of the enterprising young woman who had come from Minnesota, unprotected and alone, to pay them the rent of which some of them stood in such need.

Bawn looked at the delicate, slanting lines of the handwriting, and thought she knew exactly the estimation in which she was held by the aged gentlewoman who had penned them.

"I shall be in her eyes a bold American female, honest, perhaps, but hardly proper, tolerated and even welcomed for the sake of my usefulness to her dainty granddaughters," reflected Miss Ingram contentedly.

She wrote her acceptance of the invitation and got through her day, a little excitement at prospect of the morrow's experience just quickening her pulses. Two or three times during the course of the evening she asked herself what was the meaning of that faint qualm of fear that at intervals thrilled through her who knew

not fear ; but it was not until she awakened suddenly
in the dead of night that she was confronted by the real
shape of the thing that had been haunting her, and,
staring at the blank space of her uncurtained window,
saw the form of her latent dread.

What if the master of Tor, the cousin of her young
landlords, the man who had been in America and was
just returned from London, should prove to be one and
the same with Somerled, her friend of the steamer ?

Could anything be more unlikely ?   She had always
hitherto been quite free from nervous fancies, triumphantly believed herself utterly devoid of that kind of
imagination that raises troublesome phantoms and sees
obstacles where none exist.   Yet now it seemed that
she was learning the trick of seeing ghosts.

Into her life the truism had not yet found its way
that the world is in reality very small ; to her it still
seemed vast as an eternity.   London never seen by
her, and Paris quite unknown, both appeared as far
away from her as St Paul—even further, because she
had never travelled along the tracks that lead to them.

What evidence was there in favour of the idea that
fortune had played her such an unheard-of trick as this,
except that both men had been to America in the
interests of poor emigrants, and that each thought of
bringing their cause before the world in Parliament ?
Her visitors had not even stated that their cousin's visit
to America had been very recent.

Over and over the slight evidence she went again till
she convinced herself that she had nothing to fear from
this phantom of trouble.   For it would be a great
trouble.   Her heart beat fast in the stillness as she
thought over the maze of embarrassment in which she
should find herself involved if Fingall of Tor, nephew
of Roderick supposed to have been murdered by her

father, should prove to be one and the same with the lover whom it had cost her so much to repulse.

By an effort of will she decided to think no more about the matter, and fell asleep; but in the morning the same menacing possibility reappeared before her mind's eye, and she asked herself how could she meet the man at Tor, if he should prove to be identical with the man who had called himself by the fantastic name of Somerled? What could she venture to say to him? How could she endure his disgust at her treachery? What if he should punish her by warning his family that she was a woman who pretended to be what she was not—could insinuate falsehoods to her friends— and would probably slip away some morning without paying them the much-desired rent?

She began to cast about for some excuse for declining Gran's invitation to Tor, and, feeling that nothing short of physical incapacity would be held sufficient reason for her declining such an honour, she considered within herself how she could set about spraining her ankle. But then if she were to sprain it badly, what a complete hindrance to all cherished projects!

No. She would let no cowardly trepidation induce her to inflict a bodily hurt upon herself. She would go forth boldly; and yet—no, she would not go. Never before had she been the victim of such a fit of irresolution. At last she wrote a note giving what she perceived to be a very insufficient reason for failing to gratify the lady of Tor, and sent for Andy's little boy to act as her messenger.

No sooner was this done than the utter absurdity of her conduct struck her in the most forcible light.

She had come all the way from Minnesota to do a certain thing, she found herself excellently placed for doing it, and a good opportunity had occurred for

14

making acquaintance with people who might perhaps
unconsciously help towards the accomplishment of her
desires. And here she was withdrawing from taking a
most natural step because she saw a " bogie " in her
path.

Let her think rationally and act with common sense.
Her friend Somerled was gone out into infinite space.
Time would never bring him back to her who had
barred her heart against him. Nothing was more unlikely in the whole wide world as that they two should
ever meet again.

As for him they called Rory, he was probably in
every way the reverse of that person who was so painfully occupying her thoughts, though perhaps masterful
enough to oblige his feminine kindred to look to him as
a sort of god. At all events she must go, and see, and
know. A little change would shake her out of this
incredibly fantastic humour.

And the note was burned, and the little rosy-cheeked
lad who was to have carried it departed with his pocket
full of apples from the sweet-smelling loft.

In the afternoon, in a small vehicle drawn by Major
Batt's pony, the mistress of Shanganagh travelled the
golden valley under the long wall of purple mountain,
and felt the river flowing with her all the way to the
sea, which after a time had to be left behind while glen
after glen was threaded, before a wider, wilder, more
magnificent ocean could be sighted. The cliffs grew
steeper and bolder ; travelling the road was like climbing up and down flights of stairs ; the way went by the
edge of long headlands sweeping to waves that foamed
perpetually, and on the sides of the ravines mowers
were cutting the late grass, having been lowered by
ropes to the spot where they stood.

The deep hollows were filled with purple shadow, and

Sanda lay like a half-burnt-out cinder on the darkening sea. A bank of smouldering fire backed the murky, fantastic silhouette of Jura, and a light had sprung up on the thirteen-miles-distant Scottish coast. The roar of Tor began to be heard, and as Bawn reached the summit of a hill and felt the keen autumn air blow on her she drew her breath quickly, startled at the lowering beauty of the sunset-reddened nightfall.

CHAPTER XXIV.

STRANGERS.

A FAMILY party was assembled in the great, old-fashioned drawing-room at Tor. Gran, in her own tall-backed chair, was showing her antique watch to two of her great-grandchildren, and talking to her grandson Alister, while he lazily stroked the hair of another of his babes, reclining between his knees. Lady Flora and the young French visitor were conversing at the other side of the fireplace, and Shana and Rosheen, hovered over by Major Batt, were arranging the piano with a view to music later on.

Rory, the master of Tor, stood at a distant window looking out at the darkening sky.

"So unnecessary," Lady Flora was saying, "so overstrained of Gran to invite a young woman like that to dinner."

"My dear, I have overheard you," said Gran, smiling; "but I have acted for the best. I wish to make acquaintance with the stranger, and I cannot ask her to come all the way to Tor without putting her up for the night. As to the rest, I don't think she can contaminate our manners, judging by what the girls have told me of her."

"Oh! of course. I don't interfere," said Lady Flora. "And she may afford us a little fun. Do you know anything of American women, Manon?"

"Nothing," said Manon. And as she spoke the fire-light flashed over all the surrounding brasses, and lit up her fine, oval face, and set a red jewel in each of her languid dark eyes. She was a strikingly handsome brunette, dressed rather much for the occasion in coral silk, clouded with rare black lace, and, before speaking, had been sitting in a rather melancholy attitude, gazing at the fire with an expression of discontent on the corners of her delicate mouth.

"I shall presently win my bet," said Major Batt, sidling up to where Rory stood gazing with a frowning, anxious look out of the window. "Anything wrong with you, Fingall? I have got such an excellent joke. Haven't heard of my bet with Alister about the Minnesota farmeress? Egad, we shall see by-and-bye."

"I beg your pardon; did you speak?" said Rory, turning from the window.

"Oh! nothing; only about that bet—"

"Gran," said Rory, coming forward into the firelight, "I think something must have happened to your visitor on the way. I will go down the road and have a look about. Flora does not like waiting dinner, you know."

He was gone without waiting for an answer, and in a few minutes was driving along the road in a small, light tax-cart.

Having driven about a mile up and down hill, he descried in the still lurid semi-darkness a little, broken-down vehicle standing outside a cabin-door, through which shone the glow of burning turf.

"Hum! I thought there was a break-down," he said. "I guessed how it would be when I heard Batt had sold her the broken-kneed pony." And, calling an urchin to hold his horse, he walked up the stone causeway to the cabin-door.

There he paused a moment, raised his hat and passed

his hand over his forehead, frowned, and stepped over the threshold.

Bawn was sitting on a "creepy" stool before the blazing turf, her hat had been taken off, and her golden head was shining in the ruddy light. A barefooted child was standing before her, finger in mouth, staring with fascinated eyes at the beautiful stranger, greatly to the delight of an aged man who sat shaking his head in the chimney-corner. Two sturdy men in sou'wester hats were directing Andy where to go for the loan of a little car to carry his mistress further, and a decent-looking woman was taking oat-cakes from a "griddle."

"But, sure, here's Misther Rory himself. Never fear but the masther 'll pull ye out of the hobble."

Bawn did not hear what was said; she was talking to the child, and the master of Tor had advanced and was standing beside her before she looked up. The gentleman stood observing her with a strange look on his face, noting her fair, smooth brow, her fresh, symmetrical cheeks, her laughing lips and eyes. In her black serge dress and shawl of shepherd's plaid she was exactly the same Bawn who had wrestled for her liberty with Somerled on board the steamer.

She looked up with an unconscious, unexpecting smile, and saw the identical Somerled standing before her.

The smile died on her lips; the colour went out of her cheeks; she rose and drew back a step, and looked him in the face. Impulsively trying to speak, her ready tongue was for once at fault. She drew her shawl around her, and met his eye defiantly.

"I hope I have not startled you," he said with the manner of a perfect stranger. "I have been sent to discover if any accident had happened to Miss Ingram. You are Miss Ingram, I presume—the lady who is expected at Tor."

"Yes, I am Miss Ingram, the lady who is expected at Tor," said Bawn, mechanically.

"Will you not sit down again? Your man is making some arrangements, and then you and he can come with me in my cart."

"The shafts of mine are broken," said Bawn, "and so I must accept your kindness." And then she sat down again, feeling stunned, unable to speak more, or even to think. She heard him say he would return in a few moments, and saw him go out of the cabin-door; and then she looked round the little house desperately to see whether she could not fly out of the window or up the chimney. After he had been gone a moment or two, she asked herself if she had not been dreaming. Had her curious panic of the last two days developed this extraordinary hallucination? A gentleman who spoke to her and looked at her like a perfect stranger had appeared, standing there in the fire-light, to have the features and the proportions of her friend, her lover of the steamer. When he returned she would look at him more attentively and with all her wits about her, and doubtless she would perceive that she had never seen this Mr Rory Fingall in all her life before. She stood up, put on her hat, and wrapped the folds of her shawl tightly around her, then stepped back a little into the shadows of the cabin-ingle to watch for the reappearance of the man who had so frightened her.

She had not long to wait. Before his face appeared again within the cabin she heard his voice, speaking outside to the men—the same voice that had said to her of the enterprise on which she was now fairly embarked: "Happiness is not to be looked for from it, comfort it will have none, difficulty and disappointment will follow immediately in its train." He had said this warningly, being in all ignorance of the nature of her

enterprise. It might be that he had spoken with the
tongue of a prophet. As he stooped his head in the
doorway and came towards her a second time the
cabin disappeared from her eyes, and she saw him
coming along the deck to claim her companionship, to
offer service, to persuade her of his love. Now, however, though this was indeed Somerled, he showed no
eagerness for her company; love, or even friendship,
kindled not his features as he drew near her, and
though he was bent on service, it was tendered in
the most matter-of-fact manner, as if rather from a
chivalrous habit than as recognising a specially
interesting individuality in herself.

He lingered to say a word to the paralysed man in
the corner, and his face softened. His eyes lit up as
he patted the child's head. She noted that he spoke
to these peasants with a touch of their own brogue,
soft, rolling, and Irish, with a thread of harsher Scotch
woven through it.

"Glad to have Jim back from the land o' cakes?"
he said to the woman at the griddle.

"Ay, sur, ay. It's pleasant to have him with us
whiles," returned the woman; and the old man piped
out:

"An' yourself, sur. Won't ye tell us how ye liked
Amerikay? It's glad I am to see ye back so hearty."

"I'll look in and tell you about it another day,
Bartley. We'll smoke a pipe over it, never fear."

"God bless you, sur! an' it's you that'll be welcome."

Then he turned to the silent, shawled figure standing
back in the shadows, and, with a slightly sterner and
colder face, said:

"If you are ready, Miss Ingram, we will start."

She made her farewells to her humble entertainers
and followed him to the door. All the fiery lights

were gone now, and the stars looked as keen and high
as they used to shine a month ago above the breadth
of the Atlantic. He took her hand, helped her to her
seat in the tax-cart, and seated himself by her side.

"Your man has started before us to walk with the
pony to Tor," he said. "It is but a short distance.
We shall soon be there." And gathering up the reins,
he carried her off with him into the night.

It was a tedious bit of journey, though of no great
extent, for some of the hills appeared almost per-
pendicular. Many times Bawn's charioteer had to
alight and lead the horse up or down the steep incline,
and once or twice Bawn herself was obliged to descend
and proceed a little way on foot. It was like a travel
in a dream. The wild, romantic scenery, all so fresh
and new to her; the companion, so complete a stranger,
and yet so familiar that his personality seemed to take
something of an almost supernatural character to her
senses; the roar of Tor, growing louder every
moment; the flash of a white breaker gleaming
occasionally through the darkness on the bit of rough
sea where weird Moyle surges into the ocean; the salt,
sharp breath of the north wind on her face; the silence
of the man beside her, that man who had cried to her
but a month ago: "Unless you tell me that you hate
me, that under no circumstances could you love me,
I will exert every faculty I possess to make your future
one with mine. I cannot make up my mind to lose
you out of my life. A week has done for me what the
the rest of my years cannot undo."

The words, well remembered, were ringing in her
ears, the cry that was in them was making her heart
sore, as it had done many times since; and yet—and
yet he was here, and she was here. Fate had in an
extraordinary manner, so strange as to give to all that

was passing now an air of dream-like unreality,
delivered her a second time into his hands. It
seemed that he had lost her out of his life only to
find her again, but he did not know her, had no word
to say to her, apparently had not recognised her
features, her voice, even her dress, which was the same
she had worn when he had loved her. She was already
blotted out of his memory, and existed no more for
him than if he had crossed from America in that
steamer by which he had meant to return and had
missed.

As the impossibility of this being literally true
forced itself on her common sense she became disturbed
by two other views of the case. Either he was not
Somerled—an extraordinary resemblance had deceived
her imagination, and by and by, in many little ways,
she would perceive that a strange man, one who had
been to her neither friend nor lover for a wonderful
week, had involuntarily cheated her—or he was
Somerled, and his disgust at her deceit and treachery
was so great that he had decided to cut her, to ignore
her, to drop deliberately out of his memory that passage
of his life in which he must now admit to himself that
he had acted with extravagant folly.

This last conclusion she accepted as the correct
answer to the sum of her calculation of probabilities,
and it must be a final response to all questions in her
mind on the subject, except that one which kept asking
how it was that no involuntary start or momentary
change of countenance had betrayed even for an instant
his surprise at finding her here in the midst of his own
family. He must have seen her from the doorway,
and had time to conceal his astonishment before she
raised her eyes to look at him. Out at sea he had not
always had such complete self-control.

"Miss Ingram, I must trouble you to come down
again for a few minutes, but this is positively the last
time. When we get to the top of this hill we shall see
the lights of Tor Castle. I am sorry you have had so
uncomfortable a journey."

"Thank you; not at all. It has been very interesting to me," she answered as she touched ground
with her foot and walked on, with the horse's head
between her and him on the road. And again the
suspicion returned to her that this was not Somerled,
after all.

Had it been that friend he would, even if he had not
recognised her, have called the attention of the stranger
to the beauty of the scenery, to the dark magnificence
of the night in this wild, high region, to the burst of
strange music in the air, to the recurrent gleam of that
white breaker flashing beyond the great Tor, which
bold headland was now in view, standing up like a
black fortress of fantastic build, and scowling over the
glimmering ocean. This man, though he bore a wonderful resemblance to her former friend, and might be
good and beloved in his own place, had evidently not
that ardent love of nature, that keen appreciation of all
that is beautiful in earth, sea, and air, which had helped
to make the companionship of that other person so
attractive. Only a very few words passed between the
travellers, and merely on the commonplaces of their
journey, until they passed in at the gates and bowled
up the avenue to the low doorway of the castle on its
rock. But as he helped her down from the vehicle,
and the light from the hall within struck into their eyes,
she thought she felt a sudden flashing look turned on
her face—a look that, if it were really there, revealed
the real Somerled. Before she had decided whether
this was imagination or reality she found herself in the

hall, with Shana and Rosheen smiling on either side of her.

They took her up to a great chamber in which a mantel with carving up to the ceiling and a gaunt four-post bed at first seemed the only objects, and where candles in two tall silver branches made faint light about a narrow mirror.

"We knew something must have happened, and wasn't I right when I said Rory did not mind trouble?" said Rosheen. "Flora wanted to have a servant sent, but my cousin would go himself. And you are not to be afraid to sleep in this wilderness of a room, because there are no ghosts at Tor. Nothing evil could come near Gran. And I hope you will be nice with Gran, Miss Ingram, for everybody is. She had a great trouble once, and every one remembers it."

"Rosheen dear, let Miss Ingram get her breath and wash her hands in peace," put in Shana. And the visitor's simple toilet arranged, they proceeded down the old oak staircase, lit by oil lamps whose faint yellow flame swam ineffectually in the vault-like darkness. Bawn grudged every step she took down the black time-worn stair. Her courage seemed to have deserted her, and she would have given all her little world to avoid the necessity of walking in among these people whom she had come from Minnesota to confound. Every beat of her heart, sunk cowardly low in her breast, was telling her that Gran's trouble was the murder of a beloved son by Arthur Desmond of hateful memory, and that Rory, the grandson, who now filled the place of that son in her heart—well, was he or was he not Somerled?

"He is not," she decided; "and if he is I will ignore him as completely as he has ignored me." And then, making a large demand on that common sense of which she had plenty for small daily uses, though her plans in the main might be never so unwise, she walked into the drawing-room with head erect on her shoulders and a serene countenance.

She was conscious, first, that Somerled was not in the room ; next that every eye was turned on her ; then that Gran had risen from her great chair by the hearth to receive the stranger. Gran's individuality struck her so forcibly that for the moment she saw nothing but the fine old figure before her—a face unlike every other face ; a spotless white cap of a dignity not often attained by caps ; a rich but plain gown of well-worn Irish tabinet, the folds of which somehow suggested a train and pages. But the simplicity of character, as expressed by the eyes and by the greeting and gesture of the spare, wrinkled hand, was unmistakable, and Bawn felt herself in the presence of an unworldly soul.

" I do not apologise for my dress. I am a farmer's daughter. I have no pretty gowns," said Bawn, in a low tone to her hostess, with a desire to say the most commonplace thing that occurred to her.

" I see you as you ought to be, my dear," said Gran ; " and, for the matter of that, we are no great dressers here." But as she spoke she felt some surprise. A farmer's daughter, such as Bawn so persistently announced herself to be, would have pinned on a few coloured bows, if she had nothing else, to deck herself a little for high company. This young woman, in her black serge and high frills, was a lady, let her come from whence she might. And as for ornament, she had gold enough on her head to make a crown for a queen.

" Nice-looking, yes ; not so very handsome, but too striking an appearance to run about alone," said Lady

Flora, whose eye-glass had been levelled at the farmeress from the moment she entered the door. "I am more than ever sure she is not everything she ought to be. A cool young madam, by my word. It seems they have excellent manners in the backwoods of Minnesota."

Of all this speech Major Batt, to whom it was addressed, heard nothing. He was ejaculating to himself in the most distressed whisper:

"Egad! the witch! Small-pox. Never was so sold in all my life before!"

"Batt, I'll trouble you for that five-pound note you owe me," said Alister, crossing the room and smiling quizzically at the major's crestfallen countenance.

"Shall have it, sir—shall have it, sir!" said the major, testily.

"*I* will have it," said Rosheen, touching her brother's elbow. "I want it for the poor."

"I don't see why you should be always making a poor-box of yourself, Rosheen," said her sister-in-law, snappishly. "You will soon be as bad as Rory. Where is he, by the way? I want to hear his opinion of this wandering adventuress."

"Egad, she's a witch!" repeated Major Batt, disconsolately, watching the offender all the time with reluctant admiration.

"Flora," said her husband, "don't speak so unkindly of the girl. She may overhear—"

"Oh! nonsense. You don't suppose she is as bashful as Manon here, for instance, would be at hearing herself criticised?"

At the sound of her own name Manon started out of a reverie in which she had been gazing at Miss Ingram's face as she sat conversing easily with Gran, and her eyes were raised to the door, which opened on the instant to admit Rory. Did she also want to know his opinion of the wandering adventuress? If so, she did not learn much; she only saw his eyes turn full for a moment on the stranger, then glance away with an expression of perfect indifference.

CHAPTER XXV.

A PERPLEXING SITUATION.

DINNER, which had been waiting some time, was announced, and the company repaired to the dining-room—a long, high, haughty-looking room, if the word may be allowed, very scantily furnished, the walls hung with a few old family portraits, the windows scantily and dingily draped, but the table appointments nice and even handsome in an old-fashioned way. Rory, the master of the house, sat at one end of the table, with Manon, whom he had taken in to dinner, on one hand, and his cousin-in-law, Flora, on the other. Gran, at the opposite end of the board, had Bawn beside her, and interested herself in questioning the quiet yet audacious young woman as to her knowledge of farm-ing, her experience of America, her impressions of Ireland, &c.

"What affected me most as strange at first were the little patches of fields, the green hedges, and the gradu-ally falling twilight," said Bawn. "I stay out of doors watching the night fall, and every time it seems to me more wonderful."

Gran had laid down her knife and fork, and was looking at her visitor with a peculiar expression. She appeared absent and disturbed.

"I hope you are not unwell," said Bawn, aware of a sudden change.

"No, my dear; I am well, thank you. It was only

something in your voice. We old people get strange fancies. Our minds are full of echoes. Will you say again 'the green hedges,' just to please me?"

"The green hedges," said Bawn, smiling.

"Thank you. I am very full of fancies. I do not know of what your way of saying those words reminds me. The suggestion has passed away, whatever it was."

"The words are new to me," said Bawn, still smiling, "but they ought not to be new to you."

"No, they are not new, as you say, but at my age it is not the new things that signify. And so you intend to cut a figure in the butter-market. There is ample room for you, I own. We are open to improvement."

"Yes, I am hoping to rival the Danes," said Bawn. "I hold it a shame that Irish people continue to eat Danish butter."

"Who eats Danish butter?" asked Shana, looking shocked.

"A Dublin butter merchant assured me by letter this morning that only for Danish butter he could not supply his customers," said Bawn.

"What about Canon Bagot?" asked Alister. "I thought he had improved away all that interference."

"Canon Bagot has done a great deal," said Rory from the other end of the table, "and the dairy schools are doing more, but we had all need to be alive. A thorough revolution in our butter-making is necessary."

"Really, Rory, the idea of reform is turning your brain. Don't persuade Manon that our butter is not delicious," said Lady Flora.

"Our butter, yes," said Rory; there is none such in the world. But the butter that our farmers, especially our small farmers, make, pack, and send abroad, the butter that is to travel and to keep—that is mere money

15

thrown away by those who badly need it, capital sunk in the sea, treasure which is our national inheritance dropped into our neighbours' pockets."

Flora shrugged her shoulders. So long as the family tables were delicately supplied she cared little whether the butter of the nation was wealth-producing or not.

"Flora knows on which side her own bread is buttered, but that is all," said her husband, mischievously.

"If you mean that I don't believe in philanthropy and political economy, and that sort of thing, you are right," said Lady Flora, erecting her fan with an air of dignity. "I hold with people minding their own affairs. It is the only way to keep things going right."

"Or going wrong," said Rory, grimly.

"Come, Rory, talking of philanthropy, you have not told us anything yet about your trip to America among the emigrants. Miss De St Claire, you would scarcely believe that this elegant young man in his faultless evening dress—"

"Seven years of age," said Rory, glancing at his sleeve with the ghost of a smile.

"—Went out to New York last summer with a batch of emigrants, lived among them, ate with them, all to see how they were treated on the way. You will now know why some of us consider him the crazy member of our family."

"It must have been very nasty," said Manon, who spoke English well, with a pretty foreign accent, and she shuddered gracefully.

"It was not exactly comfortable," said Rory, "but if I had expected it to be so I should have had no reason for going. It was a useful experience, what I wanted. A man is in a better position to speak of a thing when he knows exactly what he is talking about."

"How very much pleasanter it must have been returning home!" said Manon, raising her dark eyes softly to Rory's face.

Bawn, who had regained all her usual composure, was looking at the two heads side by side, Rory's and Manon's, and thinking within herself that this Rory was certainly not Somerled. In his evening dress he looked less like her friend than in his ulster in the cabin; and she decided that Somerled never could have sat so long among his friends, even with the annoyance of her presence on his mind, without one of his brilliant smiles. When Manon said, " It must have been pleasanter coming back," she felt herself almost safe in watching to see how he would reply. He had never looked at her once, that she had observed, since they sat down to table. Why should he look at her now? What had the return journey of this crazy member of the family to do with her? Somerled was in Paris, perhaps still searching for her. " The name of a street, the number of a door "—how he had pleaded for the address of her imaginary home in Paris! A traitor she had been—that was not to be doubted; but dairy-keeping was now her rôle, and not sentimentalising, and so as a mere farmer-woman, she would have no scruple in just looking expectantly to hear how this Rory, who understood so well the necessity for improvement in Irish butter-making, had enjoyed his return journey after his quixotic excursion to America.

"Yes, it was happier coming home," he said, with a slight frown, and suddenly turning his glance full on the wide, calm, observant eyes gazing at him from the other end of the table. And then Bawn felt that she had got a blow, and sat pale to the lips, telling herself that this was indeed Somerled, and that he hated her.

Gran unconsciously came to her relief by rising from the table, and the ladies returned to the drawing-room, where Bawn was again placed by the old lady near herself as her own particular guest. As Flora and Manon kept by themselves at the other side of the apartment, it was evident that they, at least, did not intend to begin an acquaintance with the farming tenant of Shanganagh. Gran, a little tired, soon fell into a fit of abstraction, gazing into the fire from the depths of her great arm-chair, while Shana and Rosheen drew their seats as near as possible to Bawn's.

"Is it really true what Rory says, that wealth for this country can be made out of improved butter?" asked Shana eagerly.

"Rory is always right," said Rosheen.

"He is only a theorist. Miss Ingram has experience. Miss Ingram makes butter. Can a fortune really be made out of butter, Miss Ingram?" asked Shana impatiently. She was thinking that perhaps butter-making might prove a better means than story-writing of amassing that fortune which would enable her to be such a useful wife to Willie Callender. If so she would go into partnership with her tenant and hire herself as a dairymaid on the spot.

"I don't expect that I shall make a fortune," said Bawn. "I have not—" she stopped short, and then went on : "Capital would be necessary for that."

"Capital?" cried Shana, disgusted. "It is always the same answer. Capital, you are told, is needed to make money. As if capital did not mean that one had already got one's fortune. What is the difference now between our butter and the Danes', Miss Ingram?"

"The Danes do not send it out of turf-smoky cabins

where it is hoarded up from week to week. They make it better, too, and salt it better, and, of all things, pack it clean," said Rory Fingall from behind Shana. The gentlemen had come into the room while the ladies were talking. "Even the Cork merchants, who have a monopoly of the most delicious butter in the universe, pack it in such dirty old tubs as have disgraced us before the world. I hope you intend to pack clean, Miss Ingram."

"The Danes are my model in that respect," said Bawn, just raising for a moment a pair of cool, unrecognising eyes to the dark ones that had glanced at her so coldly. "I have ordered a small barrel of Cork butter and another of Danish to be sent to me, and I shall judge by my own lights of the merits of each."

"I see you are a practical woman and know what you are about," said her host; and then he turned away and left her asking herself again the question, was this man Somerled, or was he not?

"May I come to see the barrels of butter when they arrive?" Shana was pleading when the preoccupation caused by Bawn's perplexity allowed her to hear and see again what was going on around her.

"I shall be pleased, honoured, if you will come," said Miss Ingram, and she prepared to plunge once more into the butter question; but the next moment Shana was taken away abruptly by her brother to sing a duet with Rosheen, and Bawn was left to observe two things —first, that Rory was engaged in conversation with Manon, at the other end of the room, oblivious of the existence of the Minnesota farmeress; and, second, that Gran had become wide awake again and was observing her with the same peculiar look of interest which had rested on her face when she had asked her at dinner to oblige her by saying those simple words, "the green hedges," again.

Then came a "little music." Major Batt shouted in a stentorian voice his desire to "like a soldier fall," but as he followed no particular air, and all the words except the refrain were inarticulate, there was a sigh of relief when he had finished; and it occurred to Bawn that they were all thankful he had not fallen, as it would have been so difficult to pick him up again. Alister chirped an old Jacobite ditty in a weak though true tenor, and his sisters warbled sweetly enough about a bower of wild roses on Bendemeer stream, the notes of which were read from a yellow-leaved music-book which had belonged to their mother. There was no instrumental music worth listening to, for Flora played like a cat walking over the keys, and, though Bawn's fingers longed to touch the piano, no one thought of requesting the backwoodswoman to perform for the company. Even if she had been invited Miss Ingram would have thought it imprudent to betray the fact that she had received a musical education.

"Rory has a delightful baritone voice," said Rosheen, flitting back to Bawn, "but he is cross to-night, or something is the matter with him, and he won't sing."

"I am afraid the company of the emigrants has not improved his manners," said Flora to Gran, having taken up her position by the old lady, right behind Bawn. "So disappointing for Manon's sake! She will think him downright forbidding."

"Manon must take him as he is—as she must take us all," replied Gran a little stiffly, evidently thinking that Rory was good enough for anybody, even at his worst.

"Oh! of course it is only for his own sake." And Lady Flora gave her own peculiar slighting glance round the noble but not too richly furnished apartment. And by those few words, though she did not see the glance, Bawn's woman's wit apprehended at once that Manon was rich, and destined by at least some of his friends to improve Rory's decaying fortunes. With a flash of thought she remembered her own half-million lying unused in America stock, but as quickly transferred her attention from it to Rosheen.

Then the little party broke up, and Bawn lay awake in that large, sparely-appointed chamber up-stairs listening to the roar of the waves round the great Tor, the crying of the curlews and sea-gulls from the rocks below, and the swirling of the night-wind in the cavernous chimney. Projected on the darkness before her was the image of Rory Fingall, which she examined now at leisure with careful, critical eyes, and wits sharpened by the deliberate contemplation of Somerled's personality as memory presented it to her. The two were the same, and yet not the same. Rory was like Somerled's colder, harder, less amiable twin-brother. He had neither the fire, the tenderness, nor the genial good-humour of his more troublesome and more attractive double. He would not love Manon de St Claire as Somerled had loved, or had thought he had loved her, Bawn. She was too tired to follow out the strange particulars of the several coincidences that had struck her with regard to these two men who had crossed her path, but she had sufficient energy left to deny steadily the still importunate suggestion that the two individuals were one and the same. No, Somerled, her friend, was in Paris. "The name of a street, the number of a door." She heard his voice, pleading, tender, impassioned. This Rory never spoke with such a voice. The name, the number—her thoughts melted away in dreams, and she was following on his footsteps through strange streets as he knocked at door after door that would not

open to him, she herself invisible to his eyes and unable to make herself known to him ; till at last these
fantasies of approaching slumber were dissipated, and
Bawn slept the sleep of healthy fatigue.

In the morning, however, she wakened before daylight with a sense of renewed embarrassment and
trouble. Whatever or whoever he might be, she did
not want to meet again that man who tantalized her
with his likeness to Somerled. The thought of the expedition to see the caves of Cushendun gave her no pleasure, though under other circumstances she could have
delighted in it. She felt that, in spite of herself, she
should spend the hours in observing Rory Fingall from
a distance. He would be attached to Manon all the
time, guarding her delicate feet from sharp stones, and
caring for her as Somerled had cared for Bawn on
board the ocean steamer (that Bawn who could scarcely
have been herself) ; while she, though still involuntarily
and painfully on the watch for evidence for or against
her own conclusions regarding him, should find no fair
opportunity for more completely satisfying her mind on
a distressingly perplexing point. For though her doubt
had been laid to rest before she went to sleep, it would
arise again, she was aware, as soon as she found herself
in his company once more. She felt she would be glad
if, while her mind was made up against the possibilities
of his being Somerled, she could escape from Tor
Castle and get back to her solitude, her liberty of
thought, and her still immature plans at Shanganagh.

Rising early and throwing open the window, she
watched the sunrise kindling a huge fire behind the
dark shoulder of the great Tor, and caught the white
flash of those waves which had resounded in her ears all
night like thunders of doom. The fresh air of the
morning blowing in her face had already revived her

courage and enabled her to smile at the idea of trying to escape the expedition to the caves, when the sound of wheels under the window attracted her attention, and she heard the voice of Rory Fingall saying to the servant:

"You will explain to the ladies, as I told you, M'Closkey. If possible I shall be home for dinner." And then, standing near the window, she saw the master of the castle disappearing down the avenue in the vehicle in which he had carried her through his gates on the evening before.

She was now freed from the trouble of his presence for the remaining hours of her visit to Tor; also denied any further means of ascertaining whether or not he was identical with Somerled. She might go out and walk about the rocks till breakfast-time without fear of meeting him, or of wounding her own pride and dignity by trying to keep out of his way; and she did so, enjoying the splendours of the morning at Tor, with high blue skies and a gale blowing the spray over the rocks to her face.

As she walked she thought much about Rory Fingall and his emigrants, and his philanthropy, and the people who surrounded him. Gran and the two young girls were the only individuals of the family group whom she greatly liked. Alister had allowed the Shanganagh gates to hang off their hinges, and had suffered the gaps in the hedges to remain unfilled till she had come from America to stop them up. A country gentleman ought to mind his duties as a landlord first, and be a bookworm afterwards, decided Bawn. And then he had married (to save himself trouble) a woman with whom he had no sympathy, and who never let him forget for a moment that she carried his purse. While reviewing the whole circle Bawn was surprised to

observe that though Gran was the only one of these
people who had really borne a part in the cruel persecu-
tion of her father, she was precisely that one whom she
should find it most difficult to hate.

"If I can prove to her that she was in the wrong I
shall not want to make an enemy of her; but she looks
like one of those persons who have fixed ideas which
they will never consent to change. It may be that I
shall have to go back to America hating her."

This was a hurtful reflection, and when Bawn made
her appearance in the breakfast-room she was feeling a
little depressed, conscious of being here under false pre-
tences, newly assailed by a fear that she was acting a
disloyal part in accepting the hospitality of these
people, who, if they knew her as her father's daughter,
would probably shrink from her.

"But my father did them no wrong, and I am come
to prove it to them," she argued with herself, as she
took her seat by Gran's side with her usual air of cool
serenity. "And, at all events, once this visit is over I
shall come back here no more."

Only Gran and the girls breakfasted with her; and it
was resolved by these ladies that, as Rory had been
summoned away to act in his capacity as magistrate,
the expedition to the caves must be for the present
given up. Bawn steadfastly refused to wait till to-
morrow. Her affairs at Shanganagh urgently required
her presence there. She hoped to have many opportunities of visiting the beauties and curiosities of the
neighbourhood. By the way, she hoped her pony
(Shana and Rosheen exchanged glances) would not
often make a point of going down on his knees—

"If Major Batt had not believed you were marked
with small-pox he never would have sold you that
pony," observed Shana.

"Shana!" exclaimed her great-grandmother, severely, "I am shocked at your rashness. There must have been a mistake. If anything be really wrong with the pony, Rory will see that Miss Ingram gets another. Miss Ingram, you must not mind this girl. She does not mean to be uncharitable."

"O Gran, if *you* are going to take up Major Batt—"

"Good morning, ladies," said that gentleman, appearing in the doorway. "Miss Ingram, I am distressed to hear that your blundering man let the pony down last evening. I am going your way this morning, and I hope you will let me have the pleasure of driving you to Shanganagh myself."

"Thank you," said Bawn promptly. "But I am going to stay here for a week."

"Oh! ah! said the major, looking chagrined; "in that case—I—a—am sorry to say I am obliged to be off in an hour. Lord Aughrim," &c., &c.

"Have you really changed your mind, and will you stay with us?" asked Gran, when Major Batt had left the room; and the old lady looked at the girl critically, as if considering what she might have meant by her rather audacious announcement.

"Oh! no, thank you. I must indeed go this afternoon," said Bawn, earnestly. "Only not with Major Batt," she added, smiling. And she went.

CHAPTER XXVI.

SHANE'S HOLLOW.

"ARE there any wolves among the trees, Betty? Shall I be eaten up?"

"No, misthress. But sure the place is unlucky; an' if they saw you walkin' about, spyin' at the wreck an' ruin like, they'd be mortial offended maybe. There's the Fingalls themsel's daren't let on they know there's anything wrong."

"And yet they were once friends?"

"Och, dear! It was the forbears of these ones that was acquent with them. The only one alive that knowed them is the ould misthress herself at Tor; an' her an' them never was any great things of friends. They would not let her come within miles of them now, and, indeed, I think nobody vexes her by talkin' of them. You see, they were mixed up with her own trouble—"

"I know. Well, Betty, I shall die of curiosity if I do not get a peep at this mysterious place. I will keep at a distance from the house, and will take care not to frighten the old people."

Andy undertook to drive her up the mountain as far as the road went, and to wait for her at a certain cabin till she should return from exploring the Hollow. About high noon she was going through the mountain-pass on foot alone.

The sunlight irradiated the hills, and the shadows of the high white clouds floated mysteriously along their sides, casting deep, momentary frowns under the brows of the grey and purple crags. Coming to the top of the pass, she saw far beneath her a dark belt of wood out of which a thin streak of smoke was ascending. Down there lay the mystery of Shane's Hollow.

After a quarter of an hour's rapid descent she found herself standing at the top of a steep, woody incline looking sheer down on the broken roof of the dwelling-house ; and then, following a path round this hill, she went gradually lower till it brought her to a crazy gate, through which, under the wide-spreading branches of the trees, she saw the base of the gable of the ruined mansion.

It stood in an oblong hollow of the richest green. Short, close grass, verdant and sumptuous, swept away in velvety undulations under the far-reaching boughs of enormous beech and sycamore trees, which were flung out like sheltering arms, as if trying to protect and hide the wretched dwelling from the scorn and abhorrence of the world. An air of almost supernatural beauty and desolation pervaded the place, and the only sound breaking the charmed stillness was the loud, imperious cawing of the rooks, which seemed to menace the intruder, to warn him from attempting to enter these forlorn and dilapidated gates.

Bawn, however, stepped down the grass-grown path which had once been an avenue, and came slowly nearer to the home of the Adares. Three magnificent copper beeches with mossy trunks seven or eight feet in circumference stood right in front of the house, with gnarled, moss-clad roots like the velvet-sheathed claws of some gigantic animal, and with towering crowns of crimson-dashed foliage. Between two of these was an old well, surrounded with a circular wall, lichen-grown and broken down at one side, and attached to this were a bucket and windlass. Seating herself on the crumbling wall of this old well, the stranger from Minnesota surveyed the once handsome mansion of her father's enemies.

It was large, built of massive, dark grey stones, in some parts black, and over one corner of the front were splashes of dark red, as if blood had been flung on the wall. The wide hall-door stood open with a stone placed to keep it so, and the shadows of the door-way, projected by such sunbeams as could reach it, fell and veiled the depths of a hall floored with rotten boards and riddled with holes. The solid coping above the door and the pillars at each side still stood, but the roof of one side of the house was completely fallen in, and the moulding of the drawing-room walls and the fire-places of all the upper rooms were visible through the apertures where the windows once had been. Displaced beams hung by one end, pieces of zinc drooped ready to fall, the ground-floor was piled with wreckage, as could be perceived between the half-closed shutters that still clung to the lower casements ; while high aloft an open arch on the drawing-room landing, once, no doubt, shaded by silken curtains, made a striking feature in the general hideousness of this extraordinary interior.

The left wing of the house was still covered in, but the roof had already given way. From the chimney next to that sunken spot over the hall-door a little cloud of smoke was wavering upward. Almost all along that side the shutters were closed, and no light penetrated except what might enter by a few uncovered panes in two upper windows which had been gradually patched and boarded up in a manner horrible to see. Two of these windows evidently belonged to an inhabited chamber, and, if so, the floor was threatening to give way beneath, and the roof to descend upon, whatever living creature might there be unhappily housed. It was clear that this side of the house must very soon fall in as the other had done. Heavy rains or a high wind might sweep the roof away at any moment.

Behind the house rose that abrupt hill, clothed in softest green, from which Bawn had first looked down on the hollow. In the background, under the hill, lay offices, granaries, out-buildings, all in wreck, but with their mosses and ruins wrought in picturesquely with the universal greenness. Away at one end the oblong shaped itself, with crowding trees and mouldering lines of gray and olive walls. The carriage sweep was overgrown, all but a beaten cart-track past the door; for occasionally a carter would take the short cut through the Hollow, if it were not late at night, when he superstitiously shunned the spot. From one end the almost obliterated avenue pierced the distance, an irregular tunnel of cool green with a blot of purple at the end of it, and with golden light filtering down through its leafy roof, and lying in bars across the moss-spotted path bordered and embroidered with a wandering vegetation.

On the other side the oblong lost itself among thickly crowding trees, and was so green, so lovely, so rich, with golden patches and cool blue shades, and here and there a red sprinkling of fallen leaves, that one must hold one's breath contemplating it, as if some secret enchantment were at work to keep the spot so mysteriously, uncannily beautiful. At this end the hollow was finished with a low, melancholy line of wall, and a grim, tumble-down gate, of which one pillar stood erect bearing a headless animal of stone upon its shoulders. Once the traveller was without that gate, he was free of the spell of Shane's Hollow. Immediately beyond lay pleasant, open fields, where red and white cattle grazed, or drank at a sedge-bordered lakelet, which was also invaded by troops of joyous, fluttering, yellow-winged flag-lilies.

All this Bawn took in as she sat on the old well observing the details of this exquisite wilderness and feeling its weirdness to the marrow of her bones. She noticed how the trees all leaned towards the house, spreading their vast branches that way and weaving them together before the windows, as if trying to veil its ruin or to hide some secret it contained. Even on this still summer's day the breeze kept up a continual soughing in the crowns of the great trees, and the rooks clamoured incessantly. Few and faint were the notes of singing birds in the branches on the outskirts of the Hollow; evidently none harboured in the giant boughs near the house. Sometimes a small bird whirred across the hollow as if in a fright, and disappeared; and as the afternoon advanced strong sunshine fell across the great hall-door, the dining-room windows, and half of the bending roof, and threw a deeper, more sinister shadow around the building.

Turning her fascinated eyes from this sight, Bawn changed her seat and sat on the opposite side of the well, with her back to the house, and looked away to where a venerable gray wall, hoary and lichened, marked the vast square garden which sloped gradually from the hollow up a gentle incline. Tall beeches and dark chestnuts stood round it like a sombre guard, but its crumbling, gold-tipped walls were a reservoir of purest sunshine, for beyond and above them shone a world of light, just fringed with the grey foliage of a distant woodland. An old wicket, once a pleasant entrance to the garden, hung in its stone framework split and riven, and letting dazzling shafts of brightness shoot through, just where the shadows at the corner of the wall were blackest. And as her eyes roved aside from here, all around there were trees, trees, trees, weaving their branches across the sod, but leaving a delicious under-world of cool, gold-strewn grass, streaked with long, level shadows, sprinkled here and there with lush, rank weeds, and looking as if it might possibly be trodden at times by fairies, but seldom or never by foot of mortal mould.

Again Bawn altered her position. The trees at one side were now literally dripping with gold, the flickering shadows of the branches moving like living things over the great boles of the mighty beeches. One of these, split down within a few feet of the ground, had made itself into two, each of which had flung up three or four great arms, sending forth a hundred branches. Under the sycamores lay the loveliest blue-green shadows, and the roots and boles of the trees were wrapped in the most sumptuous colouring — yellow and amber and tawny brown. What majesty in the heavy draperies of those chestnuts, through which the light tried in vain to filter; what a delicate gleam of silver on those elm-trees! Now she turns slowly round towards the front of the house once more. Those lurid boughs of the copper beech stretching and straining towards the guilty house, those dark-red splashes on the corner-stones of the dwelling—what do they mean? Murder? From where she now sits only the lower half of the front is visible, from half the door downwards, by reason of the woof of the tree-branches spread across its face; but the upper part is here and there to be seen through the interlacing higher boughs which form striking ara-besques about the chimneys. They take fantastic shapes: goblin faces appear in their outlines, pointing fingers, wringing hands, gesticulating arms, all stand forth, and multiply the longer one gazes.

16

Bawn rises and walks up and down the green, mysterious sward.   How beautiful, solemn, and weird it all
is !   And this is the living tomb of the woman who for-
sook Arthur Desmond in his need, of the wretch whose
whispered calumnies had been the ruin of a good man's
life.   Truly it was easy to believe that a curse reigned
here.   God had been before her with His vengeance.
No, Heaven knew, she wished for no vengeance ; confession, restitution were all that she was seeking for.
Was it possible that a voice could ever be evoked from
that mouldering pile ?   How was she to penetrate into
whatever den Luke Adare occupied in that crumbling
ruin ; seek him in his fastness where even old friends
did not dare to intrude upon him ; wring from him the
truth that had rusted in his soul all through these long,
unhallowed years ?   Even that very night might not a
storm arise to hurl down the remainder of the falling
roof upon his head and send him to eternity with his
secret in his heart ?   Great Heaven ! to think of a
woman being housed in that rotting hole, a woman
whom her father had loved, the creature whose defec-
tion left that grey, bleak look on his face which she had
told herself a thousand times she could never forget if
she lived to be a hundred years old !   No, it must only
be a dream.   It certainly could not be——

A girl appeared coming through the trees with a
water-pail, and, using the windlass, soon filled her vessel
and rested it on the wall of the well.

"Are you not afraid to come to this strange place
alone ?" asked Bawn, watching her.

The girl eyed her, as if she would say, "I might ask
you the same."   But she only answered :

"The water is good, and it's worth coming for; but
I would not be here at night, not for all ever I saw."

And then she shouldered her pail and went her way

glancing back occasionally to see if Bawn was still sitting on the well, and gradually becoming smaller and smaller in the distance, till the last flutter of her petticoat vanished among the trees. The place felt lonelier and sadder after her coming and departure, and Bawn experienced a slight shivering sensation in spite of her vigorous physique and the fact that it was still high noon.

CHAPTER XXVII.

BAWN sat for a long time quite still on the edge of the well, overwhelmed by the enchantment of the place, and picturing to herself her father, young, ardent, happy, coming and going by those paths, now overgrown and almost lost, passing in at that dilapidated door to be welcomed by the woman he loved. What kind of place was this wilderness in those days? Lovely and pleasant, no doubt, though with a hint of coming decadence and gloom even then folded up in the boughs of these great beeches, already sinister and mighty, and threatening to shut out the light of day from the upper windows. Looking towards the avenue, she started to see a tall man, like the figure she had been picturing to herself, coming quickly through the tunnel of green. As yet he was far off, so that she could not distinguish his features. It seemed to her Arthur Desmond coming at a lover's pace into the Hollow to look for her who was the delight of his young life. Yielding to this fancy, she watched the figure without asking herself who might in reality be coming to intrude upon her solitude. Well, it was some countryman, who would pass and go out at the other end of the Hollow, as foot-passengers would sometimes do. He would disappear again like the water-carrying girl, and like her also leave the place all the more lonesome for his having passed.

As he came a little nearer something in the height

and carriage of the figure struck her as familiar. This was a gentleman, though it was not Arthur Desmond, and on his head he carried a little blue cap which Bawn had seen before. There was no mistaking the air of the man, the turn of his head, his gait, and, as he drew nearer, his features. This was indeed Somerled of the steamer, and, before she had time to think of whether she would put herself out of sight or not, she perceived that she had been recognised. He stopped, stood quite still, as if undecided what to do, and finally left the path and came across the greensward towards her. As she watched him coming with long steps across the grass a tremulous feeling came over her, as if at the approach of a vague danger. She realised that now, indeed, she had come to a difficult point in the road of her rash undertaking.

He stopped before her and removed the blue cap. "Miss Ingram," he said, "I know you are fond of solitude, but still I am surprised to find you here, so far from home, by yourself."

She was relieved to hear him speak in so easy and friendly a manner. He looked grave, but not severe and gloomy like Rory of Tor. This was really Somerled, in the very character in which he had first appeared to her.

"I have heard a great deal about this old place, and my curiosity has been excited. I am not so far from home as you suppose, for my little cart is waiting for me on the other side of the pass."

"I am well aware that you are quite able to manage your own affairs. May I sit down beside you?"

"The old well does not belong to me. I suppose any one may sit here. But as I have lingered long enough for one day, I will leave you in possession of the resting-place."

"No, stay, only for a little. It is still high noon, and the place, with all its uncanniness, is lovely. Besides, I have a question to ask which may as well be asked now. Bawn, why did you play me that cruel trick?"

He was not looking at her as he spoke, but down the long tunnel of green foliage through which he had come to her, as if he expected the answer to reach him from thence.

Bawn hesitated and collected her thoughts. She had not been prepared for so sudden and open a challenge.

"Was it cruel?" she said: "or rather was it not the best thing to do?"

"Perhaps I ought not to complain. Doubtless you found me very troublesome. Still, we had been friends —for a week—and friend expects a word of farewell at parting from friend."

"I own it looked ungrateful, but I felt no pleasure in paining you."

"You wanted to get away from me and leave no trace; that is about it. And now, by a strange freak of fortune, you have put yourself right in my path again; set up your home and hiding-place only a few miles away, as the bird flies, from mine. Fate has had a strange retribution in store for you."

"Very strange."

"Bawn—"

"Please to call me Miss Ingram."

"Well, then, Miss Ingram, why did you tell me you were going to Paris to be an actress?"

"I did not tell you so."

"You did not tell me so?"

"No; you inferred it, and I did not set you right. I humoured the idea; that was all."

"You humoured the idea, to set me further astray.

All in order that you might surely never set eyes on
me again."

" That is the very truth."

Somerled breathed a hard sigh.

"Well, it is best to be honest," he said, "And now,
have you not been greatly annoyed to find that you
have thrust your hand into the hornet's nest ? "

" If you mean was I surprised to see you, why, I was.
But then I was not quite sure it was you. Seeing that
you looked morose, and behaved to me like a perfect
stranger—"

" Both were natural, I think. I was morose, and I
had reason to be. And of course I treated you like a
stranger. When I ascertained that the person from
Minnesota whom they were all raving about was you,
after I had verified my suspicions by paying a twilight
visit to your place and seeing you standing near your
own door—"

Bawn uttered a sudden exclamation, remembering the
night after the storm when she thought her imagination
had played her a trick.

" What is the matter ? "

". Nothing. Pray go on."

"When I found you were here, you for whom I had
been searching Paris like an idiot, with thoughts—well,
thoughts that would not interest so cool and imperturb-
able a person as Miss Ingram ; when I was assured you
were indeed come among us, I resolved that I would
not subject you to the annoyance of any recognition
from me. I would spare you whatever embarrassment there might be for you in any allusion to our
acquaintance on board the steamer. That was one
reason for my greeting you as a total stranger. Another was—I will be frank and confess it—that for my
own part I could not bear to address you upon any

other terms. I even thought of continuing to ignore
our former acquaintanceship. I was not sure that I
would ever refer to it, even should the most inviting
opportunity offer, till I saw you a few minutes ago
sitting here as lonely and alone, as cool and self-
possessed, as completely yourself, in short, as when I
first beheld you in your corner on deck, with your face
turned away from the world, looking out to sea and the
future—this future which neither of us could guess."

"Who could have guessed it? But I am glad you
have spoken to me, as my mind is now made up that it
is you."

"You were not sure of my identity?"

"I still think of Mr Rory Fingall of Tor, and Mr
Somerled of the steamer, as two distinct individuals
bearing a curious likeness to each other."

"My name is Roderick Somerled Fingall. I own I
was in a savage humour that night when I found you
sitting serenely in Bartly's cabin, smiling as if you had
just newly dropped from heaven, and with apparently
no recollection whatever of an experience which had
cost so much to me. But do not be uneasy. I am not
going to renew a suit of which you gave so practical a
proof of your dislike. You are not to suppose that
because I went to Paris in search of you, I had the
intention of finding you only to persecute you. One
so self-contained as you will hardly believe me, and yet
I must clear myself on this point. The strange and
successful deception you had practised on me, whether
by false words or, as you say, by allowing me to follow
out my own inferences, had filled me with a grave uneasiness as to the future which you might be ignorantly
pressing on to meet. You will never know what I felt
when I found you were gone, what I suffered while trying to track you to Paris and through Paris. You are

not so constituted as to be able to understand it. You think, perhaps, that it was my passion for you that carried my feet over the stones of every quarter of the city I thought likely to harbour you, that strained my heart and gave my face such an expression as caused some one to say as I passed, 'That man is a mono-maniac.' No, I will not humour your vanity by leaving that impression on your mind. My love for you, as true a love as ever man felt for woman, was killed stone dead by a blow, crushed to death under your reckless foot as you left that ship, while I slept and dreamed of you. It is gone. Let it go!"

He had risen up and was standing before her. The flash of his eye, the quiver of his nostril, the nervous gesture of his hand all denounced her. He turned his face away and was silent for a moment; and then took his seat on the well again, a little further from her than before.

"I went after you as one goes after a weaker fellow-creature whom one seeks to save. That is all."

"I know you are a philanthropist," said Bawn, after a moment's pause to quell the storm in her heart, an agitation that was urging her to cry out and defend herself. "You went after me as you went after the emigrants. When a good man does these things his conscience rewards him. Believe me, I am not un-grateful, although you find this emigrant more safely settled in her new country than you had expected. If you still feel a little interest in me, is not that a thing to be pleased at?"

"I am pleased at it," he said after another pause, during which he had been adding all the meaning of her last speech to the general account of her cold-heartedness. "I am pleased to find you safe and well, and so placed that I may possibly be of some use to

you occasionally.   For in spite of your independent
spirit and your business capacity, which fit you
eminently to stand alone, you may, even in the safety
and solitude of these glens, sometimes need a helping
hand from a man.   Major Batt will overwhelm you
with attentions, but, if I know you at all, you will not
let him trespass on an inch of your land.   My cousin
Alister will promise everything, and with the best
intentions, but as soon as he gets a book between his
finger and thumb he will forget all about you.   You
may rely on me for service.   You need not be afraid
that I will ever disturb you with a renewal of my
addresses.   The past is past, and for the future we
are friends."

"I am glad of that."

"With your practical head and cool heart you are
exactly suited to be a man's friend.   I still get lost in
amazement when I think of how cleverly you kept
your own counsel all that week, how you denied my
pleading, baffled my curiosity, ignored my strong
interest in and anxiety for you, determinedly and
relentlessly put me aside—and only for this, that you
might make your way undeterred to a quiet spot, bury
yourself among hills, and lead the laborious and unexciting life of a woman-farmer.   Your mystery which
tormented me so sorely was such a little mystery, after
all.   Bawn, you might have trusted me with your secret."

"Is it not better as it is?"

"Barring my pain, perhaps it is, as you have so
completely convinced me that you could never love me.
And yet you did not tell me so outright.   Therein
lay your sin, Miss Ingram.   You did not say to me,
'You are utterly distasteful to me; I could not endure
such a companion through life.'   Nay, you gave me to
understand—"

"You forget that you said just now that the past is past and wiped out, and that we start afresh as new acquaintances. If you contradict yourself like this I shall have to reject your offer of friendship."

"True. And you are able to carry out your threats," he said, with a look of bitter mortification which transformed him from Somerled into Rory. "You would rise up some fine night and vanish back to Minnesota rather than allow me to meet you again in the character of a lover. Bawn, why cannot you love me? Am I hideous, coarse, brutal, or in any way accursed? Why did you so persistently reject me?"

The passionate pain in his voice hurt Bawn like the stroke of a rod, but she answered quickly:

"Now indeed you forget yourself, Mr Fingall. Only reflect. Suppose I had given way. Suppose I had liked you well enough, think of what it would have been. How would you have presented me to your family? A farmer's daughter, without birth or fortune; an acquaintance formed on board ship; a young woman coming alone across the sea to earn her bread by making Irish butter. Would it not all have been unfit and unfortunate?"

"Most fit, most fortunate. If you are a farmer's daughter, what am I but a farmer? If you are poor, why so am I. At Tor you could have made butter to your heart's content."

"If Lady Flora could hear you!" said Bawn with a faint smile.

"Confound Lady Flora!"

"The lady of Tor, your grandmother—what would she have said to me?"

"You do not know her. She would have made you welcome—that is, if you had loved me. But I am raving like a fool. You do not and never can like me well enough, as you say. And that is the end of it."

"I beg you will let it be the end."

"And yet, hard though you are, you will not hate me!"

"No."

"But you will not marry me?"

"No."

"You are a resolute woman. You admit, however, that we may be friends. I would like to leave myself an opening through which I may be allowed to watch that that farm of yours does not ruin you. You will permit me to befriend you?"

"Only on condition that you never speak like this again."

"Nor will I."

"If you do I shall feel myself bound to go and tell the entire story to that noble-looking old lady at Tor."

"No, Bawn, don't do that. Spare me the humiliation, at least, even if you do not care for me."

"Then I shall have to go away."

"What? Tear yourself from the little, solitary home you have taken such infinite pains to secure for yourself? Fly away over our heads like the eagles from Aura—"

At the word "Aura" Bawn's face changed. What the change was he could not tell, though he saw it, nor could he guess what had caused it. A frown came on her fair brows; her face was for the moment not Bawn's, but looked like some picture he had seen of the Angel of Judgment. She was seeing in that instant the tragedy on Aura; her father was the eagle flying from Aura, branded like Cain—Arthur Desmond, good man and true.

"Aura!" She raised her eyes to the mouldering house so near her, but in the last half-hour quite forgotten. They lit on the fallen roof-tree, the dreary frontage with the red splashes as of blood on its cornerstone. "*Murder!*" was the word which was formed by the thought in her mind—the murder of a man's good name, his heart, his hopes. That was the murder which was done upon Aura. If this man beside her, whose face, whose voice was become so dear to her that she scarcely dared to look at the one or listen to the other, were to know whose daughter stood before him, would he not turn from her in horror, would he not, with justice, reproach her for putting herself in his way, for stealing his heart in a false character? Well, had she not refused him persistently enough? Did she not act upon the knowledge that there never could be any union between Roderick Somerled Fingall and the daughter of the man who was believed to have murdered his uncle, whose name had been blasted by the Fingalls and Adares with a foul and unforgivable calumny? No, there could be nothing between them, not even friendship. Let him go back to Tor and marry Manon with her gold, as Alister had married Flora. As for her, she had done very ill in dallying with him here so long. She would go back to Betty Macalister, the one faithful soul in all this sickening world, and give all her thoughts to the Adares, and her plans for reaching them in their den.

As her eyes came back from the dreary front of the house with these thoughts in them, her companion stood gazing in wonder at their extraordinary expression. He thought he read in them a revulsion of feeling against himself.

"Pardon me," he said hoarsely; "I have tried you. Nay, I have broken my word, and I have been persecuting you. I have kept you here too long. You are angry. It was thoughtless of me. Try me again."

" I am only thinking that it is time for me to go," she said, turning away and drawing her shawl around her.

" May I not accompany you to the place where your car is waiting ? "

" No; I wish to go alone."

" But I may come to see you—when business brings me your way ? "

" Please to take no further notice of me."

He fell back and allowed her to pass, but after she had gone some distance he followed along the path she had taken, and just kept his eye on her figure in advance of him till he saw her safe across the pass and seated in her cart.

He watched the little trundling cart as far as his eye could see it, and then struck off in the opposite direction.

CHAPTER XXVIII.

"I WILL descend to my churn," said Bawn, "and there seek comfort."

She had already built herself a new dairy, upon improved principles never heard of in the glens.

"That young woman at Shanganagh is going to ruin herself," said Alister to Rory as they met in the village street. "She has taken to building. I hope the girls may get their rent, after all."

"She need not ruin herself if she is industrious and persevering," returned Rory. "She does what most of us here do not: she begins at the right end."

"I thought you would take her up, as she is evidently a reformer."

"Some people seize at once the truth that two and two make four," said Rory, "while others will stick to five till their dying day. The flavour of turf freshly burning is pleasant and aromatic enough to those who like it, but nobody likes it stale, especially on butter. Miss Ingram, in providing herself with a dairy out of the reach of her household smoke, is going the right way about securing the money for her rent."

"The last tenant of the farm could not make it pay," said Alister, "although he lost by no unnecessary outlay."

"Rather because he gained by no unnecessary outlay," said Rory. "He was too poor, or too faint-hearted or too stupid, I don't know which, to invest a little capital and trust to his own energies for the increase."

"Has Miss Ingram got capital?"

"She has plenty of it in pluck, at all events. When I last saw Shanganagh it was a deplorable sight. Eheu! the dislocated gates, the corners of land choked with weeds, the holes in the fences! Now there is a change."

"You have been there?"

"Yes, I have just been there. I wanted to bring Miss Ingram a watch-dog. Not that I imagine any one would molest her; she has already won a sort of enthusiasm from her neighbours and servants. If it be true that the Irish would either kill you or die for you, it is evident that the people of Glenmalurcan would prefer to be victims for Miss Ingram's sake."

"There is a charm about her, I own. Still, I am glad you thought of bringing her the dog."

"So am I," said Rory quietly.

"How did she receive it? I have a notion that she is not fond of being interfered with."

"She received it characteristically, I think. First she declared she had no need of him and would not have him. Then she said she would like him for a companion, if he would promise not to hurt anything harmless. Finally she smiled curiously and said, 'I hope he will take a dislike to Major Batt.'"

"The old humbug!—I mean the major. Has he been selling her any more broken-kneed cattle?"

"She is not one to be taken in twice. But I think you and I ought to look after her a little."

"You appear to have been doing it."

"I am like you: I practise as I preach," said Rory, thinking of the lop-sided gates which Bawn had had to hitch up into their places.

"She is young and fair to see, and has put herself

into rather a peculiar position," said Alister. "But of course I will stand by her whenever I can."

"She comes from a country where women are brought up to act like reasonable beings, and where, when they have not been born with silver spoons in their mouths, they proceed to do the best they can with their time and their hands."

"Perhaps she ought to have stayed there. I am not sure. Flora and Manon do not like her, somehow."

"Shana and Rosheen do. Two against two, even among the ladies," said Rory, smiling.

"And Gran ?"

"Oh! Gran says little: is for giving her a fair trial—like me," said Rory; and then, a brother landlord and magistrate having come up, the conversation turned on boycotting and other troubles of the times in the disturbed part of the country.

"Rory seems inclined to make an emigrant of Miss Ingram," said Alister, smilingly that evening as he sipped his coffee with his feet on his wife's antique brass fender, having, at the moment, one mental eye on improved Shanganagh and the other on his new *édition de luxe* of Horace, in the pages of which he had left his paper knife, intending to find it in them again as soon as he could manage to slip away from the drawing-room.

"So she is, an emigrant," said Shana.

"I wish all our emigrants had her energy," said Alister, who loved every stick and stone in the Rath, and had some misgiving that he would starve and die there, like the Adares in their ruin, rather than be driven out into a new country to put his shoulder to vulgar wheels that any man could turn as well as himself. He had a sneaking sympathy for emigrants, but it took no active form as Rory's did. He would have the people all at home and give them alms, when he

17

could spare any, to keep them alive ; but he could not do without his *édition de luxe*, and preferred it to either philanthropy or political economy.

"I wish we all had her energy, for the matter of that. It seems she is making butter already in her new dairy," he added, with a virtuous desire to say a good word for Miss Ingram here, though he had been a little hard on her to Rory.

"I have seen it and tasted it," said Shana, "and if the Danes can do better than that they deserved to conquer Ireland."

"I wish you would speak to Shana, Alister, now we are on the subject, about running so much after that American woman. I have said distinctly that I do not like her, but my feelings and opinions go for nothing. Shana is only too ready to pick up American audacity and impudence."

"Tie a string to her leg, Flora. It is the only thing to be done with young wild animals," said Alister, who was fond of his spirited little sister, and had sometimes asked himself how it would have been if he had been born with her characteristics instead of his own.

"Of course you will take her part ; but, mark my words, that Ingram girl will make mischief here yet. There she has Rory and Major Batt running after her already—"

"And Shana, which is much more improper."

"And she orders about her everywhere, and drives over the country, superintends her own buildings, for which she will probably pay no rent—"

"But then we shall have the new dairy, Flora, if she runs away, or if we evict her."

"All very fine, while she is setting her cap at Rory or Major Batt—"

"Flora, how can you be so vulgar?" burst forth

Shana. "All because Rory was thoughtful enough to bring her a watch-dog! I was there at the time, and nothing could be more unlike *that* than her manner."

"As for Batt, I believe she intends to set the dog at him," said Alister.

"If I am to be called vulgar in my own house and in my husband's presence—" began Flora, swelling with anger and injured pride.

"It is a sign you had better let the subject drop," said her husband, rising hastily and thinking of his Horace with a sensation of relief. "Evidently Shana has already been contaminated. We had better begin to kill the goose with the golden eggs, and give this Jezabel notice to quit."

It was the same day on which this conversation had taken place that Bawn had said to herself that she was resolved to look for comfort in her churn.

She acknowledged to herself that she greatly needed comfort from some quarter. The fiction that Rory was not Somerled, with which she had deceived herself, having been fully exposed, she was feeling all the reality of her uncomfortable position. She had come across the world with one settled purpose in her mind, which no counsel had been able to shake, and she found herself opposed by a difficulty of the strangest and most unexpected kind—the persevering devotion of the last person in the world who ought to have taken any notice of her.

Here was a man who fascinated her imagination and constrained her heart in a way that made her indignant with herself, and he was the namesake and nephew of that other of his family whose unfortunate and untimely death had ruined her father's life and cast a stain upon her own name. Somehow the contemplation of this fact seemed to make it suddenly become quite unlikely that she should succeed in the mission she had so boldly undertaken. The inhabitants of that rotting ruin were probably either mad or doting; and even if they had anything to tell, how were they to be forced to tell it, and who would believe them when it was told? Then if she should at some moment find herself obliged in honour to inform Rory Fingall of her identity, what would there be left for her to do but to go back whence she had come, disgraced, and perhaps —who could say?—heart-broken, leaving her task abandoned and unfinished?

Why had she not obeyed her father's wishes, followed Dr Ackroyd's counsels, and letting the past rest, set the current of her life far from the glens of Antrim and the tragedy they knew of?

She might have travelled about Europe, leading a pleasant life, in company with some respectable duenna, or she might have stayed in her own country, using her fortune to help those poor Irish emigrants of whom she had lately heard so much. She might have turned her life to account somehow, without inviting that heavy tribulation which she began to feel sorely afraid the future had in store for her. It was possible, however, that by sheer force of will she could yet come to her own assistance.

Standing alone in her dairy, so cool, spotless, and scented with the odour of fresh cream, she clasped her hands across her heart and sighed an impatient sigh. There were two ways by which she could help herself: one was by keeping Mr Fingall at an unfriendly distance; and had she not already got her feet well upon the track of this way? The other was by succeeding in her enterprise and clearing her father's character from its stain. Alas! what a moonshine dream the latter seemed at this moment, looked at with eyes enlightened

by the strong sunlight of her new experience of life.
And then her maidens came back from their dinner, and
the business of the dairy went on, till she was told that
Mr Rory Fingall was at the door, praying her to speak
with him for a few moments.

"Tell him I am busy making butter, Betty, and cannot see visitors," she said, startled at his boldness.

"He says he will call back in an hour, ma'am, when
the butter is made."

Bawn went on with her work, instructing her half
dozen maidens of the glen, who were part her servants
and part her pupils, and all the time striving to keep her
heart as hard and as firm as she was assuring her assist-
ants their butter ought to be. What was she to do with
him on his return? Great was her relief when another
message was brought to her. It was Miss Fingall who
was asking for her this time, and, while Shana remained
with her, Rory reappeared with his dog. There was now
no possibility of turning him away from the door. The
question of the dog was discussed; and Sorley Boy, a
great, tawny collie, shaggy and silky, with an intelligent
muzzle and tender eyes, was finally accepted by Miss
Ingram as the champion of her homestead.

Bawn, in her crisp calico gown and snow-white apron,
was waiting on Shana, giving the young lady a taste of
the delicious butter she had just got a lesson in making;
and, in spite of Bawn's stern resolve of an hour ago, the
giver of the dog received a cup of well-creamed tea from
the milk-white hand which had so recently been busy
with the churn.

"Rory, I wish you had not come," said **Shana**.
"You have interrupted my lesson. I know you will
not tell, but I am hoping to go into partnership with
Miss Ingram by-and-bye."

"Indeed!" said Rory 'That is your secret, is it?"

And he was careful not to look at Bawn, lest she should see dancing in his eyes the assertion that, in spite of all that had come and gone, his own hope was somewhat identical with his cousin's.

Finally Rory went away alone, satisfied inasmuch as he had left the dog behind him, and not very jealous of Shana, though she had remained where he did not venture to remain.

The car was waiting for her, Shana had said, and the day was long. It was known at home that she meant to pay a long and profitable visit to Miss Ingram.

The truth was, Shana had brought a manuscript in her pocket, and intended consulting with Bawn as to whether it was worth anything or not—the young authoress being still a little undecided between butter and literature as the means of endowing herself with a fortune before becoming a wife. Rory's provoking visit had foiled her intentions. It would soon be time to depart, and Bawn's interrupted dairy work had yet to be finished.

"What a pity you could not be here in the evening!" said Bawn, looking at the outside of the manuscript. "Of course it is impossible, but I should then be so free."

"I can wait a little longer," said Shana; and when Bawn reappeared from her dairy in the course of half an hour she found Shana looking quite at home in the little sitting-room, with her hat put away, and glancing eagerly over the pages of her formidable-looking manuscript.

"I have sent away the car, with a message that I am going to remain here all night," said Miss Fingall, quickly. "I can sleep on the floor, or anywhere."

"But Lady Flora—your family—what will they say?"

"Oh! Flora will say a great deal ; but my brother will only laugh, and can hide in his library. Rosheen is at Tor, entertaining the visitor, and so she will not be annoyed in the matter. I shall be freely condemned when I go home to-morrow ; but then I am always being freely condemned. People who are constantly grumbling do not produce as much effect, you know, as people who only scold when you do very wrong."

"I am afraid this is really wrong," said Bawn, smiling with pleasure at the prospect of having a companion for so many hours ; "but when my lady landlord chooses to sleep under her own roof—well, I cannot evict her."

The evening passed in the reading and discussion of Shana's novel. With all her boldness, Miss Fingall found it difficult to read her own paragraphs aloud.

"I never felt so with Rosheen," she said plaintively, dropping the pages in discouragement. "But then she is as ignorant as myself, and I am not afraid of her."

"I dare say you have both read more novels than I have," said Bawn, "and you ought to know quite as much of life. I shall only be able to tell you whether I think your story is like life as I have met with it."

"Oh ! it can't be at all like that," said Shana briskly, "because it is altogether about things that happened two or three hundred years ago. It is something in the style of Ossian, only in plain prose. The people are chieftains, and lofty ladies—"

"Historical ?"

"Not exactly," said Shana, changing colour rapidly "except that Sorley Boy—that is, Somerled Bhuee— the hero, was a real man."

"Was he ?"

"An ancestor of ours. Yellow haired Somerled. Rory has named your dog for him. He is named

after him himself—Roderick Somerled. Sorley Boy
is a contraction for Somerled Bhuee. It suits the
colour of the dog better than Rory, who is dark."

" But about the story ? "

" Somerled Bhuee marries a lady who plays the
harp, and of course he is very fond of her; but I am
dreadfully afraid there is not enough about that. I
want the readers to take a great deal of it for granted,
and perhaps they won't. I have some good descrip-
tions, though, and they all say such honourable things.
Do you think that will make up ? Do you believe it
will be a popular novel ? "

" I can't tell till I have heard it," said Bawn.

Shana went courageously through her work, which
was not very long, after all, though it made a great
show of foolscap. When she had finished her face
was damp, and red and white in patches, and she
dropped back into her chair as if extinguished.

" Well, what do you say ? Have you found it exciting ? "

" No," said Bawn promptly.

" Not even deeply interesting ? "

" No. I would rather have been talking to you all
the time."

Shana drew a long sigh of relief.

" On the whole I am very glad ! " And before Bawn
could stay her she had buried her manuscript in the
heart of the fire.

" I am no longer afraid that I shall be hiding a
great talent by sticking to the churn. My heart has
inclined to butter, and butter it shall be."

" But, dear Miss Fingall, why should a young lady
like you take to butter ? "

" I will tell you," said Shana, and her lips softened
and her eyes shone. " One supreme effort is enough

for this evening. But I will tell you some day when I can get myself to speak."

When Shana was tucked up in bed, and Bawn had spread a pallet for herself in a corner, she went back to her little kitchen and stood looking at Sorley Boy, the collie dog, who sat in a dignified attitude on the hearth in the red light of the sinking turf fire. A gentle snoring told that Betty and Nancy were sound asleep not far off, and Bawn and the dog were alone. She knelt down beside him and stroked his tawny silky coat. "Sorley Boy," she said to him—"Somerled Bhuee." She admired his acutely intelligent muzzle, and looked in his grave eyes, full of dog-like tenderness. Then she lifted his fore-paws, one after the other, gently, as if asking a favour, and placed them on her shoulders, and laid her hair against his ear.

"You are a fine fellow," she said, "a gift worthy of your namesake, and you and I are going to be friends. There is no reason in the world, this contrary world, why I ought not to love this Somerled, at all events."

CHAPTER XXIX.

HOLLOW PEGGY.

WHEN Bawn had got that churning of butter off her mind and had sent it away, beautifully packed, to London, she set herself to consider how she might penetrate into the recesses of the ruin of Shane's Hollow, and come face to face with its inhabitants. The first step was to make friends with "Hollow Peggy," as Betty called the poor woman who at periodical times went in and saw that the creatures were not starved in their dens. It was easy enough to persuade Betty to bring her to Shanganagh, but not so easy, said Betty, to make her talk of her poor charges to a stranger.

However, Peggy was lured to Shanganagh one evening by Betty, and came stealing in at dusk to the little kitchen, a curious figure, plain and rugged of feature, with a startled look in her eyes, but a patient brow and mouth. Her face was weather-stained to the colour of oak, her head and shoulders swathed in a woollen shawl. She supped with Betty and Nancy, and Bawn, through the open door of her sitting-room, heard the conversation that passed among them. Peggy, not being very bright-witted, had no idea she was being cross-examined for a purpose.

"You were sarvint wit' them long ago, wasn't you, Peggy?"

"I wuz," said Peggy, who was what Betty called "few-worded."

"Not when they were rich, but?"

"Na. When they were rale grand I wuz too wee. But I mind Miss Mave buyin' me a bonnet with a blue ribbon. She tied it on herself, and I niver forgot it to her."

"It was when they were gettin' poor you lived wit' them?"

"Ay."

"Till they couldn't keep ye no longer?"

"My man tuk me out of it."

"Was the roof off then, Peggy?"

"Troth then it was beginnin' to go."

"An' they always lived by themselves, in separate rooms, then?"

"'Deed an' they did. The men wuz always queer an' had ways of their own. Miss Julia got queer the soonest of the ladies, an' died the soonest. Miss Catherine wasn't long behind her. Miss Mave was the best o' the lot, an' she's not right daft yet; only whiles when the pains does be bad wit' her."

"Are you not afraid the roof will fall on her and kill her?"

"Faix an' I am. Mostly when I go in I do be expectin' to find her killed. But the Lord is good to her."

"You still go every evening to look after them?"

"I do that same, an' does what I can with Miss Mave's bed, an' makes them a sup o' tea, an' brings them an egg when I can, an' a bit o' bread. They don't eat more nor the mice would pick up in a house like this," said Peggy, looking round.

"An' you make up their fires, an' brings them coal and sticks, and leaves Miss Mave a drink of water where her hand can reach it. And then you see no more of them till the next evening again."

"Sure, you know all that."

" An' what do they ever say to you, Peggy ? "

" Mr Edmond sometimes says 'thank ye' humble enough, and Mr Luke he lets a curse at me. But he would miss me all the same if I didn't go. Miss Julia used to tell me—that's before she died—of the grand matches the ladies could 'a' had in the counthry round, only they were too grand for anybody that axed them. Miss Mave sometimes knows me and sometimes she dozzint. She tells me about her sister Catherine that's dead, and thinks she's with her still ; an' sure that's great company to her. That's when she's in her daft fits. ' Peggy,' she says to me, ' dear Catherine wakened me early this morning,' or ' she didn't call me till it was quite late. She wanted me to have a good sleep—dear Catherine ! ' She won't eat no food till I make the same for Miss Catherine, and take it to her. Then she thinks she's going out, and says to her sister, ' Now, Catherine, Margaret will take care of you while I'm away, will give you a cup of tea and an egg, and I won't be long.' "

Bawn listened, and thought of the beautiful face of the miniature, and of Arthur Desmond's love, and her heart quaked.

" It turned her brain, like, when Miss Catherine died ? "

" Sure it did. The two was always in the wan room. Miss Catherine's bed is there yet. An' Miss Mave doted on Miss Catherine. When she was dead she had her there for days tryin' to bring her to life again with turpentine. She was feared they would bury her alive, She cried and begged I would not tell outside that she was dead. But I had to tell at last, and the parish took her away and buried her. It had to be done at night. They pretended that she was goin' to the grand old burial place at Toome, where the Adares was always buried by torch-light. They have been fiercer about spakin' to any quality since then, an' Miss Mave got rale light-headed after it."

Here Bawn felt that she could keep hidden no longer, and came into the kitchen and slipped into a chair beside Peggy at the fireside.

"It's only my misthress, Peggy. Ye needn't be afraid of her. She's none o' yer grand quality; only a dacent young woman from America," said Betty.

"You're welcome to my little farmhouse, Peggy. Have you had a comfortable supper? Now don't stop talking on account of me. I wish I could do something for that poor Miss Mave of yours."

Peggy eyed Bawn all over, and did not seem so scared of her as Betty had been afraid she would be.

"I wish she would let me come to see her, Peggy. She must be terribly lonely in that ruin."

"They won't let no quality near them, ma'am, nor not a sowl at all at all but me."

"But I am not quality, only a stranger in the country, don't you see. They needn't be too proud to speak to me. I would go as a human creature to another human, creature. And I might be able to do something for Miss Mave Adare."

"If she would only look at you there would be no more trouble," said Peggy simply, "an' I'll ax her an' see what can be done. Only I don't think she'll let you cross the thrashel, ma'am."

"An' it would be the risk o' your life to do that same," said Betty.

"But Peggy does it every day?"

"She knows where to pick her steps an' put her feet. Besides, Peggy's an ould sarvint an' friend, an' you're a stranger that has no call to throw away your life on them. I'll say nothing again' Miss Mave, poor sowl, but the rest o' them don't desarve it."

"It's only Miss Mave I want to help," said Bawn, and for the moment every other feeling was swallowed up in pity for this wretched woman.

"But you could not come noways, unless Mr Luke allowed it," said Peggy.

Bawn was silent, and sat confronting in imagination Luke Adare, whom she considered her arch-enemy, and opposing her will to his.

"Try what you can do, at all events, Peggy," she said gently after a few minutes, "for my heart aches for your poor mistress."

The next evening Peggy appeared, coming towards the farmhouse with a quick step.

"She says she will see the lady from America. It was just as great a wonder to me as if a star out of the sky had dropped into my apron. When I said the lady from America had tears in her eyes talking about her, Miss Mave said, 'Tell her she may come, Peggy.' I went this morning to hear what Mr Luke would say, and he turned his back to me, and I thought it was all over. But when I was goin' out of the hall Mr Edmond follyed me an' said:

"'Tell the lady from America that it was always the custom for ladies to visit ladies. Miss Adare cannot call on Miss Ingram. Let Miss Ingram call on Miss Adare.'"

"Mr Luke said nothing?"

"Nothin' at all, ma'am: but I'm thinkin' he will not put himself in the way."

Betty threw up her hands. "It's like the end o' the world!" she cried vehemently. "Nobody would ha' believed it."

"Maybe it's death that's comin' near them," said Peggy, "but Miss Mave's wantin' you to go to see her, anyway. An', ma'am, if I might make bould to ask, if you could send her a bit of an ould nightgown, and a sheet or somethin' to dress her up, she wouldn't feel so 'shamed, I think, of your visitin' her."

Bawn turned abruptly away, and before long reappeared with various articles of linen and clothing.

"Make her as comfortable as you can," she said; "and where may I meet you to-morrow?"

"At the hall door in the Hollow, ma'am," said Peggy.

CHAPTER XXX.

NEXT morning Bawn appeared in the lights and shades of the mysterious Hollow, carrying a basket on her arm and with Sorley Boy at her heels. In picturesque contrast to the sombre shadows of the place was her gracious, womanly figure in fresh print dress and coarse straw hat, under which the twists of her golden hair caught fire from the stray sunbeams. In her basket she had various articles of light food, new laid eggs, fresh butter, cream, custard, etc.

Peggy did not keep her waiting, and, having bidden Sorley Boy lie on the doorstep till her return, she found herself crossing the unhallowed threshold and following on the faithful servant's steps into the interior of the ruin. The sunshine pursued them a little way into the wide, low-ceilinged hall, showing the jagged rents in the boards, gaps bridged over by loose planks or pieces of slate, and the open holes, pitfalls for unwary feet, through which one might fall into the cellars below. A great number of tall stakes, young trees lopped and barked, were fixed between floor and ceiling at one side to support the latter, crowding round the rusted fireplace like welcome guests after a winter's journey. Between these the splintered wood and softer stuffing of the upper floor bulged downward through the mouldered plaster. The pillars which separated the front from the back hall shook and tottered if touched, as Bawn found, having laid her hand on one while crossing a dangerous gap in the boards.

Once in the back hall she felt on more solid ground for the moment, and could observe the doors opening off on each side—massive frames deep set in the thick wall—and the passages, dripping with damp and choked with rubbish, wandering away uncannily into the darkness and dilapidation of the lower part of the ruin.

"Down there the gintlemen has their rooms," said Peggy, looking round with awe and whispering as if in a church.

"Rooms?" returned Bawn in a like whisper. "What can be down there but dens and holes?"

"Call them what you like, ma'am," said Peggy; "they're still covered in, at any rate."

"They'll be covered in more completely some day soon," reflected Bawn, and thought with a thrill of dismay of Luke Adare buried alive, and his secret with him.

From the back hall ascended gradually and slantingly a low, wide stair, with a great window gazing down the first flight, and the ascent for so far seemed easy enough. But after that came a shorter flight, slanting forward again to the centre of the house, and, having climbed this and placed her feet on the upper landing, the intruder seemed literally to carry her life in her hand.

The floor was breaking under foot, and on the totally unroofed side of the house the open arch, seen from without, yawned to heaven. Just below, an unroofed passage, barred by half-fallen beams and choked with rubbish, ran between the still covered back part of the house and the open wreck of the left front wing, and at the end of this wild corridor a crazy door hung off its hinges.

18

"That is Miss Julia's room," said Peggy. "They had hard work gettin' her out when she was dead."

To the right was a corresponding passage, roofed, and with a window at the end, an open lattice prettily contrived but dropping out of the broken wall. Through this a lovely vista of sunshine and greenery was to be seen, making the ghastly interior more deplorable by contrast. Once what a sweet green nook on a hot summer's day, full of reflections from the wavering boughs, and showing a long, delicious vista of moving gleams and shadows through the tunnel of the avenue.

Right in front as they ascended was the door of a hideous, rotting chamber, into which Bawn would have stepped to her death had not Peggy pulled her back. Floor and ceiling were both dropping down from the walls, and the crazy mass of both had hung over the intruders' heads as they entered the building. Miss Mave's room was now close at hand, to be approached by yet another venture up one more flight of shattered stair. Through the rents between the wall, and the steps on which they feared to place their feet, the hall below was plainly visible, and a heavy tread might have carried intruder and footholding into the ruin below. Peggy, accustomed to the danger, walked like a bird, and Bawn poised herself on tip-toe with vigilant care, crossing the worst bits of footing with a spring.

Even before this stair was scaled they could hear faint human wails coming through the yet closed door. Peggy pushed it cautiously and entered first, and Bawn stood on the threshold, rapidly taking in this new interior.

Though the room was large the light was obscure, because the fine windows were all blocked up with contrivances to keep out the wind and rain. The ceiling was upheld by young larch-trees, stripped, and

used as stakes as in the hall below, only here there was
a greater forest of them crowding all to one side of the
apartment, while, in spite of their efforts to delay the
descent of the ceiling, it bulged down between them,
and the straggling fragments of decay, dropping lower
and lower, gave warning of a coming crash.

Under the worst part of the ceiling, planted right
among the inefficient props, an old bed, covered with
a canopy, was placed, hardly discernible at first in the
obscurity, and behind and around it ghostly wrecks of
furniture of all kinds, encrusted with dust, rubbish, and
cobwebs, mustered in weird array, forming a grotesque,
melancholy background for the bed and its occupant.

Advancing a step, Bawn feared to put her feet
anywhere, for the floor was not only broken but sunken,
sinking towards the side where the bed stood, and
settled into a hollow, ready to slide away at any
moment into the abyss of rottenness below it. Keeping
on the threshold till invited by Peggy to advance, she
glanced round the apartment with eyes getting accustomed to the lack of light. In the safest-looking
spot opposite the door a fire burned in a rusty old
grate ; a kitchen table in a window near was littered
with a few utensils, a cup and saucer, a plate, some
rough needle-work, probably Peggy's. A hole in the
floor was evidently used as a sink, and by it were
a crock and saucepan, &c.

After one swift glance at the bed Bawn closed
her eyes a moment before looking again, and heard a
plaintive, shrieking voice wailing to Peggy, and Peggy
speaking in homely, comforting tones.

What Bawn had seen in the bed was a creature who
looked like a white witch—a skeleton covered with
white, fair skin, a small, spectral face gleaming under
the mouldy old canopy, a pair of fleshless hands like

claws, only wax white, fingering the wretched bed-clothes.

"Oh, what a dire sight! That anything human should so lie here, deserted, from morning till night, and from night till morning again, in the storm, in the rain, with this falling roof overhead and this sliding floor beneath, threatened momentarily with death from above and from below, suffering in the grip of pain, hunger, and cold, and, worst of all, face to face with the memory of joys once present in those very walls! Bawn lowered her head and covered her face; and then she heard Peggy inviting her to come near the bed.

"And this is the American lady, Peggy," said the spectral creature, leaning on her fleshless elbow and looking at Bawn's fresh beauty as if she would shade her hollow eyes from so dazzling a sight. "You are welcome, my dear; welcome to Shane's Hollow. It is but a sorry place now to receive visitors in; but our good days are over here, are they not, Peggy? We had our good days, but they are gone. Peggy, give the young lady a chair and let her talk to me a little. How many years is it, Peggy, since I have spoken to anyone outside of this house besides yourself?"

"I am sorry you are so great a sufferer, Miss Adare," said Bawn, striving to speak in the most matter-of-fact manner, to appear as if quite accustomed to sit at bed-sides like this, quite unconscious of anything out of order around her, and unaware that they were, all three occupants of the room, in danger of death at any moment from a sudden collapse of the few rotten timbers that supported them.

"I am a great sufferer, my dear. Only for this post," she said, touching one of the larch trees, that was planted as a support between ceiling and floor at her side—"only for this I should fling myself out of the

bed at night; and then there would be no one to pick
me up. I hold on by it when the pain is terrible, when
the pain is too dreadful to be borne."

Bawn looked at the stake and thought, with a new
thrill of dismay, that surely one strong shake of this
shaft, which was fastened securely to ceiling and floor,
might be enough to bring about the end, to cause this
wreck of a room with its occupant to come down like a
house of cards.

"Sometimes I scream out quite loud," the poor ghost
went on, "and then my brother Edmond comes up to
me. He is a very kind creature is my brother
Edmond."

Bawn looked at the midnight scene as presented to
her imagination by these few words, and felt her warm
blood beginning to freeze at the horror of it. She
wondered did Luke also make an ascent of that crazy
stair in the night sometimes on such an errand of mercy?
But it was her intention to ask no questions.

"Now, Miss Adare, you must forgive me for bringing
you a custard of my own making. We Americans are
handy people and think we know how to make sweets.
If you don't think it good my pride will get a fall."

"Oh, you are a kind creature; you are a nice
creature!" shrilled the bed-ridden woman. "Peggy
told me you were, or I should not have allowed you to
come here. You come from America, where everyone
is free, and there are no old families; and you are better
without them. Pride is a sin, though some people will
never believe it. And some of us must suffer for our
sins—oh! oh! oh!" she shrieked, finishing her sentence
with a prolonged wail that seemed to express something
more awful than the suffering of a body in pain.

"It's the pain that does be bad wit' her," explained
Peggy, as the poor creature began to wave her skeleton

arms, clutching the air and mourning with such cries as made Bawn think of the despair of a lost spirit.

"But God is very good when he has left me Peggy," she added, unconsciously correcting the false impression her agony had produced. "Peggy is a good creature. And you are a good creature. You are very nice—oh! oh! oh!" And again the wailing began, and her eyes rolled in her head, and she forgot everything but her anguish.

"This is dreadful!" whispered Bawn. "What does she suffer from?"

"Och, 'deed, everything," said Peggy, looking up and down. "The damp does be atin' her always, I think." And then a slight noise at the door made ·Bawn look round, and she saw that a man was standing in the doorway, but so that he could not be seen from the bed.

"It's Misther Rory Fingall from Tor," said Peggy "O Lord! I hope none o' the gintlemen will see him!"

"Tell him to go away, then," said Bawn, and turned her face to the bed.

"O Arthur Desmond, Arthur Desmond!" suddenly screamed the poor, troubled creature in the bed. "Go away, Luke, and let me speak to him. Let him touch me with his finger and the pain will go away! O Arthur! Oh! oh! oh!"

Again the wail was prolonged, and Peggy came back from the door.

"It's no use your stayin' any longer, now, ma'am," she said. "She's begun to rave, and she won't talk to ye no more."

"But I mean to come again, Peggy. I must take her out of this den."

"Ye'll be clever if ye do that same, ma'am. There's nowhere for her to go but the poorhouse, an the gintlemen would burn the counthry if ye dared to take her there. Sure herself would go anywhere, poor lady; but Misther Luke—"

Saying this Peggy signed to her to go, and, picking her steps to the door, Bawn came face to face with Somerled. She allowed him to help her down the stair and walked out into the open air with him. How sweet it tasted! How lovely was nature's wilderness after that hideous interior!

"Come out of this place!" were the first words that Fingall spoke to her, and, obeying him, she walked silently by his side till they emerged from the dilapidated gate at one end of the Hollow into the open fields where grew the yellow lilies round the sky-blue pools, and where the cattle grazed.

"Are you quite mad?" he asked, suddenly stopping and looking at her with a blaze of mingled tenderness and anger lighting up his eyes.

"Why?" asked Bawn, quietly. "Do I look very wild?"

"I will not tell you how you look," he said, feeling, indeed, that he dared not say to her that he had never seen anything look so sane, wholesome, and beautiful, unless he wanted to start another quarrel and was prepared to go seeking for another dog as an excuse for a reconciliation. "It has nothing to do with the matter. You have been wantonly risking your life in that ruined house."

"Not wantonly. I have been visiting a fellow-creature in distress."

"It was not your business. You had no right to go in there," he continued, with concentrated excitement in his voice. His eye was still burning, his heart still shuddering at the thought of the danger she had been in.

"I have assumed the right and made it my business,"

she answered. "At all events, it appears that in doing
so I have interfered with no one else, stepped officiously
into nobody's shoes. Oh! I am sick of you," kindling
into sudden anger and drawing back from him a step,
"disgusted with the whole country-side of you! If
I had been a man among you I would have walked in
there and taken that poor creature on my back, and
carried her out, and put her somewhere into a habitation
fit for human presence. I would not have left her there
screaming with pain and rotting alive in a den only fit
for rats and owls."

She paused and caught her breath. He had turned
quite pale, startled and shocked at her sudden passion.
All the indignation had gone out of his own eyes as he
watched the opening fire in hers.

"Perhaps we deserve blame," he said, "but not so
much as you, a stranger, may think. Will you sit down
here," pointing to a fallen tree, "and let me tell you
about these strange people ?"

"I am not tired. I will not sit down. I am going
home."

"You will be tired before you have accomplished
your long walk."

"You ought not to have followed me here."

"I did not follow you. I have some work going on
over yonder, and this place gives me a short cut homeward. That is how I met you here first, and how I
have happened on you to-day. I saw the dog waiting
for you at the door, and I went in to look for you,
hardly believing that you could be there. Now will
you sit down, and let us talk a little ?"

Bawn yielded and sat on the fallen tree.

"I know probably as much about these people as
you can tell me," she said. "I have been hearing of
them ever since I came. They have not been good.

They are fiercely proud, but still, as they have become old and helpless, I think their sins ought to be forgotten, and charity ought to consider their case."

" So it ought, and so it has done from time to time. But you do not understand them. They will starve, rot, die, but they will die the Adares of Shane's Hollow. Once rich, arrogant, unscrupulous, they exercised a power in the country, and for no good. Spendthrifts, they scattered their money; more dropped into their hands, and they spent that too. They acted so that the curses of the people followed them, and the sympathies of their own class dropped away from them. In their decadence they were too proud to accept any kind of work that was offered them to do. Little by little they have fallen. One by one their old neighbours and acquaintances—they never had any real friends, I believe—shrank away from them in disgust, and suffered them to wrap themselves up in their solitary pride. The people say a curse hangs over them ; and, faith it looks like it, for no effort that has been made has ever been of service to them. And efforts have been made. Some time ago Lord Aughrim offered them a comfortable cottage rent free as an inducement to them to come out of the decaying house and live like human beings, but they declined. They preferred their own house even as it was. In the course of years all the lands were sold away, parted with bit by bit, and it is through the charity of Lord Aughrim that they are not driven out of the Hollow. He leaves them the ruin and this piece of land immediately surrounding it—"

" Would it not have been greater charity to have driven them out ? "

" Perhaps so. But I suppose he is not strong-minded enough to apply his charity in such manner. The fact is, no one has cared to take the bull by the horns and struggle with their maniacal pride. Men have put money together secretly and had it conveyed to them by subterfuge, pretending it had come to them as a mysterious unpaid debt. But that sort of thing cannot always go on. Doctors and clergymen have paid visits to the house, and come out declaring that they could not risk their lives by returning there again, and that something ought to be done to relieve them of such a necessity. And yet nobody could propose the thing to do. Unless one were to set fire to the building and smoke them out they would not come ; and nobody likes to take the torch in his hands—"

For a few minutes the silence was unbroken, while Bawn recognised the ring of sincerity in his voice.

"Have they always refused help, openly given, rejected food, clothing, fire ? " she asked presently, in her gentlest tones.

" Always, and with such scorn that one fears to insult them in such a way. I have heard that a relative in a distant part of the country (for the credit of the North I am glad to say these Adares do not belong to us, only settled here fifty years ago on an inherited property)— I believe that a relative helps them from time to time by irregular doles, just sufficient to keep them alive and no more. Two or three of them have died. One man who broke his leg was stolen out of the ruin and taken to the poorhouse hospital, where he received a little humane treatment before he expired. Another died a horrible death, in a damp hole in the underground story. They said he was eaten by rats. No efforts would induce him to leave his lair. And the end came on him suddenly. But I am making you sick—"

"No ; I have heard it all before. I am thinking of that poor Miss Mave. She, I think, can have had no harm in her. What did she mean by shrieking in her pain for Arthur Desmond ? "

She had felt herself coming to this. She wanted to hear Somerled's account of the disaster on Aura.

" There you touch upon a special tragedy, and I think you have had enough of that for to-day. Cannot we talk about something pleasanter, even if it be more prosaic ? Are you getting good prices for your butter ? Will you promise to let me know if you suspect that any one is cheating you ?—I mean the tradespeople outside, for we are honest folks in the glens, as a rule. Is there anything wanting, in or out of your farmhouse, that I can get for you ? "

" I dare say there are many things, but at present I only want to know about that special tragedy. I am interested in the woman I have been visiting ? "

" I do not wonder. Doubtless she had, as you say, no harm in her, except the harm that springs from weakness of character, and weakness sometimes amounts to a crime when the weak person lives among the wicked and makes no effort to do anything but drift with them. It sometimes becomes the crime of women in this way—"

Bawn looked at him inquiringly. Was he going to condemn her for deciding against Arthur Desmond ? She held her breath.

" Inasmuch," continued Rory, " as she never appeared to wish to separate herself from the rest, and come forth into the daylight and face her reverses meekly, I hold her blameworthy."

Bawn turned away her eyes again. She knew deeper depths of weakness in Mave Adare than he was thinking of.

" But the tragedy ? " she said.

" It is a story in which our family is entangled, and

we never speak of it. Not that I have any particular feeling in the matter. I was born about the time of my uncle and namesake's death, but my grandmother still keeps a terribly vivid memory of the occurrence which was the greatest sorrow of her life. For her sake chiefly, and also because ghastly things are best forgotten, we do not refer to the murder of Roderick Fingall by Arthur Desmond, who at the time was engaged to this unfortunate Mave Adare."

"And part of her weakness, the weakness you have spoken of as characteristic of her, her crime of weakness, as you say, was in her allowing herself to be persuaded that her lover had committed this deed."

"Is that your conclusion?" he said, with a smile. "It is a woman's one, and generous, but there was no doubt, I believe, that Desmond was guilty."

"I have taken up a different impression."

"How? Why?"

"From the moment when I first heard the tale I felt that Desmond had been the victim of a plot."

"You heard it before?"

"From different quarters. I wanted to hear it from you—from a Fingall."

"Then I have had nothing new to tell you. Every peasant in the glens knows the whole history: the crime, its motive, and its consequences. The motive was part jealousy, part greed for money. My uncle stood between Desmond and a fortune—"

"Which actually fell to Luke Adare."

"I see you are really in possession of all the details," said Somerled, looking at her in surprise.

"I have been putting them together and piecing them out. It occupies me when I am lonely in the evenings—when my butter is made. We have no such tales of old families in America, you see, Mr Fingall, and so you must take my curiosity and earnestness over the matter as a product of the New World. Betty Macalister, who lives with me, is a firm believer in Arthur Desmond's innocence, and perhaps she has bitten me with her faith. Arthur Desmond has become a living hero to me, and I feel some ardour in clearing his good name."

Rory began to feel jealous of this shade of Arthur Desmond. If she would only occupy her evenings in thinking of him, a living man, with no interesting guilt upon his head! But he must be careful to keep such wishes to himself.

"I am sorry for the sake of your romance," he said, "that Mave Adare's lover will not come out of any court, even that of your charitable consideration, with clean hands. Do not look so serious over it. I did not know you felt so strongly—" as an incomprehensible expression of pain contracted her brow.

"Am I feeling strongly? It is my way."

"Is it? I wish it would come my way, then," thought Somerled.

"Well," smiling, "I am going to talk as lightly of the story as you please. One thing you can tell me. Did any one see Desmond commit the crime?"

"Certainly. There was no doubt about that."

"Who saw it?"

"I believe it was some of those wretched Adares. Of course they were respectable then."

"And good?"

"I cannot swear to that."

"Not after the account you have given of them to me just now? I think—I will make a bet of a yellow lily out of yonder pool—that it was Luke Adare who whispered away Desmond's good name."

"But Roderick Fingall was killed by him."

"Might it not be that he had fallen from the cliffs?"

"Hardly. I am afraid you will have to give up your hero. Desmond, from all I have heard, was a passionate and grasping fellow. He was too well treated, inasmuch as the thing was allowed to slide, and he got off to America. I hope, for the sake of the interest you take in his case, that he fared there better than he deserved—"

Bawn had risen up; her eyes flashed, her lips opened to speak; then she abruptly turned away and struggled to recollect herself.

"What a woman to love a man and stand by him!" thought Rory. "Well, if I have no other rival than this poor red-handed ghost, I will e'en try to be patient and bide my time."

And then he watched her as she walked a little apart from him, skirting the edge of the nearest pool, with a look on her face which he could not fathom. As the linen of her dress stirred in the breeze about her shoulders and feet, he thought her perfect enough in form to personate a goddess—Demeter's daughter, fresh and fair; or, even more fitly, Demeter herself, making the corn to grow, and the grass to thicken, and the fruit to ripen wherever she set foot. That look on her face which troubled him and seemed to push him away from her gradually failed from her brows and mouth, and as she stopped to pluck the amber lilies (whose colour was in her hair) she looked towards him with that involuntary softening of aspect which was the true source of any hope he cherished. With so much natural kindness in her towards all things, how could she continue to be hard to him? He admitted that she puzzled him more than ever. So little impressionable, so prosaically steadfast to her own simple, homely desires; so strong to conquer the weakness of her heart towards him (for there had been, he insisted, a weakness in her heart towards him that time on board the steamer); so clever in carrying out the intention with which she would not allow him to interfere—a determination merely to live solitary among these hills and to improve the manufacture of butter. And yet, in the midst of her serenity and her strength, here she was taking side passionately with an accused man, dead or blotted out from the world, of whom only a dark memory was left to the living whom he had wronged.

This last trait seemed to show her in a new light, as one who would take up fantastic ideas, a creature of imagination, impassioned, capricious; and the surprise of the discovery did not disgust him with her. He liked to think she was capable of change, for might not the next change sway her heart towards his? As he watched her he felt satisfied to think that Fate had drawn her wandering feet unawares and led them into his neighbourhood, that out there was her home, while his was over yonder, and that there was time in the years before them to win her love. Now here she was coming back with her gold-headed sheaf, and, nothing could be less flighty, less fantastic, more equable, more serene than she looked. She had forgotten the dreary shade of the unfortunate Desmond.

"Is it not curious to think," she said, "that these lilies have been going on budding and blooming every year all through that tragedy, and so near it, and even now are noway tarnished by it? For the tragedy is not over yet—not while that poor woman lives," she added, to cover her real thought, which was, "not while you and I live, who must remain parted by the cruel, ineradicable belief which exists as to Desmond's guilt."

"They are as fresh and as brilliant"—examining

them—"as though no wicked lie had ever poisoned the air that nourished them."

So she was still thinking about it. How persistent she was, whether in making her way to Ireland or in championing a ghost! Only for that look, which, unconsciously to herself, seemed to promise so much yielding where she entirely loved, a man might be afraid of her. Somerled was not afraid of her, though he wondered at her.

"Nature does not afflict herself with our tragedies," he said, replying to her as she stood sunning her eyes in the glory of the lilies. "If she did she could not keep herself so fresh, so tranquil, so ever young and strong for our benefit. We could not lay a tired head in her lap; her hand on the brow would have none of the healing touch it possesses. It is because our passions cannot wither her up, because her atmosphere is not charged with our storms, that her airs and dews have their power to soothe, that her rivers and fountains regenerate us."

As Bawn listened, she sat down again near him. "And yet there is surely a sympathy," she said. "Would you not believe that the trees in, yonder, knew all about the tragedy of the house and its inhabitants?"

"Yes; but that will not hinder their blooming on through years to come, and sheltering gladly—who knows?—perhaps a troop of sturdy children, a complete contrast to the wretched samples of humanity whom now they screen and pity, long after this hideous ruin has been levelled with the ground. This uncanny Hollow may one day be a singing grove, and people will wonder that human tribulation could ever have harboured in it. I grant you the sympathy all the same, though, for I have often thought it is that sympathy with us, that experience which has enriched without blighting, which gives Nature her mysterious influence over the soul of man."

There was again a long silence of some minutes, during which Bawn was thinking of her father's good name, swept away for ever with those ruins, while the birds sang, and children shouted, and the Hollow bloomed. Presently she said:

"Is it not believed that Mave Adare was convinced of Desmond's guilt, like the rest?"

"Certainly she proved it by her action. She never raised her voice in his defence, so far as I have heard."

"Well, then, in the course of years she has changed her mind."

"How so?"

"To-day she said a few words that carried this conviction to me. She cried out: 'Go away, Luke, and let me speak to him! Let him touch me with his finger and the pain will be cured!' Was it not a remarkable appeal, impossible if she believed him to be a murderer? It was rather like a Catholic's desire for the touch of a martyr—"

"You think she looks on him as a martyr."

"What do you think?"

"That she is a crazy woman now, and that the past supplies her delirium with fancies."

"You are terribly bigoted."

"If it would please you I would almost try to say what I do not think. But you would find me out, and it would not satisfy you."

"Nothing matters but truth."

"Nothing."

19

CHAPTER XXXI.

AN INVITATION.

AT this moment the sound of voices came towards them—not the tones of a peasant chiding his stray beast, nor of adventurous children who had wandered out of the straight way home from school, but the murmur of ladies' conversation, the last sound to be expected in these solitudes. Before they had time to wonder Lady Flora appeared in company with her young friend Manon, Major Batt following in their wake. A clump of thorn-trees had hid the approaching party till they suddenly came face to face with Rory Fingall and Miss Ingram.

Lady Flora put up her eye-glass and surveyed them both, especially Bawn, ejaculating, "Dear me!" in a tone of great surprise, while Manon turned away her head with a frown which spoiled the charming effect of her exquisite French costume. Major Batt hastened to pay his respects to Miss Ingram, over-heated and almost breathless as he was by having travelled through rude byways to which his feet were unaccustomed. Bawn and Rory had risen from their seat on the trunk of the tree, but slowly, as noway startled or disturbed.

Lady Flora had never yet addressed a word to Bawn, even at Castle Tor, and she was not going to recognise her now, when she had caught her in a most unbecoming and audacious proceeding—taking a solitary ramble with the master of Tor, a gentleman far above her in station of life. She had never liked Bawn, had never meant to like her; intended always to maintain her opinion, and prove it in the end, that the American girl was a bold creature with whom it was unfit that the family of her landlords should associate. She had come to this place at considerable pains to herself, to see whether she could not strengthen her cause against Miss Ingram by finding her in precisely the position in which she had now been discovered. There is no knowing what little bird of the air had hinted to her that Rory and Bawn had already met and conversed in Shane's Hollow, and that to-day they might possibly do so again. Thus it was that Lady Flora Fingall had penetrated to these unfrequented wilds, and now felt herself rewarded for her trouble. That Rory, who, by all the laws that regulate the fitness of things, ought now to be busily engaged in persuading Manon and her fortune to remain in and renovate and adorn his faded ancestral halls, should be frittering away his time walking and talking with a low farming girl who happened to have a striking face and that peculiar colour of hair which Lady Flora would have given three new gowns a year to possess—that Rory should so behave went to illustrate the fact that men are unaccountable and reckless in their ways, and often need to be managed for by the Lady Floras of the world. She would talk to him by and by, and meantime she thought it no harm that Manon should be a little jealous, just to keep her from tiring of the monotony of life at Tor. At present her object was to humble Miss Ingram and to gain a pretext for barring her out from all future association with the family.

"There must be something in the air to-day that draws the feet of friends one way," said Rory. First I encounter Miss Ingram in this out-of-the-way place,

and now we have another meeting quite as unexpected—"

"I suppose those are your cows," said Manon to
Bawn sweetly, having shaken off her frown, and once
more making the most of her beauty and her attire,
"and you have come here to look after them. That
must be a troublesome part of your business."

"I am sorry to say they are not my cows," said
Bawn, laughing; "I wish they were—especially that
red one. But I indulge in the extravagance of a herd."
She would not give any explanation of her presence
there. Rory, she thought, had said enough. But
Manon was no longer attending to her. She had
caught sight of Sorley Boy.

"Oh! what a beautiful dog!" she exclaimed. "Mr
Fingall, it is yours, I know, for I have seen it with you.
I am going to ask you to give it to me for my own."

"He is no longer mine," said Fingall, smiling; "I
have given him to Miss Ingram. He looks after cows
and sheep even better than his mistress."

"Oh! but I am sure another dog will do as well for
that, and I have taken a fancy to this one. Miss Ingram
will give him to me, of course, if you wish it."

It was her little way of snubbing Bawn. She thought
her host could not, even for politeness' sake, refuse
anything to a guest in his house. Here would be a
triumph, however little it might really mean.

"Can't be done," said Rory quietly. "The fellow
would bite any one who attempted the transfer. I will
get you a dog, if you wish, Miss de St Claire."

"I don't care for dogs in general, only this one," said
Manon, with a splendid fire in her dark eyes as they
turned on Roy. "I positively must have him."

Somerled caressed the dog's head. "What does Miss
Ingram say?"

"I don't think I could part with Sorley Boy," said Bawn, smiling. "Besides, it is not good manners to give away a gift. You ought to have spoken sooner, Miss de St Claire."

"You see you must be content without coveting your neighbour's goods, Miss Manon," said Rory. "I will find you a dog."

But Manon had turned away and taken a step towards Flora, who, while pretending to admire the scenery through her eye-glass, had not lost a word of the conversation.

"That young woman must be put down with a high hand," she thought; and then Major Batt, who to-day was a nuisance even to Lady Flora, and had joined her on the road, whether she would or not, began to talk.

"Ladies," he said, "I could not have secured a better opportunity—aw—for putting a little proposal before you. The weather is so charming—aw—and Lisnawilly is looking well—a small fête, a garden-party—that sort of thing—might not be amiss. If you will all favour me with your company on Thursday. Lord Aughrim has promised, and one or two others—"

"How delightful," cried Lady Flora, glad of a diversion; and Major Batt was restored to favour. She rapidly considered what Shana had got to wear. What a nice opportunity for Rory to attend on Manon! "Really, it is sweet of you, Major Batt, to arrange such a treat for us."

"So good of you to approve of my little effort. Miss Ingram, I hope, will also give me her approval and her company?"

Lady Flora's eye-glass fell from her eye, and she remained transfixed with surprise and displeasure. Now or never she must put down this presuming young woman into her place.

"I don't think Miss Ingram's engagements would allow of that," she said," slightingly.

Bawn glanced at her. Though her first impulse would have been to decline the invitation, she could not now restrain a mischievous desire to horrify Lady Flora by accepting.

"I shall not be particularly busy on Thursday," she said, quietly. "I do not churn till Friday."

Lady Flora made an indescribable movement, expressive of disgust.

"Then I shall confidently expect you," said the major, rejoicingly.

"It may rain," said Bawn, "or I may be too busy. Otherwise I shall be happy. Ah! here is Peggy, coming to fetch me home!" as, to her relief and surprise, the woman was seen coming through the dilapidated gate. "My little cart is waiting for me beyond the pass. Good morning—"

With a bow to all Bawn walked away side by side with the gaunt figure of Peggy. She was aware that by and by she might regret her mischievous impulse, but meantime she was feeling exceedingly glad. Was not Sorley Boy still following on her footsteps? And here was his namesake and former master coming after them.

"You must allow me to put you in your cart."

"What will they say?"

"Anything they like. And mind you keep the promise you were brave enough to make for Thursday. I will see you safely there and safely back."

CHAPTER XXXII.

THE MAJOR ROUTED.

ONCE at home again, Bawn felt that she had wandered out of the straight and narrow path of her intentions in giving even a half-promise to appear at the garden-party at Lisnawilly. She was consenting to play the lady by mixing with these people above the station she had chosen, and also to behave like an American woman in going independently into a large company. And yet Somerled had urged her to go. Her little triumph sank into insignificance before that one fact that Somerled wanted her to be there. Prudence, she admitted, must assure her that his desire was a strong reason why she ought to absent herself; but she had come to a point when prudence seems unnecessarily severe.

Listening to Somerled's arguments against faith in Desmond's innocence, she had almost despaired of her enterprise; and now, looking back upon her experience of the day, she told herself that in all probability the wind and rain would sweep away that ruin before she could even attempt to accomplish her object. Everything was against her—delirium, dotage, the fierce and sullen temper of Luke Adare, and the savage isolation from his kind in which he had chosen to bury himself.

The death of those old people, likely to happen any stormy night, would deprive her in a moment of any faint chance, yet existing, of that happy confession of the truth for which she had so resolutely hoped. It might be that in a few months or weeks she should find herself quite defeated and obliged to disappear from this part of the world as unexpectedly as she had come into it. She would go off some early morning and never return. At Liverpool she would arrange with a solicitor to pay a year's rent to her landlords and a year's wages to her servants, as some amends for her capricious conduct, and then she would be heard of here no more. He was not likely to follow her to America; but if such a thing were to happen, she would there tell him her true story, and he would perceive at once that marriage was impossible between them. She thought she already saw the look with which he would turn away and take final leave of Desmond's daughter. After that she would devote herself, her heart and soul, her bodily strength and her worldly possessions, to the care of those poor Irish immigrants in America of whose hard case he had taught her to think.

This was the future which she now looked in the face, and, recognising its coldness and barrenness, she asked herself should she not meanwhile enjoy this one day's pleasure which was so pressed upon her? Under the influence of such a feeling she wrote to Paris for a dress of plain white woollen material and a bonnet to match; but when the parcel arrived she was busy in her dairy among her maidens, and had returned to her senses, and resolved that she would not go to the party. The box was pushed out of sight, and when, on the morning of Major Batt's fête, Shana and Rory Fingall drove up the little by-road to Shanganagh, they found Bawn feeding her chickens, bare-armed, in the sun.

"What! not ready?" cried Shana, springing from the car.

There will be time enough," said Rory, looking at his watch. "Miss Ingram, let us feed the chickens while you dress."

"I am not going," said Bawn, standing before them, hatless, with eyes and hair full of the sunlight.

"Oh, nonsense!" said Shana, "after our long drive to fetch you! And I had to get up so early to be ready for so much travelling."

"It would be better not," said Bawn, relenting. "Why should I be so foolish as to step out of my own sphere?"

"It won't do your sphere the least harm, and will greatly improve ours," said Miss Fingall.

"Miss Ingram, I will give you just half an hour to dress," said Somerled. "Meanwhile, can I milk the cows, or anything of that kind?"

"Thank you. The only thing you could do for me would be to prop up my failing common sense, and that—"

"I have no intention of doing—at least in the way you are thinking of."

Bawn looked from one to the other of her friends and said slowly, "It is quite unwise, but I will go," and disappeared into the house to get ready.

Shana reflected, as she walked about and admired Bawn's efforts to make a garden flourish round the bleak little farmhouse, that probably most of Bawn's reluctance sprang from a difficulty about dress. But what did it matter? thought the girl. Any clean calico would be dress enough for beauty like Miss Ingram's, and nobody would expect her to be fine. Great was her surprise when Bawn stood in the doorway looking towards her shyly, dressed in the faultless array of white which she had found in her box.

"Where did it come from? You look like a princess. Are you a princess in disguise? I have thought of that before," said Shana delightedly.

"All woven of milk," said Rory, surveying her with

wonder and approval. "Miss Ingram can work any sort of magic in her dairy."

"Shall I do?" asked Bawn. "I asked for something plain. I am afraid it is a little too nice."

"Nobody will think so, except perhaps Flora," said Shana, laughing, as they seated themselves on the car, and Bawn found herself spinning along the roads, too happy almost to speak, and not daring to look back at the cast-off rags of her prudence and common sense which she had left in her little room with her work-a-day apron and gown.

Lisnawilly is a fine old place in a lovely nook of Glendun, and Major Batt had some right to be proud of his gardens and lawns, as well as of the valuables he had collected to adorn the interior of his house; and, taking into consideration all these pretty possessions, a good income, and his own great personal attractions, the major looked on himself as an enviable man, and greatly to be coveted as a son-in-law by any mother of marriageable daughters. But he was fastidious and cautious, and always on his guard against the too presuming ambition of the women of his acquaintance. Successions of girls had bloomed into matronhood around him, and in each case of the marriage of one of his favourites Major Batt had assured himself that he had had a lucky escape. Some charm had been, to him, wanting in the graceful creatures who had been found fair enough by other men. He spent most of his time driving about the country, paying visits at houses where there were ladies, and occasionally he opened his gates and invited the fair creatures to come in and see what good things were in store for that happy feminine being who might eventually persuade him that she was worthy of his hand. Meanwhile he enjoyed the thought that he was a fastidious man and an object of much

hopeless adoration. When the little party from Shanganagh arrived he was surrounded by the *élite* of the
county—Lord Aughrim and his mother, Lady Crommelin and her six daughters, the Hon. Mrs M'Quillan
and five young women, daughters and nieces, Colonel
Macaulay and three Miss M'Donnells, &c., &c. Lady
Flora Fingall and her husband, Manon, and Rosheen
were among the crowd when Bawn appeared, looking,
as Shana had said, like a strange princess in her simple
white attire, her only ornaments being her golden hair
and the bouquet of roses which had found its way to
her hands since she had left Shanganagh.

As these people all knew each other *ad nauseam*, the
appearance of a new face, and such a face, took them
by storm. There was general curiosity to know who
she might be, and for various reasons the host and the
Glenmalurcan people were careful to keep their own
counsel. "A fair American—Miss Ingram ; come to
spend some time in the neighbourhood," was the
extent of the information vouchsafed by Major Batt.

Seeing the strange behaviour of Rory and Shana,
Lady Flora was careful to keep her own counsel. For
the credit of the family it must not be known that they
were associating with a farming-girl who rented Shanganagh and made her own butter for the market. The
pleasure of the day was over for Flora as she saw Lord
Aughrim and Major Batt rivalling each other in attention to Bawn, while Rory kept hovering in her neighbourhood, giving only a passing politeness to Manon
and herself. "There is something wrong about that
girl," she said to Manon, "and I will find her out, or I
am mistaken in my own capacity."

"I like American women ; they are always so rich,"
said Colonel Macaulay, who believed himself a wag,
and speaking to the eldest Miss M'Donnell, who had

not a penny; but then she was thirty and plain, and he did not imagine she could give a thought to herself.

"In this case the riches are absent, I think," said Lady Flora sweetly.

"All the gold on her head, eh?" said the colonel. "Pity." And then he asked to be introduced to Miss de St Clair, with whom he walked away to join the lawn-tennis players.

Bawn acknowledged she could not play, and stood talking to her two evident admirers, Lord Aughrim and Major Batt, while Rory attached himself to the unimportant Miss M'Donnell, and in the pauses of her unexciting conversation about botany he observed the effect Miss Ingram was producing on the county generally.

Would her holiday end like Cinderella's ball, and would she, after this, hide herself in her farm-house and be seen no more by these people who were making such a fuss about her? It was the season of garden-parties, and, despite a little jealousy, some dowagers were thinking of inviting her to their bowers and tea-tables. How would it all answer with her butter-making, were she to get her head turned by their civilities and take to queening it about the country in that ravishing gown? She would have lovers in plenty, thought Rory, and some of them might touch the heart which he had found so hard. He began to regret the urgency with which he had insisted on her coming, and his replies to Miss M'Donnell grew a little vague. Was it only the other day that he and she were sitting in Shane's Hollow, as much apart from the world as if nobody lived on the globe but themselves He began to wish Lord Aughrim and Major Batt in Dante's Inferno, with Miss M'Donnell and botany to contribute to their amusement. How composed and unruffled she

looked—now sweet and serious, now blithely gay!
She was able to entertain both her admirers, and at the
same time to keep them in awe of her dignity. Strange
girl! Where had she come from? In the backwoods of
Minnesota how had she learned to conduct herself like
this? After all, how little he knew of her! A troubled
thought of how successfully she had always denied him
her confidence clouded his face, so much so that his
gentle companion perceived she had failed to hold his
attention and desisted from her meek endeavours to be
politely agreeable. Being accustomed to this failure,
she did not resent it, though it gave her a little familiar
pang. She withdrew and attached herself to an elderly
lady friend, and Rory found Lady Flora at his
elbow.

"Rory, I am surprised at your indiscretion with
regard to that American young woman. Mark my
words, you will regret it."

"May be so. I admit she is a woman eminently
calculated to cause regret to a good many men," he
answered, smiling. "But by the way, Flora, why do
you allow Alister to flirt so much with Miss de St
Claire?"

"Oh! come, are you jealous, after all?" she said,
brightening. "I must say Alister knows his duty to a
stranger better than you do."

"He has not done half the duty that I have done.
If you only knew all my fetching and carrying for Miss
Manon, mornings and evenings! And doesn't she know
how to take it out of a man! But all work and no play
—you know the rest."

"So the other is your play. Cruel play to Miss
Ingram, perhaps. Pity she does not hear you."

"Put it out of your head, Flora, that Miss Ingram
cares in the smallest degree for your humble servant."

"She is very deep, I think. She knows when to encourage you, and when to throw you over."

"She has never encouraged me. She has done no one any wrong. But I warn you, Flora, that a woman's tongue might work her mischief."

"So it might," thought Flora; but she did not acknowledge to herself that hers would be the tongue to do such harm.

"I want to tell you," she said, "that I am planning to have a picnic before this glorious weather breaks."

Rory reflected that Bawn would certainly not be asked to that party, and so he was indifferent on the subject, and merely said:

"Indeed!"

"Yes, and I want you to be nice with Manon. She admires you so much. And you know she is a charming girl, and such a fortune! There is Colonel Macaulay. How he would like to be in your place! And he is much richer than you."

"That is not saying much," laughed Rory. "Well, Flora, out at elbows I may be, but I am no fortune-hunter."

"Think of your ambition to go into Parliament. How are you to gratify it?"

"Not by bribery, Lady Flora. Come, let me get you a cup of tea or an ice, to refresh you after all the fatigue of this planning for a beggarly, thankless cousin. That's the way to describe me, isn't it? But if you don't talk any more about Miss de St Claire's money and admiration for me, I will promise to help her over the wet places in the bogs at your picnic. Only don't, for heaven's sake, talk to her of the poverty of the Fingalls and my admiration for her—"

Having seated her at a tea-table in Major Batt's drawing-room, and left her among some matronly acquaintances, Rory effected his escape, and, not seeing Bawn anywhere, walked away to the lawn-tennis ground. Shana and Willie Callender were among the players just then, but soon grew tired of the game and moved together to a distant part of the grounds. Among the various sauntering couples no one observed them, or could have guessed from their manner that there was a secret engagement between them.

"Shana," said Callender, "I can't endure this state of things any longer. It is not only that I do not see you, but that I feel like a sneak in not speaking boldly to your brother."

Shana turned pale. "If you could speak to my brother without giving our fate into the hands of my sister-in-law, I would gladly allow you to speak," she said ; "but Flora could ruin us."

"I have applied for that appointment in New Zealand," said Callender, "and if the answer be favourable —but, Shana, how can I take you away from all you love, perhaps to hardship ? When I think of that I almost give up hope."

"You may give up what you like, so that it is not me," laughed Shana. "I should grieve to leave Rosheen, and Alister, and Gran, and the children ; but wherever you go I will go. Some day we should come back—"

In the meantime, Lady Crommelin and her six daughters having waylaid Lord Aughrim and carried him off from Bawn, Miss Ingram had been beguiled indoors by Major Batt, and afterwards led by him through many apartments, where he displayed his various treasures, beautiful, curious, and antique, to her unaccustomed eyes.

It is impossible to say how much Miss Ingram had risen in her host's estimation since Lord Aughrim had so evidently and highly approved of her. Major **Batt** was beginning to feel that his hour was almost come, and alternated between glows of eagerness and shivers of caution, like a patient in fever and ague.

If he did not secure her at once he feared that Lord Aughrim would become a formidable rival. Lord Aughrim was just the sort of man to fall in love suddenly and want to marry at once. He had been twice engaged to actresses, and twice bought off by his mother, who might now, possibly, be thankful to have any one so every way nice for a daughter-in-law as Miss Ingram. The word " American " would answer all questions as to birth ; and was it not the fashion to marry Americans ? As for money, his lordship was, like Major Batt himself, rich enough to dispense with fortune in a bride, if he thought her worth the sacrifice. And the major was rapidly coming to the conclusion that this woman was worth her weight in gold.

Nevertheless he did not forget her poverty and her lowly station, and still felt returning qualms of fear that he was going to throw himself away. After successfully defying the feminine world for so long, it did seem hard to yield so soon before this maiden without birth or money. And yet—

"Miss Ingram, do look at this cabinet of curiosities. Here is a cup belonging to the Borgias—er—out of which all their victims were poisoned ; gold crusted with jewels. The poison was secreted in the bottom of the cup, and, by pressing a spring underneath, it was ejected from its hidden recess into the beverage contained in the cup, in sufficient quantity to destroy the drinker. Clever and neat, wasn't it ? Here is a vestment worn by the Venerable Bede ; not *beads* on the embroidery, however—ha ! ha !—but real gems, I can assure you. Perhaps you admire Indian carving.

Now, this took an Indian fellow a hundred years to finish—'pon my honour! Saw him at it myself—"

"When he was quite young?" asked Bawn, with demure wonder.

"No, come, Miss Ingram. Ha! ha! ha! Capital! He was old then, but I was told he had been young. If you come upstairs I will show you my pictures. There is a Titian that has a striking resemblance to you."

Bawn went up and saw the pictures.

"You see my house is rather complete, Miss Ingram. I may say—er—all it wants is a "—"mistress," he was going to say, but a spasm of dread choked back the fatal word, and after a long breath he added faintly, "a Claude Lorraine."

"I thought we saw one just now," said Bawn.

"Oh! ah! true. I meant a second Claude Lorraine, of course. Many collections have one, but few have two. This, now—ah—is the Titian I told you of. Isn't she a golden-haired beauty? I have long wished that I could make her Mrs Batt. But one cannot marry a woman upon canvas, now can one?"

"Hardly."

A glance at her face and her answer reassured him, for he had gone off into another fit of trepidation. And yet surely he was not going to let her depart without making his proposal. He would be brave and make another attempt. He could see Lord Aughrim from the window, looking about for some one, probably Bawn.

"All these beautiful things I have been storing up for years, Miss Ingram, for the gratification of the lady whom I might chance one day to make mistress of this house. You will easily understand how hard it has been to meet with a woman worthy enough—"

20

"I am sure of it, Major Batt. Could any one be worthy?" ("of so dreadful a fate," she added to herself.)

"I don't know that. I will not say there may not be one. Many have thought themselves admirably fitted—"

"Doubtless all these beautiful things have broken many hearts, Major Batt—"

The major glanced at himself in a strip of looking-glass, and wondered if she meant, with a sly flattery, to include him among the beautiful things. Yes, he was certainly an imposing-looking person.

"A man can only marry once, Miss Ingram. In case of death he sometimes gets a second chance; but that is a thing that cannot be depended upon. I would rather, on the whole, be satisfied with my wife" (here he surveyed Bawn with entire approval, and thought of how she would look in velvet and diamonds—the Titian would be nothing to her), "and keep her—"

"That will be a very pleasant reflection for Mrs Batt," said Bawn gravely; "but don't you think we had better go downstairs again? I think I should like another cup of tea—"

"Stay, Miss Ingram, stay. I can conceal it no longer. I fear I have unwarrantably tantalised you, kept you in suspense; but the truth will out at last. It is you whom I intend to make mistress of Lisnawilly—"

Bawn's lips parted, and her eyes opened wide with astonishment, but she quickly regained her presence of mind.

"Oh!" she said, smiling, "that is your intention, is it? I am very sorry, for it is not mine." And, sweeping him a curtsey, she tripped downstairs before him, and happily met Rosheen and Rory coming to look for her.

CHAPTER XXXIII.

NO DESERTER.

THE next day Bawn was herself again—the fine lady was gone, and the dairymaid was at her work. Into its box the pretty white dress was packed, with a regretful thought that she could never venture to wear it again. How excellently it had played its part, making her look, for one day at least, Somerled's equal in other people's eyes! How proud she had felt walking into that company with him, and feeling that she was accepted as one of themselves! It had happened once, and could never happen again. She had been quite mad in yielding to a craving for one day of delight, for taking into her heart a happiness which could never be driven out from it again, but must remain there to rust itself into sorrow.

She had finished her work and taken a book in her hand—a little old volume which had belonged to her father, and was the only book of his she had ventured to bring with her. It was so small it lay in her pocket when not at the bottom of a trunk. Now she sat with it high up in the orchard under the old apple trees, the whole wonderful panorama of the glen before her, and the mountains behind and in front of her.

It was a splendid day in early autumn; soft, rich colours seemed to move along the valley at her feet as the sunshine shifted from one lovely spot to another. Bawn's heart was full of a tumult that was half trouble and half joy. She had opened the little book to try

and still her storm by the magic of such meek lessons
as are to be found between the covers of the *Following
of Christ.* As she read she was back in the old home in
Minnesota, with the pathetic fact of her father's life-
struggle looking her in the face. She read on, hearing
his voice between the lines, and stopping occasionally
to close her eyes and recall his face, his look, his gesture.
What a miserable, weak creature was she who had
audaciously thought herself so strong—

Here she was interrupted by the voice of Betty Macalister, who came to tell her that Miss Fingall had
arrived to see her.

Bawn sprang up, dropped her little book, and,
hurrying to the house, found Shana standing in her
parlour with flushed cheeks and shining eyes.

"Miss Fingall! I am surprised."

Shana closed the door and flung herself on Bawn's
neck with a sob.

"I have come to you for refuge. I have run away."

"Oh! nonsense!" said Bawn, but holding her fast.

"I have run away," persisted Shana. "Not from
Alister, but from Flora. She sha'n't say such things to
me again. You will let me stay here with you, won't
you?"

"Of course I will. Only too glad to have you, so
long as it is right. But sit down and don't cry any
more. I shall get you some tea, and you will tell me
all about it."

Shana did not cry for long. She was so angry at the
fresh memory of whatever wrongs had driven her away
from home that her tears were dried by the heat of her
passion as fast as they fell. When she had rested
awhile and swallowed Bawn's tea her courage revived
and it was with a characteristic flash of the eyes that
she said, looking straight at her friend:

"In the first place, I must tell you I have been engaged to be married for some months unknown to my family—just as long as you have been here. The same day brought me the word I had hoped for from my love and relief from that dreadful feeling of beggary—"

She stopped, and after a few moments' silence Bawn said :

"I saw you with some one the other day."

"That was he," said Shana rapidly, a lovely smile breaking through the clouds of her anger. " Isn't he—"

She stopped short, looking at Bawn with a mixture of pride and wistfulness.

"He looked good," said Bawn quietly. "I should have said that neither of you need have been ashamed to confess the engagement."

"Ashamed!" said Shana, colouring all over her face. "No; I must make you understand. He is my equal in every way, in truth, in age, in want of means, and in determination to work for money. If I had had a mother I should not have kept my secret from her for one day, or even a father; but I have only a brother, and that, being freely translated, means a sister-in-law. The equality in want of means is the only equality Flora recognises between us. I did not need her assistance to see the difficulty it makes. I knew that my brother must be divided in the matter between his kind heart, that would sympathise with us, and his prudence and desire for a peaceful life, which would make him give way before his wife. I was not going to have his life turned into a purgatory on my account, and so I held my tongue and merely regulated my own conduct as I thought my brother would wish to see it regulated. I refrained from seeing at all the man I had promised to marry, and we did not meet except at rare intervals during our walks, when my sister or the children were always sure to be present. We believed that if we were both patient a way would be sure to open up for us. I would not let him speak. Do you think I was wrong?" asked Shana abruptly, with a look half-pleading, half-defiant.

"I would rather you could have told. I hate secrets," said Bawn, heavily aware of her own secret as she spoke. "But I can't say how wrong you have been till I hear everything you have done."

"The enormity I have committed is this: I have known for some time that he had been promised an appointment in New Zealand and that the opening was a fair one. When I saw him the other day nothing had been settled about it, but this evening I got a note asking me to meet him at the end of the avenue, as he had something particular to say. What he had to say was that he had secured the appointment, and wanted permission to speak to my brother to-morrow. I walked up and down the road with him for about a quarter of an hour, and then I got a message to say that Flora wanted me."

Shana's eyes flashed once more as she stopped, and was evidently living over again the scene that had followed her sister-in-law's summons.

She sprang up, and, clenching both her little hands, walked about Bawn's parlour with a step as light as a bird's, and the whole of her slight figure wrapped in a flame of indignation.

"I won't tell you what she said to me. My brother was away from home or she would not have dared. Clandestine meeting—secret understanding—beggary—scorn—contempt—shamelessness, were the heads of her discourse. Gracious heavens, how did I endure her!" cried Shana, quivering all over in another fiery whirlwind.

"Not very patiently, I am sure," said Bawn, sitting at the table with folded hands, watching her. "Come, Miss Fingall, confess that you did not spare her neither."

Shana calmed down instantly and stood still.

"True," she said, "I answered her fiercely. I said things to her that she will never forget. I am sorry, as she is Alister's wife."

"And then you rushed away here. Why did you not go to Tor, to your grandmother?"

"Several whys," said Shana in her most matter-of-fact manner. "In the first place, I couldn't have got so far to-night. In the next place, it was you I wanted. Gran is a good old soul, as good as gold, and kind-hearted, but she has some notions of her own which will not alter. She is a person of—"

"Fixed ideas?" suggested Bawn.

"Yes; and one of her beliefs is that girls ought never to take their affairs into their own hands, and ought always to be guided by their superiors."

"Indeed!" said Bawn reflectively.

"Flora tries her often enough, and yet she does not know my sister-in-law as I know her, and I could not grieve her by hurling my story at her as I have hurled it at you. By the time I see her I shall have calmed down and made the best of it. I will not vex her. I have never done so. Gran has had a great trial of her own. Her favourite son was murdered by his friend—"

Bawn's face, which was turned on her full, the eyes listening, full of thoughtful interest, suddenly changed, so that Shana, even in her passion, could not but notice it.

"What is the matter ? Have I tired you, frightened you ?"

Bawn passed her hand over her face, trying to sweep the look off it that had startled Shana.

"I am not easily tired or frightened. You will learn that when you know me better. I have been thinking probably your good grandmother is right in holding that young women ought not too rashly to rush into planning their own fate."

"That is the last remark I should have expected to hear from an independent woman like you," said Shana. "However, whether she is right or wrong, I shall never desert—" and her voice trembled, as if tears were coming.

"No, you are no deserter. Neither am I," said Bawn. "That is a different thing. And we can't mend matters by looking back."

CHAPTER XXXIV.

GRAN TO THE RESCUE.

EARLY the next day, when Bawn was about her business in a field near the gate of her farm, a young gentleman met her, and, removing his hat, asked if he had the pleasure of speaking to Miss Ingram.

"You are Mr Callender, I think."

"Yes. May I see Miss Fingall?"

"No."

"She is not ill?"

"No."

"She is here?"

"Yes."

"Then why cannot I see her?"

"Because I have her in charge for her family, and I cannot allow her to receive visitors."

"O Miss Ingram, are you against us, too?"

"Anything but that. But I think you are both a little reckless. It will be time enough for you to meet when Mr Alister Fingall returns home."

"That will not be for several days. And she has been made to suffer for my selfishness. You must let me speak to her for a few minutes, Miss Ingram."

"I will not, Mr Callender. I shall not let her know you are here. But I will tell you something now which I dare say is not new to you, and ought to keep you happy even if you are obliged to be patient for a day or two. You have won as true and brave a heart as exists on earth. Be careful how you give her more to suffer than must needs be. Any folly you lead her into now will be counted against you both."

Callender reflected a few minutes with a clouded countenance, then brightened up and exclaimed:

"You are right. I will not see her. Thank you for your friendly advice. Good-morning."

Then Bawn went in and told Shana who had been there and what had been done.

"It was cruel of you—cruel and inhospitable. He will think they have frightened me. He will be sure I have given him up. I wanted to tell him—"

"I told him all you wanted to say. It was much better from me than from you just at present." And then Bawn left Shana again and returned to her fields, reflecting on how wonderful a thing is human love. To her Willie Callender looked but a fair, smooth-faced boy, not much of a raft to cling to on the broad ocean of life; and yet here was Shana ready to give up home and kindred and follow him to exile in New Zealand. Unbidden the tall figure and steadfast eyes of another appeared before her in contrast, but the vision was quickly waved aside. What right had she to draw contrasts between men, to decide which was most worthy to be loved—she who would never have a mate?

Another summons soon brought her from her work. A carriage was at her gate, from which descended Gran, assisted by Rosheen, and Manon de St Claire. A lengthy epistle, sent post-haste last night by a man on horseback, had brought the old lady all the way from Tor to remonstrate with her truant grand-daughter.

As Bawn came to the gate to receive her Mrs Fingall observed her keenly. So fair, with such a look of innocence and good sense, was it possible this young woman could be compounded of cunning, audacity, and all those other bad qualities which Flora had represented her as possessing ?

"Miss Ingram," she said, looking Bawn full in the eyes, "I have come to see my granddaughter, who has been very naughty. I am obliged to you for giving her a night's lodging—that is, if you did not know of her intention, had not encouraged her to leave home."

"I would not turn away a dog who came to me for shelter," said Bawn gravely. "As for the rest, Miss Fingall will tell you everything better than I can."

Shana was standing in the middle of Bawn's parlour, her little hands wrung together and a hundred changing expressions flying over her face, when Gran appeared in the doorway.

"Shana, what is the meaning of all this ? "

Shana had been on the point of flinging herself into the old lady's arms, but Gran's stern tone restrained her.

"Why have you run away from home ? "

"Because Flora drove me out," said the girl, stoutly. "I should have gone if it had been to sleep in a ditch. As it was, I was thankful to come here."

"And you received Mr Callender here this morning. We met him—"

"He was here, but I did not see him. I wish I had ; but Miss Ingram would not allow it."

"Humph!" said Gran, and was silent for a few moments. Then she began again :

"Shana, you are the last girl in the world from whom I should have expected sly conduct."

"Right, Gran ; but don't speak in the past tense."

"I am sorry I must. To engage yourself secretly to any man, however worthy—"

"He is worthy! he is worthy!" broke out Shana.

"O my God! how Flora spoke of him! I wonder I did not kill her!"

"Shana, I am shocked beyond measure. I cannot listen to you. Come, you had better come home with me at once. You must return to your senses before we talk this matter out."

"I will go with you, Gran; you are not Flora. After you have scolded me you will listen to me. You may say anything you please of me, so that you do not attack Willie."

"My dear, I do not want to attack him. He always seemed to me a nice, gentlemanly, gentle young fellow. Why could you not have trusted the old woman with your secret, Shana?"

Shana stared and burst into tears, dropping her face into the old lady's lap.

"O Gran! Gran! I wish I had. But I did not want to bother you, and I was in dread of Flora. And I did not see him or hear from him. It was very hard, but I thought it was right; and then to be called *clan*—ugh! the horrid word, I can't say it. Only because we waited and said nothing. And last night he just came to say he had got his appointment, and might he speak to Alister. And Flora—"

Gran sighed. She could imagine all the rest. So this was all. She stroked the girl's hair and reflected.

"But, Shana, my love, are you so ready to leave us all for New Zealand?"

"I love him, Gran, and I can be of use to him, and he wants me. Anybody could wear Major Batt's jewels and things," said Shana, looking up contemptuously and flinging back her hair, "but nobody but me could make Willie happy, or help him on through the world."

"Major Batt?" said Gran, inquiringly.

"Yes, that is what Flora is so wild about. She had

a fancy to marry me to Lisnawilly.   And I assure you,
Gran, even if I did not hate him, he would not think of
me.   It is Miss Ingram."

" Humph !" said Gran again.

" I will go home with you, Gran, **as soon as you please,
and I have written a letter to Alister."**

CHAPTER XXXV.

KIDNAPPING.

ALL that was over. Shana had been carried away to Tor, and Bawn's thoughts had again set towards the mysterious Hollow. As the autumn, with its brilliant colours streaming down the glen, and its glorious clouds banked behind the mountains, advanced in beauty, the nights became more stormy; fierce squalls would swoop down from the high crags about midnight, burying the moon in darkness, and playing mad pranks over hill and dale till the morning dawned. On such mornings Bawn wakened unrefreshed after uneasy sleep, in which she had imagined the entire collapse of the old house in the Hollow under the assaults of the gale.

"Betty," she said, "I have made up my mind to do something, and I rely on your help."

"Anything I can, misthress."

"I am going to bring Miss Mave Adare here, to this house."

"Misthress !"

"I will give her my room, and I shall sleep on the sofa here till we see further. The truth is, I can't rest for fear of the roof falling on her."

"God bless you, misthress, for taking that thought! But she will not come."

"I am not so sure of that, Betty. Coming here to me, knowing how I feel for her, is different from going to the poorhouse hospital. I may as well do it as soon as I can, for I shall have no peace till it is done."

Betty looked at her young mistress, shook her head many times, clapped her hands, groaned, frowned, finally snatched Bawn's hands and kissed them, and, throwing her apron over her face, fled from the room.

In this pantomime she expressed her still lingering disgust at the Adares, her dislike to having the dreadful invalid in the pretty little, cheerful house, her pity for and sympathy with the sufferer, and finally her rapturous appreciation of her mistress' superior charity and courage in proposing to harbour so undesirable a guest. Bawn, looking after her, felt a sudden sting of pain as the old woman's last action reminded her of the words in her father's notes descriptive of Betty's conduct towards himself when every other creature had turned against him ; of how, having offered her sympathy, she had flung her apron over her face, turned into her house, and shut the door. Desmond's daughter now longed to follow the old woman and hug her, but prudence restrained her from behaviour so remarkable.

That afternoon she proceeded, in a peculiar, very old-fashioned, almost obsolete vehicle known in Ireland as a " covered car," to the Hollow, consenting to a longer journey than usual in order that she might bring the conveyance near to the house. Alighting in the avenue, she bade Andy wait there till she signalled him to approach the door; then, meeting Peggy by appointment, she dived with her into the ruin as before.

The interior looked, if possible, even more appalling than when Bawn had visited it last. There had been much rain in the nights, and a slimy wetness was over everything, making it doubly dangerous to take a step in any direction. Each of the larch tree props had carried its own stream of ooze from above, to lie in a pool around it on the spot where it had been fixed.

As they climbed the shaky stair Peggy kept assuring

Bawn in low tones that Miss Mave would never consent to come with her, and that if she attempted to carry her off the brothers would rise out of their dens and interfere.

"I am going to try, however, Peggy. Just you go presently and ask Mr Luke if he has any objection to his sister's taking a drive with the lady from America. Put it in the most respectful way you can."

As soon as Bawn was seated at Miss Adare's ghastly bedside Peggy went on her errand. It seemed to the girl, sitting there face to face with this awful example of death in life, that the woman in the bed was more weird, more skeleton-like, more pitiable even than she had appeared to her at first. And yet when the poor creature greeted her with weak cries of welcome, and at the same time made a sort of effort at lady-like courtesy which had an indescribably strange effect in the midst of such surroundings, Bawn soon found her more human, more real than she had once thought possible.

"Now, Miss Adare, you are coming with me for a drive. I have got a conveyance for you, and the air will do you good."

"Out?" shrieked the poor creature. "I to go out! Oh! you must be dreaming or raving. I rave and I dream myself, and I can understand it. You think you see me riding and driving as I used to do, my dear—indeed I used, though it is so long, long ago, and seems only yesterday."

"But I mean not yesterday but to-day, Miss Adare. Peggy and I will wrap you up in cloaks and rugs—we have brought plenty—and you can't think how sweet the air is."

"Oh! don't I know? Why do you tell me? Why do you talk about it? What have I to do with fresh air now? Leave me alone with the rats and the owls.

I see them, my dear, at night—indeed I do, and there is a rat I am afraid of—and ghosts ; though I don't mind them so much—"

She was wandering now, but Bawn recalled her to herself by saying : " You will come with me, I know, Miss Adare. You won't disappoint me ? "

"You don't know what you are saying," shrieked the sufferer. " Luke never would permit such a thing."

" Peggy has gone to ask your brothers," said Bawn gently. " And I am sure they will not be so unkind as to refuse. Here is Peggy."

"I saw Mr Edmund, ma'am, and he spoke to Mr Luke, and then he comes an' he says, 'We see no objection,' says he, 'to a lady goin' out for a carriage drive wid another lady. We only hope our sister will not be kept out too late in the night air,' says Mr Edmund, says he."

There was in all this assumption of pride and stateliness something so ludicrous and grotesque, when contrasted with the utter desolation of everything she saw around her, that for a moment Bawn was overwhelmed by a sense of complete unreality, of impossibility, such as she had experienced before in that place. She sat silent, struggling with an inclination to laugh and weep together, when Miss Adare's voice recalled her attention to the facts of the situation.

"That is a different thing, Peggy. That puts it in quite another light. And oh! how glad I should be to go. But how will you get me out of this, Peggy ? O my God! Shall I really go out into the sunshine again?"

"No doubt of it," said Bawn, triumphantly, and she stood up and looked at Peggy for a hint as to how to proceed, while the weird invalid stretched out her lean arms towards them from under cover of her hideous çanopy.

21

"Go down now, miss," whispered Peggy; "away and hide among the trees, and I'll get Mr Edmund coaxed to come and help me down wid her. You an' me couldn't be sure of not lettin' her fall. If he doesn't see you he'll do it. When we have her in the car I'll call ye."

Bawn obeyed, having first helped to wrap Miss Adare up in the comfortable clothing she had brought, and slipped away and left Peggy to manage the rest.

She went across the sward, away under the great spreading trees, and hid herself behind the trunk of one of the giant beeches. "I shall be within earshot here," she thought, "and shall neither see nor be seen." Scarcely had she taken up her position, however, when she saw and was seen by one person whom she had not expected—Rory Fingall, who was approaching from the direction of the old garden.

"Miss Ingram!" he said, coming quickly near and standing before her.

"Hush!" she said. "Stand well behind the tree, or you will spoil everything."

"What do you mean? What are you doing here, if I may venture to ask?"

"Kidnapping."

"Kidnapping what? Crows, owls, rats? Have you set snares anywhere?" looking round.

"I am kidnapping Mave Adare. Hush! it is a deep-laid plot. She thinks I am taking her for a drive only, but I mean to carry her off to Shanganagh and keep her."

"You are a strange girl."

"Am I? So strange that I do not like waiting calmly to see a broken roof drop down upon a fellow-creature. I ought to have been born in a place like Ireland, in order to be able to take such things philo-

sophically. In America we have no such roofs and no
suffering humanity mouldering away under them un-
heeded. My 'American audacity'—I think that is
what I heard a lady call it—has prompted me to
make a raid upon this ruin while it is still accessible ;
to snatch a poor woman from a horrible death."

"It ought to have been done some other way. I
have been thinking about it; but meanwhile you have
acted, though not, I fear, much for your own comfort.
God bless you, Bawn! you are good—"

"Don't praise me," she said, throwing back her head
quickly and thinking of all the motives that had
been at work within her, leading her to do what she
was doing. "I am not so good as you think."

She had drawn back a step, as all her mixed feelings
toward the creature she was now trying to benefit, her
abhorrence of Luke Adare, her disgust and dislike to
even his, Rory's family, rose distinctly in her mind.

"You are not to credit me with goodness—you who
know so little of me. I am doing what I choose to do,
and that is about all."

"It is true that I do know little about you, but I am
willing to believe all that is noblest and best."

"Ah!" she said, with sudden sadness, "don't believe
too much. Judge me not at all till I am dead or gone
from here. But hush-sh-sh! I hear them coming
Oh, pray, pray do not let yourself be seen!"

He moved a step and they stood close together,
hiding behind the great beech-tree, wrapped in its blue
shade, looking out on the golden moss and grass, and
through rifts in the drooping foliage ahead of them,
away to the blackened and broken and sun-pierced
garden-walls—a wide well of sunshine against grey and
distant woods.

"Who are coming? By what witchcraft are you

conveying Miss Adare down those crazy stairs in the teeth of her brothers' opposition ? "

"Her brothers have consented to allow their lady sister to go for a carriage drive with another lady. It is with their permission ; indeed, Mr Edmund himself is carrying her down, and that is why we must not be in sight. They will not endure to be seen. Have you ever beheld these men ? "

"Edmund I have seen ; Luke, never. Edmund occupied himself for years breaking stones in a hole at the back of those ruined out-buildings, which he sold for the mending of the roads. He used to keep up a little play in the matter by pretending he had bought the stones, and would oblige us by supplying them when wanted. I found him out by accident, poor old fellow ! coming on him one day as he stood on the top of his heap of broken stones, with an old riddle in his hands which he had just emptied on the heap. He was a very queer figure—tight clothes and stockings, an old dress-coat, and a little black skull-cap on his head. He is a small man with a large white beard. When he saw me he vanished, and never came near me again for an order for stones to mend my roads. He is not the worst of the Adares."

"I can see him now. He is carrying his sister into the car. He is not so well dressed as you describe him. He looks like a little wizard. Now she is in, and he has fled back to his den. Good-bye, Mr Fingall. You are on your way home, I suppose. So am I. You had better not come near the car. Good-bye."

She gave him her hand hurriedly ; he raised his hat, and she was gone.

Miss Adare was lying in the car, wrapped about with the rugs and cushions Bawn had brought for her. At first Bawn thought she was dead or in a swoon, till

Peggy whispered that the creature was only tired with the moving, and was resting herself. Bawn had read somewhere of a waxen image, made to the likeness of a human creature, to be wasted before a fire for purposes of witchcraft, and she thought now that such an image, already half-wasted, might this poor Miss Adare have been taken for. The car proceeded slowly, the sweet mountain air penetrated through the open door of the vehicle, and the ghastly invalid breathed deeply and revived. A wild glance from Bawn to Peggy, a murmured "Don't keep me long or they will be angry. O my God, the delicious breeze!" and she lapsed into seeming death. Later in the evening she recovered from her trance, and saw Peggy sitting by her bedside in Bawn's little lavender-scented bed-chamber.

"Peggy," she whispered, "where are we now? Are we in heaven?"

"No, ma'am, not just yet," said Peggy, cheerfully; "but, faix, I think we are the next door by. It's at home wid the American lady ye are. You're goin' to stay on a visit wid her."

"O Peggy, I must go back at once. Luke will never allow it. O my God, what will Luke do to me?"

"Now whisht, ma'am, and lie back and rest yerself. Sure the gintlemen gave me leave to lave ye for a while wid her. Never fear but she made it all right wid Mr Luke. It's herself knows how to bring wan thing straight along wid another, so she does. An' she has the beautifullest little taste of a supper ready for ye, an' if ye don't try to eat it ye'll just break her heart."

Then Peggy had to go home, and Bawn and Betty stood at the kitchen fire holding council over their charge.

"We must nurse her between us, Betty. And you'll be good to her?"

"Och, ay! I'll do what I can, poor body! But she needn't ha' come to this if she had 'a' stood up for Mr Arthur. It's the good home he would have give her somewhere, forbye rottin' herself off the face o' creation wid damp and hunger."

"Well, Betty, I may tell you that I think she believes now that your Mr Arthur was innocent."

"Thank her for nothing," said Betty, scornfully. "It's time she found it out. But never fear, ma'am; I amn't such a haythen monstier as not to be as good to her as I can."

The little household settled to rest; the strange guest had relapsed into her swoon of peace; only Bawn was awake and up, feeling still too much excitement after the events of the day to be ready for sleep. Her fire was expiring, her lamp burning low; she had opened the blind to see the horn of the late-risen moon appear above the curve of the black-purple mountain opposite, and was walking up and down the floor, her hands locked behind her back, her head upraised, thinking over her success with regard to Mave, her conversation with Somerled, his persistence in meeting her. Did he wait and watch for her, or was it always chance that brought him through the Hollow just as she appeared in it? Say what she might to her own heart, it would feel glad at the sight of his face and the sound of his voice. By the pain that passing gladness left behind it let her expiate the sin of her weakness in loving one of the family of her father's enemies. As for him, he had been warned, and why could he not keep out of her way? Why could he not stay at Tor and learn to love Manon de St Claire? And then Bawn paused in her walk, and her heart winced. Of course that would naturally be the end of it all. After she had gone back over the sea she had so confidently crossed; after the ruin in the Hollow had been levelled with the ground, burying under it the ashes of the Adares; after the Hollow had bloomed again, as Rory himself had predicted it would bloom, in that time Rory would dwell among these hills a contented man, husband of a suitable wife.

Bawn, choking a little over the sadness of her own fate, acknowledged that she had one cause for self-congratulation, in that she could not be called on to witness that admirable state of things; that there was still a merciful ocean within reach, ever ready to carry her back to the unknown.

The moon had risen above the mountain-ridge, a clear crescent, and clouds were drifting towards it. Bawn stood in the middle of the floor looking at it, her meditations broken by the fancies it suggested. It was the diadem of the queen of night, more like half of the golden ring that romantic lovers break between them; but here a long, streaming cloud, dark and filmy, with a weird outline, reminding one of a banshee with outstretched arm and threatening finger, came hurrying towards it, pounced on the jewel, and hid it in her mysterious draperies. At the same moment a loud sob escaped the wind, which had been whispering complainingly around the corners of the house, and among the old thorn and alder trees, and a sense of uncanny solitariness just touched Bawn, who was accustomed to sleep early and soundly, and had no timorous associations with the dead of night.

She had just shaken off the feeling, and was approaching the window to draw down the blind before taking refuge in her pillows, when something she saw struck her intelligence like a blow and froze up the

blood in her veins. A figure was distinctly visible at
the window, strange and uncouth; a ghastly and
malignant face was pressed against the pane, the
hollow eyes straining out of their sockets, trying to see
into the room. A pair of long, claw-like hands
grasped the upper sash, and the figure seemed to hang
by them, as if weak and wanting support. Dusty-
looking hair, in shaggy masses; long gray jaws and a
hungry mouth—these details of the countenance im-
printed themselves on her imagination as the creature,
whatever it was, crushed itself against the window-
frame, like a beast struggling behind the bars of a cage.

"Good God!" muttered Bawn, and waited to see if
the thing would try the fastenings of the window or
make an attempt to get in. If so she would quickly
shut the shutters and put up the bar. But if this
should be only some poor tramp, hungering for a sight
of fire on the hearth, or out of mere curiosity peering
with all the fascination of the homeless for a look into
a home, why need she be afraid of him?

He might be a lunatic escaped from control; and if
he were to prove too quick for her? She thought of
the horror of a midnight alarm, the possible effect on
the sufferer within, the excitement of her women, and
decided to fasten the shutter without further delay.
As she stepped to the window the pale ray of the
moon, now free of the gathering clouds, fell on her and
revealed her dimly to the creature outside the pane,
and its gaze, fastening on her at once, seemed straining
to distinguish her features, as if the sight of the hollow
eyes was imperfect as well as the light. Bawn's vision
being strong, she was able to see more clearly than
before as loathsome a human face as imagination ever
pictured. A ravening desire for something unattain-
able, a malignant cunning, a wicked despair, were the

passions suggested by the expression of the visage. Shuddering she put forth her hand and drew the blind, and then stood waiting for the look or word that might possibly follow her action. Some minutes passed before she ventured to lift a corner of the blind and look out, and when she did so the strange visitor had disappeared.

She closed the shutters quickly, saw to all the fastenings of the house, and hurried to bed, where she lay long awake, unable to blot the image of that ghastly countenance from her mind. Something inexpressibly evil in the eyes that had strained in at her had stifled the ready pity in her breast. Whosoever her strange visitor might have been, she felt certain that he was nothing good.

CHAPTER XXXVI.

SLANDER.

AUTUMN was beautiful at Tor, even though the melancholy sea of Moyle muttered its never-ending dirge with white lips, wailing for the children of Lir, and round the knees of the great Tor breakers climbed and were repulsed with a noise like recurrent peals of thunder. Bright-eyed, bare-kneed children hanging into the ravines almost, as it seemed, by the hair of their heads, snatched the last of the luscious blackberries growing in those long, slanting hollows, yawning greenly from cliff to wave; and if sunset overtook earlier than heretofore the footsteps of a chilled noon, its own magnificent pageantry gave sufficient splendour to the day. As Shana sat up in the little turret-room, that had always been hers at Tor, looking through the long, narrow slits of her windows, the twilight fell so fast that Scotland's cliffs had taken their forbidding, war-like aspect, and the beacon-light on Mull of Cantire had sprung up red as Mars before she had finished the letter she was writing to Bawn. The letter was to tell her friend that her happiness was secured, that Gran had proved herself a darling, that Alister and Willie had come to a satisfactory understanding, and that, consequently, New Zealand was soon to be the writer's home.

Having befriended her so far, Shana's twilight failed utterly, and as she would not go down stairs till the moment of dinner, because Flora was in the drawing-room, punishing Gran (so Shana put it to herself), the girl lit her candles to finish the epistle.

" I cannot go to see you now," she wrote, " because they will not let me, and I must be obedient after all I have gained ; but I shall never forget your goodness in taking me in, and standing up for me, will never believe anything against you, no matter what they say."

For much was being said by Lady Flora to Gran in the drawing-room, where Flora had seized the leisure hour of the day to pour out her tale of long-cherished distrust and dislike of the tenant of Shanganagh. Gran was listening to her with bent brows and compressed lips, that showed her vexation of spirit. Seeing that Flora was intent on saying much that she was not willing to hear, the old lady tried to speak her own mind beforehand.

" I saw nothing about her conduct that was not nice. You have been too much displeased with Shana to allow the child to tell you the part Miss Ingram played in the matter. She knew nothing about the affair till Shana ran to her, and then she received her as a matter of course. When all this annoyance has subsided you will be in a better position to do justice to that girl—"

" Justice ! " echoed Flora, contemptuously. " My dear Gran, you are running away with the question. I am not going to make vague accusations against Miss Ingram. If you will kindly listen to me with patience, I will tell you my various reasons for wishing that this young woman should be kept at a distance by the family, if not warned to return to where she came from. You are not, perhaps, aware that she is passing under an assumed name—"

" No ; I am not aware of it."

" But I can tell you it is true. Manon is my authority, and I hope you will admit that she, at least, is an unprejudiced observer."

" Humph!" said Gran.

" If you doubt that, your mind is indeed becoming warped. I never saw any one behave so nicely, seeing that her lover is being actually enticed away from under her very eyes.

" Who is her lover ? "

" Why, Rory, of course."

" That fact, if fact it be, is as new to me as the false-ness of Miss Ingram's name."

" You do not see everything, and Manon has given me her confidence. You do not appreciate the com-pliment she pays him. That a girl, with such a fortune as hers, so well born, so handsome, should be willing to content herself with Rory at Tor—"

Gran bristled. " In my young day a girl did not make any such contentment known until she was in-vited from the right quarter to do so. I do not think the more of her for displaying it. I repeat that I have never seen Rory take the attitude of her lover."

Flora made an impatient gesture, as if to say that Gran, choosing to be blind, could not be expected to see.

" You were always prejudiced against her."

" Perhaps I was, a little, till I saw her ; but I can truly say that since then I have been ready to believe her everything delightful. Of late the idea has grown upon me that she can be sly."

" Nonsense!" said Flora.

" I do not like her hints about Miss Ingram. This fancy about the name—"

" The story is simple enough. On the day you went for Shana to Shanganagh, Manon and Rosheen were left to walk about the farm with Miss Ingram while you talked to—to the future Mrs Callender," said Flora, with an ill-natured little laugh.

"I believe they were. What then?"

"At the foot of a tree Manon picked up a small book, apparently dropped and overlooked there, and saw on the title-page Miss Ingram's Christian name—if so outlandish a name can be so described. With it was joined a surname which was not Ingram. Manon would have kept the book, but the young woman espied it in her hand, and demanded to have it on the spot."

"What was the name in the book?"

"Oh! it began with a D, and was of a different shape from Ingram. Manon, being a foreigner, could not seize it at a glance. But she knows it was not Ingram."

"The book may have belonged to her mother, or to her mother's sister for whom she was named. Names go in families, especially out-of-the-way names like Bawn."

"I guessed you would see a way out of the difficulty," sneered Lady Flora; "but from her anxiety to regain possession of the book Manon felt assured there was something wrong. And so do I. My idea is that she is married."

"You think she has escaped from an unhappy marriage to bury herself here. Poor young creature! I sincerely hope you may be wrong."

"I do not say what I think, but I know that a married woman ought to make it known that she is married, and that if she does not there is something amiss. For a long time I have felt that there was something wrong about this so-called Miss Ingram, and her behaviour from beginning to end has gone to prove it. She arrives here in the most unprotected manner, pretending to be a common farmer's daughter, when it is evident she belongs to quite another class. She

passes under an assumed name, and before many weeks
has all the gentlemen in the neighbourhood flying after
her."

"What!"

"Certainly. In the first place, she scraped up some
kind of acquaintance with Major Batt on her way
here, and ever since she arrived he has not been the
same person. Before that he was desperately in love
with Shana, and I had it from her own lips that she
was willing to accept him. In the course of a few
months he forgets her very existence, and Shana, in
despair, is going off to New Zealand, assisted in such
madness by the so-called Miss Ingram's co-operation
and advice. Lord Aughrim, I know on good authority,
has been to visit her; and as for Rory—I must say,
Gran, on that subject your obtuseness is very remarkable. He meets her frequently. Did I not tell you
before, that Manon and I met them in the fields near
Shane's Hollow, in the most out-of-the-way spot,
perfectly suitable for a romantic walk—"

"Stop, Flora, stop! You bewilder me."

"I want to enlighten, not to bewilder you. I have
put the matter bluntly before you."

"Very bluntly."

"Only that you may speak to Rory and warn him
before he is hopelessly entangled. A person whose
conduct is so open to criticism is not a suitable wife for
him."

"But I thought you said she was married," said
Gran.

"Oh! I dare say she is divorced. In America that is
very easy."

"But—Lord Aughrim! Major Batt! Which does she
intend to marry?"

"The lord, no doubt, if she can. If not, the wealthy

Major Batt; failing all else, the not very wealthy but otherwise desirable master of Tor. Now, I have put it all before you, Gran, and I leave it to you to work the question out. My own suggestion would be that Miss Ingram should get notice to quit before Manon returns to Paris, believing herself rejected for the sake of a creature—"

Here Flora rose, and, dropping her energetic manner, sauntered to the window, finally quitting the room without another word, leaving Gran leaning back in her chair, her brow on her hand, thinking deeply of all she had just been forced to listen to.

Unwillingly she was obliged to admit that there might be something in all that Flora had been saying, and that to save Rory from great unhappiness later she ought to speak to him about the matter. Of all her grandchildren Rory was the dearest. More like a son than a grandson, he had lived with her always since the death of his parents, except during his years at college. He was named for that favourite son who had met his death so cruelly on Aura long ago, and there was, besides, something in his nature that was akin to her own. An unfortunate marriage for him would be an unspeakable misfortune to her. A penniless, friendless girl, working for her own independence, however praise-worthily, was not exactly a mate for the representative of the elder branch of the Fingalls. She could not bear the idea of his marrying for money; the mere sound of Flora's voice was enough to remind her that even an income drawn from the three per cents might be secured at too great a sacrifice of domestic joys. And yet his noble ambitions were dear to her heart. She had hoped to see him in Parliament, feeling sure that wherever there was a good cause to be worked for, all over the world, and especially at home, his vote and his energies would be at its service. Yet how, on this barren rock of Tor, was money to be found to enable him to gratify all his honourable desires?

He was too kind and conscientious a landlord to exact from his serfs that heavy toll on the land they tilled, which they must hunger that he might spend. She had often feared that he would never marry—that, following his philanthropic instincts, with such small means as Providence had placed in his hands, he would be satisfied to fill his good years with unselfish activity, and find himself, when too late to remedy the mischief, with a lonely hearth and heart.

Now Bawn's noble, candid face rose before her, and the old woman was ready to avow that the girl was as good as she was fair. But are faces always to be trusted? The world is deceitful, and American women are known, thought Gran in her old-fashioned way, to be strange. And there was Manon. Of the two countenances before her mind's eye she infinitely preferred Bawn's; and then the old woman sighed with a sense of baffled intelligence. Was she indeed prejudiced against Flora's *protégée*, and was any fair-faced stranger preferable in her esteem to the granddaughter of the friend of her youth? Manon would be suitable in birth and position, and her large fortune would put power into Rory's hands. Was not Flora right, after all, and might not Rory have been satisfied with Manon if the tenant of Shanganagh had never appeared on the scene? However that might be, the question now was of wrong and misfortune that might come upon the old house of Tor through Miss Ingram's possible dishonesty. It was clearly her duty to speak to Rory, and speak to him she would, even at the cost of exceeding pain to herself.

The evening passed slowly for her. Rory was be-

having admirably, said Flora, who flitted to and from
the billiard-room, where the young people were amusing themselves. He was taking great pains to improve
Manon's style of playing, and Manon was looking so
pretty. Of Shana and Callender Flora had less gracious words to say; and as her husband was also in
disgrace with her for permitting their engagement, her
remarks on his want of skill in the game were of a
cutting character.

That night, when Rory had gone to his own particular den to smoke and read in solitude after the
household had gone to rest, Gran gathered up her long
skirts and her courage, and climbed slowly and with an
anxious heart to her grandson's retreat.

"Gran! why, this is an unexpected pleasure!" cried
Rory, springing from his arm-chair and placing it at
her disposal. "Why did you not send for me? It is
too late for you to mount up here."

"No, no. I wanted to ask you quietly about this
affair of Miss Ingram and the Adares. Is it true she
has taken Miss Adare to Shanganagh?"

"Perfectly true. She has done at once what some of
us ought to have done long ago."

"What was impossible to us may have been made
easy to her, being a stranger. But it is a good deed,
though it may bring trouble on her."

"She is very good."

Gran felt puzzled how to proceed further. She was
ashamed of what she had got to say, and peered wistfully through her spectacles at the manly face turned
towards her with an expectant look in the eyes."

"Come, Gran, out with it! You have something
more to say to me."

"I have something more to say, and I would rather
not say it, only it appears to me now to be my duty.
This Miss Ingram, Rory, of whom you think so highly

22

—is it wise to see her so often, to concern yourself so much with her affairs?"

"I am hoping to make Miss Ingram my wife," said Rory gently, after a moment's pause.

"That is what I have thought," said Gran, quelling her agitation and trying to speak as calmly as he did; "and therefore I feel bound to warn you."

"Warn me of what?"

"Are you aware that she is living here under an assumed name?"

"No."

"I have heard that it is so. You will, of course, be able to ascertain whether or not the report is true. The evidence is hardly conclusive, I am bound to admit, merely that a different name coupled with her Christian name has been found in a book—"

"A clever suggestion!—coming, I should say, from Flora or Miss Manon de St Claire. And even granted that Miss Ingram should for some good reason of her own have changed her name, had she not a right to do so if she pleased?"

"It has been suggested that she is married."

Rory started, and grew a little pale under his bronzed complexion. Then he laughed and said good-humouredly:

"What an ingenious romance!"

"It has been observed that she is absolutely silent, even with the girls, as to her antecedents. Shana herself admits that she pretends to be of a different class from that to which she evidently belongs; that she has money for every purpose, though supposed to be working for her bread; finally, that she is seen to be somewhat light in her conduct—"

Rory walked up and down the room with a flushed and troubled countenance.

"I am not blushing for you, Gran," he said, suddenly

stopping before her, "only for some of your sex. I do not feel that I need defend Miss Ingram to you. All this is said by you against the grain, is it not? I need only say, for your comfort, that I have had better opportunity of observing Miss Ingram's character than either Flora or her friend, and that I believe in her. As to the lightness of conduct, it is a lie. If it be light-behaved to work hard, to improve every one and everything she comes in contact with, to make the wilderness bloom, and two blades of grass to grow where only one grew before, to feel for the poor and sick, to risk her life out of charity to a wretched dying fellow-creature, giving up her own comforts to nurse so unpleasant an invalid—well, don't you see, dear Gran, how atrociously ridiculous the entire charge must be? And as for your anxiety about me," he added, more quietly, "it ought to take the form of concern that the woman I love should completely deny and ignore my suit—"

There was that in his voice, as he broke off abruptly, which kept Gran silent for some minutes. In spite of her prudence her heart was cheered by his faith. Might it not be true that he had had better means of judging than those others; and, besides, being of a nobler nature, might he not possess a truer instinct? But yet ought she to venture to encourage him? Poverty is a stern fact. She must think of his honourable ambition.

"My lad," she said, "my heart goes with you. But think a little of your future. You had plans of your own. You hoped to be of use in your generation. Will marriage compensate you for all you will give up?"

Rory passed his hand across his brow, and thought a moment before he replied:

"When I formed those plans I did not expect to meet in this way the one woman I could mate with; and, though you affectionately call me your lad, I have

met her at a ripe age. I love her more, after all, than
Parliament and the emigrants, though I do not mean
to say that I lose sight of a career of usefulness among
the possibilities of the future. According to my theory
a noble wife will help a man more greatly than gold.
And now, dear Gran, you must go to your rest.
Trouble your head no more about Flora's inventions."

After she had left him Rory sat gazing at the wall
with the eyes of a man considering a hateful contin-
gency. He had spoken bravely, for he would share his
uneasiness with no one; nevertheless was it not true
that he knew absolutely nothing of this woman who
had gained such a hold upon his life? His memory
went back to her conversation on board the steamer,
and revived the strong impression he had then received
that some painful circumstance which she would not
allow to be discovered influenced her movements and
obliged her to reject his friendship. She had certainly
stated that she was not married. He remembered with
what evident surprise she had answered his question on
the subject. Could she, after all, have deceived him?
Could some strong and terrible dread have driven her
to a falsehood under which she might have thought
herself justified in taking shelter? Never for one
moment, he admitted, had she given him to suppose
that she might alter from the mood of mind in which
she had rejected him as a husband. Latterly he had
comfortably made up his mind to forget those strong
first impressions which had seized him on board ship,
which had seemed to surround her with mystery, and
place her in imminent danger. And now he asked
himself, What if they had been true, if behind her
frank, smiling aspect there lay the consciousness of
some erring or tragic past which practically deprived
him of a future? After all, what had brought her here

with her beauty and her breeding, to bury herself, if not some necessity for escape, to hide herself from something?

He sat half the night lost in troubled thought, and towards morning left the house and walked the cliffs, unable to shake off the fears that had laid hold of his imagination. If Bawn was not good and true, then good-bye to goodness and truth. His love for her was no boy's fancy to be replaced later by a more genuine feeling. He had passed the age for caprices, and, as he had said, in his ripe years he had met with the ideal of his manhood. His heart, his mind, his soul all approved of her, and everything in nature seemed to declare her worth. Her flowers bloomed, her beasts throve, her industries were productive, all that she touched prospered. The first time he had met her eyes they had revealed to him a spirit more noble than that of ordinary women. And here he paused, asking himself, was this not the very madness of love which poets rave of and wise men distrust? Had infatuation blinded him, and in looking on her did he see something which had no actual existence? In this state of mind he felt he could not breathe till he had seen her again, spoken with her, questioned her closely, and sat in judgment on her replies.

He forgot that as a man who had been rejected, who had never been encouraged, he had no kind of right to question her. He only felt now as if his very life depended on her answer. To-morrow he would go to her; yet where? Over and above the fact that she had forbidden him to come to see her, he could not, after all that Gran had said, insist on paying a visit at the farm. And now that she had Mave Adare under her roof, she had no longer a reason for haunting among the trees, and lingering about the fields that skirted the mysterious regions of Shane's Hollow.

CHAPTER XXXVII.

ESCAPED.

IF Bawn had cherished a faint hope that Mave Adare might yet regain strength of mind and body, and that from her she might learn something profitable to her enterprise, she was doomed to disappointment. The poor creature, all whose energy seemed to have been spent in her desperate struggle with lonely suffering in the ruin, had, now that she was in comfort and at peace, collapsed into a state of chronic lethargy from which she only wakened up occasionally to declare her belief that she was in heaven. All Bawn's gentle ministrations failed to win any demonstration from her except the whispered assurance to Peggy that in her absence she was tended by an angel.

"That is why I know I am in heaven, Peggy; and I am always going to ask about some one I wanted to meet here, but at the right moment I forget. The angel has a voice like his, and that is why I forget, because when the angel speaks I think it is Arthur himself, and I am content. But it is not himself. And I wonder he does not come to me, for I know he must be here."

Bawn, watching for these gleams of the spirit from the poor worn-out clay, and listening to the wild words, concluded that the invalid had recognised Desmond's tones in his daughter's voice, and she resolved to endeavour to gain some advantage from this fact. One night, sitting alone by Mave's bedside in semi-darkness she reflected on the means that might best be taken to coax some admission from her patient's lips; and as she watched the last vestige of the landscape without disappear from beyond the window, an idea came to her and she repeated aloud, softly but distinctly:

"Arthur Desmond! Arthur Desmond! Arthur Desmond!"

There was a movement in the bed, the waxen face turned towards her, and the eyes unclosed.

"Where is Arthur Desmond?" asked Mave Adare in a voice that sounded quite sane and conscious. "I have been looking for him everywhere and I cannot find him. Yet I know he must be here."

Bawn replied, almost without thought, so naturally did the words come:

"How can you expect to see him here, you who believed him guilty?"

And then she held her breath, fearing a burst of excitement or some wandering, meaningless reply; but, to her great surprise, the answer came distinctly and reasoningly:

"Because I have expiated my sin, through the mercy of my Redeemer, by long years of suffering, and both God and my beloved have forgiven me. I know you are an angel and I deserve your reproach, but there are thoughts between God and the soul which even angels do not see."

Bawn's heart melted within her at the strange, solemn, comforting words.

"You are right," she said. "You shall see Arthur Desmond presently. You are not in heaven yet, but in a place of peace that is close to it. In the meantime will you tell me why you ever believed him guilty? Who told you he committed that crime?"

The dying woman shuddered. "Luke said he saw

it," she said. "Luke thought he saw it. But Arthur's spirit came to me in the night, one of those terrible nights when the roof was falling in, and he told me he was innocent and in heaven. That is why I have been willing to suffer; that is how I am so content—"

She dropped back into her slumber, and Bawn was left in possession of the truth she had spoken. Luke had said he saw him do it. Then her instinct had not been at fault, and it was with Luke only she should have to deal. She sat for half an hour thinking intensely of the likelihood or unlikelihood of her being able to make any use of the knowledge she had just acquired. When and where could she expect to penetrate to the conscience of Luke Adare? Was there any hope that the tongue that had now uttered so important a revelation might yet direct her further? Suddenly feeling a desire to continue her thinking in the cool night-air, she rose softly, and, placing a small lighted lamp behind the bed so that the light might not disturb the sleeper, she went out of the room and out of the house, and felt the breeze quiet her pulses and brace her excited nerves. Having lingered a short time on the verge of the orchard slope, she had returned and was about to re-enter the house, when her step was arrested by the sight of a moving shadow, visible through the window, flitting across the walls within the invalid's room.

She had believed that Betty was in bed. Could that good woman have heard Mave Adare cry out in pain, and have got up to attend to her? Bawn went close to the window and looked in.

The gaunt, uncouth figure of a man, weirdly out of place in the neat chamber, was bending over the bed, and then followed a scene like the horror that happens in a nightmare. The intruder seized the sick woman's hand, and shook her by the shoulder, and called her by her name, till she awoke and lay staring at him helplessly.

He put his long arms round her and attempted to lift her out of the bed. And then her cry broke forth:

"O Luke! Oh! no. O! not back there!"

Then followed curses, stamping on the floor, and an unequal struggle: but suddenly the intruder, man or fiend, dropped his prey and stood listening. In doing so he turned his face now towards the door, now towards the window, and revealed to Bawn the same awful countenance that had looked at her through the pane a few nights ago. It was Luke Adare come to recapture his sister. Before Bawn had time to move Betty was in the room in answer to the patient's cry, and Luke, seeing his attempt was baffled, skurried away past her like a startled wild animal, and fled from the house.

The next minute Bawn was following him swiftly down the path to the orchard, calling him in a voice clear as a silver trumpet.

"Luke Adare! Stop! I have something to say to you!"

She expected he would fly the faster for her call, but he stopped, he stood still and waited for her.

"What do you want with me?" he asked roughly.

"I want you to come back and have some supper. You have allowed your sister to be my guest. Will you not accept my hospitality for yourself? It is late at night and you have far to go. It is not friendly of you to take leave of us like this."

"Curses on your falsehood!" he said savagely. "You did not get my permission to take her away and expend your insolent charity upon her. You were suffered to have the pleasure of her company for a carriage drive, and no more. Why did you not bring her back to her ancestral residence?"

Bawn could see but dimly the expression of the hideous face, which matched with the contemptuous fierceness and ludicrous pomposity of the creature's tone.

"It was late," she urged, "and your sister was tired, and there are reasons why I was proud and glad to receive her under my roof—reasons which I will tell you some day, if you will allow me to see you again."

"What are your reasons? Cannot you tell them now?"

"It is too late, for, since you will not come into my house, I must bid you good-night. But, believe me, you would be interested in hearing something I could tell you."

"It is false!" he shouted furiously. "I knew you were a coward and an impostor from the first moment I heard your voice. How dare you go about mimicking the voice, the very tones of—"

"Of whom?" asked Bawn, with a sudden leap of the heart.

"Of a reprobate long in his grave, no doubt, but who will not lie there always. Tush! do you think I am afraid of spirits? A man who lives with rats is not much in fear of ghosts. All I have got to say to you is this: don't dare to meddle further with the Adares than you have done. To-morrow I will make arrangements for bringing my sister home. And, after that, come no more to the Hollow at your peril!"

With this he turned from her, and the gray face, just gleaming with awful indistinctness through the darkness, vanished, and she was alone, realising with difficulty that she had held her first interview with Luke Adare—her first but not her last, as she assured herself in spite of his threats. She remembered with exultation how his conscience had already betrayed him. The vibration of her father's tones which was in her voice, which had perplexed without enlightening Gran, which had acted like a charm on the diseased imagination of Mave Adare, had evidently caught the ear of this wretch and aroused his hatred—a hatred for which there was no reason, but that it sprang from injury done by the hater to its object. Horror of the memory of the man he had ruined accounted for his hatred of herself. Oh ! if Mave Adare would but live, and prove a link between her and this monster !

Reminded by this thought of the position in which she had last seen the suffering woman, she went quickly back to the house and entered the sick-room on tip-toe. As she did so she was instantly aware of a new state of things. Betty was on her knees by the bed praying aloud, and the rigidity of the figure in the bed struck her fearfully as expressive of a ghastly change. The little spark of vitality that had lingered in the wasted frame of Mave Adare had been rudely quenched. The long-suffering soul was released and at rest.

" Och, misthress, sure she's gone ! " sobbed Betty rising from her knees. " The villain just frightened the life out o' her ! "

Next morning a scrap of ragged paper was found under the door, and on it was scrawled :

" The Adares were always buried by torchlight in their ancestral burial-place in the old graveyard at Toome."

Bawn rightly concluded that the words had been written by Luke Adare and were intended as an instruction for her.

" It was always one of their mad whimsies," said Betty. " You or me might be put in the ground while the sun was shinin', but not an Adare. They were always taken away in the night with torches, and the flames of their funerals could be seen over the country-side."

Bawn saw no reason why she should not act upon the hint, and arranged that her father's early love should be laid among her kindred in the ancient grave-yard, and by night. And there was one at least who did not think her action extravagant—the gaunt, ragged creature who followed the little procession unperceived in the darkness, and to whom it was probably a satisfaction that the ancient glory of the Adares was thus properly maintained in his sister's case to the last.

CHAPTER XXXVIII.

RUIN.

RORY, having resolved that he would speak plainly to Bawn, make one more endeavour to learn something positive concerning her past, was yet undecided as to the means he would take thus to try to obtain her confidence.

Thinking it all over, he came through the Hollow one wet, windy autumn morning, and was startled to see her standing under the beech-trees in front of the ruin, her shawl folded tightly round her, her eyes raised to the shattered windows, and an expression on her face and in her whole figure and attitude of the deepest and sternest despondency.

Her presence here on such a morning struck him as strange and inexplicable. Mave Adare was dead. In her she had expressed a deep interest, and on her she had expended her charity. What further did she seek in haunting this uncanny hole? How did she expect to reach or influence the half-savage old men who hid among these mouldering walls? What could she hope to gain by coming in contact with them? Why need she concern herself about them, and their sins, and misfortunes?

With his mind full of such questions he approached and saw her start of surprise, and her involuntary shrinking from him when she suddenly became aware of his presence.

She had just been realising the extreme unlikelihood

of any ultimate success for her romantic enterprise. Autumn gales, the forerunner of winter storms, had already set in, and she had hastened here this morning fearing to find the ruin reduced to a heap of rubbish and at last become Luke Adare's unholy grave. That the end had not yet come seemed a miracle. To-morrow, next week, would this miraculous delay be still prolonged? In the meantime his hatred of her presence and his suspicion of her identity would certainly keep him carefully concealed from her.

Was there any hope left of refuting that calumny which had blasted her father's life, and was now darkening her own by raising an insuperable barrier between her and the man she loved?—for, without further effort to ignore or deny the truth, she owned to herself now freely, that she loved him.

For that very reason she was bound to keep out of his way, to do him as little injury as possible, to force him to feel more and more assured that there never could be a marriage, that it was not natural there should be even friendship between them.

And so, suddenly seeing him beside her, she shrank from him. He saw the movement, and it hurt and angered him.

"Miss Ingram, forgive me for interrupting your meditations. I did not expect to find you here this wild morning."

"I can believe that," said Bawn, recovering her self-possession; "but the fascination of the place is too much for me. I cannot keep myself from coming."

"Are you not satisfied with the work you have done? What further do you imagine you can do?"

"There are other lives in danger in yonder."

"What are they to you? How can you expect to in·

fluence two obstinate old men? You cannot kidnap
them as you kidnapped their sister."

"I fear not. That is what I fear."

"Why should it be so much to you?"

"Ah!—why?"

"They cannot live long, in any case, and life to them
is misery. A sudden death might not be the worst
that could befall them."

Bawn shivered and drew her shawl around her, and
as she did so it struck Rory painfully that she had
grown thinner, and that there was a shadow of trouble
deepening in her face—that bright face which, even
one month ago, no one could have associated with a
sorrowful thought.

"Bawn," he burst forth, "for God's sake let them
alone! Put them out of your thoughts, and think of
yourself and think of me. I believe you come here
merely for an excitement; that you give your mind to
these wretched people only to keep other matters out
of it. You have some sorrow, some secret, and you
will share it with no one, not even with me, who love
you better than my life—me, whom you trust, whom
you love—"

She made a gesture to silence him, but she did not
speak.

"You dare not deny it. You know that you love
me. And either you have some terrible secret which I
have a right to learn, or you are breaking your own
heart wantonly, wickedly—"

He broke off abruptly, and after the storm of passion
in his voice Bawn's words came slowly, a mere whisper
of pain:

"It is true I have a terrible secret."

The rustling of the dead leaves and the drip of the
boughs on the path seemed to catch up the murmur
and spread it all through the Hollow.

"I have a hideous, intolerable secret," continued Bawn—"a sorrow that brought me across the sea and brought me here. I know what people are saying of me, and what you would ask me. Ingram is not my name, and I am not what I pretend to be. I thought to wash a stain off my real name, but I have lost hope, and stained it must remain, I have reason to fear. This is what I want you to understand. I thought I had made you understand it on board ship, but you have seemed to forget it."

"I have forgotten it. I will forget it again, if you will let me."

"I must not let you. You must keep away from me and think of me no more. If you knew who I am you would turn away and never ask to see me again—"

"That I will not believe till you tell me what you mean, till you give up talking in mystery, till you explain the exact meaning of your hints—your probably misleading hints. Girls have often exaggerated ideas of things. I myself must judge of your case. As for what others think or say of you, that is nothing to me so that you are personally what I believe you to be. If you tell me you are not good I shall conclude you are mad—"

Bawn gave him a startled look and coloured faintly.

"I do not think I am very good—not good enough for you," she said; "but yet I believe there is no wickedness in me so great that you could not forgive it. Yet the barrier remains, as you will one day admit."

"Why not give me an opportunity this day, this hour?"

"I cannot. On the day I tell you I shall go. I will not wait here to see you turn from me—"

"Turn from you! Bawn—"

"No! no! You must not come near me. There is

something that stands between. You must not look at me so—"

"I will not even ask to touch your hand, if you will not fly from me. But, however all this may end, Bawn, will you say to me just three words: 'I love you'?"

"To my sore sorrow I do love you."

"After that I will not lose you. You cannot dare to leave me."

"After that I must leave you all the more surely, but not until—"

She stopped and involuntarily cast an eager glance at the dripping ruin before them.

"Till what?"

"I cannot tell you; not now. I have already said too much. If you love me at all, let me go. Think of me as dead."

She turned away with a quick step, and he remained standing where she had left him. He felt it useless to pursue her. In this mood she was impracticable, and he feared to press her too far, to scare her to a longer flight, out of his neighbourhood, out of his reach for evermore. He had lost her once; he would not lose her again, if he could help it.

He remained pacing up and down the Hollow, reflecting on all her enigmatical words and looks. Flora, even Gran, would consider that he ought to be quite satisfied with her admissions, quite sure that she was one whom he could never think of as his wife. She had spoken of a stain upon her name which could never be wiped out, yet she had hoped to see it wiped out. How could that hope have any connection with her coming here? Had she come merely to hide, and from what? Was she waiting for tidings of some kind, in suspense as to the ending of a lawsuit, of an in-

23

vestigation, in expectation of somebody's death ? The
longer he pondered the more puzzled he became. Of
one thing he felt sure : he must let things drift as they
were drifting, unless he meant to drive her out of the
little harbour in which she had anchored. She had
said, and she was capable of keeping her word, that on
the day on which she told him the story of her antecedents and circumstances she must quit this spot and
be seen by him no more. He would not push her to
that alternative. At all costs he would be patient and
wait for her to speak.

After he had walked about, he knew not how long,
lost in his thoughts, the rain began to fall heavily, and
mechanically he moved into shelter of a gable of the
ruined house and continued his walk under cover of the
dense trees and the dismal stone wall, the monotonous
surface of which was broken here and there by a few
dilapidated windows. The gable was a remote one at
the back of the ruin, and the lower windows were evidently those of domestic offices, lumber rooms, pantries,
and servants' apartments. As Somerled passed one of
these he thought he heard a voice speaking loudly in a
peremptory manner, and he stood still in great surprise,
wondering from whence it could come. The wind was
high, and the trees kept up a soughing sound, crossed
every minute by the swish of the rain as it swept
through the heaving branches.

He thought he had been mistaken, and proceeded
with his walk, asking himself how long it would be
worth while to linger here in expectation of an improvement in the weather, when a second time the gruff
tones, unmistakably human and having a strange
suggestion of uncanny meaning, startled the silence and
solitariness of the place. This time he satisfied himself
that the sounds proceeded from a particular window,

small and low, and barred with rusty iron, out of which all the glass had been shattered long ago.

Convinced that this was the utterance of one of the self-imprisoned souls hidden in the ruin, he remained standing where he was, with some expectation of seeing a face come to the window, and of finding himself subject to the wrath of an Adare for trespassing on the ancient family demesne.

No face appeared, but after another pause the snarling voice went on, pouring forth speech so vehemently that Somerled's next conclusion was that a quarrel must have arisen between the two wretched old men in the ruin, and that he had accidentally come within hearing of the sound, while out of reach of the meaning, of what was said. As he could distinguish no word he did not feel that he was eavesdropping, and listened with a keen appreciation of the mingled grotesqueness and fearfulness of the situation. Presently he began to perceive that there was only one voice, and that its owner, if quarrelling, was quarrelling with himself. Now a loud harangue was poured forth in sonorous, arrogant-sounding tones, and then after a silence came snarling remarks, and groans, and sharp, short cries. The listener was aware that miserable solitaries will sometimes talk aloud for their own hearing alone. No doubt Luke Adare—yes, he thought it must be Luke rather than Edmund—was uttering the bitterness of his soul in the hideous solitude to which he had condemned himself.

He had just turned, disgusted and pitying, to go on his way when the voice was raised again, this time with a shriller clearness which carried a few words to his ear, an utterance with shape and meaning. Only two of the words remained in his mind the next moment when the voice had ceased, and so strange were they that though they rang through his brain, he could scarcely believe he had really heard them. Yet how could his imagination have suggested them?

"Desmond's daughter!" were the words, angrily and contemptuously spoken, which startled his ear like the blast of a trumpet.

Where did they come from? What did they mean? Why, even if they had been uttered by Luke Adare in his savage ravings, should they bear any particular meaning for him, Somerled? Why should he consider them as of the slightest importance? While he reflected thus they came towards him again, loudly and gruffly spoken, as if the speaker had drawn nearer to the aperture in the wall and was striving to drive some one, or something, forth.

"Desmond's daughter! Begone, begone! Desmond's daughter, come to spy and persecute—" And then a wild laugh ending in wrathful growling and muttering.

Fingall came close to the window and listened with all his ears and with all his brain; but that last burst had ended Luke's outpourings (could the speaker be any one but Luke?), and complete silence had settled once more upon the ruin, while the wind, which was rising, howled round the tottering chimneys and lashed the trees against the streaming gable.

Relaxed from the strained tension of listening, Somerled's mind began to work on the ideas suggested to him by those few wild words. Ravings—yes, they might be ravings, but what was the fancy that had run through the raving? Desmond's daughter! Who was Desmond's daughter?

"Desmond's daughter, come to spy and persecute." Why, Bawn!

With a flash of understanding, of recognition, Fingall saw Bawn, her circumstances, her enterprise, her dream,

in the lurid light of the truth. She was Desmond's
daughter. Her intention in coming here had been to
learn, on the very scene of her father's crime, that there
had been no crime at all. In this she had failed. She
was the daughter of the man who had murdered his
uncle.

She had hoped for some light on the subject from
these miserable Adares. With her firm will and her
high spirit she had thought to be able to make black
white. And yet could it not be done? There was
some mystery to which she had the clue, else why this
fury of Luke Adare at her appearance? After all, he
had jumped to a conclusion. He would not sleep, at
all events, till he had ascertained from Bawn herself
whether or not she was Desmond's daughter.

He walked to the place where he had left his horse
in shelter, and rode straight through wind and rain to
Shanganagh.

Bawn's little cart had reached home only a short
time before his arrival, and Bawn was feeling an
anguish and utter forlornness so new to her in its in-
tensity that she did not know how to deal with it.
The admission she had made to-day seemed to have
altered her very nature. She had confessed what
hitherto it had been her strength to deny. It was
right and fit that the crushing of her own happiness
should be involved in the total ruin that had destroyed
her father's life, but what was she to do with this new
want that had sprung up in her life, where was she to
carry it, how was she to rid herself of it? Her romantic
devotion to her dead father had carried her across the
sea and urged her through an army of difficulties; but
when her final defeat was consummated—and it was
near now, very near—what was she to do with the
burden of living love which a broken heart must carry

with it over land and sea through an incalculable number of years, perhaps to the end of a long life-time?

Her women were out milking, and she was alone in the house and was kneeling on the tiles of her little kitchen before the hearth, the blaze from which illumined the place fitfully as the dusk began to fall. The door, which had not been quite fastened, was pushed open, and Somerled stood before her.

Her heart leaped up for a moment with dangerous gladness, then failed within her. The next moment she had perceived his dripping condition, and, woman-like, was only concerned for his present comfort.

"Mr Fingall, you are shockingly wet. Take off that drenched ulster."

"There!" he said, and, flinging the garment on the back of a wooden chair, advanced to her with outstretched hands.

"Bawn, you will think I have done a wild thing. I have come here out of all season and in the storm, but it is to ask you a question which you will not refuse to answer me. Is this woman who has denied me so long, who has spoken to me of a secret sorrow and a stained name—is she Arthur Desmond's daughter?"

Bawn's eyes, which had widened with startled amazement, remained fixed on his, answering him sorrowfully out of their grey depths. She drew a long breath, said "yes" simply, and then moved away a step and put her hands behind her back—involuntary movements expressive of separation and departure.

"I would have kept the secret a little longer," she said quietly, with pale lips. "Who has told you? It must have come from Luke Adare. He is the only person who guessed me. I have been very rash and daring, and I am punished. I thought to overcome Luke Adare, but he has overcome me."

"What did you expect from him?"

" Confession. Reparation of the wrong he did to my father."

" Do you mean that he, Luke Adare, did that thing for which your father suffered the blame ? "

" No, I do not mean that. I know how the thing happened. If he would speak he could clear my father's name. He will not speak. He will die without speaking. How the wind roars ! "

" Did your father accuse him ? "

" He accused no one. He only suffered and made no complaint."

" How, then, do you imagine that you know ? "

" Know what ? My father's innocence ? You would have known it, too, if you had known him, his spotless life, his tender heart, his honourable nature. You would have felt him to be incapable of the motives you ascribed to him the other day when you spoke of him."

" Few are incapable of sudden passion."

" He was incapable of that. I do not expect you to believe it. You gave credit to the whispered calumnies that destroyed his good name ; you drove him out from among you—"

" Stay, Bawn, stay ! I did not do it. I am guiltless of what my people did in that day, as you are of your father's actions."

" I take them all on my head."

" That you must not do. Now listen to me, my dearest, dearest love. You have dreamed a wild dream in imagining that Luke Adare would assist you in this touching, this noble enterprise. I am the only other person in possession of your secret, and it shall be as if I did not know it. I am willing to believe that Arthur Desmond is all you describe him to be, and that a passionate quarrel (my uncle, I know, was a hot-headed man) had fatal and unpremeditated consequences.

More it is not necessary for me to ascertain. It is a tragedy long past and almost forgotten. Marry me, Bawn, and trust me. No one save myself shall ever know that Arthur Desmond was your father."

Bawn's lips and eye-lids trembled, but she kept her attitude of aloofness and shook her head.

"You do not trust me."

"I cannot trust either you or myself so far. I dare not put either of us in such an unnatural position. I fear there would come a day when I should see something in your eyes—should see you ask yourself, 'Why is the daughter of a murderer sitting at my fireside?' and I do not so trust myself as to feel sure that I should not get up and fly from you in despair which even now I can realise. When I go away from you, as I shall go soon, I shall at least take with me a sweet memory to live with all my life, and the knowledge that I have not destroyed your happiness. I shall not leave you bound to a horror from which you cannot escape."

"You have no knowledge of what you may leave me bound to. If you can imagine a despair you could not brave, why so can I. As for the change in me you fear might come with the future, that is nothing but a foolish scare. You should never see anything in my eyes but what you see now—love, tenderness, worship of yourself, admiration of your brave efforts, pity for what you have suffered. Bawn—"

She breathed a long sigh, and let her hand remain in his grasp for a few moments while she looked in his eyes with a wistful, far.seeing gaze, and then drew it slowly away and again retreated a step or two.

"Could I, for my own selfish happiness, consent to live, denying, ignoring my father's memory, sinking my own knowledge of his goodness and innocence and the testimony I could bear to them? Could I hear his story alluded to, hear him spoken of as a guilty man and never cry out? It could not be. You must let me go."

"I will not let you go." His eyes flashed, and he advanced towards her; but she suddenly threw out both her hands and pushed him away, then turned and disappeared into her little parlour, closing the door behind her.

Rory, not venturing to follow her, walked up and down the kitchen trying to calm his agitation, and with a faint hope that she might return. But she made no sign. Then he threw on his wet ulster again, and went out of the house into the storm.

He rode against the storm towards the Rath, where he had intended to spend the night, but soon had to dismount and lead his horse, which was terrified at the uproar of the elements. Peals of thunder now resounded from mountain to mountain, and in the glare of the lightning he saw the troubled valley below him and the dark rack of clouds trailing over the pass leading to Shane's Hollow. He thought of Luke Adare and Bawn's abandoned hope perishing together in the ruin, and for a time urged on his horse towards the pass with the intention of making a desperate effort to reach the Hollow, to drag the wretched solitary out of the jaws of death; for must not a night like this be his certain doom? Baffled in this attempt, he was forced at last to rouse the inmates of a cabin on the roadside, and to ask for shelter for the remaining hours of the night. The good people of the cabin, amazed to see Mr Rory from Tor in such a plight, did their best to make him comfortable on some straw by the fireside, and here he remained till daylight brought a lull in the tempest, and he was able to proceed towards the Hollow.

Approaching the uncanny spot, he soon began to see

signs of the night's ravages. Fallen trees lay across the
beaten track leading to the house, and a wreck of
broken branches strewed the wilderness. Making his
way through these in the grey mist of the morning,
Somerled arrived at the ruin, and saw at a glance that
the long-threatened end had at last arrived, that the
portion of the building which yesterday was standing
had fallen in, and that the home of the Adares was now
a pile of shapeless rubbish.

The catastrophe which Bawn had foreseen and sought
to avert had come to pass, and with it had probably
perished her hope, and his, Somerled's prospect of happiness. Confronted by this fact, yet unwilling to
acknowledge it, he walked round the melancholy pile,
seeking for the window through which only yesterday
the voice of Luke Adare had reached him with its
extraordinary revelation. Was that voice now silenced
for evermore? It was at least possible that the creature
might be still alive, though buried in his den, still
capable of uttering a truth, of answering a question.

If he, Rory, could find him now alive, and take his
dying deposition, receive his confession—if, indeed, he
had such to make—all might yet be well. For the
moment Fingall had adopted Bawn's belief, and all the
happiness of the future seemed to hang on a chance—
the chance that this miserable soul might not yet have
been summoned before judgment.

He found the window now almost blocked up from
within by fallen rubbish, and wrenching away the rusted
bars, climbed in through the aperture that remained.
Having carefully observed the interior as far as was
possible, he ventured to enter further, and made his way
into a small space which, from the smoke-blackened
wreck of a fireplace visible, he judged to be the remnant
of a room lately inhabited. Sure that he had penetrated

to the unfortunate Luke's retreat, he forgot the danger to which he was exposing his own life, and groped in the semi-darkness, calling loudly, in the hope that a living voice might respond to his cry; but in vain. Exploring on every side as far as was possible, he was about to give up his search and return to the light of day when he stumbled over something less resistant than the stones and wreckage through which he had been moving.

The spot was so dark that he could not see what he had touched till he struck a match, which only made a faint, evanescent gleam of light, but sufficient to show him a human arm outstretched and clothed in rags, a clenched hand rigid in death, protruding from a mound of stones and rubbish, under which, evidently, a corpse lay buried.

Sickening with the sight, and satisfied that he had seen all that remained of Luke Adare, he groped his way to the window again and stood once more under the heavens in the wind-swept wilderness.

Men were soon at work digging away the rubbish, and the crushed and disfigured body was laid on a bier on the grass, while the excavators proceeded to make search for Edmund Adare, the only other person who had lately inhabited the ruin. Their search was in vain, and after some days it was given up, the conclusion having been arrived at that Edmund, too, had perished in the catastrophe which had closed the last chapter in the history of the Adares. An inquest was held upon the body of Luke, and he was buried with his fathers at Toome.

CHAPTER XXXIX.

A GHOST.

WHEN Bawn learned the news she was not taken by surprise, and yet the blow fell as heavily as if it had been unexpected. In a week the colour had left her lips and her dress hung loosely upon her. It was a week of rain and tempest, and Betty Macalister thought her young mistress had been suddenly seized with a fit of loneliness and fright of the storm.

"I was feared, always feared, that the winter 'd be heavy on you," said Betty. "In summer time a body doesn't feel the loneliness; but winter up here is a trial, I can tell you."

"Perhaps I'm homesick," said Bawn, trying to smile. "I believe I am going back to America, Betty. This climate does not seem to agree with me. What do you think of coming with me—you and Nancy?"

"Och, misthress, I'm too ould for changes; and it's too short a time you've given to the ould country—you that was so brave at the first and had such plans. Why would you give up for a bit of a storm that'll blow over."

Bawn lowered her head and made no reply. The storm she must fly from would never blow over, she feared—not, at all events, as long as she lingered here; for the storm was in her own heart. Back in America, with the ocean between her and this temptation, it might be that in years hence her old courage would

return. The question now was how to depart quickly
enough.

She must not give cause for wonder by a too pre-
cipitate flight; must give timely notice to her landlord,
alleging that the Irish winter did not agree with her
health. She must think of her handmaidens and their
disappointment, and make them some amends. In the
meantime she must not see Rory.

He had come many times to her door, but had
always been told in answer to his inquiries that she was
ill and in her room ; as indeed she was—ill with sorrow
because she dared not run to him ; shut up in her room
as in a prison from which she could not escape to freedom.

He had written her an urgent and impassioned letter,
in which he bade her forget everything but his love, and
end this tragedy with a word ; but to all his pleading
she had answered only that she was quite unmoved in
her resolve.

One day, when all her preparations for departure
were almost made, Gran's ancient carriage arrived at
the Shanganagh door, and Gran herself entered with
trembling steps, uttering a little cry of dismay as her
eyes fell on Bawn's altered face and figure.

"My dear," she said, "how ill you are looking!
What is it all about? Can an old woman help to
make things straight? Have we been unkind to you?
Has any one hurt you, that you so persist in running
away from us?"

"No," said Bawn sadly—"no, indeed. It is only that
I am a capricious American and want to go home."

The old lady spread her thin hands before the fire
and looked thoughtfully at the girl.

"My dear, I want you to understand me. I have
not come here without a purpose. My grandson is
very dear to me. You are making him unhappy."

"I am still more unhappy," said Bawn, standing before the old woman with her head lowered and her hands hanging by her side.

"There is a mystery somewhere," continued Gran, having studied Bawn's face eagerly for a few moments. "I cannot think of anything, except that some of our family have offended you, and that pride is in the way."

"It is not that. If I ever had any pride it is gone. And every one here has been only too good to me."

"What is it, then? Will you not confide in me? Is there a difficulty which cannot be overcome?"

Gran's face twitched and her voice quivered. Bawn dropped on her knees and covered the wrinkled hands with kisses.

"It cannot be overcome," she said. "If I were to tell you, you would be the first to bid me go."

Then Bawn burst into uncontrollable weeping, and the old woman drew her to her heart and wept with her.

"I feared there was something," she said. "But you will trust me, will you not, if you can? How can you be sure of what I shall tell you to do till you try me? I know you are noble and good, and that this trouble which is on your mind, this hindrance to my grandson's happiness and your own, is nothing personal to yourself. He knows what it is, and he is not daunted. Why will you not be satisfied, too?"

"I will save him from himself," said Bawn, regaining her courage, but holding fast by the tender old hands that clasped her own. "I will not condemn him to a future of bitterness."

"We are talking in riddles," said Gran, "and nothing comes of that but deeper bewilderment. I was hoping you would have given me an explanation which Rory in honour cannot make."

"When I have got to the other side of the ocean I

will write it to you. Yes, I have made up my mind to
that. I will write you the whole story, of what brought
me here, and of what has driven me away again. And
you will never ask me to come back."

" But if I should ask you ?"

"You are putting an impossible case; and I cannot
see further than just this, that I must go."

Gran went away at last with a sorrowful yearning in
her heart towards the girl, but with a fear that there
must be something very terrible to be revealed, as no
woman, except under pressure of dreadful circumstances,
could so withstand Rory.

She went on to the Rath, where she had promised to
stay a few days. Rory, who was there to meet her, was
the only person who knew of her visit to Shanganagh.
He was eager to hear the result of her interview with
Bawn.

" I have gained nothing by going," said the old lady,
"except that I understand what you feel in losing her.
There must be some insurmountable bar, for she loves
you dearly. But you must let her go."

" I do not consider it insurmountable," said Rory.
And yet, as he went out of the old woman's presence
and walked alone down the glen in the twilight, he
admitted to himself that Bawn had reason on her side
in fearing to become his wife, now that the stain of
murder could never be wiped from her father's name.
He felt that Gran would believe she was right ; and
that if ever she received that letter which Bawn had
promised to send her from America, his grandmother
would applaud the resolution of the writer, and would
never, as Bawn had predicted, ask her to come back.

Even for himself in the far future could he so
assuredly answer ? How could he tell that a terrible
repugnance might not one day spring up within him

—repugnance to the idea that the grandfather of his
children had been the murderer of his uncle?
What reason had he for accepting the theory of
Desmond's innocence beyond the impression made on
his imagination by the passionate loyalty and faith of
the daughter whom Desmond had reared, but who
might have inherited her noble nature from a mother o
whom she had no recollection?

Angry now with himself and now with her, and all
the time sick at heart under the pressure of uncompro-
mising circumstances, he walked on half-blindly, while
the twilight gradually deepened. He tried to put himself back into the place he had occupied among all
things just before he had first seen Bawn—a place
which had held him well enough, and with which he
had been tolerably satisfied. But he owned bitterly to
himself that he could no longer fit into that place,
having outgrown it. The general altruism which had
once wholly occupied and interested him had all
centred in the desire to have one loving creature always
by his side. He thought he perceived that he could
never again be a contented man. Had she been unable
to love him, or had she proved worthless, he might
have hoped to put her out of his life and forget her;
but the knowledge that her life, too, was broken by the
love that had driven her away from him must forbid
him ever to forget what might have been, would take
the sap out of his energies and sour the flavour of his
daily bread.

It had grown quite dark except for a faint gleam from
the moon—the same moon, now on the wane, that had
lighted him to Shane's Hollow after the storm; a
watery, red-eyed moon, trailing forlornly through
clouds, like a weeping woman moving through the
world alone with sable veils around her.

As Somerled walked on observing her he struck against somebody right in his path.

"I beg your pardon. I believe it is I who am to blame." And then he saw, by the pale ray from behind the roadside trees, what a fanciful person might have taken for the ghost of Edmund Adare.

"My God, man!" he exclaimed, "where have you come from?"

"Where should I come from but from Shane's Hollow, my ancient home?" answered the strange figure, which a brighter gleam of moonlight now revealed more distinctly. "Perhaps you do not know that you are speaking to an Adare."

"Excuse me," said Somerled; "the night is dark." And then he stood still a moment, feeling curiously embarrassed in presence of this wretched wreck of humanity.

"I excuse you," said Edmund Adare loftily, and passed on, and Somerled turned his steps and walked with him in the direction of the Rath.

"I must congratulate you, Mr Adare, on your singular escape. We feared you had perished in the accident of a week ago."

"Thank you," said Edmund, mollified. "It was a terrible accident, but not perhaps unexpected. My poor brother persisted in living in a dangerous part of the house. These old ancestral houses always become dangerous with time. My preservation is due to my wariness in selecting my own apartments. I have still ample accommodation—" Here he was interrupted by a frightful fit of coughing, followed by a faintness which obliged him to lean against a tree.

Somerled surveyed him with infinite pity. His small, shrunken frame, his streaming white beard, his hollow, glassy eyes contrasted strangely with the self-

24

satisfied pomposity of his manner of speaking, which would have been ludicrous only for an occasional pathetic break in the voice and sob in the articulation which hinted that a long-suffering patience had almost given way; that a monstrously bolstered-up pride had nearly broken down. Fingall remembered that this man was he who had always been considered the gentlest and least forbidding of the brothers. Struggle as the poor creature might, death was very near him. Was there nothing that charity could do for his relief, to soften the parting pangs of humanity yet to be endured by him?

"Mr Adare, I fear you are ill," he said kindly. "Will you not accept a neighbour's hospitality for a little time —just for change of air?" he added, feeling that he was humouring the strange creature's pride, but unable to help it.

"You are good," said the poor ghost, pulling himself together and trying to move on, "but the Adares have always been stay-at-home people. Just now I am going to the Rath on business, to pay a strictly business visit to Mr Alister Fingall—your cousin, sir, I believe."

"Yes," said Rory; "and as I am going there now myself, we may walk together, if you have no objection. Perhaps you will take my arm, as you seem a little weak."

"Old age, sir—old age!" said Edmund as Rory drew the death-cold, trembling hand within his arm, and suited his steps to the tottering steps that shuffled on beside him; and the last of the Adares, taken by surprise, allowed himself to be led along through the chill darkness, like a father by a son.

Impressed with the feeling that something strange was about to happen, Rory hastened to tell his cousin Alister of the curious resurrection that had taken place, informing him that the one survivor of all the Adares was waiting in the library, seeking an interview with him.

" Poor old creature! has he come to beg at last?"
exclaimed Alister. "Well, we must see what can be
done for him."

" I do not think that is what has brought him," said
Somerled ; "but if you can force a glass of wine down
his throat, do it without delay."

Having seen Alister to the library-door, he went
to the drawing-room, where he found Flora talking
excitedly to Gran, who looked bewildered—and no
wonder ; for the subject of Flora's eloquence was the
engagement of Manon to Major Batt, an event which
had been announced to her only that morning.
Somerled, on hearing the news, expected to be overwhelmed with Flora's scorn of his want of taste and
enterprise in allowing so disappointing a state of things
to arise ; but, to his great surprise, her greetings took
the form of congratulation.

Only yesterday she had learned that Manon, so far
from being an heiress, was utterly penniless, having so
greatly displeased her grandfather just before his death
that he had left her nothing.

"So her sly mother sent her here, hoping that
something would turn up for her ; and undoubtedly
something has turned up. The question is, will Major
Batt marry her when he hears the truth?"

" Undoubtedly he will, Flora. He is not so bad as
you paint him."

" There is no knowing what he may do under the
influence of his disappointment, after the way Shana
has treated him," said Flora, determined to keep hold
of one grievance, at least. "I must say you take
it very coolly, Rory. Just imagine what it would have
been if you now stood in Major Batt's place."

" My imagination is not so elastic as yours ; it won't
take in such a possibility. As for Miss Manon, I can

only say that in future I shall back Gran as a judge of character, rather than you. But, on the whole, it is a good thing to have Batt married, and he has money enough to afford a penniless wife, even looking at the matter from your point of view, Flora."

"Money enough? I should think so. But why should it fall to the lot of that designing little foreigner?" said Flora, thinking bitterly of Shana preparing for exile in New Zealand, and Rosheen unprovided for. "However, I have done with all attempts to improve the condition of my husband's family. It seems to me that the Fingalls have a constitutional objection to possessing the good things of this world."

Rory reflected that when his cousin Alister took to himself Lady Flora's handsome dowry and pretty face he had not secured all the good things of the world by that act. And Gran, being too generous to exult over Flora, too tired to speak at all, merely looked at her favourite grandson with a wistful, sympathetic gaze which at once approved of his conduct and deplored that it had not met with the reward it deserved.

Interrupting the conversation came a message from the master of the Rath requesting Rory's presence in the library.

CHAPTER XL.

WHEN Somerled entered the library Alister was standing on the fireplace holding a piece of paper in his hands, and with a disturbed look on his usually placid countenance, while Edmund Adare sat at the table, drooping towards it, with his arms folded upon it and his chest supported on his arms. A glass of wine stood untasted before him, and a tray with other refreshments was near.

"I have asked you to come here to support me in my magisterial capacity," said Alister. "This gentleman, Mr Adare, has brought me some curious information; has placed this document in my hands, which, though very interesting, would be rather enigmatical if not explained by his testimony. I wish you to hear his explanations. But, Mr Adare, will you not oblige me by drinking that glass of wine before we go further?"

"Thank you; I never eat or drink except at home," said the famished-looking visitor, shaking himself out of a sort of collapse which seemed to have fallen on him from the warmth and comfort of the room. "I am an abstemious man, Mr Fingall, and if I were to partake of your refreshments I could not afterwards dine."

Alister and Rory exchanged glances as the wretched man uttered the above words with a gasping effort, and at the same time an attempt at flourish which was pitiful in the extreme, seeing the very low ebb to which his physical strength had sunk; and Alister hastened to get the business of the moment over.

"This is a statement made by the late Mr Luke Adare," he said—"a very singular statement. Mr Edmund Adare tells me that he himself wrote it at his brother's dictation—some years ago, was it not, Mr Adare? Perhaps you will kindly tell my cousin how the statement came to be made."

Edmund Adare shook himself up again with another great effort, and lifted his pallid face, looking from one to the other of the two men standing before him.

"It was about four years ago," he said. "My brother Luke was suffering in body, and haunted by an idea that he must make a confession, and he called on me to write it down for him."

"You consider that he was of sound mind at the time?"

"I am sure of that, or I should not have come to you. Since then his mind has sometimes been a little astray, but not then—certainly it was not so then."

"Will you tell us what occurred between you?" said Alister, while Rory glanced over the soiled and crumpled paper which he had taken from Alister's hand, and turned pale.

"He came one day to my apartments. At that time we occupied rooms in different wings of the house, and had not met for a year. My brother Luke was always a peculiar person, but very clever, Mr Fingall, and very clear-headed. Had it not been for misfortune—such misfortune as often overtakes the best ancient families —my brother Luke would have made a figure in the world. He came to me that day and said: 'I have something on my mind which will not let me rest night or day. It is like a rat gnawing me. I cannot tell why it is,' he said, 'for I do not believe in conscience, but I have a feeling that if you were to write down what I have to say I shall get better.'

"I said, 'What is it about?' He said, 'It is about Arthur Desmond.' I said, 'The man who murdered Roderick Fingall long ago?'

"'He did not murder him,' said Luke. 'Roderick Fingall fell down the cliff. That is what I want you to write.'"

"Yes," said Rory. "Go on."

Edmund Adare passed his heavy, colourless hand over his sunken eyes, and with another great demand upon the remnant of vitality within him, spoke again:

"I said, 'Who is able to tell about that now?'

"He said, 'I am, because I saw how the thing happened. I was on the mountain that evening by chance, and I saw the two men meet, and I heard their conversation. I saw Arthur Desmond stretch out his hands to Fingall, and Fingall draw back and fall headlong over the precipice. It was an accident, and Desmond had no fault in it.'

"I said to Luke, 'Why did you not speak at the time?'

"'I did speak,' he said. 'I spoke to some purpose. I whispered in everybody's ear that Roderick had been murdered and that Desmond was the murderer. I had excellent reasons for it. I never did anything without an excellent reason. I wanted the money that old Barbadoes was on the point of bestowing on Arthur Desmond, and I got it. It is all gone now, like everything else, and nothing matters except to stop this buzzing in my brain whenever I think of it. And I can't get rid of thinking of it. Write it all down that I may get rid of it.'

"I wrote it down as you see, gentlemen, and Luke

was satisfied. I put away the paper, and never should have troubled any more about it, for I thought no good could come of showing it to any one now, only for certain matters which occurred during the last year."

" What are those matters ? " asked Rory, with eyes fixed intently on Edmund's face.

" A young lady came visiting at Shane's Hollow," continued Edmund, with another faint attempt at his grandiose manner which failed pathetically as he went on, " and she was an angel of goodness to my poor sister, who was a great sufferer owing to our reverses, and had not all those comforts which an invalid requires. This girl, gentlemen, nursed her like a daughter, gave her hospitality, and buried her in our ancestral burial place as befitted an Adare. I never saw the young lady's face, but I have heard her voice as she passed down our staircase, and there was a tone in it that reminded me of the ill-treated Arthur Desmond. This I might not have dwelt upon, only that of late my brother Luke fell to raving about Desmond's daughter who had come to persecute him. After coming to the conclusion that the girl must be Desmond's daughter, I had some struggle with myself as to whether I should or should not come forward and lay this statement before a magistrate ; for the step I am taking now, gentlemen, is a difficult one to a person of my recluse-like habits, but ever since my poor brother's death I have felt a great anxiety to make known his confession. I have felt it, to use his own words, ' like a rat gnawing me' ; and so I have come—"

He stopped abruptly and cast a wild, wandering look around the room, as if, now that all was said, and urgent need for effort was over, he knew not how to pull body and mind together any more ; and before Alister or Rory could reach him he had fallen forward on the table in a state of unconsciousness.

They did all in their power to revive him and sent in haste for a doctor, but before the doctor could arrive to tell them that he had only a few hours to live, the last denizen of the ruined home of the Adares was lying in Lady Flora's best bed-room, scarcely aware of the long-unwonted comfort with which he was surrounded.

An hour before death he had a return of conscious-ness, and renewed in presence of the doctor, clergyman, and others, the statement he had already made to Alister and Somerled; but by midnight the last of the Adares was no more.

LEAVING Alister to tell Edmund Adare's story to Gran and Flora, Somerled rode off early in the morning to Shanganagh. Walking up to the farm-house he saw signs of preparation for departure and Bawn's little cart waiting at the open door, and at the same moment Bawn herself appeared on the threshold, dressed for travel.

"Unkind," he said, "trying to steal away from us without a word of farewell!"

He was smiling jubilantly as he took her half-reluctant hand, and Bawn, who had plotted to escape this last trial, felt herself turn sick and faint at seeing his unconcern. After all his urgency and insistance it was she who would have to suffer now and in the future. He would easily reconcile himself to the in-evitable, and forget.

She looked pale, weary, beaten. Knowing to what a pass things had come with her, feeling that she was unable to struggle longer without crying out, she had been trying to escape quietly in her weakness and sorrow without going through the ordeal of spoken farewells. Caught on the very threshold, she would have to make one last, almost impossible call on her courage.

"I have been obliged to make my arrangements hastily," she said, "and to write my farewells and thanks for all kindnesses. Betty is coming with me. Nancy will stay till all is wound up finally here, and will follow us. I have written to Mr Fingall of the Rath—"

"Come in, Bawn; come in, and give me one last half-hour of your company. The pony can wait. Your steamer does not sail for two days to come. Don't be afraid—I am not going to ask leave to cross the ocean with you a second time."

She returned into the little parlour which she had just quitted, as she had thought, for the last time, feeling the joy of seeing him again embittered, the acute pain of parting infinitely aggravated by the strange delight in his eyes and in his voice. Had he cruelly come here to punish her by showing how little he cared, how, having come to listen to reason at last, he was rejoiced to make an end of folly?

She stood in the middle of the dismantled room with a wretched consciousness that she was unable to hide the grief in her eyes, that her face, her attitude, her very hands were treacherously making confession that she was escaping away from the scene of her wild enterprise, vanquished and with a broken heart. Not that she cared now if he knew it, only he might have spared her. He was so much the stronger, after all. Her strength, which he had so talked about, was such a sham, his fancied love for her had been so short and so easily dismissed. How could he stand smiling at her misery thus, if he had ever for one hour really cared for her?

"Bawn, take off your gloves and your hat, for I have a great deal to say to you."

"Would it not be kinder to let me go?" she said, and she felt that her pride was gone, and that she had said it piteously. "I have been very foolish, very daring, and I and my cause are shipwrecked. I have done no one harm but myself, for which I ought to be thankful; but say good-bye quickly and let me go."

He had taken her hands and held them tightly, and tried to look in her eyes, which were turned steadily away from the gladness in his.

"Bawn, I swear to you solemnly that you must not, need not go."

She looked at him startled, suddenly struck with the fact that his manner seemed to imply a certainty which could only come from a change in circumstances; but, remembering that such change was impossible, she said sadly:

"Nothing could persuade me of that unless the clouds were to open and drop down the truth, or a message were to come back from the dead—"

"My dearest, the clouds have opened; a message has come from the dead. I have been all night entertaining the king's messenger who brought us miraculous tidings. Luke Adare has spoken."

Bawn's lips parted, and in her eyes, which were fixed on Somerled's, amazement, hope, and incredulity succeeded each other swiftly.

"Impossible!" she said faintly. "The heavens were opened to convert Saul, but that does not happen now. The dead do not come back. Why need you torture me?"

"Luke Adare has spoken."

"I saw him dead."

"So have I seen Edmund Adare, but only a few hours ago. He is the king's messenger I told you of, and here is the message he brought for you and me."

He drew the paper containing Luke's confession from his breast and put it in her trembling hands, but, seeing she could neither hold nor decipher it, he took it back and read it aloud to her. Hearing him, she looked straight before her with bewildered eyes, tried to take the document to read it for herself, but suddenly turned blind, and the next moment Bawn the strong-hearted had fainted in her lover's arms.

THE END.

www.ingramcontent.com/pod-product-compliance
Lightning Source LLC
Chambersburg PA
CBHW032143010726
47494CB00002B/331